PRAISE FOR WILLIAM BERNHARDT AND PLOT/COUNTERPLOT

"A man on the run... a woman on the run... in a thriller that hits the ground running... then running faster... then absolutely flying. And you're flying, too, flying through the pages with one of the masters of the modern thriller at the controls. William Bernhardt knows when to soar and when to dive, when to make you sweat and when to let you breathe, when to throw this flying machine into a barrel roll that will absolutely shock you and when to bring you home safe and satisfied. A terrific entertainment."

WILLIAM MARTIN, *NEW YORK TIMES-*
BESTSELLING AUTHOR OF *THE LINCOLN
LETTER* AND *DECEMBER '41*

"*Exposed* has everything I love in a thriller: intricate plot twists, an ensemble of brilliant heroines, and jaw-dropping drama both in and out of the courtroom. William Bernhardt knows how to make the law come alive."

TESS GERRITSEN, *NEW YORK TIMES-*
BESTSELLING AUTHOR OF THE RIZZOLI
& ISLES THRILLERS

"*Splitsville* is a winner—well-written, with fully developed characters and a narrative thrust that keeps you turning the pages."

GARY BRAVER, BESTSELLING AUTHOR
OF *TUNNEL VISION*

"William Bernhardt is a born stylist, and his writing through the years has aged like a fine wine...."

STEVE BERRY, BESTSELLING AUTHOR
OF *THE KAISER'S WEB*

"Once started, it is hard to let [*The Last Chance Lawyer*] go, since the characters are inviting, engaging, and complicated....You will enjoy it."

CHICAGO DAILY LAW BULLETIN

"[*Court of Killers*] is a wonderful second book in the Daniel Pike series...[A] top-notch, suspenseful crime thriller with excellent character development..."

TIMOTHY HOOVER, FICTION AND
NONFICTION AUTHOR

"I could not put *Trial by Blood* down. The plot is riveting—with a surprise after the ending, when I thought it was all over....This book is special."

NIKKI HANNA, AUTHOR OF *CAPTURE LIFE*

"*Judge and Jury is* a fast-paced, well-crafted story that challenges each major character to adapt to escalating attacks that threaten the very existence of their unique law firm."

RJ JOHNSON, AUTHOR OF
DREAMSLINGER

"*Final Verdict* is a must read with a brilliant main character and surprises and twists that keep you turning pages. One of the best novels I've read in a while."

ALICIA DEAN, AWARD-WINNING
AUTHOR OF *THE NORTHLAND CRIME
CHRONICLES*

"Thrillingly interwoven plots are Bernhardt's forte, a talent he once again demonstrates full-blown in his latest superb thriller..."

BOOKLIST (FOR *DARK JUSTICE*)

"Bernhardt keeps his readers coming back for more."

LIBRARY JOURNAL

PLOT/COUNTERPLOT

WILLIAM BERNHARDT

NATIONAL BESTSELLING AUTHOR

PLOT

COUNTERPLOT

BABYLON BOOKS

For my mother

PROLOGUE

Three Months Before

THE BITTER SUBZERO wind chilled Dr. Scheimer—but not nearly so much as the thought of what they were about to do. Ice pelted his cheeks like shrapnel. He could taste the cold. He could feel it at the base of his spine. But the shivers rippling through his body could not be blamed on the temperature.

He stood on the edge of a snow-covered precipice, 2200 feet above the shoreline, staring out into the Pacific Ocean. For the first time in his life, he was glad Liesel was no longer with him. He would be ashamed for her to see him here, so lost, so far astray.

"PROTECTIVE HEADGEAR ON," read the text message on his iPhone. The shrieking wind made audio communication impossible. So the greatest minds in the world of physics exchanged messages by text, as if they were teenagers. Perhaps they were, at least in terms of emotional maturity. How could such well-educated people be so easily manipulated? How could they be so smart about science but so ignorant about the lessons of history?

He gazed out at the target on Kudil Island. Kudil was one of the larger uninhabited islands in the Aleutian chain, but it was not connected to the Alaska Marine Highway. Kudil had the advantage of being far from the view of any casual observer. Even shock waves of enormous intensity would not be felt outside this remote wilderness. Perfect for a test that must be shielded from public view.

On the island, they constructed a small town of facades and shacks in a field of endless white. They positioned a scarecrow in the dead center. The object of the experiment was to see how close they could come to hitting the scarecrow. The goal was to do as little collateral damage as possible while still eliminating the primary target.

Scheimer and his fellow scientists were dressed in protective suits covered by insulated cold-weather clothing. They hoped that would be enough. But no one was entirely sure what they were protecting themselves against. Solar flares? Heat? Tornado-velocity winds? A space-time wormhole? Scheimer had read that when Oppenheimer and his colleagues conducted the first atomic bomb test, some believed the explosion would ignite the atmosphere and incinerate the earth. That did not happen.

But this time, anything was possible. The science was so new, and the anomaly that made it possible was so unpredictable. The only fact Scheimer could be sure of was that his work had made possible this gigantic advance in the destructive power of mankind.

"KEY HAS BEEN INSERTED."

He knew what that meant. Somewhere in Hawaii, at the base of a massive volcano, a project technician had initiated the activation sequence. The coordinates would be delivered wirelessly through a linked laptop. The tip of the firing mechanism would glow a hellish red as it pivoted into position.

They were actually going to do this. This was going to happen.

He felt a padded glove on his arm. "Be still, old friend. All will be well."

He wished he shared Dr. Johann Karelis' barely audible optimism. He and Karelis had been colleagues since their college days in Berlin. They had both come to America after the Wall fell. Karelis resisted the lure of government employment for years. The advantages—ready financing, plentiful resources, and a certain degree of autonomy—were not enough. The disadvantages were well known to every scientist since Galileo's time. Eventually, the financiers would expect results, and establishing the tenets of the physical world would be insufficient to keep them happy.

The generals wanted something they could use.

Scheimer passed the infrared binoculars to his friend. "You tell me what happens."

"As you wish." Karelis raised the glasses to his eyes.

"TARGETING   IS   COMPLETE.   COUNTDOWN INITIATED."

Targeting the energy required a series of coupled, encrypted equations to be entered into a targeting device—the Key. With the Key, the device could be used by those who did not have a Ph.D. in Physics. It could be used by anyone who knew how to type coordinates into a computer.

Developing those equations had been the primary focus of Scheimer's work. The work he now regretted more than anything he had done in his entire life.

Scheimer's stomach ached. He knew the beam's journey would be virtually instantaneous. It would rematerialize directly over the target. If it traveled any longer it would acquire too much energy. They wanted this to be a controlled test. They wanted to measure its potential. Without igniting the atmosphere and destroying the world.

According to Oppenheimer, while observing the Trinity test, he was reminded of a line from Hindu scripture: *If the radiance of a thousand suns were to burst at once into the sky, that would be like the splendor of the mighty one. Now I am become Death, the destroyer of worlds.*

But this was so much more.

Without warning, the steel gray sky exploded with a sudden flash of bright white light. Even though he wore protective goggles, Scheimer covered his eyes. The light still penetrated to his brain. It turned golden, then an intense violet. He was buffeted by a gale force wind that rocked him to his knees.

And then, just as suddenly as it had begun, it ended. The sky returned to its previous gray. There was no smoke, no dust, no mushroom cloud. The air had an eerie calm, like the moment after a thunderstorm when the coppery smell still lingered.

Karelis held the binoculars to his eyes. His face was expressionless.

Scheimer rose and gazed at the island. "Was the town destroyed?"

Karelis' lips moved wordlessly, as if he could not form an answer. At last he shook his head.

"Was the test a failure?"

No response.

Scheimer grabbed the binoculars and looked for himself.

At first, nothing appeared to have changed. The town still stood. Every façade remained upright. Every shack was in place.

Then he looked closer.

The scarecrow was gone.

The beam had reached its target with preternatural accuracy. And eliminated it. Without causing the slightest damage to the surrounding area. As if Zeus had cast down a lightning bolt from Olympus.

The experiment had succeeded beyond their greatest expectations. *Now I am become death...*

Scheimer felt his iPhone vibrate. He glanced down at the message.

"THE BEAM WILL BE RELEASED IN FIVE SECONDS."

In five seconds? But—

Scheimer's eyes widened. He felt himself teeter, stagger to one side, as the full magnitude of what they had done, what they had created, hammered into his brain.

They had become more than mere harbingers of death. With the turn of a key, they had transcended one of the fundamental dimensions of the physical world—time—and created a weapon capable of destroying anyone, anyplace.

They had become destroyers of worlds.

One Month Before

WE'RE SCREWED, Xavier thought, even before the building exploded and the corpses fell like rain. He'd seen it coming. The Supervisor was playing his usual nasty tricks and X was little more than a puppet. He'd thought all along that the planning for this mission was unimaginative and the intel was weak. When he drove his black Hummer into the parking garage, his concerns were confirmed. Only one guard should be on duty, and that guard should be on his afternoon break. Instead there were two, ready and watching. When a job began this poorly, it was impossible to reliably predict the outcome.

Except—he knew he would survive. He always did. Even as a puny five-year old boy in a Siberian workhouse. He survived then and he would again. But he couldn't make any promises about anyone else.

That was the story of his life, wasn't it? Everyone around him fell. But never Xavier. He was something different from the rest. They had made him into something different.

He would have to improvise. Fortunately, he was good at that. He'd had years of training and covert-ops experience with the KGB. On one mission, he was shot three times in the chest—and still took down the intercept base on schedule. After the Wall fell he worked for *Bratva*— the Russian mafia--where he had the pleasure of eliminating three rival gunrunners with a single swing of a baseball bat. After that, he'd served a brief stint training Pakistan-based militants in the Lashkar-e-Taiba, but he found them weak and unprofessional. He spent years working for Islamic extremists in Afghanistan, surprising his enemies by leaping unassisted across desert crevasses. He might still be there, in his little adobe home on the outskirts of Sabaa, if—but he couldn't let himself be distracted. He needed to focus, even though his skills and experience made the infiltration of a US scientific instillation about as difficult as killing kittens.

It only took twelve seconds to get inside this innocent looking building on the outskirts of Honolulu. While the first sentry explained that he didn't sell parking permits, Xavier grabbed the half-door between them and rammed it into the man's stomach. Careful to keep the guard between himself and the surveillance camera, Xavier kicked him in the ribs with ten-pound leaded boots. The useless functionary crumpled to the ground.

The second guard reacted almost immediately—which wasn't fast enough. Xavier's dark goggles prevented the guard from knowing where he was looking—which put the man at an extreme disadvantage. Xavier started toward the door, then pivoted abruptly and rammed the flat of his hand into the guard's face, shattering his nose. Bloody cartilage splintered and splattered through the air as the man reeled backward. Xavier clutched him around the neck and hoisted him effortlessly into the air. The guard's feet thrashed, unable to find purchase. His arms flailed, unable to break the grip of Xavier's bulging arms.

"You're...not human," the guard sputtered.

"Correct." With his spare hand, Xavier thrust his gut-hook hunting knife into the guard's throat and skewered him against the back wall. The guard thrashed spastically for a few seconds before dying.

A voice crackled over Xavier's earpiece. "All good?" Tomas asked.

"All good," Xavier subvocalized. The transceiver sewn to the inside of his cheek conveyed his response. "We move in."

DR. KARELIS GLANCED at his Steinhausen chronograph. Time moved so slowly these days. He was behind on the work that had brought him to the innocuously and deceptively named Cartwright Institute for Hawaiian Antiquities. But he couldn't concentrate. Even though the project had been shut down, he knew that would only be temporary, only until he completed his post-test analysis. They had discovered something wondrous—and potentially terrifying. His friend Scheimer wanted to turn his back on the project altogether. But not Karelis. Their achievements mesmerized him with such intensity that he could think of almost nothing else.

His tendency toward obsession had begun back in the old country, when he was still young, when his scientific genius began to reveal itself. He'd had a long and distinguished career at the Berlin Academy for Theoretical Physics, both as a researcher and teacher. He'd almost single-handedly developed the quantum chromodynamics theory of strong interactions. He'd been quite content, until his long-standing colleague, Louis Scheimer, contacted him about an astounding discovery—and a research opportunity. Karelis could not resist.

Karelis crossed his apartment and stroked the papers spread across his drafting-table style desk. A faint mustiness spiked the air, permeating the preexisting odors of unwashed laundry and uncleared breakfast. The papers were reproductions, of course, but he still treated them with delicacy. To him, there was nothing more valuable in the universe. The greatest wealth was knowledge. And knowledge was power. In this case, the power to reshape the world.

Several years ago, construction workers in Manhattan made a startling discovery. While restoring and renovating the New Yorker Hotel, they discovered a hidden annex, a hideaway between the top floor and the roof that no one—at least no one alive—knew existed. Inside, they found a cache of documents and handwritten notes, some in English, some in a Slavic language, some in code. The papers had been deliberately hidden. They were extensively damaged by water, heat, and insects. But following an intense restoration process, they were now 67% legible. And in the Master's own hand.

What Karelis discovered in that 67% was the Holy Grail of physics. Breakthrough scientific research, hidden for decades. And a description of a bizarre anomaly hidden here in the Hawaiian islands. President McKinley's foresight made everything they'd accomplished possible.

Karelis knew the world would be safer if the project remained inactive, if they buried the anomaly and destroyed the accelerator and targeting mechanism. But he couldn't resist the opportunity to expand the boundaries of known science. Since the dawn of enlightenment, there had been people all too ready to misuse scientific advances. The same equations that put men on the moon also created offensive-strike missiles. But you could not allow the evil motives of some to impede the acquisition of knowledge by all. The destiny of humanity was to understand the world in which we live. That was a sacred quest and Karelis would not forsake it.

He was not above taking precautions, however. A smart man could prevent his discoveries from being misused. He had a touch of Hypatia in him, though he doubted he shared her capacity for sacrifice.

Karelis was tired and he needed a bath. The water would refresh him. Perhaps he could continue a few more hours before he slept. Perhaps he would work all night.

He had job security, work that he loved, and a comfortable place to live. Best of all, he was safe, securely ensconced in this high-security facility. No one could harm him here.

THE STEEL-REINFORCED door to the Institute required a key card, but a single grenade from Xavier's Russian GP-30 turned it into a revolving door. As he and his team entered, someone turned the corner and headed down the corridor toward them. A scientist, judging from the white coat and the preposterously unkempt hair.

The staff were supposed to be out of the office today. Another screw-up.

The scientist stared at them, seemingly perplexed. "*What do you think—*"

Xavier lifted his Bushmaster XM-15 carbine rifle and gunned the man down before he could finish his sentence. He fell face forward onto the floor. Blood seeped through the coat, spreading like a viral infection. Xavier never slowed his stride.

"Keep moving," he said, waving Tomas and the others forward.

The second door on the left was supposed to be a security control room, but when Xavier opened it, all he found were brooms and cleaning supplies.

Xavier's fist clenched around his rifle. He could survive bazookas, butchers, and badasses—but no one could survive poor planning. At least not for long.

It took them almost eight minutes to determine the actual location of the security control room, and that was about seven-and-a-half minutes too long. The door was locked and a grenade might damage the equipment, so Xavier used the latest CIA-developed toy: K4. Essentially a paper-thin sheet of C-4 that could be inserted into the jamb to "unlock" the door. After they stepped through the wreckage, Xavier was forced to kill four more people, which was not only inefficient but greatly increased the chances of premature detection. Someone surely heard the explosions or the gunfire and called the authorities.

So the countdown had begun. They did not have much time.

Xavier located the target on the monitors, then used his rifle to disable all internal communications and video surveillance throughout the entire building.

He hurried his team to their quarry's lab and found— *Chyort voz'mi! Who was running this place?*—only one guard posted outside the door. The egghead inside possessed knowledge that could alter the geopolitical balance of power. So the government gave him one guard? They deserved what was about to happen.

Xavier strode forward. "Show me identification!" he bellowed. The obviously rattled MP fumbled for his papers. As soon as the man lowered his eyes, Xavier twisted the rifle out of his hands and hammered him with the butt. The guard's head slammed back against the wall. He still struggled. Xavier grabbed his head by the ears and pulled so hard a piece of his right ear tore off. The guard screamed.

"You supposed to watch?" Xavier asked. "Watch this." He pressed his thumbs against the base of the sentry's eyeballs and avulsed both at once. The man's cries were choked in gurgled blood. A fitting end to a poor watchman.

Xavier opened the door and pulled the dead guard in so he would not be spotted by any passersby.

"Wait outside," Xavier told Tomas. "Act like guarding Karelis. If someone asks, tell them was break-in, so boss brought more security. If they don't buy it, kill them."

"Understood," Tomas said with a curt nod.

Inside the apartment, Xavier detected no sign of his prey. "Dr. Karelis?"

No answer. Xavier entered the small apartment. An Edith Piaf recording played. He was assaulted by the odiferous evidence of a life-long bachelor. Apparently the good doctor lived as well as worked here. But where was he?

Xavier tripped a switch on the side of his goggles, activating the thermal imaging function. What would they do without the CIA to steal gadgets from? These goggles were so sensitive to heat differentials that they could not only detect where someone was but where they had been. He spotted a strong purple thermal reading from the desk in the corner. Karelis had sat there for some time. In the distance, faint footsteps luminesced on the carpet. The target had walked down the corridor. Recently.

He followed the heat readings until he heard splashing.

Karelis was in the bathtub. This would be even easier than he imagined.

Xavier quickly entered the bathroom, pressed down on the man's shoulders and held him underwater. Karelis writhed beneath Xavier's grip but in this position, the scientist had the same defensive capacity as a newborn baby—none. Nothing to grasp for leverage, no means of overcoming the strong arms holding him down.

"Stop splashing."

Perhaps Karelis didn't hear well, given the circumstances. Xavier wondered if his accent might be impeding communication. He was still insecure about his English and consequently never spoke unless it was unavoidable. Besides, a thick Russian accent made him too easily identifiable.

He tried to imagine what must be running through Karelis' brain as he stared up through the water at the blurry image of a stranger with a stubbled complexion, buzzcut hair, and a weather-worn face. Xavier could almost feel sorry for him—if he weren't working for the biggest murderers who ever strode across the globe as if they owned it.

"If you resist, you cannot hear what I say."

And still the man splashed like a seven-year-old in a backyard inflatable pool. How could a genius be so stupid?

"Stop or I slit throat." He drew his knife with his left hand, still holding the man down with his right. "Immediately."

The thrashing stopped. That was more like it.

Xavier hauled Karelis' head out of the water. He gasped for air so desperately he began dry heaving.

"You have thirty seconds to tell everything you know about Kronos Key."

More than ten passed before Karelis was able to speak. "I—I—don't know what you mean."

"Do not treat me like fool. I took papers on desk. And research notes. Tell me about Key."

"I don't—I—I never—heard of it. I'm working on a theoretical problem in chromodynamic--"

Xavier shoved him back into the water. It hadn't been thirty seconds. But he had a low tolerance for lying. His time was limited. Reinforcements could arrive at any moment.

He left Karelis under until he was on the brink of unconsciousness.

"I'm telling you," Karelis said, when the sputtering was done and he'd recovered his voice. "I've never heard of any...Kronos Key. I don't know—"

Xavier hit him in the stomach so hard it broke a rib. Then he hit him again, in the same place, so he would not only have a broken rib, he would know he had a broken rib. Karelis probably never had experienced anything like it. He was in poor shape, even for a man in his sixties. This flabby body spent its days in the lab, not the gym.

He hit Karelis again and this time, just as the man's eyes bulged, Xavier thrust him back under the surface.

Karelis' lungs sucked in water. He couldn't last long. Xavier had probably torn the pleural membrane. A collapsed lung was the likely result. The doctor must know that if he stalled much longer, he might suffer brain damage.

"You will tell what you know," Xavier explained when he hauled him out of the water again. "If necessary, I hurt you more first. But you will tell."

Karelis gasped for breath, blood oozing through his teeth. "When the hordes invaded the great Library at Alexandria...the librarian Hypatia stood firm against them. They stripped her naked, ripped her flesh from her bones with dull pot shards, then burned her alive. But by delaying them, she saved hundreds of scrolls, knowledge that later generations used to haul mankind out of savagery."

Xavier shook Karelis' head by the hair, ripping strands out by their roots. "You will tell what I want to know. I am your master."

"You are the barbarian at the gate, trying to drag humanity back to the primordial slime. We have always fought your kind. We always will."

Xavier crushed Karelis' skull between his hands.

OUT THE WINDOW OF KARELIS' apartment, Xavier saw two trucks filled with armed troops pull up to the front door of the Institute. Military police. Wouldn't take them long to get up here. He needed a diversion.

He took more K4 from his pack and pressed it into place, then added the blasting caps, then inserted a radio-controlled detonator. He unwound the silken cord wrapped around his waist and tied it to the shower head.

"Tomas! Get in here!"

"Will be ten or so men surrounding corridor in less than one minute. You hold them off."

"What's our extraction route?" Tomas asked.

"Rear stairwell. After I clear it, I call for you. Pull your men back and follow downstairs. I wait for you in garage."

"Yes, sir. But—"

Xavier raised his voice several notches. "*Do you understand orders?*"

"Yes, sir!"

Tomas positioned his men around the corridor. A moment later they were firing. Xavier retreated into the bathroom.

There was no rear stairwell, of course. His men were already dead, even if they didn't know it. But Xavier was excellent at repelling. He lowered himself out the window and down the side of the building, pushing off the brick wall to maintain momentum. He touched pavement in fewer than ten seconds. No one spotted him.

Until he reached the parking garage.

"Freeze!"

Xavier's hands rose. Damn. They left a man behind to guard the back door. A sensible precaution.

"Down on the floor. *Now!*"

As he dropped to the pavement, Xavier scrutinized the uniformed MP holding an assault rifle on him. He looked young and nervous. Good.

"Just stay put till I—" The MP scrutinized Xavier's face. "Wait a minute. I've seen you before. On the barge. I know where you live. Good God, I've got to tell—"

Xavier pivoted on one arm and swung his legs around like a Cuisinart blade, knocking the MP off his feet. Before the man hit the ground, Xavier had his head in both hands and pounded it against the concrete.

Xavier took the last of the K4 from his pack and rolled it like a cigarette with a fuse. He stuck it inside the MP's mouth, then duct-taped his mouth closed.

"You will tell nothing to no one," he murmured, igniting the fuse. He moved away to escape the blast. The K4 exploded with the muffled pop of a thousand firecrackers, blasting the young MP's head into a million pieces.

Never threaten my home, Xavier thought, as he made his way back to the Hummer. Your people took that from me once, in Sabaa. Never again.

He slid behind the wheel and drove.

Just before Xavier pulled out of range, he triggered the detonator, igniting the K4 in Karelis' bathroom.

The entire fourth floor of the Institute exploded with a thunderous din that hurt Xavier's ears even from a distance. Huge chunks of the building flew through the air. Sonic vibrations made his car shudder. The crumbling fourth floor tumbled into the third, the foundation weakened, and barely a heartbeat later the left side of the building was dust. The Cartwright Institute looked as if a giant cake-cutter had sliced out the westmost wedge.

Tomas and the others had always been expendable. The objective had been to obtain information. And he had accomplished that, with the documents, though Karelis failed to tell him all he knew about the Key. Xavier could not escape his own harsh judgment. This mission was not a success. And given the massive destruction, the military would be alerted to the potential threat—an unnecessary complication created because their plan had been clumsy and unimaginative from the start.

He knew where to go for schematics, details, everything they would need to use the Key or to build their own. But extracting that information would require careful planning, ingenuity, and specialized skills. They needed finesse, not brute force. They needed to take what they wanted without the government realizing it was missing. They needed to do the impossible.

They needed new ideas.

And Xavier was going to find them.

PART ONE
THE COURTSHIP

"The role of a writer is not to say what we all can say, but what we are unable to say."

ANAIS NIN

CHAPTER
ONE

Present Day

DYLAN LOVED it when Leilani purred. He reached upward to the soft swell of her breasts. He tickled her on the underside and she curled up, pushing her velvety bottom into the air. He knew what that meant. She wanted to be taken from behind.

Dylan was happy to oblige.

When he first met Leilani, he had no idea she would be the woman with whom he wanted to spend the rest of his life. They were introduced at the book-release party for his fifth Fargo Cody thriller, *The Venetian Vendetta*. During the years after his second novel hit *The New York Times*-bestseller list, he'd been through more women than he cared to recall. It was an embarrassment, the way he'd let success give him the social maturity of a teenager. He thought of himself as a caring, sensitive human being. He never meant to be shallow. But that's exactly what he became.

Until he met Leilani. They were an unlikely pair. She was a paramedic, he was an artist. When he asked her out that first night—actually, he asked if she wanted to join him in his hot tub, he recalled with a cringe—she'd stared into his eyes with an unaccustomed directness, held his gaze, and said:

"Are you ready to evolve?"

He didn't have to ask what that meant. As it turned out, he was ready, and they'd shared the best two years of his life mutually discovering what it meant to be not just lovers but partners. She made him a better person. He was better with her than without her.

He had a brother here in Honolulu and a father somewhere, but he rarely saw either. He had a few friends, none of them close. His world was his fiction, his college mentor, and Leilani. He cared more about her than anyone he'd ever known.

Dylan stroked and teased her for a long time, until her arousal reached a level so intense she could no longer remain still. He knew she liked to feel his lips on her, not just at the usual points of interest but everywhere, on the nape of her neck, across her arms, between each knuckle, across her soft belly, up and down her legs. He sucked on her toes, gently at first, then with increasing pressure. Only a few moments of that and she was moaning, undulating her hips, wanting him.

"Ready?"

"Yes," she whispered. "Please, yes."

He resisted the temptation to take her hard and fast. There were times when she liked that, but this was not one of them. Instead, he entered slowly. A sudden gasping told him he had touched exactly the right spot. He gently massaged her from the inside out. Only when her cries of ecstasy resounded did he plunge. He leaned forward powerfully, squeezing her buttocks together, pushing with increasing force. She screamed and he began pounding, strong and rhythmically. Her head turned sideways and she whimpered while he continued thrusting with thighs muscled by daily long-distance power runs. Running was Dylan's other passion. He strove for stamina and style. Just as he did now.

Leilani's cries echoed through the dark bedroom. He knew it would not be long now. She flung her head back, urgently, her long black hair flying. She gripped his hand and pulled him closer, harder, faster. He grabbed her hair, tugging her head toward him, and that clinched it. They both exploded at the same time, crying out to the heavens, totally immersed in a shared moment of bliss.

When enough time had passed, he rolled her over gently and wrapped his arms around her. It was a full minute before either spoke.

"My God, Dylan. Oh my God."

Not scintillating dialogue, but he knew what she was saying. "I feel the same way. You're wonderful."

"*You're* wonderful. I remember imagining what you would be like when we first met. I mean, you're a writer. I expected you to be timid and to use words like, 'Indubitably.' But a part of me still wondered—could he make love like Fargo Cody does?" She purred again. "No scene in a book could ever be as powerful as what we share."

Dylan stroked her cheek. This was a problem he often faced—people expecting the creator to be as incredible as his fictional creation. Dylan enjoyed writing those books, trying to recreate the works that had sustained him in his youth—John Buchan, Graham Greene, Ian Fleming, Trevanian. But even though he took pride in his creations, Fargo Cody was only fiction. No one could be so clever, brave, and thoroughly fantastic in real life. Certainly not Dylan.

"We're writing our own book," he replied. "And it's the greatest story ever told." He stood up, naked, and opened the rear window so the breeze would cool them. The palm trees on the beach below swayed mysteriously, silhouetted against the cerulean blue of the Hawaiian night sky. The fronds seemed to slither toward him like undulating arms threatening to seize him and carry him away. He'd taken this pricey penthouse condo for the view, the security, and the privacy. He preferred his hidden cabin in the wilds of Pupukea, on the North Shore, but when he had to be in Honolulu, this was a place he and Leilani could stay free from prying eyes and autograph hounds.

"Dylan, I--I feel...very close to you right now."

He flipped his tousled black hair out of his gray eyes. "That's the oxytocin talking."

"No. I'm having very...serious thoughts. About us. You meant it, didn't you? When you said you wanted to be with me always?"

He returned to the bed and gazed into her lovely Hawaiian eyes. "Just because I'm a fiction writer doesn't mean I make everything up."

"I'm glad to hear it," she said. "I've been with you two years and I've still never met your family."

"Believe me, you don't want to."

"I'd like to have your father's blessing."

"I don't know why. I never did." Dylan's mother died when he was six. He and his brother had been raised by their father, in a manner of speaking. "I have a better idea. Let's start our own family."

She threw her arms around him. "Do you mean it?"

"I mean it."

The instant his lips touched hers, the bedroom door slammed open with such speed and force that Dylan involuntarily dug his fingers into Leilani's flesh. Before he could see anything, he heard the rush of movement. Heavy footsteps. A shadowy figure at the end of the bed. No, there were three figures moving rapidly across the room. How did they get in?

Dylan sat up, positioning himself between the intruders and Leilani. "What the hell is—"

Dylan never finished. Something hard hit him in the jaw, slamming his upper body against the headboard.

"Dylan!" Leilani touched his face. "Dylan!"

A barely visible hand turned on the lamp on Dylan's side of the bed.

Blinking rapidly, struggling to remain conscious, Dylan saw a fair-haired giant with a buzzcut. From Dylan's perspective, he seemed huge, massively built, with arms like barbells and a neck as thick as a pipeline. Dylan exercised regularly, but this man looked superhuman. Sinewy veins snaked through his muscled arms like corded rope. The two other men were smaller but obviously strong. One looked as if he'd come from India, or perhaps Pakistan. The other was Caucasian with a face horribly scarred by acne.

The buzzcut grinned in a manner reminiscent of a dog baring its teeth. "Nice home." He spoke with an accent—Russian, Dylan thought. "Nice woman."

Dylan motioned for Leilani to stay behind him. He felt a sudden rush of fear—but that was good. Fear was a stimulant that sharpened his mind. He would need to think fast to protect Leilani and himself. This was like something out of one of his books. Except he would never have used the thug with the acne-scarred face. Too cliché—the scars on the outside reflect the evil within, so banal and almost—

"You listen?" Buzzcut said, shaking Dylan by the shoulders. He had a growling voice, like aural sandpaper. "You come with me."

"What are you doing in my home?" Dylan kept his voice firm. He'd read that psychopaths could smell fear, like wild beasts. He needed to remain calm, to buy time until he could think his way out, or find a weapon, or help arrived.

"No questions. Come—"

Somewhere nearby, probably the corridor outside the front door, Dylan heard a creaking sound.

Leilani sat up, the bedsheet pulled around her chest, and screamed. *"Help!"*

Buzzcut snapped his fingers, then pointed at his acne-scarred accomplice. He grabbed Leilani by the neck, lifted her naked body into the air and hurled her across the room. She hit the mirror over Dylan's dresser, shattering it into pieces. She fell down onto the dresser amidst a hail of glass shards, then bounced and rolled onto the floor. The top drawer shot out, spilling its contents onto Leilani's limp body.

"*Leilani!* Can you hear me?" Dylan started forward, but the two thugs raised large guns and pointed them at his face.

Leilani's legs and arms were cut and bleeding, twisted at unnatural angles. She did not move. Her eyes were closed.

Dylan froze, suppressing his rage. Getting himself killed would not help Leilani. Surely someone outside heard the crash.

"Stay where you are," Buzzcut said. "You cannot help. You only make it worse. If you do not do what I tell you—my friend slices up her pretty naked body. She dies. You watch."

CHAPTER
TWO

DYLAN STARED at the three men, his brain scrambling for a plan of action. He was accustomed to orchestrating dramatic situations, rearranging facts and characters to suit his purposes. He was a planner, not an improviser. But here he didn't have time to plan, and worse, he couldn't control the characters. He didn't even know who they were.

And Leilani lay on the floor, not moving.

"All right then," Buzzcut said. "If you keep voice low, you can talk. We have maybe one minute before we leave." He paused. "You may call me Xavier."

Dylan took advantage of the opening. "Okay...Xavier. Why did you attack Leilani?"

"She compromised mission."

"You hurt her."

"Collateral damage."

"You *hurt* her."

"And?"

Dylan watched the man carefully, gathering information from the way he talked, the way he carried himself, the way he dressed, even down to his thick-dialed wristwatch. This man was a soldier, one who'd seen combat. He was not afraid to hurt people. He would do whatever was required to obtain his objective. "What do you want?"

"My associate has proposition for you."

My associate? Dylan forced himself to think clearly. He needed to remember every detail about everything that happened, every word, every facial expression, every gesture. You can't write a character until you understand how he thinks. If Dylan paid close attention, he might glean information this man would never tell him.

The way Xavier just said "my associate" told Dylan what he really meant was "my boss." Xavier might be in charge of this assault, but he was not in command.

"Whatever your associate is offering," Dylan said, "I'm not interested."

"I use word 'proposition' to be nice. You have no choice." Xavier glanced at his watch. "Time is up. We should go."

"I'm not going anywhere with you."

"You can walk on own feet, or I can have friend work you over and drag you out. Your choice."

"I can't leave Leilani. I don't know how badly she's hurt."

"What do you care? We waited till you finished, right?" Xavier grinned, but on him, the expression was chilling. "Even let you cuddle some, yes?" He laughed. "Bitch squeals like pig."

Dylan's voice went cold. "You were watching us?"

"We watch for long time."

"That's impossible."

"That's easy. Just like breaking in here."

So they have high-tech surveillance equipment and the ability to override a top-of-the-line security system. Xavier was not employed by amateurs.

Keep him talking, Dylan. The more he talks, the more you'll learn. "Who is this associate of yours?"

"I cannot give you name."

"Then what should I call him?"

"How about...Mr. X? Like in *The Diogenes Deception.*"

Dylan's lips parted. This cretin who broke into his condo—*reads his books?*

"Let us do this easy way. My associate thinks you work better if not crippled." He paused. "But I will do whatever it takes to get job done. I—"

He stopped in mid-sentence. Dylan heard the squeaking noise outside again, but this time, it was much closer. Someone was heading this way.

"Dylan? Everything all right in there?"

Dylan recognized the voice. It was Kai Fielding, the building's night watchman. This was Dylan's chance—possibly the only one he would get. They would be reluctant to shoot with a security guard nearby. But it was still dangerous.

What would Fargo Cody do?

He'd take any chance he got.

Dylan leapt from the bed, grabbed the lamp on the end table and swung it hard at Xavier's hand, sending his gun flying. While the man was momentarily distracted, Dylan raced past him, grabbed a bottle of cologne from the dresser and sprayed it into the other gunman's face. He shouted and tumbled backward into his associate.

The path was clear. Dylan darted toward the door, plunged through the threshold—

And two large hands clapped down onto his shoulders, pulling him back into the room. They wrenched his right arm backward, sending lightning bolts of pain rippling through him. Someone kicked his knees out from behind and he fell hard. More pain shot up his spine.

"Big mistake, Dylan," Xavier whispered.

Dylan couldn't budge, much less escape.

He heard more noise outside. "Dylan, are you okay?"

Fielding stepped into the bedroom, saw the shattered glass, saw Leilani on the floor, saw Dylan pinned down and three men standing behind him. "What in the—"

He reached for his weapon, but Xavier grabbed his hand, twisted his arm behind his back, and pressed down on the pressure point of his palm. Fielding dropped his gun and fell to his knees.

"You make mistake, Dylan," Xavier grunted. "Now this man pays for it." Xavier picked up his gun from the floor.

"Why?" Dylan said. "He hasn't done anything. Don't—"

Xavier fired. The gun had a suppresser, but Dylan was so close he could still hear it, could feel the bullet whiz past him. The shot ripped the top of Fielding's skull off like the lid of a tin can. Fielding made a gurgling noise and toppled, blood and viscous cranial matter spilling out of his head.

"Oh my God," Dylan whispered under his breath.

"His death—your fault," Xavier said, yanking Dylan to his feet. "I hope you not make me do anything worse. We leave now. Stay silent or I silence you." He nodded to his associate. "Take care of girl." He pushed Dylan out of the bedroom.

"Take care of her? What does that mean? What are you going to do to her?"

Xavier clenched his teeth. "I tell you to keep goddamn mouth shut."

His fist rocketed toward Dylan, a barely visible blur. It appeared huge, like a missile heat-seeking its way toward him.

Dylan felt the fist hit his neck, felt the air rush out of his lungs, felt the dry, sucking sensation in his throat. I can't breathe, he thought, but before he could focus on that, he felt a boot to the solar plexus and after that, he felt nothing at all.

CHAPTER
THREE

DYLAN AWOKE IN DARKNESS.

His neck hurt. He wanted to massage it, but he was unable to move his arms—or anything else. The air seemed hot and thick. He had trouble breathing. Sweat trickled down his face, creating an itch he was unable to scratch.

Several seconds passed before he realized his hands were tied behind his back. His feet were also bound. Something pulled on his arms, stretching them backward, and it hurt. He was wearing some sort of loose-fitting garment, like a hospital gown. Something covered his head.

What was going on?

His first attempt to speak failed. His jaw felt as if it had been wired together and his tongue was drier than dirt.

He tried again. "Where...am I?"

"You really think we tell you?" Xavier's voice. "Why you think we put hood over head?"

"We?" Dylan said weakly.

"Pardon poor manners." Dylan sensed movement behind him, and a moment later, felt the brush of burlap against his face.

Light assaulted him. He squinted until his eyes adjusted to the sudden harsh illumination.

Four walls, one light overhead, no furniture. A stripped hotel room?

A warehouse? A storage locker? Impossible to know.

Xavier slipped a loop of rope around Dylan's neck. The rope ran upward to a square block fastened to a hook on the ceiling. A simple block and tackle apparatus, with potentially lethal applications.

Xavier pulled on his end of the rope. The noose tightened around Dylan's neck. It cut into his flesh. It burned, and worse, cut off his breathing. Adrenaline rushed through his veins. He rose to his feet, creating slack in the line, but Xavier pulled harder to compensate. Dylan pushed up on his toes. Xavier yanked even harder. When the noose was tight enough to constrict his breathing again, Xavier tied it to another hook in the wall to maintain the tension. Dylan was forced to remain on his toes, gasping for air. He could feel his face reddening, the rope rubbing his neck raw.

"Mr. X also here with us."

"Yeah? Where?" Dylan asked, in short bursts of expelled air.

"Very pleased to meet you, Mr. Taggart."

Dylan's eyebrows rose an inch. Mr. X was a woman.

Dylan reined in his surprise and put his brain back into first gear. Despite the fact that he was being tortured, he had to focus his attention, collect all possible data. Remember everything, he told himself. Every detail.

She was middle-aged, with vivid red hair that fell below her shoulders. The left side of her face was horribly scarred. The skin beneath her left eye drooped, revealing the underside of her eyeball. The scars were white and thick—keloids, he suspected.

"I do hope your head doesn't hurt too badly." She spoke with an Irish brogue. "We gave you an injection before you awoke. It should alleviate some of the pain."

If she was so concerned about his pain, why were they torturing him? "You gave me...an injection?"

"It's rather difficult to have a serious conversation with someone whose head is in a pea-souper."

"Where's Leilani? How is she?"

"She's fine," Mr. X answered. "Xavier left someone to watch over her. All she needed were bandages and a few choice drugs from the chemist. She may limp for a bit, but it will pass."

"Where am I?"

"It doesn't matter."

It did to him. He shouldn't have been unconsciousness for more than a few minutes, certainly no more than half an hour. And they had apparently used some sort of stimulant to rouse him. So they couldn't have taken him far. He must still be on Oahu, probably still in Honolulu.

"What is it you want?" Dylan asked.

"I want us to be friends."

And the bizarre thing was, she acted as if she meant it. Her tone was, if not friendly, perfectly businesslike. He needed more information.

"I guessing you didn't have a lot of friends when you were growing up," Dylan said, straining against the noose. "You don't seem to have a grasp of the fundamentals."

"Ah, the mordant wit of the artist. I should've expected as much."

"I'm guessing you're not renowned for your sense of humor."

"'Tis true. Not many playmates in Belfast back in the day. Not many laughs, either. I did eventually muster a few mates, when I was older."

"And your friends were, what? IRA?"

She tried to smile, but the scar damage on the left side of her face made it lop-sided and disturbing. "Given your current situation, I would think you'd have more pressing interests than my autobiography."

"You're wrong. I want to know all about you. I might use you in a novel."

"I wouldn't be good for fiction. I can't be reduced to a single traumatic childhood incident. My backstory is dull."

"Life in the IRA was dull? That's hard to imagine."

"I suppose there were moments. When things went right."

"They didn't always?"

"You don't find the pot of gold every day."

"And you're wearing the proof of that on your face?"

Her neck stiffened. She gazed at him levelly. "I know what you're doing. Don't waste your breath. I've had a great deal more experience extracting information than you have."

"I don't know what you're talking about."

"Just relax and listen, Taggart. Do you have your listening ears on?"

He twisted his neck around, struggling to breathe. He flexed his toes to reduce the strain. "Always."

"Is there anything I can get you?"

"Ten minutes with the bastard who hurt Leilani."

He felt the noose tighten. Apparently this was the wrong thing to say.

"That request I cannot grant. Is there anything else you would like?"

"My freedom."

"You'll have your freedom. After we're done talking."

That threw him. But he didn't let it show. "All right. Talk."

"I've heard that all writing is autobiography, on some level," she continued. "So I read one of your books. Xavier selected it for me. He's more familiar with this genre. It was called *The Singapore Sanction*. Clever premise, and Fargo Cody's plan to infiltrate the Japanese Yakuza was ingenious. One can only admire the way he defeats his enemies without a gun, without resorting to violence. But I thought you let your liberal politics get in the way of your storytelling."

"I'm supposed to take literary criticism from a...a..." He was fishing under the guise of floundering.

"Freelance terrorist," Mr. X supplied. "Someone who knows a good deal about real-world politics and consequently doesn't care to read superficial, ill-informed polemics in escapist fiction."

"'Freelance terrorist?' Meaning, you operate independent of any government?"

"Meaning I work for hire," she replied. "As you surmised, I learned my trade in my homeland. With the IRA. Until I met with an unfortunate accident." He tried not to look at her scars as she said it. "And then your President Clinton entered the fray and the next thing you know, the fighting is over. What's a working girl to do? I had to repurpose myself."

Dylan watched her eyes carefully and read between the lines. Xavier was not the boss of this operation—and neither was she. Someone hired her. Someone was pulling both their strings. "So you don't care what the cause is. You're just in it for money."

Xavier and Mr. X looked at one another for a long moment. The expression on Mr. X's face changed.

"No," she replied. "I wouldn't say that." Dylan detected a slight tension in her neck. "We are both highly motivated to complete this mission. So don't delude yourself into thinking we're going to give you any choice about helping us."

"You've committed actual acts of terrorism? For your current employer?"

"Yes." She did not correct his use of the word "employer."

"Prove it. Give me an example."

"Not that I need to prove anything to you. But did you read about the explosion at the Cartwright Institute of Hawaiian Antiquities a few weeks ago? Not far from where you live?"

"Some kind of gas main explosion."

"Yes. Triggered by two pounds of K4."

"That was your organization?"

"That was me," Xavier said.

Dylan's toes hurt and his head felt as if it would implode from insufficient oxygenation. But he knew he needed to keep them talking. "Why the explosion?"

"Unexpected problems. Big disaster. We lose four men. I barely escape. But I got intel."

"And attracted far too much attention in the process," Mr. X said. "We should've gone in quietly and we should've had a contingency evac plan more sophisticated than blowing the place to bits. One clever idea would've been more useful—and less obtrusive—than six pounds of K4." She pursed her lips. "Please don't misunderstand me, Taggart. We're very good at what we do. But for the task we will next undertake, we need to be better than very good. We need to accomplish the impossible."

"Sounds like time to quit."

"No. Time for fresh perspectives. New ideas."

"I don't see what this has to do with me."

"Isn't it obvious? We need a new idea man, Dylan. And we choose...you."

CHAPTER
FOUR

LEILANI WOKE SCREAMING.

Her throat was so raw it hurt. Where was she?

It took her several moments to realize she was still in Dylan's condo. In the living room on the sofa opposite the kitchen. Her entire body ached and her left leg throbbed and—

She looked down at herself. She'd been naked before, but now she was wearing a nightgown, *her* nightgown, the pink lacy number she'd worn earlier that night. Before Dylan took it off.

Every muscle in her body stiffened. *Who put it back on?*

She pulled up the nightgown and stared at her legs. Her left leg had been bandaged. A three-by-three-inch air-permeable gauze bandage covered what must be the worst laceration. All the wounds had been cleaned.

Had she gone to a hospital? If so, how did she get there? Was she discharged?

"Dylan?"

"He ain't here."

She bolted upright, eyes wide, hands crossed over her breasts.

Someone sat on the other side of the coffee table. In the armchair, slouching. The man with the scarred face. The one who hoisted her by the neck and—

She pushed onto her feet, desperate to get away, to create as much space as possible between herself and that hideous man. The moment she put weight on her left leg, a painful jolt radiated through her femur. She hobbled forward, ignoring the hurt, rounding the sofa and heading toward the door—

"You can't get out."

She grabbed the doorknob and pulled, but it was locked. Where was the key? She had to get out of here before that madman came after her and—

"I'm not gonna hurt you. Probably."

She paused, took a breath, and noticed that he was still sitting in the armchair. He hadn't moved.

"I'm not gonna do anythin' to you. Not that I wouldn't enjoy it. Xavier left me here to give you a message."

Leilani grabbed the back of the sofa. Whether he was moving or not, she felt better with a large object between them. Her heart pounded and the agony intensified every second she stood. "I—don't believe you."

"Look, you've been out for hours. If I wanted to do somethin' to you, it'd already be done. Who do you think got you looked after?"

Someone *had* treated her wounds. That she could not deny. "Why would you want to help me?"

"I don't. I'm a soldier. I do what I'm told. Xavier said to take care of you, so I called in a doc who works for us. He looked you over good, got you all cleaned up. Got the glass out. Gave you a shot of somethin'. I don't know what it was."

Leilani had to control her gag reflex to keep from vomiting. A stranger—some criminal doctor—injected a foreign substance into her body. She didn't know what it was and she had no way of learning. She felt dirty. She didn't think she'd been sexually assaulted. But she felt as if she had.

"Where's Dylan?"

"I can't tell you that, or why they took him or who we work for, so don't bother asking. Here's the message." He rose slowly to his feet. Leilani reflexively took a step back. "After I leave, you're gonna be tempted to call the cops. Don't. If you tell anything to anyone, we kill you." He smiled. "After we have some fun with you."

"I'm not afraid of you."

"You should be, sister, because this operation is bigger than you can imagine. We're everywhere. If you call someone, we'll know. If you write anyone, we'll know. If you so much as drop a hint, we'll know. You'll die a horrible death. And so will your boyfriend."

She glared at him, her lips curled.

"I'm gettin' the impression you're not convinced you oughta keep your trap shut. So let me show you somethin'. Go take a look in the bedroom."

Cautiously, keeping her eyes on him at all times, she edged into the bedroom.

All the air rushed out of her lungs.

"Bad, ain't it?"

Leilani had met Fielding, the security guard, on several occasions. He was a friendly, easy-going man. She liked him.

His brains were spilled out on the floor surrounded by a pool of his own blood. The top of his head was missing. His face was a ghastly turquoise.

While she stared at the decaying corpse, the scarred man grabbed her neck and shoved her downward. Her face was only inches from the corpse, the splattered brains.

She held her breath. She was a paramedic. She was used to blood. But not this. Never anything like this.

The man shoved her even closer. "That's what happens if you open your mouth."

He released her, then pressed his hands together. "Lemme give you somethin' else to think about. You call the cops, they'll think your boy plugged the guard."

"They wouldn't be so stupid. Dylan doesn't even own a gun."

"The records will show he bought a gun two years ago and that gun plugged the guard. His prints are on it, and we'll arrange for the police to find it. They'll assume the guard stumbled onto your loverboy's cocaine racket—"

"What?"

"—when they find the huge stash we planted. They'll think he killed the guard to keep him from exposin' that druggie side hustle. Considerin' all the people we own in the police force and the courtroom, I can guarantee your boy spends the rest of his life in prison. Where I understand sensitive writer-types don't do so hot."

"It'll never work. I'll tell the police what I know."

"You go anywhere near the police station, you're dead."

Leilani didn't know what to say. She felt trapped, boxed in, unable to think of a way out. She'd forced herself to be tough her entire life. She'd had no choice--no parents since the age of ten, never fitting in anywhere. She'd always managed to brazen out a solution, no matter what problems confronted her. But her mind was blank. She was just as powerless as she'd been when this gargoyle threw her across the room. Totally vulnerable, utterly exposed.

"I'm outta here." He grinned. "Unless maybe you'd like to go a few rounds with me on the sheets. I hear you're pretty hot stuff."

Her eyes narrowed. "Go."

He leaned in so close she could feel his fetid breath on her face. "How about a French kiss, sweetheart? You'll like it. I promise. You think that queer-ass writer-boy of yours is hot stuff? I could show you what it feels like to have a real man between your legs."

Without thinking about it, Leilani slapped him across the face.

He massaged the sore spot, laughing. "Gotta hand it to you, baby. You got a pretty mean swing." He laughed some more, then he wrapped his hand around her throat and shoved her back against the wall. With his other hand, he grabbed her waist and hoisted her into the air.

Don't throw me! she thought, her eyes clenched shut. *Please don't throw me!*

"Do you know how badly I could hurt you?" he bellowed. "I could cut you in places you didn't know you had. I could do you till there's nothin' left to do!"

She felt his elbows bend and braced herself for impact.

He dropped her onto the sofa.

"But the boss says no." His voice resumed its previous tone. "Not now, anyway." He winked, then walked to the door and unlocked it. "So remember. Not a word to anyone. Or I'll be back." He closed the door behind him.

Leilani curled up into a fetal position, arms wrapped around her legs, hugging herself tightly. She told herself to be strong, told herself to be brave, but no matter what she did or thought, she couldn't stop the trembling.

CHAPTER
FIVE

"ME? WORK FOR TERRORISTS?" Dylan wanted to laugh in her disfigured face, but he knew that wouldn't be smart, especially with this noose wrapped tightly around his neck. Play along with her, he told himself. The more you learn, the better you'll be able to fight them. To formulate a plan. That was what he did best.

But a plan required information. "What is it you want to do?"

"You didn't answer my question. Will you help us?"

"I don't know whether I can help until I know what you want."

"I'd rather have you on board before I reveal all the details."

"I understand your reticence, but I can't give any meaningful consent until you tell me more about the operation."

"The details of the operation are what we want you to devise."

"Tell me the objective and I'll tell you whether I can achieve it."

She laughed, but there was no merriment in it. "You're good, Taggart. But I've been in this game a long time, so don't waste your energy trying to outthink me." She ran a long black fingernail down the side of his cheek. "Our immediate objective is to steal military intelligence that will allow us to control a radical new weapon of enormous power."

Something about the way she said it—devoid of inflection yet teeming with phrases like "enormous power"—made it impossible to doubt her. She wasn't just delusional, though insanity was a definite possibility. He wondered how much more he could get her to say. "What do you plan to do with this...weapon?"

She broke eye contact and paced around him in small circles. He couldn't turn his neck far enough to follow her movements. "There's a conference being held in Hawaii in about two months. Many important people will be there."

"Tell me you're not talking about the G20 summit." Dylan stayed well informed on world affairs—his job required it—and he knew the annual summit of the leaders of the greatest economic powers was being held on Oahu in a few weeks.

"Very astute."

His neck was raw from the rope and he didn't think he could remain on his toes much longer. "Which leader are you planning to assassinate?"

"Does it matter? Someone wants a job done. We're going to do it."

"I didn't know political assassinations could be outsourced."

"How naïve. Have you heard of Blackwater USA?"

He had, of course. "Weren't they a private security firm?"

"That would be a generous way of putting it. They're the consortium the CIA hired in '04 to locate and assassinate top Al-Qaeda operatives. Since 1976, the CIA has been barred by executive order from carrying out assassinations—so they hired someone else to do it. Blackwater also guarded American diplomats in Iraq, using extreme force on several occasions. Seventeen civilians were killed. After the political donnybrook and a few mergers, Blackwater changed its name to Constellis Holdings." She paused. "But if the CIA can outsource assassination..."

"So can your employer." He listened to her voice carefully. He had good reason to believe she wasn't telling him everything. She had broken eye contact just before Dylan mentioned the G20. This alleged assassination plan might be a total fabrication. At best, it was a small part of the overall scheme. "Why do you need a new weapon? Wouldn't a few well-placed snipers suffice?"

"Still baiting me, aren't you?" Her eyelids fluttered. "Or perhaps you're simply unfamiliar with the level of security the G20 summit will have. Snipers could never get anywhere near the leaders. The entire city block will be cordoned off and anyone entering will be subjected to high-security searches. Airspace will be restricted. Any plane or copter attempting to violate it will be shot down on sight. To get near these leaders, we would need a small army. Possibly a large army. And every soldier involved would know that he or she was on a suicide mission. Hard to find paid employees willing to do that."

Dylan wasn't buying it. Granted, the G20 would be tough to infiltrate, but these people seemed extremely resourceful. There was something she wasn't telling him. Probably a great deal she wasn't telling him.

"Who are you working for?" Dylan asked. "Al-Qaeda? The Taliban? China? Pakistan? Russia? North Korea?" Dylan watched her face as he rattled off each potential employer, but he didn't detect any meaningful reaction.

"All you need to know is that we require your help."

"And you think I'd be useful? That's absurd." Dylan drew in his breath. "I've never held a gun in my life. I just make up that stuff in my books."

"Writers have been very useful to people in my line of work in the past." Dylan wondered what she meant by that. "And they will be again."

Dylan's body ached and his neck bled. But he kept moving the conversation forward. "Okay, but why me? There are lots of writers out there."

"It's convenient that you live in Hawaii, near the weapon's installation site. But there's more to our selection than that. There are many people writing exciting adventures with stalwart heroes running and jumping and shooting. But your Fargo Cody is different. Like you, he doesn't own a gun. He says reliance on guns makes people sloppy. He relies on his brain. And in book after book, he ingeniously concocts nonviolent plans for breaking into supposedly secure places, getting what he wants, and getting out again. Without detection." She paused. "That's the one thing you write better than anyone else. And that's what we need."

"I'm flattered. But I already have a job."

"What if I told you working with us could be quite lucrative?"

"I've got plenty of money."

"What if I said you'd never have to write again?"

"I like writing. It's what I do."

Xavier cut in. "What if she said, if you not do it, I make your life endless misery?"

Xavier pulled on the rope, hoisting Dylan into the air. He felt his neck burn as the noose seared his throat, choking him and gashing him at the same time. His legs flailed. He grabbed the rope with both hands, trying to create some slack, but he could not fight gravity. He could feel blood on his fingers.

"Stop," Mr. X said. "Let him down."

Xavier obeyed with a grunt. Dylan fell to the ground on his hands and knees. He remained there for several moments, gasping, trying to clear his head.

Imagination. Use your imagination. Find a way out.

"You're planning an escape, aren't you?" Mr. X crouched down beside him, pressing her face close to his. "I can see the wheels turning behind your eyes. I can see the plot twists and character reversals falling into place. But they won't help you here. And besides, I already told you —once we're done chatting, I'm letting you go."

Dylan felt a stiffening of the rope, requiring him to get back on his feet. "If you're going to release me," Dylan asked, still short of breath, "why would you tell me about your plans?"

"Because you won't be able to tell anyone. Or stop us."

"How can you be sure?"

"You'll never have a chance." Her thin sliver of a smile was a knife gash across her face. "In fact, I'm so certain you won't be able to stop us, I'll tell you even more. We're not just killing one of the twenty world leaders. We're killing all of them. And thousands of other people who will be in attendance at the opening press conference. Journalists, security officers, attachés, protesters, spectators. All dead in an instant. We'll create a new world order—one that isn't dominated by the current superpowers." She paused. "And I for one will be a very happy woman."

Dylan kept a straight face, but he mentally made copious notes. When Mr. X was agitated, she talked more.

"You think you're smart, Dylan, very smart and oh so wise about the world. Let me tell you something. You know nothing. Your lack of real-world experience permeates your books. All you have is a clever imagination. I'm going to take that imagination, introduce it to the real world, and create an ingenious means to an impossible end. And you will not be able to stop me."

"Tell me who you are. Then I'll decide whether I want to help you."

With frightening suddenness, Mr. X clenched her fist and launched it. The blow landed in the soft part of Dylan's stomach with such explosive force that his head rocketed forward.

The next blow also hit his stomach, but lower, closer to the groin. As badly as the first blow had hurt, this one stung a hundred times more. Adrenaline rushed to his head, blotting out other thoughts, making it difficult to think.

Mr. X's whispered voice was so near it made him start. Her face was contorted, twisted. Her eyes were colorless black holes. "You want to know who I am?"

Dylan inhaled in short bursts, trying to subdue the pain. "Yes."

Dylan felt a strong hand clutch his crotch with a crushing grip. "I'm the woman with your balls in the palm of her hand."

She squeezed.

The pain was intense, crippling, unbearable. And when he thought it couldn't get any worse, she squeezed even harder.

"I hope you and that bitch you're screwing aren't planning on children," Mr. X said, her voice right in his ear.

Dylan's eyes watered. He kept his lips shut tight, refusing to make a sound. He was not giving her what she wanted. He would not give her the pleasure.

"I will have what I want, Taggart. Or I will rip your balls off and use them for earrings."

He forced his lips to move. "Is—the chat over? Can I go now?"

"Listen to me very carefully," she said, still squeezing with maximum force. "If you do not agree to work for us in twelve hours—everyone you love will be killed. Or worse."

Beads of sweat trickled down his face. "Are—we—done yet?"

"Twelve hours. And the longer you delay the inevitable, the more you will see your life fall apart. You will lose everything. Your lover, your mentor, your family, your friends. And you will still work for us. You will simply do so knowing your stubborn stupidity destroyed everyone you care about."

Even though he would've thought it impossible, she squeezed even tighter. And then, all at once, she released him.

Before he had a chance to recover, Xavier pounded his ham-thick fist into the side of Dylan's head. The pain seared through his skull, and a second later, the noose stiffened around his throat. He fell backward, struggling. The constriction on his neck increased, choking the life out of him. He tried to speak, but the words bounced off his oxygen-deprived brain.

From the fading click of her heels, he realized that Mr. X was leaving the room. "Twelve hours."

"Thought...you...were letting me go."

He heard a door close and realized she'd left the room.

Xavier hoisted him into the air.

The rope lacerated his flesh. It felt as if the rope went straight to the bone. He pulled futilely on the noose, but his brain was so fogged he could barely think straight. The room swirled and his eyelids were impossibly heavy.

Xavier pressed a sheet of cellophane over his face. Dylan inhaled and the thin plastic film was drawn into his mouth. He couldn't breathe at all now, couldn't even try. Bright flashes of light erupted behind his eyes. He felt sick and knew his head would explode at any moment.

Just before Dylan's consciousness mercifully faded, Xavier leaned forward, his lips twisted in perverse pleasure, and whispered into his ears the last words he would hear, words with absolutely no comfort in them.

How much are you willing to lose?

CHAPTER
SIX

LEILANI SCRUBBED blood off the hardwood floor, using an industrial strength cleaner to eliminate all traces. The work took hours. The blood and cranial matter stained the throw rug under the bed. She'd have to get rid of that. But she couldn't discard the floor. So she cleaned. She knew crime scene techs could use luminol to reveal traces. But she hoped they would never have any reason to do that.

After that monster left, she huddled on the sofa for a long time. But even though those feelings of fear were intense, they could not suppress an even more intense emotion, the most powerful she had ever experienced.

She loved Dylan Taggart. She loved him with an intensity that gave meaning to the word she had never before understood. He was the family she'd never had, and they were on the verge of planning a family even larger. She was not going to let these bastards take that away from her.

Leilani knew that this time, finally, she was not alone. Dylan would be doing whatever he could to escape. He was smart. He would come up with something. And when he did, she wouldn't let these people frame him, not for murder or anything else.

She would protect him, whatever the cost. She would fight for him. She would fight for *them*.

She'd already disposed of the corpse, in the dead of night.

Many years ago, she'd seen a movie where someone rolled a corpse up in a rug and carried it off. She never expected to be doing it herself, but since she had a rug that had to go, it seemed the logical approach. Unfortunately, the corpse was too stiff and heavy for her to get it over her shoulder, so she had to go down to the gardener's shed and retrieve a wheelbarrow. Even then it was tough. But she'd been making her own way in this world since she was fourteen and she'd been a paramedic for eleven years. She was accustomed to tough, to dealing with the dead and dying, to performing unpleasant tasks.

She did it at three a.m., when everyone else in the building was asleep. Moving the corpse wasn't the hardest part. Doing it quietly was the biggest challenge, especially given her leg injury. But she got the corpse into her van and drove to the far end of the island, to a secluded area near nothing and no one.

Then she set Fielding on fire.

She used gasoline and a match and let him burn until she was certain he'd be unidentifiable. The stench was revolting—Barbeque of the Damned, she kept thinking. The sight of melting flesh was so horrifying that after a few minutes she couldn't watch any longer. But she got the job done.

She dumped Fielding off a roadside cliff into one of those wonder-fully still-wild parts of Hawaii inaccessible by foot or automobile. She knew it would not be long before the wild pigs found him. His remains would probably never be discovered, but even if he were, no one would be able to identify him. There'd be no crime to pin on Dylan.

French kiss that, you asshole.

Just to be safe, she cleaned her van and searched Dylan's condo top to bottom for a cocaine stash. She didn't find one.

So sometimes these people bluffed. That was useful to know.

By the time the floor was scrubbed clean, every task she needed to accomplish was completed, except one. Contacting the authorities.

That was exactly what Pock-Face had warned her not to do. He'd threatened to kill her if she did, if she even tried.

But if she didn't, what would happen to Dylan? She was certain he would find a way to escape—but she didn't know how long it would take. Or what it might cost him. Better if someone was also working on this end. His chances of success might increase.

She was going to the police. What could Pock-Face do to her once she was inside the station? She drove to the local police headquarters. Even if that goon squad had some people on the inside, they couldn't have everyone. She'd take her case straight to the Chief of Police. She'd met him several times at charity functions she'd attended with Dylan. She didn't believe he could be on anyone's payroll. He would listen to her.

She parked her car on the street and walked up the stone steps toward the front door.

Her fingers froze just before she opened it.

If you tell anything to anyone, we kill you. After we have some fun with you.

That's what the man had said. But how could he know? What could he do about it even if he did know?

Not a word to anyone. Or I'll be back.

Leilani took a deep breath, steeled herself. She'd come this far. She would not stop now.

She opened the door.

Pock-Face stood just inside.

"Miss me, cunt?" He wagged his tongue at her.

She braced herself against the door. *How did he know?*

"You look good enough to eat, you know it, baby? And yeah, that's an offer."

She backed away, but he followed her, down the steps, then onto the street.

"I know what you're wonderin'," he continued. "If you scream, will someone come in time? The answer is, no. I've got a knife in my pocket and you'll be dead before you get the scream out. I got two guys to help me carry your body to the truck. You'll disappear and never be heard from again."

She stared at him, lips pressed tightly together. Could she make a run for it? Not likely.

"You're not gonna talk to anyone, got it? Not the cops, not your friends, not even a goddamn dog. You get one mistake—and you just made it. You won't get another one."

"I—I didn't—"

"And here's the other thing you need to know. Your Dylan is havin' a very bad night. But we're gonna make it three hundred times worse now. We're gonna do that because you screwed up."

"No! Please don't hurt him."

"Too late. Listen, I didn't care about you cleaning up the mess in the condo. Hell, someone had to do it. You showed spunk."

"I—I—"

"Spunk is what gets people killed. Spunk is what gets little girls fucked in the ass fifteen times over and then slowly cut into pieces. And that's what's gonna happen to you if you ever try anything like this again. You understand me?"

"I—understand."

"I hope so. For your sake. Not that I wouldn't mind havin' a go at that sweet ass of yours. But I don't think you'd enjoy it much. So get the hell out of here."

Leilani ran away as fast as she could.

She crawled into the car, put her head on the steering wheel, and closed her eyes. She hadn't helped Dylan. She hadn't helped anyone.

Her mind flashed on her parents, bleeding, their lives slowly oozing away, while she watched. She hadn't helped them, either. And now they were gone. She'd spent her entire adult life helping people, saving lives. But it seemed she could never save the ones who mattered most.

She'd done everything she knew how to do. But she hadn't helped Dylan. She'd made whatever torture he was going through worse.

That was the reality she had to face. She'd hurt the man she was trying to protect. That was her fate, the story of her life. She always hurt most the ones she loved best.

CHAPTER
SEVEN

DYLAN STOOD on the coffee table in the living room wearing nothing but his underwear, holding a ten-pound rock over his head. He'd been standing there for almost four hours. He'd wet himself. He tried not to, but after three hours, he couldn't hold it anymore.

People came and went. They saw him, but they had the courtesy not to say anything. They knew how ashamed he was, how utterly humiliated. Bobby saw him and ran, terrified he would be next. The mailman knocked on the door and Dylan knew that he saw. He didn't say anything. At least he showed that kindness. But he saw. Soon everyone in town would know. Everyone on the base, everyone in school.

Dylan was twelve years old.

He'd tried to sit down, but every time he did, the man in the uniform whipped him with a riding crop. The back of Dylan's legs bore harsh red marks. He dropped the rock several times, which also earned him a whipping. And then the man in the uniform put the rock back in his hands.

"You've earned this punishment."

Dylan knew better than to argue.

"You showed weakness. Weakness is cowardice. And the only cure for cowardice is shame. When the fear of shame becomes more powerful than the cowardice, the weakness ends."

Dylan's legs ached so badly he could no longer feel his feet. The rest of the world faded in and out. He heard voices calling to him, but he ignored them. He didn't want to talk to anyone. He didn't want them to know he was here. He was so ashamed, wishing he could be anywhere else. And so he let his mind wander, let it take him to a better place, a safer place, filled with love and adventure and thrills, far away from the Shame Table and the bitter humiliation that haunted him and—

The phone rang.

Dylan woke up, startled, naked, in his own bed.

His temples throbbed. He pressed his hand against his head, trying to erase the pain. His stomach and crotch ached. His neck was raw. He tried to pull his head together while he took his cellphone from the end table.

There was no mistaking the thick Russian accent on the other end of the line. "Your twelve hours began at noon. You have till midnight."

Dylan checked his watch. It was 12:05 p.m.

He was tempted to act defiant, but he knew that would not help him. He had to be clever. They were playing mind games with him. He would play right back. "I need more time," Dylan said. "To tie up loose ends. Say goodbye to my loved ones."

Xavier chuckled. "Don't take too long. Or you will have no loved ones left." The line went dead.

Dylan swore under his breath. Only twelve hours. He would have to make the most of it.

Every possible scenario ran through his brain. It was like plotting a story—but with a deadline far harsher than usual. He had to see the plot holes in advance and avoid them. There would be no chance for revision. He had to get it right the first time.

Despite the danger and the repulsiveness of his opponents, Dylan couldn't deny a certain frisson tingling down his spine. He was caught in the midst of an impossible situation—the sort of dilemma he created for Fargo Cody. He wasn't Fargo Cody, he knew that, not by a long shot. But he had to figure out what Fargo would do in this situation. He had to devise a Fargo Cody plan for accomplishing the impossible. The only problem was time. What Fargo Cody improvised, Dylan Taggart spent weeks devising.

He didn't have weeks now. He had twelve hours. To plan. To *plot*.

Because working for these people was not an option. Even if he gave them what they wanted, he knew what would happen when they were done with him.

Xavier and Mr. X were no different from the playground bullies he'd had to deal with during his navy-base schooldays. All bullies are ultimately driven by one thing: a deep, underlying feeling of inadequacy. Insecurity. No matter how many people they hurt, deep down, they suffered from a profound lack of self-esteem.

He could use that.

He saved Xavier's number and added it to his contacts list. If the bastard called again from that number, he'd know. Then he dialed Leilani's cell. Even as he did, he realized his phone was probably bugged or tagged. Maybe hers, too. Mr. X was convinced he wouldn't be able to talk to anyone. They probably also put surveillance cameras in the condo. Maybe had people out on the street, watching for him.

It would not be hard to contact the authorities. All it took was one phone call. He knew the Chief of Police personally. Knew a few people at the local NCTC office, too. He'd used them as technical advisors. He'd even taken them out for dinner. They liked him. They would know he wasn't just pulling their chain. They would start investigating. Xavier must've left a thousand traces a trained investigator could detect. They'd locate him and his dominatrix gal pal and shut down their whole insane scheme.

But first he had to make some phone calls. Without getting caught. Mr. X had threatened everyone he loved. Leilani, obviously. And Mr. X had specifically referenced his "mentor," so they must know about Dobie.

He picked up his cellphone and dialed Leilani. He knew they were probably listening. So he chose his words with precision.

"Hello?"

"Leilani, is it you? Are you okay?"

"Dylan, oh my God! Is it really you?"

"It's me, baby."

"I was so worried. They said—" She paused. He could hear her voice crack. "Dylan—did they hurt you?"

"I'll live. But I need you to listen to me. Very carefully."

"Dylan, I want to see you. I *need* to see you."

"Leilani, that just..." Think. If you give in too easily, they won't buy it. They need to hear you wrestling with the decision. "I have a difficult choice to make."

"What is it?"

"These people—they want me to do something. Something that goes against everything I believe in."

"Then tell them to go to hell. We have plans, Dylan. We have a family to—"

"But if I don't agree, they say horrible things will happen."

"Like what?"

"They said...They said..." He put a little choke into his voice. Not too much. He wasn't going for the Oscar. Just enough to make it believable. "No. I can't take the risk. I've made up my mind, Leilani. I'm going to help them. I'll be gone for a while. I just have to tie up a few loose ends first." Let the eavesdroppers think he was caving. "In the meantime, I need you to be strong."

"I want to see you."

"I can't do that, Leilani. I can't talk to anyone. I'm going away and —well, I think it's time for us to say goodbye."

"But—Dylan! We just said—"

"And I don't think we should talk anymore."

"Dylan—"

"And you can't talk to anyone about this. You must be strong, Leilani. Strong like Stacy."

Short pause. "But why?"

"I want you to be just like her. Do you hear me? Just. Like. Her. Twelve hours from now—well, it won't matter. I wish you all the best, Leilani."

Silence on the other end of the line.

"All right, Dylan. Whatever you say."

"Thank you. It's been great. Really great."

"Be careful, Dylan."

"I will. Bye now."

He hung up the phone. She would understand. But Xavier and his murderous monsters would be clueless. They'd think he'd just given her the big heave-ho.

Until she disappeared.

He looked around the bedroom. Someone had cleaned up the mess —including Fielding's corpse. Leilani, he'd be willing to bet. She was strong enough to get the job done.

He put on some clothes, making his selections carefully, but without appearing to do anything out of the ordinary. He counted all the cash in his wallet—about a hundred dollars. Better bring credit cards. And a checkbook. Then he went to the bathroom to clean up, casually shoving a few key items into his pockets.

From the closet in the living room, he grabbed a lightweight windbreaker. It was Hawaii, after all—you never knew when it might rain. Then he left the condo.

He could not know exactly where they might have hidden cameras. But he was certain he knew one place they would not have a camera.

The elevator. Because there was already one there. And for people at Xavier's tech level, it would be much simpler to hack into the existing closed-circuit signal than to install a new camera.

Dylan pushed the elevator button and waited. The doors opened and he stepped inside.

His penthouse condo was on the forty-second floor. That gave him about thirty seconds before he reached the parking garage.

As soon as the doors closed, he jumped up on the metal handrail, using it as a platform to spring even higher. While balanced precariously on the rail, he reached behind the security camera and pulled out the power cord. The red light at the base of the camera faded.

He checked the declining floor number readout. 38, 37, 36.

He pulled a battery-powered hair clipper out of his pocket, a remnant of the brief pre-Leilani period when he decided he was going to save himself a trip downtown by cutting his own hair—with disastrous results. Today he didn't care if it looked pretty. Watching his blurry reflection in the silver metal doors, he sheared off his hair, starting at the top, right through the center.

31, 30, 29.

Black curly locks tumbled to the floor, leaving only the thinnest layer of stubble behind. First the top, then the sides. He knew he prob-ably missed a few spots in the back. But it would do. He'd entered the elevator with long wavy hair. He would leave buzzed to the scalp.

22, 21, 20.

He tore off his jacket, then his shirt, then his undershirt. He'd chosen a dress shirt, still stiff from dry-cleaner starch. He wadded the shirt up, then wrapped the undershirt around it like a balloon, then tucked the open end under his belt so the bulk hung just above his belt. He reversed the jacket and zipped it up. He'd entered the elevator wearing red. He would leave wearing black. And he looked as if he had a pot belly, especially when he slouched.

15, 14, 13.

He shoved cotton balls into his mouth to change the shape of his face. He put on a pair of black horn-rimmed glasses he used to wear after his first book was published, primarily to make himself look smart and literary. Leilani had convinced him he didn't need a disguise to be what he already was—but fortunately, he still had the glasses.

He checked his reflection in the doors. He looked like a different person.

8, 7, 6.

He'd bought these khakis for his trek up Mt. Kilimanjaro, where it was cold in the morning but hot by midday. They were called convert-ible pants. A zipper in the middle of the pant leg allowed you to remove the bottom half, which he did.

He'd entered the elevator wearing long pants. He would leave wearing shorts.

5, 4, 3.

He stopped the elevator on 2—because they would expect him to ride all the way to the parking garage where he kept his Bentley. He hurried out of the elevator to the rear stairs, which took him to the opposite side of the building. They'd be watching the parking garage for a slender writer with unruly curly hair, a red jacket, and slacks. They would not notice the shaved head guy on the other side of the building with a black jacket, a pot belly, a pudgy face, eyeglasses, and shorts.

He walked along the cars parked on the street, scanning for an unlocked door. The first one he saw was a Corvette. He passed it by—

too flashy, too much what they would expect him to drive. And so new it might have a LoJack system—a GPS tracker to reveal its location if it was stolen. He kept looking. A few moments later he found an unlocked door on an old brown pickup—something he would never drive. It wouldn't have a LoJack. Probably had an 8-track tape player.

He slid into the driver's seat, reached under the console and hot-wired the ignition, a skill he'd acquired because Fargo Cody had to do it in his third book. Thirty seconds later, the engine fired.

He pulled onto Kalakaua, looking all around, checking his rear view mirror. No one was watching him. No one was following him.

He allowed himself a small smile. He'd given them the slip.

Mr. X said he would have no chance to tell anyone about their plans. But Leilani was already safe, and once he knew Dobie was protected, he would prove just how wrong that psychotic witch really was.

Fargo Cody was rolling into action again. But this time, for real.

CHAPTER
EIGHT

12:20 p.m.
Eleven hours, forty minutes left

LEILANI SAT at the kitchen table, cellphone in her hand, trying to decide what she should do next.

The last few hours had been the most challenging of her life—and that was saying quite a bit, given that she'd worked as a paramedic for eleven years. Someone with less fortitude might already be shell-shocked. And now she got a call from Dylan, free but inexplicably breaking up with her after professing his love and making future commitments the night before. A lesser woman might be spinning in circles.

But not Leilani. She was fortified by two facts she could not forget.

First, Dylan Taggart loved her. What she saw when she looked into his gray eyes could not be faked.

Second, she knew Dylan was not a quitter. He was one of the precious few who knew tenacity was the secret to life, the secret of creating a life worth living. Despite coming from a military environment and a father who never offered encouragement, he'd made himself one of the handful of people in the world who could support themselves writing fiction. That accomplishment required a special kind of resilience. It was not on the resume of a quitter.

Dylan had said these people wanted him to do something. Leilani didn't know what it was, but she knew this: it had to be illegal. Dylan would never do that willingly. She doubted he would do it at all.

So when he told her he was giving in to them, he was lying. The whole conversation was riddled with obfuscation and cryptic references. Why?

Only one possible answer. Someone was listening. And Dylan wanted them to believe he was joining them.

Because that was the exact opposite of what he planned to do.

He wasn't breaking up with her. He was protecting her. He was convincing the eavesdroppers she was out of the picture, so hurting her would not hurt him. When he said he didn't think they should talk anymore, he was saying, Don't call me. Don't talk to anyone else, either.

And when Dylan said he wanted her to be "just like Stacy," he was giving her an action plan. Only three words. But they told her everything she needed to know.

The reference to Stacy was something the eavesdroppers couldn't possibly understand, even if they had the condo under surveillance. Even if they'd researched Dylan's background extensively. Even if they'd read every book he ever wrote.

Because Stacy was a fictional character in a book that had not been published. In the book he was writing now.

No one had read the manuscript except Dylan and Leilani. Not his publisher, not his editor, not his agent. It was still in the rough-draft stage. They did not discuss it in the condo. They never talked business at home. Anytime she had suggestions, she gave them to him while they took their power walks. Even if Xavier had mirrored Dylan's hard drive, he wouldn't get it. Dylan knew other writers who'd been burned when their work-in-progress leaked prematurely. He took no chances. He wrote on a non-networked iPad and he locked it every night in a safe that could not be opened—even with the combination--without triggering an alarm.

No one else could know that when Dylan told her to be strong like Stacy, he was telling her to do what Stacy, the girlfriend of Fargo Cody, did. Which was first, ditch the thugs tailing her, and second, get to a safe place.

In the manuscript, Stacy fled to a cabin in the wilds of Oahu. Dylan was telling Leilani to go to the real-life equivalent. The cabin Dylan kept on the North Shore. The cabin that was almost as secret as the manuscript.

Dylan wanted a place out of the city, a retreat, a place to gather his thoughts and write. He didn't want to be followed by fans, critics, inter-viewers, or anyone else. Except her, of course—and there were limits to that. Dylan's lawyer bought the place in the name of a shell corporation created just for this purpose. Dylan was careful that no one saw him in the area. The Realtor had no contact with anyone but the lawyer. The money filtered through two offshore banks after it left the dummy corp's account. The title was not in Dylan's name.

No one knew about the cabin and no one, no matter how good they were, could find it. Dylan and Leilani hadn't been there for months, so even if these people had been following him for weeks, they wouldn't have seen the cabin. It was his sanctum sanctorum, he called it. His fortress of solitude.

And he wanted her to go there. So she would.

She'd rather be with him. She didn't know how he would foil these killers, but they were a team, and she knew they were stronger together than apart. So she respected his wishes. He knew much more about the situation than she did. If he wanted her to disappear, she would disappear.

Twelve hours, he'd said. She hoped that meant he would join her at the cabin in twelve hours. She'd be waiting for him.

She grabbed her purse and headed for the door. Before she went anywhere near the cabin, she'd have to lose anyone who might be following her. She didn't knew her driving skills weren't up to that job. Her paramedic team wouldn't even let her drive the ambulance. She needed help.

She had a few thoughts on how she might pull that off. But in the meantime, she had to act as if she were doing nothing suspicious. She had to play her part—the jilted girlfriend, distressed, injured, scared, but nonetheless going to work on time. Doing what was expected of her.

And then, just when they thought they had Dylan and Leilani trapped, she would disappear.

She didn't know who these people were. She didn't know what kind of monsters would employ a sleazebag like Pock-Face. But she knew this.

If they thought they could screw with Dylan Taggart and Leilani Kahale and get away with it, they had another think coming.

CHAPTER NINE

2:50 p.m.
Eleven hours, ten minutes left

DYLAN PARKED THE PICKUP, constantly scanning in all directions. It was remotely possible Mr. X had someone watching the place. Dylan's change of appearance had been sufficient to escape the condo, but he knew it wouldn't fool anyone who took a close look.

The attending nurse at the receiving desk of the Mahoe Assisted Living Center blinked twice, her eyes squinting, before she recognized him. "Mr. Taggart?"

He lifted the glasses so she could see his face more clearly. "It's me. And please call me Dylan."

"I'll try. But it's hard! I was reading your books even before Dobie came to stay with us. To me, you'll always be that handsome man on the dust jacket with the piercing grey eyes."

"Oh, I put my pants on in the morning one leg at a time, just like everyone else."

The nurse's eyes widened slightly. Her pupils dilated. Dylan got the distinct impression that putting his pants on in the morning was something she might like to observe first-hand. "I need to meet with your boss. And you, and any other staff members who have contact with Dobie."

As she gathered everyone, Dylan considered how best to approach this. How could he explain why he thought Dobie might be in danger? Even if he told them the whole story, they wouldn't believe it—and there was always a chance that one of Xavier's friends was listening. How could he persuade them to institute new security protocols without telling them what the threat was?

By the time everyone gathered in the manager's office, he had a plan. "I'll pay for it."

The manager, Joe Bendis, a balding man with poor posture, did not appear to welcome any interruption to the normal course of business. "But—why?"

"Have you read the papers lately? Honolulu is becoming a dangerous place."

"But we have twenty-four-hour security."

"I want you to double your security staff. In fact, I want you to triple it. Effective today. I'll give you a five-thousand-dollar bonus if you can implement this immediately."

Bendis brightened. "Well, yes then, of course. But—"

"I want Dobie watched at all times. And I mean all times. Even when he's sleeping. You don't have to hover over him, he won't like that. Just make sure he's watched. At least four guards, specifically assigned to protect him. And I want those four guards chosen randomly. No one who shows any interest. No one you've used in the past."

"Do you have some reason to think—"

"I'm the only family he has."

"Yes, but—"

"There's nothing more important than family. I have to take care of him. So I want you to go into lockdown mode. All doors secured. No strangers admitted. Until I say otherwise."

"How will I explain this to the other residents?"

"I don't care how you explain it. Tell them a hurricane's coming. Tell them you had a bad horoscope. Just do it."

"Well..."

Dylan took out his checkbook. "I'm making a five-thousand-dollar donation, right now. As a way of showing my appreciation for these extra efforts."

Bendis snapped up the check. That was easy enough. Dylan was glad to see he'd read the character correctly.

"How long will these heightened measures last?" Bendis asked.

"I'm not sure. I hope it will be over soon, but I can't make any guarantees. Surely that check covers the inconvenience."

Bendis gazed at it as if it were his long-lost son. "I suppose it does."

"Let me ask you a question. Have you added any new staff recently? Have you noticed anyone watching the facility? Has anyone shown a particular interest in Dobie?"

The attending nurse shook her head. "We haven't had any new hires for more than six months. I certainly haven't had any indication we're being watched. I would've reported it if I had. And the only outsider who seems to have any interest in Dobie is you."

Dylan nodded. "Mr. Bendis, I'm only going to be here about ten minutes. I'd like you to have those guards on Dobie before I leave."

"But that's impossible!"

"And if you can make it happen, I'll write another five-thousand-dollar check on my way out."

Bendis grabbed his phone. "I'll make the arrangements."

"Excellent. Now, can someone show me where Dobie is?"

"You're late," Dr. Iaukea said as Leilani entered the front office of the paramedics station at Kekekolio Hospital.

"I've had kind of a rough night," Leilani replied.

"I don't want to hear it," Iaukea said, raising a hand. "Just get to work. You're behind on your paperwork and I'm sure we'll get a call any minute. How long can this town go without a knifing or a shooting or a tourist falling off a surfboard into shark-infested waters?"

Leilani leaned across her superior's desk. "Liane, I need help."

Dr. Iaukea peered through her reading glasses. "Is this about that guy you're seeing?" She did not appear sympathetic. Leilani wondered if this was because she'd never been interested in seeing a guy, but Iaukea's personal life was her own business. "You're still with the writer, right? The one with the ridiculously expensive foreign car?"

"We're having...troubles," Leilani said.

Dr. Iaukea fell back into her chair. "Do I look like Dr. Phil?" She was in her mid-to-late forties and wore her crusty exterior like a raincoat. Despite the curmudgeonly attitude, most of which Leilani suspected was feigned, Leilani trusted her. She was intelligent—you didn't get through medical school if you weren't. And she was flinty. Wimps did not go into emergency medicine, easily the most stressful field in the healing arts. She'd not only chosen this practice, she'd excelled in it. That spoke to a level of competence that was exactly what Leilani needed right now. "I'm here to save lives, not to mend broken hearts."

"It's nothing like that. It's much more complicated."

"Okay, I'll bite. What's going on?"

"We're in danger."

"You and your writer? What, you're being stalked by a psychotic book critic?"

"No."

"Then what?"

"That's the trouble. I don't know much about it. And the less you know the better."

Dr. Iaukea removed her glasses and tossed them down on the desk. "Then what the hell am I supposed to do?"

"I need a favor," Leilani said. "One only you can provide."

"And that would be?"

"I need to disappear."

CHAPTER
TEN

1:32 p.m.
Ten hours, twenty-eight minutes left

DYLAN KNEW that Dobie loved the beach, even years before when he lived in California and taught at Stanford. Back then, Dylan spent many an oceanfront evening with his favorite professor, talking about books, dreaming of a life as a writer. Dobie had written a book in his youth, a brilliant novel called *Challengers of the Abyss*. It was highly acclaimed and nominated for the Pulitzer—but he never wrote again. He didn't seem to have a second book in him. So he focused on his teaching, mentoring the next generation of writers—like Dylan.

When the time came, Dylan brought him to Oahu and found this place for him—and a room with a lanai facing the beach. Excellent care-givers, the kind who didn't butt in when they weren't needed. If Dobie had to be in a home, this was the best possible choice. Dylan made sure he was always given first-rate attention.

Dobie sat upright in a wooden chair, slightly hunched but clean-shaven, wearing suspenders and a brown bow tie. He was eighty-nine years old, but he looked as if he were ready to go into the classroom and teach Modernist Literature.

"Dylan! What a delightful surprise!"

Dylan halted Dobie's attempt to stand and pulled a chair beside him. Dobie was in astonishing shape for his age, but Dylan was well aware that the doctors had diagnosed him with early-stage Alzheimer's. Every day his memories remained was a blessing.

"How are you, Dobie?"

"Oh fine, fine. Just watching the tides. Same old same old. Has anything exciting happened to you lately?"

Dylan almost laughed. "You could say that. But I can't go into the details. Sorry."

"You don't have to apologize to me. Have you read the new Michael Chabon?"

Dylan was startled, though not surprised, by the sudden change of subject. "Naturally." He couldn't help scanning as he talked. Hard to concentrate on literature when he knew killers were searching for him—and possibly for Dobie, too. He thought they were safe, but he couldn't risk overconfidence.

"And your thoughts?"

"Ingenious. As always."

Dobie nodded enthusiastically. His eyes lit, as they always did when he talked about books. "It's his best work yet. Why more people don't read him, I'll never understand. He's one for the ages. I know talent when I see it."

"I know you do," Dylan said, suppressing a smile.

"Back in the day, I was telling everyone in the faculty lounge to read James Joyce's *Ulysses*. Did they listen? No. They went on reading John Galsworthy and John Q. Marchand and a lot of other claptrap. And who was right, eh? Who was right?"

"*Ulysses* was the most important book of the century."

"Damn straight." Dobie tucked a thumb under a suspender strap and snapped it. "I was right, that's who." His eyes narrowed a bit. "I was right about you, too, Dylan."

"I'm hardly James Joyce."

"You write a damn good book."

"I'm pretty certain James Joyce never wrote gunfights, terrorist masterminds, or the world on the brink of an apocalypse."

"Don't sell yourself short. You've learned the fundamentals of storytelling and transformed them into a higher form of literature."

"I write adventure stories."

"So did Conrad. So did London. They took the conventions of the genre and infused them with new levels of meaning. You're still searching for your voice, true. But when you find it, you're going to write something important." He leaned forward. "You have something profound to say, Dylan. You just don't know it yet."

Behind Dobie, Dylan saw activity at the front door. The new security team had arrived. "I've still got the fountain pen you gave me when I graduated. Remember?" Dylan removed the Delta Dolcevita from his pocket. Gorgeous orange and black resin, a sharp fine nib. "When you gave it to me, you said, 'Every time you pick up a pen, you have the power to change the world.'"

"I meant it. And I still believe it."

"I'm having some books sent to you."

Dobie's eyes lit. "New masterpieces?"

He nodded. "Anne Tyler. Dennis Lehane. Jonathan Lethem."

"Brilliant?"

"That's what the critics say. But of course, you're the final arbiter."

"As it should be." He made a sniffing sound, straightened himself. "Thank you, Dylan. For everything."

"Dobie—I may have to go away for a while." He thought it best to reveal as little of his plan as possible. Just prepare him for the worst possible contingency. "I'm not sure when I might be able to return. So I've arranged for people to watch you."

"I don't need more keepers!"

"It's just temporary."

"I suppose I can put up with it if I have to." He paused. "Thanks for coming to see me. You're the only one who does, you know."

"I know," Dylan replied quietly.

"That boy of mine never visits. Just lives twenty minutes away." His hand twitched. He almost reached out—then stopped. "You're...my real son, Dylan."

"And you're the father I—well, you know."

They looked at one another for a long moment.

"Yes, indeed," Dobie said. "I know."

AFTER DOBIE'S new security team arrived and Dylan wrote another check, he spotted a phone on the reception desk by the front door.

All he had to do was make one phone call to the proper authorities. One call and Xavier and Mr. X's sick game would be over.

His hand hovered over the phone.

Could he be certain they weren't watching? Could he be certain they hadn't bugged this phone? They knew about Dobie.

No. He couldn't be certain. And he couldn't take any risks until Leilani had time to get to the cabin.

He'd like to get it over with, but he had to be careful. Stick to the plan. No improvising. There was still plenty of time left before the twelve hours expired. He would do this right and make sure no one got hurt in the process.

He left the retirement center and returned to his hijacked pickup. No one was watching. No one was following him.

Dobie was safe now. Leilani would be soon.

And then he would strike at the heart of this nest of vipers. Mr. X had squeezed him, hard. Now he was going to squeeze back.

LEILANI HAD BARELY BEEN at her desk for twenty minutes when the call came in—a shooting in Kalihi Valley, one of the poorest districts in the Honolulu area, perpetually troubled by street gangs. A teenage boy was down.

She usually paired with Michael Anders, a heavy-set and relentlessly amiable paramedic a couple of graduating classes ahead of her. This time, at Dr. Iaukea's direction, Maria Cameretti came as well. She was a dark-haired woman about Leilani's age.

"What are the odds?" Michael said, as he flipped on the siren and tore down the driveway. Leilani knew what he meant. What were the odds the kid would still be alive by the time they arrived?

"We can hope for the best," Maria replied. And that was the truth. They always hoped for the best. Because hoping didn't cost you anything. She would not have mentioned prayer. Because if they started praying for good results, soon every paramedic on earth would be an atheist.

"Sometimes I think they ought to board up the whole neighborhood and shut it down," Michael said. "Send everyone away."

"Are you kidding?" Maria replied. "I don't want thugs coming to my neighborhood."

"I'm sure they wouldn't all come. Just the ones who like petite raven-haired paramedics. That would be maybe half the thugs, tops."

"You can't cure crime by forced relocation. You cure it with education and job opportunities."

"Right. If those gang homeboys just had Ph.D.'s, crime would evaporate."

Leilani closed her eyes. She couldn't drum up any interest in what passed for current-events discussions in the front seat of an ambulance. She had far more pressing problems.

"What did you do to yourself, Leilani?" Maria asked.

Leilani was startled by the sudden digression. "Me? I'm fine."

"You're limping, girl. And I can see the cuts on your neck and arms."

"Oh, that. It's too stupid. I was stumbling around in the dark last night and I walked into a mirror."

Michael whistled. "Do you sleepwalk?"

"No, we were still up. It was just...an exciting evening."

"Oh ho ho. I'm getting the idea now. You and your writer were having wild-and-crazy monkey sex and he gave it to you so good you couldn't walk a straight line afterward."

Leilani liked Michael, but he had the emotional maturity of a fourteen-year-old. "That wasn't exactly it."

"What part did I get wrong?"

"The part about the monkey. There is no monkey in Dylan. It was more like wild-and-crazy Adonis god-like sex. All night long lollipop sex. Multi-orgasmic, ultra-intense, can't-get-enough-of-him, I'm-begging-for-more, do-him-till-candy-drops-out sex." She paused. "But I'm sure you know what that's like."

Michael fell silent. Maria grinned from ear-to-ear.

CHAPTER
ELEVEN

2:51 p.m.
Nine hours, nine minutes left

DYLAN ROUNDED the corner onto Smith Street, then pulled into the only available parking space and waited.

He didn't think anyone was following him. But he was cautious. If he had a tail, they would round the corner and not see him until they were already past him. He would get a good look at them and know from their reaction whether they were tracking him.

He waited two minutes, then three, then five. Only one car rounded the corner and it was driven by an elderly woman who did not appear remotely interested in him. She drove down the street, then took the first left toward Bishop.

He was not being followed.

He could go to the police station, or the local FBI or CIA office. But that was where Mr. X would expect him to go. They might be watching, waiting for him, especially now, after he'd given them the slip. A phone call would be safer. Especially since Leilani had not had time to get to the cabin yet.

Dylan ditched the fake pot belly, the cotton balls in his cheeks and the glasses, jumped out of the pickup, and headed toward Keona's Spy

Shop. Dylan had been here on numerous previous occasions conducting research, checking out the latest high-tech gizmos and quizzing Keona about spyware too expensive or restricted for retail sales.

He pushed open the door and stepped inside. He loved this place. He could easily pass an afternoon browsing. But this wasn't going to be one of those afternoons. He had a much more focused goal.

Keona's had the look and feel of a pawn shop, that dusty, low-rent, anything-goes ambiance. The shop smelled like its clientele, which was not a selling point. Even the air had a certain oiliness that made Dylan want to shower immediately. But he could tolerate that if it got him what he needed.

He surveyed the cards on the endcaps. Recording devices, some so small as to be virtually invisible. Vehicle trackers. Spy cameras. Listening devices. Night-vision optics. Voice distorters. Bug sweeping gear. Computer-monitoring thumb drives. A paradise for those with a desire to snoop.

Keona sat behind the front counter eating. He looked as if he hadn't shaved in a week or washed his hair or changed his shirt, which bore distinct traces of the last four hula burgers he'd consumed.

He didn't recognize Dylan at first. Only when he was a few feet away did Dylan see the light of recognition dawn in the proprietor's eyes.

"Whoa, Dylan—is that you? Extreme haircut, dude."

"It's me."

"How the hell are you?"

"You don't want to know. I'm in a hurry. I need to make a phone call."

Keona pushed forward the phone beside the cash register. "Go ahead. I assume you're not calling Marrakesh."

Dylan thought for a moment. What if he did use Keona's phone? They couldn't possibly anticipate that move. They couldn't pick up a landline on a frequency scanner. But it was still risky. No improvising, he told himself. He had a safer plan in mind.

"Listen to me carefully. I need to make a phone call without the slightest chance that the phone could be bugged, the line could be tapped, or the call could be overheard."

"Don't you have a cellphone?"

"Not secure."

"Buy a burner phone at ABC."

"Still not necessarily safe. Especially if I'm being monitored."

Keona grinned. "What kind of trouble has Fargo Cody gotten himself into this time?"

"This isn't about Fargo, Keona. This is about me."

———

THE KID WAS dead before Leilani and her colleagues found him sprawled across the front seat of the car. The kid's face was a ghastly translucent pale blue and his wound had stopped bleeding.

Leilani couldn't look at him without flashing on her parents, trapped in the front seat, their prostrate position and blood-caked faces all too similar. She washed it out of her brain. She needed to focus on what she was doing.

After the investigators finished their work, the body needed transport to the ME's office. Michael got the gurney out of the ambulance and they lifted the body onto it. A few minutes later they had the corpse wrapped in the standard black zipper-up-the-front body bag. They lowered the ramp and wheeled it into the ambulance.

A small crowd stood on the outskirts of the crime scene. Others watched from their porches. At least one woman cried. Leilani wondered if she knew the victim, or if she was lamenting what had happened to this once-respectable neighborhood.

Police officers arrived from the downtown headquarters and asked questions. Leilani was tempted to grab one of them and tell her story. But who would believe it? And what if Pock-Face was watching? No, Dylan knew more about the situation than she did. She would play this his way.

"I'll ride in the back," Maria said.

"Me too," Leilani replied.

Michael frowned. "You don't both need to attend a corpse."

"Is there a rule against it?"

"No. But I thought we might play the alphabet game during the drive back."

"You can play with yourself. I imagine you're used to it." Maria grabbed Leilani's arm. "We need some girl-talk time." She and Leilani jumped into the back of the ambulance and took their seats on either side of the gurney.

Michael was disappointed, but not entirely surprised. The surprise came when he pulled into the driveway outside the ME's office, got out, and opened the back doors.

There was only one woman in the back of the ambulance.

Leilani was gone.

CHAPTER
TWELVE

3:24 p.m.
Eight hours, thirty-six minutes left

"SO CAN YOU HELP ME?" Dylan asked Keona. "Can you get me a phone that cannot possibly be traced or overheard?"

"What's going on, Dylan?"

"I don't have time to explain."

"Trying to duck the NSA?"

"A much more dangerous organization."

Keona's bushy eyebrows knitted together. "Whatever. Want a weapon to go with that?"

"I don't use guns."

Keona gave him a look he didn't like. "You said this wasn't about Fargo Cody. So why are you playing by Fargo Cody rules?"

Dylan drew in his breath. "I know what I'm doing. Can you just get me the phone?"

Keona disappeared into the back room. Dylan heard furious rummaging, followed by a murmured, "Where did I put that?" A few moments later, he reemerged.

He plopped two objects down on the counter. One looked like an ordinary cellphone. The other was a small metal capsule, about the size of a fortune cookie. "That's what you want."

Dylan picked up the phone. "This can make calls? Safely?"

"Guaranteed. In the first place, the phone is clean. No one knows the number until you open this sealed canister. So no one is listening. The only possible problem would be if they know who you're going to call and they're monitoring that line, or if they scan the airwaves and pick up your frequency. But we can prevent that, too."

Keona pulled a small flat rectangular object out of his pocket. It was the same length as the phone and had a metal input plug at the bottom. Keona plugged it into the earphone jack.

"That's a Belmont RF-52 frequency scrambler. It's automatically active anytime you have it plugged into the phone. Someone tries to trace your signal or eavesdrop, either by working backwards from the line you've called or by using a frequency scanner—they get gibberish."

"What about the FBI's 'hot mike' technology? I understand it can trace any cellphone. Can even turn a cellphone into a listening device they can activate at will."

"That's true—but it requires a special SIM card, and they have to know your number or trace it back from someone you've called. I'm telling you, this phone is safe."

"Sounds good." Dylan studied the apparatus carefully. "But I know that if something like this exists, the CIA is working on a countermeasure to beat it. Probably already have something."

"You're right. They could beat this by monitoring the signals at the cellular server tower. That would give them the frequency and enable them to pinpoint your location, even if you use the scrambler. But it takes at least an hour, even assuming they're ready and waiting for you." He paused. "Dylan—are you hiding from the FBI?"

"No."

"Good. No one else has the right to monitor calls coming in or out of server towers. Even the cellular companies that own them can't."

He hoped Keona was right. But even if Xavier and his gang could hijack a tower, he wouldn't give them an hour. Five minutes would be long enough to reveal the essential details and arrange a meeting at a safe place. Then the authorities could take him into custody and he would talk his head off.

"What else can I get you, dude? If you're in trouble, I want to help."

"Just the phone and the scrambler."

"What about a nonlethal weapon? An air gun that shoots tranquilizer darts?"

"Tempting, but no."

"Directional shotgun microphone. Can pinpoint and pick up a conversation half a mile away."

"I'm traveling light."

"How about this?" Keona picked up what looked like a black magic wand.

"I write Fargo Cody, not Harry Potter."

"It's a metal detector. Like they use at the airport, but smaller." He pointed it at Dylan and a ringing sound immediately emerged from its base. "Dylan—are you packing?"

"Of course not."

Keona moved the wand upward and it sounded even louder. "Have you got a metal plate in your head?"

"Don't be—oh." His necklace. Leilani had given it to him for the three-month anniversary of their first date. She bought it at Tiffany's on the Beach Walk. An Atlas clock face in white gold. She said it meant they had all the time in the world.

"Mahalo, Keona, but all I need is the phone. How much?"

"Four grand."

Dylan blinked. This would be the most expensive phone call of his life. He handed Keona his credit card.

Keona ran it through his Square scanner. "Been living large, Dylan?"

"Not the way you mean. Why?"

"Credit card's been declined."

"That's impossible. Try this one."

Keona ran the second card. Same result.

Dylan swore under his breath. This couldn't be a coincidence. Xavier and his people were screwing with him. "Fine. Just use my ATM/debit card. Take it straight out of my checking account."

Keona ran the third card. And a moment later, he shook his head. "Sorry, Dylan."

"Declined?"

"Actually, it says they don't recognize the account number. You don't seem to exist, at least as far as your bank is concerned."

Last he checked, he had sixty thousand dollars in that bank account. Somehow, Xavier erased it. He wondered if the blond giant had gotten to his savings accounts, too. That would really hurt.

He still had some cash, but not enough for this purchase. Fortunately, he'd brought his checkbook to use at the retirement home. "Look, Keona, can I just write you a check?"

Keona put his hand on his chin and batted a finger against his lips. "Will I take a check from a guy who just had two credit cards declined written on a bank account that doesn't seem to know he exists?" He grinned. "Sure, dude. I know you're good for it."

"You're a prince, Keona. I won't forget this."

He wrote the check, grabbed the phone, and ran out of the spyware emporium. His plan was back on track. Now he would make Xavier and Mr. X see what plotting was all about.

MICHAEL ANDERS' mouth gaped as he peered into the rear of the ambulance. This was impossible. "Where is she?"

"Not here," Maria replied. "C'mon, help me with the gurney."

"That corpse isn't going anywhere."

"Not without your help. Grab the other end."

"But—what about Leilani?"

"She stopped off for doughnuts."

"There's no way—"

Maria put a finger across her lips. "Michael, shush!" She gave him her sternest glare. "Don't you know when you're being given the international signal to shut the hell up?"

"But Leilani's disappeared!"

"Intentionally. And if anyone comes around asking, she was never there. They must've seen me and thought it was her."

"But—"

"Michael, listen to my words. She was never there. Now grab the gurney. We have work to do."

"I'm...confused."

"Life is like that. Let's get this body to the morgue. If you're a good boy, later on I'll buy you an ice cream."

"And then you'll tell me what's going on?"

"No. But at least you'll have an ice cream. Now lower the ramp. We can't afford to be lollygagging."

Michael did as instructed. "I hate my job. I must be the most miserable person on this island."

Maria sighed. "I'm pretty certain you're not...."

CHAPTER
THIRTEEN

4:01 p.m.
Seven hours, fifty-nine minutes left

DYLAN DUCKED into an alleyway across the street from Keona's Spy Shop. He could smell the enticing aroma from Little Village Noodle Shop, one of the best and most economical restaurants in Honolulu. Unfortunately, he didn't have time for food.

He pressed his back against the brick wall. He looked up and down the alley. He even looked above. No one was watching. No one could possibly be watching.

He pulled out the high-tech super-secure phone and dialed. He decided to try the police. Despite Mr. X's grandiose claims, Dylan could not prove there was any international terrorism in play. But he could prove there'd been an assault and a murder. Extortion, threats. And those were police matters. He would start there, with his good buddy, the Chief of Police.

Someone picked up the phone on the second ring.

"Hello?"

"Is this Chief Fernandez?

"No, he's out today. This is Detective Michael Li. Who's calling?"

Of all the days for Bill Fernandez to be absent. But Dylan knew Li, at least by reputation. He was a high-flyer, frequently in the paper heading important investigations. He had to be trustworthy. "I need your help. People are trying to blackmail me. To force me to participate in an insane criminal scheme against my will. They hurt my girlfriend. They killed a security guard. They—" He realized how loudly he was speaking and lowered his voice. Could anyone hear him? There was no one in sight, but what if they used a directional microphone like the one Keona offered him?

Stay cool, Dylan. That was not possible. No one followed you. No one knows where you are.

"What did you say? What are you reporting?"

"Murder. Extortion."

"Where?"

"It started at the Splintered Paddle condo building. It's—"

"I know where it is. Near the Outrigger Canoe Club."

"Exactly."

"How many witnesses?"

"Just me and my girlfriend."

"When did it happen?"

"It started last night. A little after midnight."

The detective's voice rose. "This happened more than twelve hours ago and you're just now calling?"

"They were holding me captive. Threatening me."

"But now they've released you."

"Yes."

"So what's the problem?"

"I'm trying to explain—"

In his pocket, Dylan's cellphone vibrated.

He picked it up and looked at the Caller ID screen.

Xavier.

Dylan's pulse pounded as he stared at the name on the Caller ID screen.

They knew.

Dylan hung up on the detective and answered his cellphone.

No one said hello. Instead, he heard his own voice.

"I need your help. People are trying to blackmail me. To force me to participate in an insane criminal scheme against my will."

The sound quality was imperfect. There was a hollow echoing tone, as if he were speaking in a wind tunnel. But he could hear every word.

And apparently, so could they.

"This happened more than twelve hours ago and you're just now calling?"

"They were holding me captive. Threatening me."

The recording was replaced by a male voice with a Russian accent he knew all too well. "Only reason you're not dead is you did not give names and you ended call before you said anything important."

"Is Detective Li...one of you?"

"All you need understand is I know everything you do. Everywhere you go. Mr. X tried to tell you. You cannot contact anyone."

"Where are you? How are you doing this?"

He heard Xavier chuckling, a sound rapidly becoming his least favorite in the known universe. "You disobeyed. Now bad things happen."

"They already have. You screwed up my credit cards. My bank account."

"It will get worse. Try to talk again and someone will die." He paused. "You have seven hours, twenty-two minutes."

CHAPTER
FOURTEEN

4:38 p.m.

Seven hours, twenty-two minutes

DYLAN PRESSED BACK against the wall of the alleyway, breathing in short, quick huffs.

How had they found him? How had they traced the call?

Think. Don't get rattled. Keep plotting. That plan didn't work. You still have time. Come up with another one.

They must be monitoring all calls coming to the police station. It seemed incredible, but that was the only possible explanation. They could easily anticipate that he might call the police. So they tapped those lines. Maybe they had an operative on the inside.

Another disturbing possibility popped into his head. His necklace had set off Keona's metal detector. That had never happened before. He'd worn it through airport metal detectors and never had a problem.

Maybe this wasn't the necklace Leilani gave him. Maybe Mr. X made a switch while he was unconscious. Maybe it was a listening device or a tracking device. Or both.

He ripped the necklace off, snapping the clasp. Sorry, Leilani. He'd always loved this gift. But he was going to have to part with it. He hurled it down the alley into a nearby Dumpster. He tossed the four-thousand-dollar cellphone after it. It had been compromised. They knew the number. It was useless to him now and possibly could be used to trace his movements.

He raced back to Keona's Shop, pushed through the door, and ran to the counter. Keona was still eating.

"I decided to take you up on your offer."

"You want the air gun?"

"No. I want to use your phone. The land line."

"But I sold you—"

"Just give me the phone, okay?"

Keona slid it over to him. Dylan dialed. He knew the number of his NCTC contact, Eustace Doss. He was a middle-management desk jockey, but he could get Dylan somewhere safe and take his statement. He'd know how to mobilize troops to round up Mr. X and everyone working with her.

"Hello. National Counterterrorism Center."

"Eustace Doss, please."

And just as soon as he said it, he felt the buzzing in his pocket. He pulled out his cell and looked at the screen.

Xavier.

Damn! He didn't answer the phone. He knew nothing good could come of it. How were they doing this? Were they using hot-mike technology to turn his cell into a listening device, even when he wasn't using it?

"Keona, is that a hammer on the shelf behind you?"

"Ye-es..."

"Give it to me."

Keona complied. Dylan put his cellphone on the counter and smashed it. With great vigor.

Keona jumped. "Whoa! Extreme action, dude."

"These are extreme times. Can I borrow your laptop?"

"If you promise not to smash it."

"I assume it's secure. All the top spyware installed?"

"Of course."

He opened Keona's Chrome browser, entered his Gmail account, and typed. There was more than one way to contact someone. Even if

Xavier was capable of tracing email, he couldn't possibly anticipate that Dylan would use Keona's email account. The question was: Who to email? The police weren't safe. He knew all law enforcement agencies had websites, but he would just be sending a message to some anonymous email monitor. He couldn't expect a fast response. So what was left?

Think! If ever you needed an ingenious plot twist, it was now.

When the idea came to him, the cleverness made his heart race.

Forget law enforcement. Contacting them was too dangerous. He'd try someone else.

The fourth estate.

Leilani had been inside the body bag for more than two hours.

Michael hadn't noticed the extra weight. He wasn't lifting the gurney, only pushing it. Maria disguised the weight by pushing extra hard.

Leilani had the easy job. All she had to do was cling like Saran Wrap to this kid's dead body.

Unfortunately, she couldn't take the next step alone. She couldn't unzip the bag from the inside, and Maria couldn't do it with Michael and the ME's people watching. After depositing the body in the morgue, she'd left. Leilani would have to wait until someone let her out.

That would be some time yet.

Stay calm, Leilani, stay calm. If you lose your head, you're no use to Dylan. Eyes on the prize. We have a future together. And no one is going to take that future away.

But the corpse was starting to slime. The ooze, the dead kid's sweat —whatever you wanted to call it—was all over the left side of her face. She couldn't risk moving. Couldn't even risk wiping it off her face. She didn't know who might be in the morgue. She had heard the door open and shut a few times. She thought the room was empty, but she didn't want to take any chances. If the body bag started moving, she might give some young ME intern a coronary.

Or she might tell Pock-Face where she was hiding.

Either way, she was toughing it out.

She might've pursued a simpler way of disappearing. She and Liane considered all the possibilities. Jumping out the rear of the ambulance at a stoplight. Hiding under the gurney. But none of those ideas was foolproof, not if the people watching her were observant and smart. And she believed they were both. So she chose the path that was revolting but certain to give the appearance she'd disappeared. Because in a very true way, she had.

In the early stages of decomposition, Leilani knew, a dead body breaks down proteins, lipids, and carbohydrates, producing new acids and gases which form VOCs—volatile organic compounds. Some caused the body to ooze. It seeped through the pores. Skin developed blisters containing cerous fluid. Those blisters would burst and...the result was currently smeared all over her face. She was desperate to wash. Sometime. Soon. When it was safe to move.

It wasn't as if she could go anywhere. She was stuck here until someone released her. She'd known all along it would take a while. She didn't think it would take two hours, though. Two hours that passed like twenty.

One happy note—she was wearing a luminous glow-in-the-dark watch, so she knew how much time had passed. She could count every minute, every passing second. Which made time pass all the slower. While corpse ooze crept all over her body.

The glow from her watch provided not much light, but enough to reveal a small patch of the body's increasingly green skin. She knew why this was happening. Homeostasis ended at the time of death, which resulted in increased bacterial activity in the cecum. Those bacteria converted hemoglobin into sulfhemoglobin, which caused the body to turn green. But knowing why it was happening didn't make it any more pleasant to observe. Or to smell. She didn't know why his eyes were bloating or why something black was seeping out of his ears. Guess she should've gone to medical school after all...

Wait. Somewhere outside, she heard a door open.

Leilani stiffened, although she was still nowhere nearly as stiff as her current companion. She heard footsteps crossing the room.

They were coming closer.

She felt a hand on the bag. Someone was manipulating the zipper. But who? She'd lost Pock-Face this time, hadn't she? He couldn't possibly be here now. *Right?*

She prayed to God for one small favor—that when the light flooded in, she saw the face of the person she wanted to see. Not the face of the person she wanted to kill.

CHAPTER
FIFTEEN

5:05 p.m.
Six hours, fifty-five minutes left

"CARLTON REYNOLDS," Dylan murmured under his breath.

"Is he the dude you're running from?" Keona asked.

"No. He's a reporter." A pale, heavy-set reporter who carried his Chihuahua in his messenger bag. Had no living family. Never been married. Pretentious snob. But a fine reporter. His story last year on the slumlords of West Oahu was nominated for a Pulitzer.

But the most important thing Dylan knew about Carlton Reynolds was: he can't cook. And has no one to cook for him. So he eats at Taormina's, a lovely Italian restaurant on Lewers, near the upscale Beach Walk shopping district. Eats there every night. Has his own designated table where everything is just as he likes it. Probably has OCD issues. But the salient point was—Dylan could count on him being there tonight. Even without contacting him.

Carlton could get him to a safe house. Dylan knew he'd done it before for mob squealers and corporate whistle-blowers. Why couldn't he do it for Dylan?

And then they could bring in Dobie and Leilani. Dylan would tell

Carlton everything. And the authorities could stomp out Xavier and Mr. X like the cockroaches they were.

He checked his watch. Carlton had probably left the office. Dylan knew he ate early, as soon as the place opened, and generally made it last all night long. Beat going home to an empty house, he supposed.

It would take him a good while to get downtown. So he sent an email to the restaurant. He knew who would get it: Paolo, the maître d'. He knew Dylan and he knew how to be discreet.

Dylan typed the message quickly but carefully: TELL CARLTON REYNOLDS TO GO TO MEN'S ROOM AT 8. I WILL MEET HIM THERE. BIG STORY—MAJOR CRIMINAL OPERATION. PEOPLE ARE WATCHING. TELL NO ONE. TAGGART.

That ought to be sufficiently mysterious to get them all wondering. Reynolds couldn't resist this. And even if Xavier somehow tumbled onto the meeting, what could he do with a reporter and a hundred other people in the restaurant? Nothing.

He'd had two strikes. But he was not going to strike out. He would go on swinging. And this time, he would hit the ball out of the park.

The New York Times said Dylan was a master storyteller. He was about to prove them correct.

JUST THIS ONCE, Leilani's prayers were answered. In a good way.

Someone unzipped the body bag and parted the sides.

Her boss, Dr. Iaukea, peered down at her.

"You two look cozy. Does the writer know you're sleeping around?"

Leilani didn't reply. Her first priority was getting out of the bag and she did so with all possible alacrity. She hoped she didn't tear the corpse's skin or body hair in the process, but that concern dwarfed beside her extreme need to get out of the bag.

"Sorry I took so long," Iaukea said. "Never imagined it would be so hard to get in here. The ME's receptionist is a real pain. Didn't care who I was, wasn't letting me through. When I finally threatened her into submission, who do I meet in the hallway but the ME himself? He was pleased with my interest in the case and wanted to come in with me.

That wouldn't work. So I made all kinds of excuses. Promised I wouldn't disturb the body. Just wanted to search the pockets. And I didn't want him with me because I didn't want a witness if I found something unhelpful. Yadda, yadda, yadda. Never knew how quick I was on my feet till today."

Leilani wasn't hearing much of the soliloquy. She rubbed her hands up and down her body. She ran to a nearby sink and held her face under it, wiping away the slime. She was probably taking off a few layers of skin as well, but at the moment, she didn't care.

"Anyway, you're free and you need to get the hell away from here." Liane held out her car keys. "My car is on level five of the parking garage. Blue Ford Explorer. Decent gas mileage, very dependable. Get wherever it is you're going and don't come back till it's safe. I have a junker at home. I'll make do."

Leilani snatched the car keys. "I don't know how to thank you, Liane."

She held out her arms as if to give her boss a hug, but Liane waved it away. "Oh, don't start that. I don't date people from work."

"I wasn't—"

"That was a joke."

"Right. Sorry. Guess I'm not in a jolly mood."

"Understandable. So go already. I'll distract the receptionist. You can sneak past to the elevator, take it straight to P5. Three minutes and you'll be a mile away."

"Perfect." Leilani started toward the door.

"One thing, though, Leilani."

She slowed, doorknob in her hand.

"I talked to Michael, after he returned to the station. He was distraught. Thought he'd lost you somewhere. I convinced him that you and Maria were playing an elaborate practical joke and that the best thing he could do was ignore it and not give you two the satisfaction of enjoying his befuddlement."

"Sound advice."

"But he told me about something else that bothered him. Even more than your vanishing act."

Leilani's pulse quickened. "Yes?"

"Michael thought someone was following him. When he drove back to the hospital. He couldn't figure out why anyone would want to follow an ambulance."

Leilani's lips pursed tightly together.

"Here's the curious thing. He saw them as he left the crime scene, with you in the back. But he didn't see anyone when he left the ME's office."

"Which means?"

Liane took her hand and squeezed it. "Be careful, Leilani. Sit low in the car. Wear my sunglasses. I've got a ball cap in the glove box—tuck your hair up into it. And don't stop till you've arrived at your destination. You've got a full tank of gas. Use it."

"Understood."

"I'll cover for you at work." Liane hesitated, but Leilani didn't know why. Then, all at once, her boss wrapped her arms around her. The squeeze was so tight Leilani temporarily lost her breath. "One little platonic hug. For luck." She pulled back and held Leilani by the arms. "You're the best medic I have. I don't know what you've gotten yourself into—but I can tell it's serious. So get in that car and drive. Don't stop until you're someplace safe. I know you're a caregiver by nature, but for the moment you need to take care of yourself. And most importantly--" She peered directly into Leilani's eyes. "Don't trust anyone."

CHAPTER
SIXTEEN

6:00 p.m.
Six hours left

TAORMINA'S WAS on a side street just off the busiest section of
the famed Beach Walk—not Dylan's favorite part of the city. It used to
be a place couples walked hand-in-hand to gaze at the Pacific shore.
Now it was a place tourists went to buy ridiculously overpriced designer
goods. Dylan hated watching honeymooners in matching outfits, or
tourists in aloha shirts and cowboy hats, blowing big bucks to get status-
symbol labels on their shoes and purses. People who wasted money like
that shouldn't be allowed to have any.

Of course, if it was something truly valuable, like his 175-thousand-
dollar Bentley GTD convertible, it was justifiable...

Paolo, the maître d', didn't say a word out of the ordinary when
Dylan entered. He was being discreet. Didn't mention Dylan's hair buzz
or his lacerated neck. But Dylan was certain the message had been delivered. And he suspected it was no coincidence that, as Paolo led Dylan to
his table, they passed right by Carlton Reynolds.

Without making it obvious, Dylan nudged the table as he passed.

The Chihuahua yipped.

"Oh, I'm so sorry." Dylan feigned a double-take. "Carlton—is that you?"

"Dylan. What a surprise." With his bow tie, linen jacket, and brown Oxfords, he looked like a reporter from another era. "How's the world of fiction treating you?"

"Like you wouldn't believe."

Reynolds made a harrumphing sound. "Wish I could make up my stories. Would save a lot of time."

"No doubt. Still working the city beat?"

"In a sense. I have my own column now, you know."

In fact, Dylan didn't. He rarely read the paper. "Of course. Best thing in the whole damn rag."

Reynolds tucked in his chin and acted as if he was embarrassed by the flattery. "It does have its followers."

"Pardon me, but I have to rush." Dylan didn't think anyone could be watching, now that he'd ditched the necklace and the cellphones, but he wasn't taking any chances. He wouldn't do anything that might make an observer suspicious. He was tempted to talk to Carlton now, or to make some excuse to get him into the men's room, but that wasn't the smart play. He'd devised a plan. He would stick to it.

Carlton had been calm and cool and detached. He didn't give the slightest indication that anything was out of the ordinary. But Dylan was good at reading people. He'd trained himself to pay attention to details. And he saw something extra in the man's eyes, an unspoken message that said, I'll be there.

Dylan would be ready.

As Leilani pulled beside the skyscraper office building in downtown Honolulu, she knew instinctively what Dylan would think about her current activities.

He would be seriously pissed.

His instructions had been explicit, even though they were coded and cryptic. Ditch your tail. Don't talk to anyone. Get to the cabin and stay there.

She'd eluded all potential pursuers. Even those who helped her dodge her tails, Maria and Liane, had no idea why she wanted to disappear. Dylan couldn't fault her performance so far. But he could now. Because she was making a stop before she left town.

She drove down a side street and parked in the rear where she should be safe from prying eyes, not that anyone could possibly expect to see her emerge from Liane's car. She found the rear entrance open and wound her way up the stairs to the fourth floor. Thank goodness they kept late hours.

"Is Mark Haliani still here?"

The receptionist at Bixby, Haliani & Chaffee, P.C., peered at her through half-glasses. "He's with a client," she said, with a clipped British accent. "Do you have an appointment?"

"No, but he has to see me anyway."

The receptionist arched an eyebrow. "Is there an emergency?"

"Yes. Tell him Leilani Kahale needs to speak with him right now."

"I'll tell him you're here. As soon as he comes out of his conference."

"I'm sorry, but I need to speak to him now." She lowered her voice. "And don't tell anyone else I'm here."

Leilani could see her curiosity was piqued, but her British upbringing restrained her. "I understand you believe this is urgent, but I can't interrupt Mark's meeting."

Leilani's tolerance for chitchat had reached its limit. Every moment she stood exposed in the lobby she was potentially in danger. "I can." She marched past the receptionist and breezed down the corridor.

The receptionist jumped out of her chair, but Leilani had a head start and knew where she was going. She raced to Mark's office, opened the closed door, and stepped inside.

Mark sat in an armchair opposite his desk. Another man she did not know was speaking with him. They both stopped talking as soon as she entered.

"Mark, I need you. And it has to be now."

The lawyer looked back and forth between her and the man in the chair. He seemed confused about what to do next. Or perhaps he was just mentally calculating which client was more valuable to him—Dylan Taggart or the guy in the chair.

Thank goodness for big royalty checks. "Sam...I'm really sorry, but I'm going to have to take this. Would you mind...?"

"No, of course not," the man said. His creased brow suggested he wasn't as amiable about it as he acted, but he rose anyway.

"This won't take ten minutes," Leilani said. The man nodded and left the office.

Leilani closed the door behind him. "I'm sorry, but it's an emergency."

Mark retreated behind his desk and picked up a pen, apparently unfazed by her dramatic entrance. "What do you need?"

She looked at him earnestly, eye-to-eye. "I need you to save my life. And Dylan's, too."

CHAPTER
SEVENTEEN

7:55 p.m.
Four hours, five minutes left

ALMOST TIME.

The Uni Pasta Sea Urchin was one of Dylan's favorite dishes, not that he was currently in a mood to appreciate it. He had no appetite. His nerves were on edge and all he could think about was getting the message out about the human vermin on his tail. He assumed Leilani was safely at the cabin by now. But he would feel better about it when he saw her there himself.

Dylan almost placed his credit card on the tray—then thought better of it and retrieved some cash. That left him almost broke. This plan had better work—for more reasons than one.

He checked the corner table. Carlton Reynolds was not there, though his place had not been cleared.

He must be waiting in the men's room.

Dylan drew in his breath, then slowly released it. He knew he was taking a risk. But he had to stay strong. *Weakness is cowardice.* And he was not a coward.

He left the table and walked down the stairs, confident that this ordeal was coming to a close. He'd finally outflanked them and it felt good.

He pushed open the door to the men's room.

No one was there. At least no one he could see.

"Carlton?"

No answer.

No one at the sink. No one at the urinals.

A pair of shoes were visible under the door of the farthest stall. Brown Oxfords.

He walked to the door, dropping his voice.

"Carlton? Are you in there?"

No reply. He tapped on the door. It wasn't bolted.

He pushed the door open. And gasped.

Most of Carlton Reynolds was sitting on the toilet. His neck was severed at its base. His head dangled downward, barely attached. Blood and brain matter were sprayed across the tile wall behind him.

There was a note pinned to his shirt.

HOW MUCH ARE YOU WILLING TO LOSE?

Dylan stepped backward, stumbling. Jesus God. They killed him. Xavier had said someone would die if Dylan tried to contact anyone again and they really did it. *They really did it.*

If they would do that, they were capable of anything. Anything at all.

It seemed as if the bathroom walls were closing in on him. Think fast, Dylan. *Think!* He had to get out of here before someone else came in and thought he'd done this. He only had so much time before the twelve hours elapsed. He didn't want to spend them trying to explain what happened to the police.

He tore out of the bathroom. No, stop. Don't run. The body will be found, probably soon. He didn't want people to remember seeing him bolt out of the restaurant. He slowed down, nodded at the waiter, smiled at Paolo, and got the hell out of there, sweat streaming down the sides of his face.

He walked onto the sidewalk, hand covering his mouth. He felt like he was going to be sick.

A moment later, a black Hummer speeded in front of him, then skidded to a stop.

"Like new haircut, Dylan. Ready to go?"

It was Xavier, smiling that sickening smile, the one that gave Dylan the nearly irresistible impulse to knock all his teeth out.

He turned left. Xavier's associate, the dark-skinned one, was heading his way, with two other men following in lockstep. They were obviously together.

Dylan turned the other way but saw the same configuration with different faces. They were going to grab him, force him into the Hummer.

He glanced back at the restaurant. There was a commotion in the front lobby, people pointing and shouting. Someone must've discovered the corpse in the bathroom. He couldn't go back.

He could feel the seeds of panic churning in his stomach. He ignored them. He needed to focus. *Think*! He might be trapped like a rat in a maze but, he reminded himself, even the rat will eventually find an exit, if he's smart enough.

On the opposite side of the street, Dylan spotted a uniformed police officer.

"Dylan," Xavier said. "Do not do that." Xavier reached inside his windbreaker. He was carrying a gun.

A thousand thoughts raced through Dylan's mind. If he shouted for help, could the police officer get to him before Xavier plugged him? Xavier would shoot first then speed away, and his thugs would disperse. But what would happen if Dylan got in Xavier's car? His goons had just decapitated a reporter in the men's room.

"Calm down, Dylan. Take drink." Xavier pulled a silver flask out of his pocket.

In less time than it had taken Dylan to subvocalize all the options, he made a decision.

"Do not be stupid, Dylan. Get in car."

"Sure." Dylan grabbed the flask—and poured it over his head. Whiskey, if he wasn't mistaken, the smelliest of liquors. Xavier gritted his teeth and opened his car door. The men on opposite sides closed in.

Dylan leaped up and raced across the hood of the Hummer.

"*Chto za huy!*" he heard Xavier growl, but Dylan didn't slow. He jumped off the opposite end of the car and raced into traffic, weaving and bobbing between cars driving much faster than they should.

He didn't know if Xavier's goons were following him, but he saw that he'd caught the police officer's attention. Time to start his performance.

He and his older brother had both been in high school drama, an activity his father did not feel had much merit. In the eleventh grade, they were in *The Silver Whistle*, and he had the pleasure of playing an elderly character who was drunk throughout the pivotal Act Two scene. At the time, Dylan had never actually been drunk, but his performance was sensational—or at least that's what his friends said.

Time to see if he could revive his thespian gifts.

"Whass with all the carsss?" Dylan said, tripping in the middle of the street. "Where'sss my car?"

"Get out of the road!" someone yelled.

"I jusss wanna go home," Dylan mumbled, punctuating it with a loud hiccup. He raised his voice. "Where'sss my home?"

He didn't look directly, but out the corner of his eye he saw the police officer moving toward him. "Come on, buddy. Get out of the street." When he got close enough to smell Dylan, he winced. "I think you've had one too many, pal. Maybe six too many."

Dylan shuffled sideways. "I jusss need to find my car."

"No way you're driving home tonight. I'm taking you to the station for your own safety." He ushered Dylan to the curb.

"You cannn't do that!" Dylan said, plastering a goofy expression on his face, his eyes never focusing. "I dinn't do anything."

"Drunk and disorderly ought to cover it. At least until you've slept this off. Come on." He escorted Dylan to his patrol car parked at the end of the street.

Glancing behind him, Dylan saw Xavier and his goon pack staring at him, pissed as hell. He smiled and waved at them.

The officer opened the back door of the car and steered Dylan in, pushing his head down and through the door. "Just two minutes to the station, pal. They're keeping a cell warm for you." He pulled Dylan up, cuffed his hands, and buckled his seat belt.

Dylan grabbed the wire cage separating the front and back seats, as if using it to stay upright. "What'ssss going on?"

"Standard procedure." The officer climbed into the driver's seat and started the car. "Booking, printing. Then you get one phone call."

Dylan closed his eyes and smiled. One phone call.

Perfect.

CHAPTER
EIGHTEEN

9:28 p.m.
Two hours, thirty-two minutes

AFTER THEY BOOKED Dylan and snapped the mug shots, a black-haired baby-faced police officer escorted him to a holding cell. Dylan was still handcuffed.

"Wait a minute." Dylan saw no point in continuing the drunk act now that he was where he wanted to be. He suspected his time here would be limited. He'd refused the breathalyzer test—possibly the first person in history to refuse because he knew he would pass—so they took blood. Soon they would run the blood test and realize he was not intoxicated. They might have questions, but they wouldn't have a case. He didn't want to get kicked before he'd had a chance to do what he came to do. "Don't I get one phone call?"

"You get to make your call inside the cell."

"Inside? But—" Dylan pointed to a phone bank in the waiting area, in front of about fifty hardshell chairs occupied by minor criminals watching *CSI* on the overhead television. "Everyone makes their phone calls over there."

"Not you." He opened the cell door. "I have a friend who's arranged special privileges for you."

Dylan didn't like the sound of that. But before he could reply, the officer grabbed his arm and shoved him. The baby face contorted into something far less innocent. "Get in the cell."

"You're with them. You're working for Xavier."

"Get in the cell or I'll be forced to persuade you." He placed his hand on his nightstick. "I'd enjoy that. Haven't gotten to beat anyone all day."

"I want to speak to the duty officer. I—"

The kid cut him off. "Open your mouth and I'll knock your teeth out. I'll say you went for my gun and I had no choice." Before Dylan could think what to do, the officer pushed him into a cell. He took the cuffs off and locked the door behind him.

Dylan pounded on the cell door. "What about my phone call?"

The officer walked away. "We'll get there, chump. Have fun."

Dylan paced in circles, teeth gritted. His brilliant master stroke had turned into a disaster. Instead of setting himself free, he'd given up his freedom. He couldn't do anything in here. He couldn't contact the FBI or the press. He couldn't check on Leilani or Dobie.

He'd tried everything Fargo Cody would do. The instant disguise from *The Sisyphean Sanction*. The car heist from *The Calcutta Conundrum*. The untraceable cell phone from *The Koljack Killing*. None of it worked as well when he couldn't rearrange the world to fit his plot.

What now?

Think. That's what you do best. *Think!*

He surveyed his new surroundings. The holding cell was miserable: one sink, an unbreakable sheet metal mirror fused to the wall, and a toilet. Not even a chair. Just a bench nailed to the floor. His chances of escaping were zero. His opportunities to talk to anyone were even smaller. And—

He checked his watch. Fewer than three hours until his twelve hours ran out.

Think hard, Dylan. Think clearly.

There were two primary problems. First, Xavier always seemed to know when he was trying to contact someone. Second, Xavier always seemed to know where he was. How?

They could have anticipated that he would contact the police. So they tapped the lines, or arranged for someone to monitor incoming calls. But he didn't believe they could have anticipated that he would contact the NCTC. Perhaps they had a listening device in his necklace. But how did they know about the rendezvous with Carlton Reynolds? Xavier couldn't possibly foresee that Dylan would attempt to contact Carlton. Why would they go there?

He was certain he hadn't been followed. Not when he snuck out of his condo, not when he left Keona's, never. He had utilized all the professional techniques for avoiding and spotting a tail. They couldn't put a tracking device on his car. He chose it at random. Did they plant that pickup for him to steal? No way. Even assuming they were that smart, they would have bugged the Corvette he passed on. They couldn't have predicted what clothes he would wear. He'd ditched the phone and the necklace. They could not track him.

And yet, somehow, they had.

What was it Sherlock Holmes used to say, back in those stories he loved when he was a kid? When you have eliminated the impossible, whatever remains, however improbable, must be true.

They always knew where he was, always knew what he was saying. That was a fact. So what could he deduce from that fact?

Dylan's eyes flew open. He stared into the mirror.

They didn't bug his car. They didn't bug his clothes.

They bugged him.

"SAVE YOUR LIVES?" Now Leilani had the attorney's attention. "How can I do that?"

"Two ways. You've still got power of attorney, right? You can rearrange Dylan's finances?" Dylan was out-of-town frequently, sometimes for long periods of time on research trips—what he called extended tax-free vacations. He gave his attorney POA so he could pay the bills and manage investments.

"Yes. And?"

This wasn't going to be easy. But she had never let the lack of "easy" stop her. "I want a hundred thousand dollars transferred out of investments and into Dylan's checking account."

"That's a lot of money. Is he planning to make a large purchase? Another Bentley, perhaps?"

"No. I just want the money there. In case Dylan needs it." Which was the literal truth. She didn't know where Dylan was or what he might have to do to get free of those people. But if he needed money, she wanted him to be able to get it with a phone call. If he needed an emergency first-class fare to Shanghai, he could get it. If he needed a military-grade supersonic bazooka, he could get it.

"Okay. Is Dylan with you? I'll need his authorization, of course."

"No, Dylan isn't here, and he isn't going to be anytime soon. I need you to arrange it anyway."

"Leilani—I can't do that. I need Dylan to sign off on it."

"Mark, I know for a fact that you can do it. You may not want to. But you can."

"I'd feel more comfortable if—"

"I'd feel more comfortable if I weren't here at all. But this is an emergency and we all have to do our part. Including you."

"Leilani, you're not even on the account."

"I don't have time for a debate. Let me bottom line this. I sleep with Dylan. I think you know how tight we are. If you don't do this for me, I guarantee he fires your ass before the end of the week. So you choose. Are you going to transfer the money or not?"

He pondered a moment. "Let me make a call." He took a file out of his credenza, picked up his desk phone and dialed a number. "Bank of Hawaii, please."

She listened patiently while he talked to the banker in charge. A minute later, she heard, "That's funny."

"What?"

Mark held a hand over the receiver. "Did Dylan move his account to another bank?"

"No. Why?"

"They say he has no account there."

"That's not possible."

"That's what they say. In fact—" He paused and listened another minute. "They're saying there's no record that he ever had an account there. I know he did, though. I've got it right here in my file. Must be some kind of bureaucratic snafu."

Leilani could think of another explanation. Identity theft must be a cinch for people who could break into a penthouse condo, tap phones, and put someone like Pock-Face on their payroll.

"Okay," Mark replied, "then I want you to open an account. You can do that, right? Sell the bonds in investment account H46732X and transfer the proceeds. No, it isn't in his name. It's a holding company. I'll give you the routing number. Make sure the money is ready for Mr. Taggart when he needs it." He chattered a while longer to complete all the arrangements.

"The money should be there within the hour," Mark said as he hung up the phone. "Anything else?"

"Yes. Put this in a safe place." She pulled a folded envelope out of her back pocket. She'd handwritten the document back at her office, while she waited for a likely DBA (dead before arrival) call to come in. She sealed it in an envelope to protect it from prying eyes. She'd written down everything that had happened, everything she knew and every-thing she guessed, with detailed descriptions of the three men who broke into Dylan's condo. "In the event that anything should happen to Dylan or me, or both of us, you open this, send a copy to the *Star-Advertiser*, and hand-deliver another copy to someone in the police department you know is trustworthy."

"In the event that anything should happen to you. Like what?"

"Mysterious death. Sudden disappearance. Violent assault resulting in vegetative state."

"Leilani—what's going on?"

"I wish I could tell you, but I can't. And I can't stay, either. Get it done."

"I will." He rose to his feet. "Take care of yourself. Dylan, too."

"We will." She rushed out of the office—then decided to make a quick stop at the ladies before she left.

While she was in there, she remembered something else she wanted to discuss with Mark. He'd supervised the creation of the dummy corporation that purchased the cabin. She wanted to remind him he was not to tell anyone about it. In fact, she wanted him to destroy his records.

She left the ladies room and reentered his office. "Mark, you need to—"

She froze. Her heart raced out of control.

Mark was sitting in his desk chair—what was left of him. His assailant must have put the gun in his mouth, because what remained of his head was unrecognizable.

A thick pool of blood puddled on his desktop. Blood splatters sprayed the wall behind him like a Jackson Pollock painting.

The envelope she'd given Mark was gone.

They'd found her.

CHAPTER
NINETEEN

9:47 p.m.
Two hours, thirteen minutes left

THEY MUST'VE PLANTED something on him while he was unconscious, Dylan reasoned, staring at his image in the jail-cell mirror. Mr. X said she gave him an injection. He assumed it was a stimulant, but it could've been an anesthetic.

The reflection in the metallic mirror was poor. His face shimmered from the harsh overhead light shining on the silvery plating. But he could see himself.

Where was it?

He stripped off all his clothes, down to his underwear. He didn't see anything unusual. No signs of scars or incisions. But that could simply mean they were good at what they did. Or that they'd planted something very small. Where?

Think!

At Keona's, he'd set off the metal detector. His necklace had never done that before.

The alarm sounded when the wand passed over his head.

He took a step closer to the mirror and scrutinized his face.

What was his first thought, the moment he awoke in his condo after his job interview with Mr. X?

His head hurt. To be more specific—his temples throbbed.

He raised both hands and massaged both sides of his head.

He felt it. On the left side, below the surface of his skin.

There was something in there.

That was why Xavier clubbed him on the side of the head before he passed out. So the bruise would disguise the incision.

He cursed himself for not thinking of this sooner. But he didn't have time to waste. He wanted to be able to travel freely, without being tracked.

He paced frantically around the tiny cell, searching for some way to get this thing out of his head. Holding cells were designed to give those incarcerated no opportunity to harm themselves. The sink was riveted into the wall. He couldn't budge the mirror. Since it wasn't made of glass, he couldn't shatter it. He couldn't do anything with the toilet. Drowning himself wouldn't get that thing out. The bench was nailed down firmly, sanded and painted. There were no rough edges or—

Wait a minute. Nailed down.

Dylan crouched on the floor and examined the four nails pinioning the bench on opposite ends. They were in firmly and painted over, the same muddy gray as the bench.

Except one of them. The head of one of the nails was tilted upward slightly. Just enough.

He pinched the head between his fingers but it didn't budge. They'd taken everything from him that might be useful, like pocket change or keys. They even took his belt.

They hadn't taken his shoes.

What can you do with a pair of shoes, Mr. Novelist?

He unlaced his right sneaker. The shoes were new and the laces were sturdy. He wrapped the lace around the head of the nail, knotted it, knotted it again on the opposite end so he could get a firm grip, and pulled.

Nothing happened.

At first. As he continued tugging, he felt the slightest give. Not much. But enough to convince him that this was not impossible.

He used both hands and pulled with all the strength he could muster. He clenched his teeth. Harder. *Harder.* He feared the lace would snap before the nail gave any more. He could feel sweat trickling down his brow. He continued pulling. He knew from weight training that once he untensed those key muscles, he would probably never be able to mount the same magnitude of strength. He pressed his feet against the bench to increase his pulling power.

The nail gave again. It poked up at least an eighth of an inch above the floor.

He pulled even harder. He closed his eyes tight. He tasted blood in his mouth. But still he pulled. Fargo Cody wouldn't quit and neither would he.

The nail shot upward, so quickly he lost his balance and fell backward onto the floor.

The nail was halfway out.

From that point on, he could work it out with his hands. It took a while. He yanked, twisting it back and forth, moving in a circular pattern, widening ever so slightly the hole into which it had been drilled. He pulled at it, then gave it a sudden jerk.

He had the nail. Rusted at the tip and spotted with paint. But his.

Now for the hard part.

He washed the nail off in the sink, but it didn't make much difference. The paint and the rust remained. Didn't matter. He had no time to worry about germs and infection.

He felt his temple, reminding himself where the foreign object had been implanted.

He pressed the tip of the nail against his left temple and pushed it in.

It was a strange and challenging thing, poking an iron object toward your skull. It went against all instinct. Particularly at the temples, the softest part of the head, the part humans instinctively protected. He'd be lucky if he didn't die of tetanus.

He pushed harder. Blood spurted out.

Ignore the blood, he told himself, just as you ignored the pain. Head wounds always bled excessively. The fact that blood rippled around his hand did not mean he was doing himself any permanent injury.

His hand shook. Steady, Dylan. Keep it steady. He could feel the nail penetrating layers of flesh, as if a worm were squirming into him, burrowing toward his brain. Like a doctor was performing surgery while he was still awake.

He felt a pop. The nail entered what felt like empty space, an air pocket between his flesh and his skull. Somehow, that was even worse than inching through his flesh. He slowly moved the nail in a circle. The tip of the nail brushed against his skull, sending a chill up his spine.

And then he felt it. The nail touched something solid. Something that didn't belong there.

He tilted the nail so that the tip came down between his skull and the foreign object. The shaft of the nail tore at his flesh, widening the hole it made entering. Hurt like hell, but he kept on working. Slowly, a little bit at a time, he pushed the object outward. It was wider than the nail, so it made a larger tear in his flesh. But it was moving.

Sweat and blood comingled. His hand was sticky, making it harder to grip the nail. He concentrated and forced the object through his flesh, one millimeter at a time.

When at last it poked through the surface, he dropped the nail and seized the object. It was about half the size of the fingernail on his pinky and covered with blood and flesh. Careful not to drop it, he wiped it off in the sink, then took a closer look.

He'd read about devices like this. It was an incredibly small polymer transponder. A listening and tracking device, imbedded subcutaneously. He'd also read about nano-radios—transmitters too small to be observed by the naked eye. This one was huge by comparison.

He saw holes on one side—a tiny microphone, no doubt. He remembered the recording they'd played for him and the echo-chamber quality it had. Because the sound was being transmitted from within his own head.

On the other side, a tiny red light still lit. A GPS tracker. That's why he never saw them following him. They didn't have to follow him. They knew exactly where he was at all times. And they could hear it every time he dialed a phone, every time he started to talk to someone.

He threw the object into the toilet and flushed it. He hoped that sent Xavier and his friends scurrying into the sewers.

The cell door opened, revealing the unctuous young officer who had thrown him in here. "What the hell have you done to yourself?"

Dylan glanced into the mirror. The blood on his head wound was coagulating, but he still looked as if he'd been on the losing side of a gang rumble. The skin surrounding his left eye was darkening. And he was wearing nothing but his underwear.

"I tripped," he said, pressing his hand against the side of his head. "Is it time for my phone call?"

CHAPTER
TWENTY

9:55 p.m.
Two hours, five minutes left

LEILANI BACK-STEPPED out of Mark's office. She'd seen dead bodies before. In fact, she'd recently cuddled with one. But that was seeing them where she expected to see them. Not in a lawyer's office. Not a man she'd been speaking with five minutes ago. Not splattered against the wall.

In the distance, she heard voices. She raced down the corridor in the opposite direction and ducked into the ladies room. Barely a second later, she heard them just outside the door.

"The bitch was here all right." She involuntarily cringed. She knew the voice. Pock-Face. "Look what I found on the guy's desk."

He'd found her statement. So her back-up plan was history. Worse, they knew she'd tried to do exactly what they'd warned her not to do.

She had no illusions about what would happen if they found her.

"I searched the floor. Didn't find her. Had to get rough with the receptionist."

"We know she's somewhere in this building. If we don't find her, Xavier's gonna go roid rage on us."

How did they know she was here? And Xavier—was that the name of the buzzcut giant who led the assault into Dylan's bedroom? What did they want?

"Marco, I'll take the north end, you go south."

So Pock-Face's name was actually Marco. As if a monster like that deserved a real name.

"Got it. What do I do when I find her?"

"Make sure she doesn't open her mouth again."

"Can I have some fun with her first?"

"You know the timetable. If you've got the minutes, you can do anything you want."

"Good. That uppity bitch needs to be taken down a few pegs."

Leilani held her breath as the two men dispersed. She didn't know exactly where they were headed, but she was certain it wasn't safe to leave the way she'd come. She was also sure that eventually they'd think to search the ladies room.

She had to get out of here, and fast. But how?

There was a window in the rear of the bathroom, just over the sink. It was an old-fashioned, square, tenement-style window, maybe a foot long on each side. Not exactly roomy. But it was not hermetically sealed. She pushed up the handle on the sash. It budged slightly. She shoved even harder, doing her best to apply force without making noise.

She jumped up on the sink, testing to see if it would support her weight. It did. Now she had more leverage.

She didn't relish the thought of squeezing through that opening. But she liked the prospect of ending up like Dylan's lawyer even less. She didn't want to die, but more importantly, she didn't want to let Dylan down. These sewer rats were not going to steal her future.

The window budged another inch. Now she could get some strength behind it. She gritted her teeth and pounded the handle. It broke free and slid all the way upward.

She had her escape route, assuming she had the slithering ability of a small python. Thank goodness she'd skipped breakfast this morning. Come to think of it, she couldn't remember the last time she ate. Just as well.

She stuck her arms and head through the opening, then squirmed through the window enough to push her hands against the outside wall. The head was easy. The hips would be the hardest part.

Then she made the mistake of looking down.

No, the hips would not be the hardest part. Avoiding falling would be the hardest part. She'd forgotten she was on the fourth floor.

The pavement was a long way down.

There was a short ledge beneath the window but no balcony, certainly nothing she could walk or even stand on.

So once she was through the window, then what? Her body still ached from the injuries sustained the night before. Her left leg was particularly vulnerable.

But she had no choice, did she?

Once she was out as far as her waist, she grabbed the ledge and pulled. She had strong gym-girl arms. She worked out four times a week. But her fingers scraped against the abrasive stone.

She gritted her teeth and toughed it out. Better than being shot by psychotic criminals.

She pulled her legs through, then executed a perfect gymnast's pull. Using both arms, she brought her legs over her head, then downward. She flipped her hands around, one at a time, till she was dangling from the ledge, facing the outer wall of the building.

Thank God for abs workouts. They'd just saved her life. Except it wasn't much of a save, because she was still four stories up. There was a similar ledge beneath her on each of the succeeding levels. But the distance between them was daunting. She might hit the next ledge with her legs, but she couldn't balance there for long. Her best hope would be to slow her descent, then grab the ledge with her hands.

And if she survived, she would be only three stories up.

In movies, when people jumped out of windows, there was always a conveniently placed Dumpster full of cushy garbage bags, or a passing truck filled with foam rubber.

All she saw below her was hard pavement.

Then she heard Marco enter the bathroom.

"God, I'd like to find her. Just thinkin' about it gets my blood boilin'."

"Is she in here?"

"Nah. Wait—the window's open."

That made the decision for her. Leilani let go of the ledge.

CHAPTER
TWENTY-ONE

10:04 p.m.
One hour, fifty-six minutes left

THE SMARMY OFFICER standing by the cell door held a phone. "This is for your call. You want it?"

Dylan wiped his hands on his shirt. He thought the bleeding was mostly done. He took the phone.

The sergeant left the cell. Dylan immediately dialed—

But someone was already on the phone.

"Is prison food bad as I remember?"

Xavier. Dylan's fingers tightened. This was his one phone call?

"How you doing, Dylan?"

"I've been better."

"You should've gotten into car with me."

"I preferred the ride I took."

"Nice playacting, too. But big mistake. We control more people in police station than chief does."

"You murdered Carlton Reynolds."

"Man was what we call, *buttinsky*."

"You didn't have to murder him."

"I did. Because you broke rules. I understand. You had to make attempts, with your little spy phone and your reporter. You may be writer, but you are not wimp. I admire that. But you failed. Just as Mr. X said you would fail. And innocent, if insufferable, man dead as result."

"You made that happen. Not me."

"Was your fault."

"I will never give in to you."

"You will. Just matter of how much you lose in process. Have you learned nothing?"

"Yeah. I've learned that you and your friends can be real sons-of-bitches."

"Time running out. Make this easy. Work with us."

"Become a terrorist? *No!*"

The line went silent for a long time.

"I am sorry. Very sorry."

"Sorry about what?"

"I have actually read *Challengers of the Abyss*. Hell of good book. Shame he never wrote another."

The air in the cell thickened. Time slowed and Dylan felt as if he were moving in slow motion. "What...are you...talking about?"

"I give you chance to prevent. This on your head."

Icy fingers clutched Dylan's heart.

"Have fun in jail. I take leettle trip to beach. Take my sand shovel and pail. Your one phone call over."

"If you touch Dobie I swear to God I will rip out your heart with—"

The line was dead. A thunderous silence replaced Xavier's voice. Dylan was shouting at a piece of plastic.

He pushed the Callback button, but it didn't work. He dialed the assisted living home, then Leilani, but it still didn't work. Apparently this phone had been good for one call only.

He threw it down and banged on the door. "Let me out of here!"

The desk sergeant glanced up, scowled, then returned his attention to the newspaper.

Dylan grabbed the door. "Do you hear me? They're going to kill someone!"

No use. They ignored him.

This wasn't possible, Dylan thought, pounding with all his strength. He'd thought everything out. He made his plan, a good one, a clever one. A plan worthy of Fargo Cody. But it had failed. And now—

Dylan fell against the wall and closed his eyes. Please God, not Dobie.

But even though he was talking to God, the only voice he heard had a Russian accent and a sneering tone.

How much are you willing to lose?

LEILANI PLUMMETED from the fourth-floor ledge. As she predicted, her legs hit the lower ledge, but they didn't hold and they didn't slow her descent much either. She kept falling till her hands slapped the concrete ledge.

Her arms felt as if they were being pulled out of their sockets. Her whole upper abdomen stretched and split like someone had run a sword through her. Her hands scraped down the side of the ledge, ripping her skin. Blood slickened her grip. She was hanging on for dear life. She couldn't stand to fall another flight, much less all the way down. She would have to think of another way...

Marco poked his ugly head through the window.

"There she is!"

Leilani let go of the ledge. Her legs missed the next ledge altogether. She grabbed it with her hands but they were too sore, too bloody from the last fall. Her chin slammed down on it. Her head swam. Black patches appeared before her eyes. She was losing consciousness but falling backwards at the same time.

Get it together, she told herself. You cannot pass out!

In the split second before she hit the pavement, Leilani twisted her body around. She wanted to land on her lower back or buttocks, to absorb the impact and roll with it.

She almost made it. She hit sideways, taking too much on her right arm, but she did roll, legs over her head, then downward again. The pain was instant and excruciating. That leg had already taken a beating. She hoped it wasn't broken.

She pulled herself to her feet just as she heard the first gunshot ring out.

"Drill the bitch!"

Another bullet impacted the wall of the alley, so close to her a brick chip slapped her neck.

She clung to the wall, making it difficult for them to get an angle on her. She hobbled down the alley with a speed that surprised even her. Amazing what you can do when people are trying to kill you.

She headed toward the rear lot where she'd left Liane's car. The shooting stopped, but that didn't comfort her. She knew they were making their way downstairs as fast as possible. She had to get out of there. They were going to come out of this nightmare alive and together and damn it all they were going to start a family.

A family. She lost that once. Not again. Never again.

She slid into the car and started the engine. She didn't think they could know what car she was driving. But just in case she was wrong, she decided she wouldn't take it all the way to the cabin. She knew a place by the beach where she could ditch the car. If she shortcut through the uncleared area between the beach and the cabin, away from the roads, no one could see her. The hike to the cabin would be less than three miles. Even if by some freaky chance they tagged her car, they couldn't possibly know where she went after she left it behind.

She would be safe in the cabin. Waiting for Dylan to arrive and tumble into her arms.

Those bastards could trace a call or even a car, but they couldn't possibly trace her.

CHAPTER
TWENTY-TWO

11:01 p.m.
Fifty-nine minutes left

"CAN'T YOU WORK FASTER?" Dylan asked the wizened man behind the Detention Center processing desk.

He did not appear perturbed. Nor did he increase his speed. "I didn't invent the rules, but I got to follow them."

"Please hurry."

"You don't want me to lose my job, do you?"

Frankly, Dylan didn't care. He just wanted to get to Dobie as quickly as possible. He'd felt a surge of relief when the desk sergeant—not the punk who brought him the cellphone--finally opened the cell door and told him he'd been cleared for release. He didn't know that they would make him go to the infirmary so they could bandage his head wound, or that it would take them half an hour to process all the paperwork.

"Sign this form." The clerk pushed a piece of paper and pen across the desk under the acrylic divider. "Says you got back everything they took from you."

And he was supposed to sign it before they gave anything back to him, as if that made any sense. Dylan scrawled his name on the bottom line. The clerk pushed through a Ziploc containing his wallet and keys, then jabbed a button under the counter. Dylan heard the exit door latch release. He pushed his way into the front lobby.

"Can I use your phone?" he asked the attendant.

"Sorry. Office use only."

He didn't have time to engage in what would likely be a fruitless argument. He raced into the parking lot and searched for a car with unlocked doors.

DOBIE DIDN'T UNDERSTAND what all the fuss was about. One minute, he was telling his new keepers about the time his paper on *Light in August* trumped the so-called foremost Faulkner scholar from Harvard, and the next, everyone was running and screaming. He was having a hard time following it all.

"Fire!" someone screamed. "In the East wing! Fire!"

So that was what all the bother was about. He didn't kid himself that he could be any help, not when it was so difficult to walk. He would have to amuse himself until the hubbub ended. Maybe a quick hand of solitaire...

"Hey. Old man."

Dobie looked up. The darkness made it difficult to see and the face was unfamiliar. Big build, thick neck. Hair cut close, like he wore his in the fifties. A prominent birthmark and a ruddy face that had seen too much weather.

"You Dobie Bellinger?"

"You have the advantage of me. May I ask whom I am addressing?"

"Does not matter, old man. Just wanted to make sure." He grabbed Dobie's right arm.

"Just a minute. What are you doing?"

"Not much, old man." His upper lip curled. "Just thought we might play in sand."

Dylan saw the billowing smoke at least a mile before he reached the Mahoe Assisted Living Center. By the time he was in the parking lot, the smoke and ash were so thick it was difficult to breathe. He pulled the collar of his shirt over his mouth and parked the hotwired Pontiac Aztec —possibly the ugliest car he had driven in his entire life.

Two fire trucks were parked in front of the east wing. The entire section was black with flames illuminating the insides. Windows were shattered. Only skeletal traces of the woodwork remained. A large group of elderly residents huddled in nightclothes watching the firemen fight the blaze.

Dylan approached the nearest staff person. "What happened?"

The orderly shrugged. "Fire came out of nowhere. We did everything we could to stop it. But we were too late."

Dylan raced past him toward the front door.

"Hey, wait, mister! No one's supposed to go inside!"

Dylan didn't stop running. Fortunately, the fire was off to the left, so the main entrance was untouched by flame, though thick with smoke and soot. He bolted through the lobby searching for someone he knew.

He didn't have to look long. Despite the black haze, Dylan spotted a group of people gathered around the back door. The manager, Bendis, covered his mouth and nose with a handkerchief. Dylan grabbed his arm.

"Where's Dobie?"

Bendis' face told the whole story.

"You were supposed to have people watching him at all times! I paid for extra security!"

Bendis stared back, his lips parted, a helpless expression on his face. Dylan couldn't tell if he was crying or if the smoke made his eyes water. "We did everything you asked. But when the fire broke, everyone raced to get the patients out."

"What caused the fire?"

"I don't know. All at once, the east wing was ablaze. Like it exploded or something."

Dylan cursed silently. "Where's Dobie?"

"I think it would be best if you didn't—"

"*Where is he?*" Dylan grabbed the man by his arms.

"I'll show you." It was the nurse, the one who'd greeted him at the door earlier. "But I warn you—it's ugly."

Dylan followed her through the rear door onto the lanai, every nerve ending tingling, every synapse firing. It was drizzling outside, the daily Hawaiian shower, but the combination of soot and rain made breathing labored and difficult. Dylan trudged ahead.

A group of police officers huddled in a circle. Dylan's throat contracted and his mouth went dry.

Wet caked sand clumped in a heap in the center of the circle. On one end, Dylan saw several locks of gray hair above the sandy outline of a face. On the other, the points of two shoes.

Dobie's Hush Puppies.

An upended pail rested in the center with a little blue flag poking out of it.

"We can only speculate about how it happened," the nurse explained. "When his guards left to deal with the fire, he must've wandered off. He did have his bouts of dementia, as you know. And he loved the beach. We think he came out here, maybe attracted by the pail, and laid down. Perhaps even fell asleep. And then the tide came in. You know how quickly the tide can change. And how much sand it brings. Sinkholes form in seconds."

Dylan knew all that, having lived in Hawaii most of his life. But he also knew this was the wrong time for the tide to come in. And even if it had—it wouldn't explain this.

Dobie's face was almost entirely buried. His mouth was open.

They had pushed him down, or held him down. Then they shoveled sand into his face. Into his mouth, his throat, his lungs.

They buried him alive.

An eighty-nine-year-old man. The man who turned Dylan into a writer. The man who considered Dylan his son.

They buried him alive and they made a goddamn sandcastle out of him.

Dylan had failed. He thought he was being clever, outsmarting the bad guys. But the only person he'd outsmarted was himself.

"Leilani," he whispered. But that wasn't possible. She was safe and sound, hidden away at the cabin, unless—

His neck muscles stiffened.

Unless they planted one of those damn trackers in her skull, too.

One of the police officers turned toward him. "Sir, I'm sorry for your loss. I'd like to ask you a few—"

"I've got to leave."

"But, sir—"

Dylan bolted away, his feet sinking into the wet sand, slowing his progress. He was fairly sure the policeman wouldn't shoot. It normally took him an hour to get to the cabin. He would have to break a few traffic regulations this time. Maybe all of them.

He jumped into the Aztec, gunned the engine, pulled out of the driveway, and careened onto the H3, his eyes glued to the road, his hands clenching the steering wheel so tightly they turned a bloodless white.

CHAPTER
TWENTY-THREE

11:55 p.m.
Five minutes left

LEILANI DIDN'T THINK she could stand to wait any longer. But she would. For Dylan.

She wanted to flee. She wanted to hop the first plane off the island, fly somewhere untraceable. That last encounter with Marco and his friend was too close. She was still battered and bloodied and bruised from her flight out the window. Her hands were scraped and her left leg still hurt. But she wasn't going anywhere without Dylan.

She'd driven north toward Pupukea, just as he'd instructed her, dumped Liane's car on the side of the road, then hiked three miles to the cabin. She'd been watching the clock ever since. She couldn't wait till she heard his voice. She couldn't wait till she flung open that locked door and wrapped her arms around him.

Then the nightmare would be over. Then, finally, they would be safe.

DYLAN BLITZED down the private road that led to the cabin. He'd made it there in record time. The unspoiled rain forest environment was beautiful, but he couldn't appreciate it now. He'd circled around several times, making sure there were no suspiciously parked cars or vans with fogged glass, no one watching and waiting.

The cabin was simple enough—one story, three rooms plus kitchen, Polynesian façade. The secluded location was the main reason for the purchase. No neighbors.

No witnesses.

He bounded out of the car, raced up the front steps and pounded on the door. "Leilani!"

He heard a familiar voice inside. "Dylan!"

"Leilani! I'm here!"

And just after he said it, a hand clamped over his mouth with a grip so strong he couldn't break it. Four other arms grabbed his, immobilizing him. He tried to struggle, but there were more of them and they were much stronger.

Xavier's head appeared in his field of vision. "Thank you, Dylan," he whispered. "That was all we needed you to do."

They heard the click of the lock turning.

Leilani never had a chance to speak. The gun fired the instant she opened the door. The bullet hit her in the stomach. She collapsed onto the floor, gurgling blood.

Xavier grabbed her by her hair and dragged her inside. The other two men shoved Dylan forward. Xavier closed the door behind them.

Dylan's eyes bulged. *They shot her! They shot her before she could say hello.*

Despite the hand wrapped around his face, he could see Leilani was still conscious. And he could see she was in pain. Intense, immense pain. She pressed her fingers against her wound, as if trying to massage the searing agony from her body. No doubt her paramedic training told her she needed to staunch the bleeding, but she had no way to do it. Her face was locked in a contorted grimace.

"I try to warn you, Dylan," Xavier said. "But you would not listen."

Dylan wanted to reply, but the hand on his mouth prevented it.

Xavier held a small digital camera.

The acne-scarred man jerked Dylan toward a chair on the other side of the coffee table, just a few feet from where Leilani lay bleeding on the floor. He struggled and fought, but Xavier wrapped his thick oversize arm around Dylan's throat and jerked him downward. Then he pulled out a roll of duct tape and wrapped it around Dylan twice, binding him to the chair. Only when he was securely immobilized did the hand come off his mouth.

"Mr. X said if you do not cooperate, all your loved ones die—or worse," Xavier said. "The reporter die. The old man die. Now the girl— she get the worse."

"We have to call a doctor," Dylan said. "She's bleeding. She won't last long."

Xavier ignored him. "I could have killed her. But that would be too easy. Instead, I sever her spine. Cripple her for life. Because that is worse." Xavier grabbed Dylan's jaw, forcing him to look at Leilani. "I want her to see what happens next. I want her to feel it happening."

While Dylan watched, the acne-scarred man knelt down into Leilani's face. Her eyelids fluttered. He wagged his tongue at her.

"Puh-Puh—Puh-lese," she managed to sputter out. "Don't..."

"Not such an uppity bitch now, are you?" the man said. "You were too good for me before. Now maybe you'll have a diff'rent attitude."

"Leave her alone," Dylan growled.

"Or what?" the man replied. "What are you gonna do about it?" He cuffed Dylan on the side of his face, making blood trickle. "All you can do is watch, writer-boy. I hope you enjoy the show."

"Leave her alone or I will kill you. That's a promise."

"Kill me? You can't even stand up."

"Stop this, Xavier," Dylan said. "Stop it."

"Too late." He pulled a small black box-shaped object out of his pocket. "Know what this is? Used this in any of your books?"

Dylan's teeth clenched. "It's a taser."

"Got it in one." Without warning, he jabbed the weapon into Leilani's side, only inches from where the bullet had entered.

Leilani shrieked, a sound more horrible than anything Dylan had ever heard. She thrashed spasmodically, like a marionette whose strings were controlled by a madman. Her eyeballs rolled up into her head.

Think. There must be something you can do. There's always something you can do. Remember Fargo Cody's motto. There's always a way out. You just have to figure out what it is.

Xavier jabbed Leilani again with the taser. This time, she began to convulse. She choked up blood, spit it out, gasped for air. If he jabbed her with that again, she would surely die.

Dylan focused on the immediate task before him—escape. He'd read once that Houdini escaped from straitjackets by dislocating his left shoulder. It created enough slack for him to slither out.

Could Dylan use that here? If he could pull off Houdini's stunt, he might create enough wiggle room to get a hand free and rip off the tape. Even if he only weakened it, he might be able to escape.

He focused on his shoulder. He knew human anatomy well. He knew exactly what he had to do, exactly where he needed to separate the ball from the socket.

"Do not let horrible thing happen, Dylan. Give us what we want."

"Help you kill thousands of people?" That's it, keep talking. Don't give the homunculus any idea what you're doing. Dylan could feel his tendons straining, the ball trying to break away from his shoulder socket. "Help you assassinate world leaders?"

Xavier shrugged. "As you wish. Go ahead, Marco."

The acne-scarred man unzipped his pants.

Leilani cried out in terror, wide-eyed and horrified. "*No!*"

Dylan strained with all his might. Come on, shoulder. Separate! Set me free!

The man—Marco, apparently—grabbed Leilani's slacks and tore them off her.

Dylan continued straining, working with all his might to dislocate the shoulder. He couldn't be weak, not now. *Weakness is cowardice.*

"S-s-s-stop it," Leilani said, her voice fading, her eyes filled with horror. "Please...stop it..."

Marco ripped off her panties. The third man took the camera, hovered over his partner's shoulder, and recorded.

"First my comrade do her," Xavier explained. "Hard, ugly. Then we put video up on dark web. Your girlfriend will be more famous than you."

"Wait a minute," Marco said, grinning. "She likes it from behind, don't she?" He grabbed Leilani by the hips and flipped her over onto her stomach.

Leilani screamed. Dylan could almost feel the pain rushing through her body. He knew that sudden movement must have been excruciating —though not as much as the contemplation of what was about to happen.

Damn it—why couldn't he get that shoulder to pop?

"I wanna hear you purr, sweetheart. That's when I'll know you like it."

Dylan gritted his teeth.

"You ain't purrin', you bitch. Purr!" He slapped her on the side of her head. Leilani made a hideous gurgling sound. Dylan knew she was trying to comply, but the pain and the blood in her mouth made it impossible.

Dylan mustered his strength. All at once, with a single excruciating jerk, his shoulder joint popped free. He clenched his teeth together, stifling the instinct to cry out.

His left arm dangled, useless. But a small amount of leeway now existed. His right arm could move. He twisted sideways, snaking his good arm out from under the tape.

"Hey, sweetcakes," Marco said. "How 'bout I give you that French kiss now? How 'bout I give it to you where you'll really like it?"

Dylan pried the tape off his body without making a sound. He needed more time. Just a little more time...

Marco had his pants off. He was lowering himself, erect, ready to go, inches from making contact. "Here I come, you snotty cunt."

"Dylan!" Leilani screamed. "Help me!"

"All right! Stop it already! I give up. You win!"

Xavier raised a hand, halting his accomplice. "What are you saying, Dylan?"

"I'll work for you. I'll help you kill people. I'll do anything you want. Just—don't do this to Leilani."

"How do I know I can trust you?"

"Do I have any choice?"

Xavier nodded. "Cut him from chair."

Marco was enraged. "You can't stop me now!"

"Do as I say."

"But—"

"Cut him free."

Dylan tucked his arm inside so they wouldn't see what he'd tried to do. His left shoulder was useless, but he didn't let it show. If he'd only had a little more time—

But he didn't. He'd been forced to choose between Leilani—and the world. He chose Leilani.

The would-be rapist grudgingly pulled his pants back on, his face contorted with anger. The other man cut Dylan free.

"D-Dylan..."

Dylan could tell Leilani's consciousness was fading. Now that the assault was over, whatever adrenaline surge had kept her alert was fading. If medical help didn't arrive soon, she had no hope of survival.

"One condition, Xavier," Dylan said. "You call 911. Get her medical help."

"That I can do," he replied. "When we are gone." He took Dylan by the arm and led him toward the door. "But remember, if she talks to anyone, we will be back to finish what we started."

"Dylan?" he heard Leilani whimper behind him, her voice almost gone. "Dylan?"

He clenched his eyes shut. "Goodbye," he whispered.

Xavier led Dylan to his Hummer and shoved him into the passenger seat. The other two men climbed in behind. Dylan listened as Xavier called 911.

Xavier slid into the driver's side and turned the ignition. "You held up better than most," he added, as they pulled away. "Longer than anyone thought you could."

"Just drive," Dylan said, staring straight ahead. He'd failed. Failed Dobie, and Leilani, and himself. He'd tried every gimmick in his bag of tricks—and come up short. Fargo Cody's nonviolent schemes only worked because the author rearranged the universe. In the real world, where Dylan couldn't control everyone and everything, those shenanigans were a dismal failure. Fargo Cody was a lie. His whole life was a lie.

"That last business—dislocating shoulder. Very brave. Not many could do that."

"You knew about that?"

"My business to know everything. It would not have helped you. But valiant effort. You show much courage. What I would expect from creator of Fargo Cody. I look forward to working with you. I help you pop shoulder back into place."

Dylan's speech was so clipped it was as if each word were its own sentence. "Just. Drive."

Xavier nodded, pulled onto the main road, and headed toward the ocean.

PART TWO
THE SEDUCTION

"When a man knows he is to be hanged in a fortnight, it concentrates the mind wonderfully."

SAMUEL JOHNSON

CHAPTER
TWENTY-FOUR

Three weeks later

"I HAVE A PLAN," Dylan announced.

Xavier, Mr. X, and several of their associates sat around the conference table. From some, Dylan detected a perceptible release of tension. He knew that, despite his reassurances, they'd wondered if he would ever actually help them. He was happy to put their minds at rest. And their suspicions.

"'Bout damn time," Xavier grunted. "Summit less than month away."

"Hush," Mr. X said, swiveling around in her chair at the head of the table. "Share with us, Dylan. We've been anxiously waiting for inspiration to strike."

"The task you set for me was considerably more complicated than cooking up another thriller," Dylan replied. "This job is, to be blunt, impossible."

Mr. X's lids lowered in a manner that was all too familiar to Dylan. It was the first indicator of her Jekyll-Hyde transformation from semirational ex-IRA operative to maniacal monster. Since Xavier brought him to their compound, Dylan had learned to watch for it and to choose his words accordingly. "I don't much care for that word, Dylan. We consulted you to make the impossible possible."

"Consulted?"

"Just trying to keep it professional."

"Or trying to keep it...distant. What happens if you let people get close?"

"This is a strategic planning meeting," she said. "Not a therapy session. Do you have a plan or not?"

"As I see it, we have three primary problems, all of them impossible to resolve. First, based upon the intelligence Xavier gathered at the Cartwright Institute, the only person possessing the information we seek is Dr. Louis Scheimer, a physicist who works at a university research facility covertly funded by the US military. He is closely guarded at all times, making access to him impossible. Second, even if we could get to him, Scheimer will not voluntarily give us the information we seek and he is impervious to torture."

"I can get information from anyone," Xavier said. "Just give me few hours."

"Felix hacked into his CIA dossier. In the wake of the death of Dr. Karelis at your hands, Scheimer was given a post-hypnotic suggestion that will cause him to forget everything he knows if anyone tries to force him to talk. So your usual 'blunt instrument' approach will not succeed."

Xavier made a grunting sound and folded his arms across his chest.

"The third problem is that we have to extract this unextractable information from this intractable egghead without the government knowing it has been taken."

"So what's the solution?" Mr. X asked.

"By definition, there is no solution to an impossible problem," Dylan replied. "So we have to change the problem. We have to alter the variables to make the impossible at least slightly possible. If improbable."

"And how do we do that?"

"Since he can't be forced to talk, we have to make Scheimer want to talk."

"Now that really is impossible."

"No. That's why you need a storyteller who understands how to motivate a character." He slid copies of his plan across the table.

Mr. X looked at the cover summary. A tiny smile slowly crept across her disfigured face. "Yes." Her voice suggested inner excitement. "This is exactly why we wanted you. Only you could have devised this. Finesse. Cleverness. We get in, we get out, and no one is the wiser."

"I'll need five specialists," Dylan continued, passing out a list. "Five men or women with unique talents. I've done the necessary research and compiled a short list of candidates for each position."

"I don't like this part." Mr. X frowned. "The more people involved, the greater the risk of detection."

Dylan didn't love the idea of involving others either, but in this case, he had no choice. "You involved me because I was a specialist. Now we need more." He spread his hands. "Shall we get started?"

THE SMILES and nods around the table suggested that, overall, Dylan's ideas were being received with approval. Good. That was exactly what he wanted.

They thought they'd beaten him. They thought he was totally under their control. But they were wrong.

His first plot failed. That was a fact. He wasn't Fargo Cody and his attempt to pretend to be Fargo Cody ended in miserable failure. But he and Fargo did share one useful trait. Neither of them were quitters.

Another chapter was being written. Mr. X won the first round. She had a great advantage--a willingness to do anything to anyone at any time, no matter how cruel. But she hadn't beaten him. He would still find a way to stop these people. He would make sure what happened to Leilani and Dobie was not in vain.

You may be the cruelest bastard on the face of the earth, he thought, staring at Mr. X. You may outgun me, outman me, and outspend me. But I'm a writer. I will out*plot* you.

You think you're the ones writing this story. But you're not. And I'm going to write a better story than you do.

CHAPTER
TWENTY-FIVE

TIMOTHY HARDCASTLE WONDERED if he should have another Jack and Coke. He liked the way bourbon felt as it burned its way down his throat and nestled in the pit of his belly. He didn't mind what it did to his head, either. He had so much stress in his life these days. He needed a little liquid comfort. He didn't want to get drunk. Just a little something to take the edge off. That's what he told himself.

Next week would be even worse, with PFD fast approaching. The annual madhouse. An excuse for some of the brightest young minds in the islands to act like total ignoramuses, running about in stereotypical island garb, sporting masks and giant plastic heads. Halloween for grownups. And a pain in the ass for campus security.

Yes, he definitely deserved another drink. Even if that did put him over his predetermined booze limit.

What did it matter? No one was waiting for him. Only the dog would notice if he came home wobbly. It had been six years since Stella left, unable to live on an assistant director of campus security's income. He'd had no one in his life since. Not even a memorable one-night stand. He was beginning to give up hope. Maybe everything Stella said about him was true. Maybe he wasn't good for anything except ticketing poorly parked Porsches and breaking up frat parties. Maybe he didn't deserve anything better.

Except—there was one detail that mitigated against all Stella's criticisms and complaints, one factor that a little booze always helped recall to mind. Stella was a chronic complainer. Believing anything she said was like letting Satan select your socks. Fact was, he liked his job, he was good at it, and he made more than enough for any normal couple to get by, even here in the islands where prices were well above the national average. Meeting women was hard. He just had to be patient.

That was why he'd come here tonight. That, plus the desire to imbibe bourbon. The two goals were not mutually exclusive.

He'd hoped some nice female number might take one of the barstools on either side of him, but he'd been here more than an hour and it hadn't happened yet. These days, women always traveled in packs. He'd have more luck if he had a wingman.

He glanced at the rough-hewn man sitting two stools to his left chugging whiskey. He was older and bigger, but maybe if they linked up, he'd have more success.

He turned the man. "Don't take this the wrong way, but I've got a proposition for you, buddy."

The man nodded. "Have proposition for you also, comrade."

XAVIER LAID the inebriated security officer across his kitchen table, then wrapped duct tape around him to ensure he could not move. Xavier had a Sig Sauer under his windbreaker, but he wasn't going to need it. Once, in the outskirts of Baghdad, he'd taken down four highly trained agents single-handedly with no weapons other than his fists. Duct tape would be enough to handle this preposterous alcoholic.

"Whaddre ya doin'?" Hardcostle asked, blinking.

"Just making you comfortable," Xavier said. "Then we have leetle chat."

"I donnunderstand."

"You will, my friend. Very soon."

This op had been even easier than Xavier imagined. Hardcastle was at least two sheets to the wind before he arrived. After Xavier magnanimously bought the next three rounds, he was pure putty. Hardcastle wanted to hit a dance club and cruise for babushkas, so Xavier had spilled a drink on him, necessitating a trip home for a change of shirt.

Hardcastle would never leave his home alive.

Xavier retrieved a small medikit from his car. He removed a syringe and filled it with fluid from a small ampule. He pushed the plunger till a bit of the fluid spurted out to insure there were no air bubbles. Then he took Hardcastle's right arm and flicked it with his middle finger to bring out a vein.

Hardcastle was slow, but not totally numb. "What're ya doin'?"

"Giving you stimulant. Clear your head. Neutralize alcohol."

Hardcastle winced as the needle entered his vein. "But I like my alcohol." He hiccupped again.

"That obvious." Xavier withdrew the syringe, applied a cotton ball, then held it in place with a bandage. "Head is clearing?"

"I guess so."

Xavier could see the man's expression alter as his heart pumped the serum through his system. He became more alert and aware—specifically, more aware of the fact that he was affixed to his own kitchen table. "What's goin' on here?"

"We will have conversation," Xavier explained. "I ask questions. You answer."

"Whaddaya wanna know?"

"Has numbness gone?"

"I—I don't know."

"Easy test." Xavier closed both fists and hammered them into the soft part of Hardcastle's stomach. His head—the only part of his body that could move—lurched forward, coughing and gagging. Convulsive noises rose out of his throat. Xavier suspected he was close to vomiting.

"What—the hell was that?"

"Experiment," Xavier replied. "I think you not numb." He pounded Hardcastle again, this time harder than before.

Hardcastle coughed up blood in uncontrollable spurts. With a gloved hand, Xavier stuck a swab in his mouth to clear it. He did not want the man to aspirate on his own blood or vomit. That would be much too quick and would impede communication.

"What was that for?" Hardcastle gasped.

"So you understand how serious situation is. And how badly I hurt you if you do not answer questions."

"I don't know anything important."

"You are assistant director of security at university?"

Hardcastle's eyes narrowed. "Is this about that kid who cheated on his Spanish final?"

"No. More concerned with Physical Sciences building. Lab and living quarters next door."

"What do you want to know?"

"Everything. Every detail."

"I can't help you. The government controls that building. I'm out of the loop."

"I think you lie. Do you enjoy pain?"

Hardcastle swallowed. "No. But I can't pretend to know what I don't know!"

Xavier did not argue. Instead, he reopened his medikit and withdrew a plastic tube and another syringe.

"Wha—What's that for?"

Xavier wrapped the tube tightly around Hardcastle's right arm and brought out another vein. The man tried to struggle, but Xavier held his arm firmly. "Will hurt more if you move."

Xavier jabbed him with the syringe.

"What are you putting in me this time?"

"Not making deposit. Making withdrawal."

"You're—what?"

"Drawing blood out. Slowly."

Hardcastle squirmed, but the duct tape left him no room to maneuver. "You're...taking a blood sample?"

"Not taking sample. Taking all. Do you feel yet? Trickling onto arm?" Xavier put his finger in a puddle of blood and smeared it across Hardcastle's face. "You now universal donor. Donating blood to universe."

"I don't understand."

"If I do not stop it, you dead in forty minutes."

"F-Forty minutes!"

"But will be so light-headed in twenty minutes that you be useless.

So you have twenty minutes to tell everything I want. Or you bleed out. All over lovely kitchen linoleum."

"I—I can't do that. They'll know it was me."

"You answer questions, I remove needle. You don't, you die."

"Go ahead. Kill me. I don't have anything to live for."

Xavier paused. "There are worse things than dying."

For the first time, Hardcastle's voice trembled. "Like—Like what?"

Xavier put his hand in the puddling blood, then smeared it on his own face. A streak of red across his forehead. Thick lines down each side of his nose "We are at war, fool, and I am warrior." He jabbed his fingers into his mouth, licking them. "I will drink your blood, then I will eat your flesh. *After* I have my fill, I will kill you." He grabbed the tube and drank the collected blood in a single swallow, then wiped his mouth with the back of his hand. "The feast begins."

BEFORE THE TWENTY minutes were over, Xavier had all the information he sought and then some. He'd chosen the assistant director, rather than the director himself, because his death would be less cause for suspicion, especially given his troubled emotional history.

After Hardcastle finished talking, Xavier removed the needle, as promised. And then he used a razor blade to slash the man's wrists. When the body was found, which would likely take days, he would appear to have committed suicide.

Just before he lost consciousness, Hardcastle spoke one final time. "Why...are you so interested in...some physics geek?"

There was no harm in answering. Hardcastle would be dead in minutes. "Because geek holds power to destroy nations."

"Who—are you working for? A...foreign power?"

Xavier couldn't help but grin as he packed away his tools. "No. A writer."

CHAPTER
TWENTY-SIX

SEAMUS MCKAY HEARD footsteps approaching his office. He flipped over his legal pad and tucked it into his top desk drawer. Close call—he was almost caught.

"Morning, Seamus. Hard at work, I see."

"No rest for the wicked," Seamus grumbled.

"Or the workaholic." Seamus's new superior, Eustace Doss, was nothing if not blunt. Some people thought he was rude, even mean, but Seamus knew that, as an experienced counterintelligence operative, he had simply learned to be direct. "Still working the Cartwright case?"

Seamus grunted his reply.

"Don't feel bad, Seamus. Half the CIA, as well as a good portion of the FBI, the NSA, and Homeland Security, are working this case. And no one knows anything."

"Usually some group—or several—call in to take credit. This time, no one's talking. Not even a half-credible crackpot."

"Maybe no one wants to take credit for a failure. All the terrorists died in the explosion." Eustace paused. "But if the perpetrators don't take credit, doesn't that make the op pointless?"

"If you assume this was a standard terrorist operation—death and destruction for the purpose of instilling fear, sending a message, or attaining political retribution."

"Are you suggesting it wasn't?"

This is where it got tricky. If Seamus had learned anything during his long tenure in the intelligence business, it was the prudence of not telling people what they didn't want to hear—unless it was essential. And you were certain.

"What if this is only the first step?" Seamus suggested. "The warm-up act. Part of a much larger operation. What if they don't want us to know who they are because if we did, we might figure out what they're trying to do and prevent it."

"Do you have any evidence of this?"

"It makes sense."

"But do you have any evidence?"

"I'm working on it."

Not for the first time, Seamus wondered if it had been a mistake to get out of the field and put in for a desk job with the National Counterterrorism Center office in Honolulu. He'd spent almost his entire adult life doing the nasty to insure the security of the greatest nation in the history of mankind. He'd spent sixteen years working for the CIA, most of that time in the Middle East. He was probably the most fluent speaker of Farsi they ever had. He organized and led the counterintelligence deployment in East Africa following the attack on the US embassy in Dar es Salaam. After 9/11, he hunted down Osama bin Laden in Afghanistan and had him trapped within a mountainous twenty-mile radius. He would've gotten the bastard, too, if their focus hadn't shifted to Iraq.

After Afghanistan Seamus had a series of missions in the Middle East, Pakistan, and Bangladesh. He dealt with Russian arms dealers and a dangerously unstable Uzbekistan bio-weapons research facility. He infiltrated a Libyan prison to extract an American journalist. His last foreign assignment was to Iran, where his Farsi was most useful. He successfully thwarted an impending attack on the US water supply—and in the process lost everything. At least everything that mattered.

He received the CIA's Intelligence Star, the highest award they offered. It wasn't enough. He put in for a stateside transfer, hoping a change of scenery might help him recover his focus. They reassigned him to D.C.—and that turned out to be the worst job of his career. The one that almost killed him. So he asked for this desk job out in the middle of the Pacific Ocean. He wasn't hiding. He wasn't isolating. He simply wanted a calmer life. One that would give him time to pursue his secret dream. He was living in paradise, for God's sake. This was going to be the happiest time of his life. Soon.

"When I have something, I'll let you know," Seamus told his boss. He didn't say "if." He said "when."

"I would hope so. In the meantime, can you take a look at this incident report?" He passed Seamus a gray file. "Looks like a home invasion gone bad. Woman was severely injured, boyfriend purportedly kidnapped or killed, no ransom request."

Seamus took the file but did not open it. "Kidnapping is the FBI's turf. What's our involvement?"

"May not be any. But I also gave you a report about an explosion, fire, and death at the Mahoe Assisted Living Center."

"Why?"

"The arson investigator says the fire was triggered by a controlled detonation of K4."

Seamus sat up. "At an old folks' home?"

"Subsequent investigation revealed the place was in full lockdown mode with beefed-up security. The arsonists obtained access by disabling the perimeter security alarms and motion detectors with a digital mutating code generator. Preliminary computer analysis by the new Aprilynne decryption program suggests the generator used an algorithm designed by Hans Ringold at the Swiss Institute of Technology. Not something found in the toolkit of your average cat burglar."

Seamus and Eustace looked at one another. For two men who had served in this business so long, a look was often enough. Eustace knew Seamus would recall that the people who broke into the Cartwright Institute had used a similar device.

Aprilynne was new. Few people knew about it. Especially—God willing—the enemies of the United States. So even the most sophisticated terrorist might use the Ringold algorithm thinking it was untraceable.

And it had turned up twice in the same general area in a relatively brief period of time.

That fact alone was more than enough reason for Seamus to look into this incident report.

"Why was Mahoe in lockdown?"

"The manager ordered it, but he did so at the request of a friend of one of the retirees. The one who turned up dead on the beach."

"Murdered?"

"Unclear. The manager thinks it was an accident—brain-addled resident wandered off and drowned. But the whole situation sounds about a dozen alarms in my head. His friend orders more security for the old guy, and a few hours later, he's dead."

"Who is this mysterious benefactor?"

"The same person who disappeared after the home invasion."

"Weird."

"It gets weirder. We have witnesses who say they saw the same guy arrested on the Beach Walk and taken in custody maybe an hour or so before the old guy croaked. But there's no record of his arrest at the police station."

Seamus opened the file and scanned the contents. The woman was in critical condition. She was known to be dating the man who beefed up security at Mahoe. Lots of booze at the scene, broken furniture. Police suspect that the boyfriend might've lost control, attacked the woman, staged it to look like a home invasion, and fled.

"What's the guy's name?"

"Dylan Kane Taggart." The Hawaiian middle name was pronounced "Kah-nay."

Seamus blinked. "Wait a minute. Not Dylan Taggart."

"Name rings a bell?"

Seamus flipped through the file. "Dylan Taggart? The writer?"

"What, like in a rodeo?"

"Not rider. Wri-*ter*."

"Oh. What's he write?"

"Novels. Thrillers. Big action stuff. Battling superpowers. World on the brink of disaster. Except his hero, Fargo Cody, always swoops in and sets things right at the last possible moment."

"Huh." Eustace was beginning to look bored. "I don't have much time for fiction. Is this guy famous?"

"Compared to whom? He's a writer, not something really important, like a Beverly Hills heiress or an *American Idol* finalist. Look, I'll get right on this."

"Good. But remember—the focus is on Cartwright, not this writer. The military brass are concerned. Lots of top-secret stuff going on there, apparently." He started toward the door, then stopped. "Oh, by the way —hear anything from Ingrid?"

"Oddly enough, we haven't stayed in touch."

"Shame."

"I prefer it that way."

"I can see where you might be bitter. But even after all that happened, you have to admit—she's a hell of a woman."

"She is that."

"Everybody loves Ingrid," Eustace said, as he left the office.

Yeah. That was the problem.

As soon as Eustace was gone, Seamus opened his desk, removed the legal pad and placed it in the silver metallic trimline attaché he carried with him at all times. He kept his desk locked, but given his experience in the world of secrets, he wouldn't leave anything this important to the protection of a flimsy desk drawer lock. It would stay with him. Always.

Taggart's behavior prior to the break-in suggested someone was out to get him and the people close to him. And now Taggart was gone. Maybe he was dead. But if so, where was the body? And why go after a writer? Seamus didn't have the answers, but given the connection to the Cartwright Institute, he suspected he should. And the only way to get those answers would be to find Taggart. Immediately.

If he could track down Osama bin Laden, how hard could it be to find some writer?

CHAPTER
TWENTY-SEVEN

"YOU HAVE the information about university security that Xavier provided," Mr. X said, swiveling around in her chair at the conference table. "Did you get everything else you needed?"

"Yes," Dylan replied. Xavier's intelligence-gathering assignment verged on the impossible—and the Russian had completed it in fewer than twenty-four hours. He'd always known the man was a brute, but the report he received made him aware of another dangerous fact. Xavier had a gift for perceiving what scared people most—and using it to get what he wanted. Whatever he took to pump up those enormous muscles hadn't addled his brain. Dylan couldn't let himself be fooled by Xavier's broken English and his Boris-and-Natasha accent. He was a formidable man.

"When will we be ready to proceed?"

"Soon. But I want to take this one step at a time."

"Sod that," she said levelly. "I want to move within the week. So that's what we're going to do."

"Of course," Dylan replied, as always giving the appearance of compliance. She didn't believe it, but she expected it. Kept her from detecting where the real resistance lie. "But we still need to recruit the other specialists. And I will need equipment."

"We'll get it." Mr. X's lids fluttered. "Have we not given you everything you desire?"

In some respects, that was true. Dylan had his own office with an excellent support staff. They brought him meals and offered him tea at midday. The food was superb. They had a gym for exercise. They had a masseuse available in the afternoons. He could requisition anything he needed and had never been turned down. They treated him like a prince.

He was a prisoner.

The guards maintained a discreet distance, but Dylan knew he was being watched every second. During every meeting, there were four armed thugs in the room. Two were posted outside his room at all times, even when he was sleeping.

After Xavier drove him away from the cabin, three weeks ago, he'd squirted an aerosol anesthetic in Dylan's face. He had no idea how long he was out. He woke up here, at their headquarters hidden away in the dense rain forest of—someplace. He thought he was still in the Hawaiian islands, judging by the vegetation and climate. But he couldn't be certain. And it really didn't matter. He could be in the heart of Waikiki and it wouldn't make any difference. They weren't letting him go anywhere.

On the outside, the compound looked like a dilapidated old warehouse overgrown with vegetation. That was the disguise. On the inside it was a networked control center rivaling NORAD. They had well-furnished offices with the latest and greatest technological devices, computers, wi-fi, satellite links, digital displays, the works. He knew there was a scientific laboratory and an armory, though he didn't have access to those areas. There were at least two dozen people on staff, including a medical team. They'd even given him a tetanus shot. It was like working in a corporate office. It had the same ant-colony feel, everyone moving in their orbits accomplishing their specialized tasks. Except this office was in the business of creating terror.

"What gave you the idea of targeting me?" he asked Mr. X shortly after he arrived. "Why do you think I can help you?"

Eventually, she offered him a clue.

"In 1995, an uneducated jackal executes a bombing plan that

destroys a federal installation in Oklahoma City and kills 168 people. Where did this backwoods moron get his inspiration? Do you know?"

Dylan searched his memory...

"From a book. A novel, to be specific. A poorly written piece of shite called *The Turner Diaries*. It wasn't worth the paper it was printed on, but it was popular on the underground militia circuit. Timothy McVeigh read it—and the result was written in blood."

"That's an isolated example."

"Skyjacking. Who came up with that idea? Rod Serling, the *Twilight Zone* creator, for a television drama. He regretted it the rest of his life. 9/11. Where did the idea for that come from?"

"Al-Qaeda operatives—"

"No. Tom Clancy wrote a book called *Debt of Honor* that portrayed a terrorist flying a jumbo jet into Capitol Hill. Sound familiar? What's more, in March of 2001, the pilot episode of a television program called *The Lone Gunmen* featured a plot to hijack a commercial airliner and fly it into the World Trade Center. Six months later, Al-Qaeda did it for real."

Dylan had no reply.

"Hence, Analytic Code Red. A government program initiated by Homeland Security. They contacted Brad Thor and other writers to brainstorm about how terrorists might next attack the country. They were searching for *ideas*, Dylan. And if they can do it, why can't we?"

Dylan hadn't forgotten what she said they were planning. Whether he believed it or not, she wanted this so-called super-weapon for a reason, and it wasn't to satisfy her intellectual curiosity. They planned to use it. And when they did, people would die.

That sobering thought brought him back to the present. "Did we get the university schematics?"

"I had to work my butt off," X's assistant replied. He seemed to be X's top assistant. "Tightly restricted. The IP was masked, but I ran a traceroute to get a list of the network devices—all the routers and switches that connected their machine—"

"I don't need all the details," Dylan said. "Did you get the schematics?"

"Of course." Felix never looked up. His eyes were glued to his laptop. Felix was at best twenty-five, possibly younger, with a shaved head, a butterfly tattoo on the back of his neck, a soul patch, and a silver ring through one ear. He had an off-the-charts IQ and a hacking ability that could bring down third-world nations. And if that didn't provide Dylan all the character detail he needed to understand this young man —Felix wore a T-shirt that read: OBI-WAN FOR PRESIDENT. HE'S OUR ONLY HOPE.

"Can you get me dossiers on the people working security? Both the campus cops and the government ones."

Felix clicked a few keys. "No problem. I'm linked to the big boy in their computer room." He smiled like a man in love. "I could conquer the world with our IBM Blue Gene/L. Processing speed 12.18 peta-FLOPS. I didn't think anyone but the government could afford these babies."

Dylan wondered if Felix had surrendered to the dark side for polit-ical purposes, money, or just so he could play on Mr. X's cool computer.

"Please have the files sent to my office. Here's the list of equipment my team will need.'

Mr. X picked it up, glanced over it. "Dylan...you're expensive."

"You want a Wal-Mart plan or a Tiffany's plan? You people don't seem to be hurting for cash."

"If it will get us Scheimer's files--consider it done."

Marco peered over her shoulder at the list. "Plastic heads? Fake vomit? Is this an infiltration or a practical joke?"

A little of both, Dylan thought. But he didn't grin. Dylan didn't like any of these people, but he found it hard to be in the same room with Marco without ripping his eyes out.

He closed his eyes, blotting out the memory of when he had seen Leilani last. She'd called out his name—as he walked away.

He'd had no choice. But it didn't make it hurt any less.

He'd asked them for status reports. Did she make it to the hospital? Was she still alive? They refused to answer. Said it wouldn't be good for morale.

They were probably right about that.

"You'll need to rent some space near the university," Dylan reminded her. "Best to get started on it now."

"As you say. And we need—a chemist?"

"I'm going to require some drugs."

"I hope you don't imagine that truth serum will persuade Scheimer to talk. Even if he's drugged, as soon as we start interrogating him, the post-hypnotic suggestion will be triggered."

"I understand. No, that's not part of the plan."

She stared at the list. "A contortionist?"

"Someone extremely flexible. And small. And an encryption expert."

"Is that it?"

"No. I also need...you."

Mr. X's eyes squinted slightly. "I don't go into the field."

"Your participation is essential."

"We have many operatives."

"For this job, you are uniquely qualified."

"How so?"

"You speak fluent German."

"As do millions of people. I...attract too much attention."

"Please don't take this personally...but I wondered if you'd ever considered seeing a plastic surgeon?"

"I haven't," she said, raising her chin. "I don't need one. I like my scars. I *earned* my scars."

"No one deserves...that."

"You're not taking them from me."

"Because you earned them in pursuit of a noble cause?"

"Stop fishing."

"Because that's how you punish yourself? How you remind yourself to experience guilt on a daily basis?"

"I didn't do this to myself."

"I understand that."

"And it could have been much worse."

"And for someone else—it was. Right?"

"He—" She stopped short. Her lids lowered to such an extent that her eyes were almost imperceptible. "Very good, Dylan. Well played. But your job is to get information from Scheimer. Not me."

Which told him he was definitely on the trail of something useful.

"Whether you want surgery or not, I need a German-speaking female about your size, and all things considered, you're the best choice. I've selected a doctor. My research indicates that he is adept in the use of several invaluable new techniques and chemical agents—some not yet approved for use in the United States."

"This is becoming increasingly complicated. I do hope you're not just busting my balls." Her voice deepened, and her hand flexed open and shut, as if she were squeezing invisible genitals. "I can't be put at risk."

"You didn't recruit me to give you anything ordinary."

She pushed herself to her feet. "Indeed not. Let me think about it. In the meantime, proceed with your plan."

As soon as she left the room, Xavier pressed his hands down on Dylan's shoulders.

"I hope you take this serious."

"Believe me, I do."

"This my home now. Do not want to lose."

What did that mean? Dylan filed it away for future use.

"I have news," Xavier continued. "Your woman. Bitch that squeals like pig."

Dylan contained his emotions. Poker face. "Yes?"

"She lived."

A surge of adrenaline coursed through his body. "Is she...well?"

"Dead below waist. Will be in wheelchair all life. Squealing days are done."

Dylan nodded. "Thank you for the update. If you'll excuse me, I have work to do."

Dylan rose from the table, but Xavier shoved him back down. "This mission must be accomplished. Soon."

"I understand. And I will do my level best to—"

Xavier squeezed his shoulders with bone-crushing intensity. "If you fail, I will let Marco have way with your girl. Then I will strangle her slowly with bare hands." He leaned in close. "Your idea better work."

"It will, Xavier. Trust me." His eyes drifted to the side as he added, "It will work exactly as I've planned."

CHAPTER
TWENTY-EIGHT

THE POLICE HAD ALREADY WORKED the Mahoe Center with every crime-scene tech they had and the reports were reasonably thorough. Dobie Bellinger died from asphyxiation, wet sand blocking his windpipe. Attributed to dementia and a sudden tide. The only part Seamus found of interest was the ME's report. There were slight bruise marks on both sides of the victim's neck. The ME assumed he ran into something, slipped, fell, couldn't get up, and was killed when the tide rushed in.

But Seamus wasn't buying it. That fire had been set for a reason, and given that only one person was harmed, he had to believe the arsonist wanted to create an opportunity to get to the target. The victim was found on his back, face up. If he had fallen, any bruises would be on the back, not the front.

Someone had pushed him down. Held him down. It wouldn't take much. The man was eighty-nine years old, infirm, barely able to walk. A child could've restrained him—while his accomplice shoveled sand into the man's mouth.

And this all happened just a few hours after Dylan Taggart bribed the manager to ramp up security.

Seamus wondered if Taggart had taken any other precautions to protect Bellinger or himself. So he called Taggart's publisher and got the name of his lawyer. Tried to call him, but there was a problem.

The lawyer had been murdered three weeks ago. Same day the old man died. Same day Taggart's girlfriend was attacked.

This plot was thickening in a way that only made it appear darker and more dangerous than Seamus had imagined.

After Mahoe, Seamus went somewhere the police hadn't been—Dylan Taggart's penthouse condo. None of his neighbors had seen him for weeks, not since that memorable night when he was apparently arrested, the retirement home burned, his girlfriend was assaulted, and he disappeared.

There was another intriguing detail Seamus uncovered. The night security guard at the condo had disappeared the night before all this excitement. He still hadn't turned up.

Curiouser and curiouser.

After he broke in with his lockpick, Seamus spent almost an hour examining the condo. It was spacious but sparsely furnished. A bachelor pad, Seamus thought. A place that lacked a woman's touch. The kind of place a single man who has experienced great success buys—and then doesn't know what to do with it. Reminded Seamus of his own place, except he didn't have any of the expensive toys. Looked as if he and Taggart had the same taste in books, though. Robert Louis Stevenson, John Buchan, Conan Doyle, Baroness Orczy, Rider Haggard. The adventure classics of a previous century. The heroes of a bygone era.

Seamus was about to abandon the search when, on the window beside the bed, he found the trace of a distinctive oval outline. Something had been affixed by suction cup.

He pulled a digital camera out of his pocket, removed the infrared filter, and took a picture. A tiny red dot was apparent in the digital display. That was the sign of an optical listening device, probably a Digitel XL-5. It transmitted a pulsing signal through a pane of glass that converted sound vibrations in the glass into speech. The suction cup probably held a fiber optic camera.

Someone had been spying on Dylan Taggart, even in his bedroom. Someone sophisticated. They watched, waited, and then at the moment when he was most vulnerable, used stormtrooper shock-and-awe tactics to crush resistance before it began. Taggart probably never stood a chance.

Except...

If they were watching this condo, and they grabbed Taggart here—why did the medics find the girlfriend at a cabin out in Pupukea?

Seamus needed to talk to the girlfriend.

MR. X WAS FUMING.

"I am not happy about this part you've written for me, Dylan."

"If you'll recall, I didn't choose my role in this drama, either."

"I told you I don't wish to lose my scars. I earned them."

"Sort of like an IRA merit badge?"

"Would you believe me if I told you my injury had nothing to do with the IRA?"

"Jilted lover?"

"Don't be preposterous."

"Is it preposterous to suggest that you once had a lover?"

She drummed her fingers on the conference table.

"To answer your question," he said, filling the gap, "of course I would believe you. I believe everything you tell me."

"That's good to know."

"So if it had nothing to do with the IRA, how did it happen?"

"Let's return our attention to the matter at hand. I don't want this procedure."

"Dr. Giep is a miracle worker."

"Find someone else for him to wreak his miracles upon."

"Do you want to have the weapon when the summit brings all those important people to Honolulu?"

She folded her arms across her chest.

"Then we'd better get Scheimer's files, hadn't we? The sooner the better. PDF is fast approaching. I know you're not happy about this. But you're a trouper. So you're going to take one for the team."

Somehow, she managed to purse her lips and snarl at the same time.

"Suck my dick." She paced around the table. "This operation must be performed today?"

"Immediately."

"I've lined up the Hollywood people you wanted," she said. "The art director. He's a two-time Oscar winner."

"That should do."

"And I've got one of the top set design and construction experts in business. Stole him right off a Steven Spielberg set."

"How?"

She shrugged. "He has a gambling problem. Large debts. The art director is attached to his mother and doesn't want to see anything happen to her. Worse than what already happened."

Dylan felt his teeth grinding. She was targeting more victims. Exploiting weaknesses. Destroying lives. But this time, she was going after people he requested. This time, he was the mastermind behind the evil.

In the story he was writing, he'd become Mr. X.

CHAPTER
TWENTY-NINE

SEAMUS HAD INTERROGATED terrorists who were not as intransigent, or as tough, as Dr. Evan Fender, the emergency-room surgeon who supervised Leilani Kahale after the ambulance brought her to Leahi Hospital. The gruff, balding doctor had presumably been toughened by years of service. Seamus guessed he was at a point in his life—mid-sixties at least—where he didn't have to work to live so he wasn't going to be bullied by anyone. Flashing a badge wasn't enough to get the man talking. Fender spent fifteen minutes calling the NCTC to make sure they had a Seamus McKay on the payroll. Even after confirmation, he remained guarded.

"Nothing personal," Fender grunted. "It's a matter of confidentiality."

"It's also a matter of national security," Seamus replied.

"You government boys always act as if it's the end of the world."

"it is serious. I'd like to know about Leilani Kahale's condition."

"I need her to waive confidentiality."

"I'm going to talk to her. But I want to hear from you first."

"Doctor-patient privilege—"

"Has been totally overridden by the Freedom Act and we both know it. Do you want me to have your files subpoenaed? Have you hauled down for questioning? You'd be tied up for days."

Fender squinted in a way that made his eyes disappear. All that remained were bushy gray eyebrows. "What is it you want to know?"

"What happened to this woman?"

Fender plopped into the chair behind his desk. "Someone shot her in the stomach, that's what. She damn near bled out before the paramedics arrived. And that's just for starters."

"What else?"

"We found an abnormal electrolyte profile. Acute muscle inflammation. Elevated lactic acid levels in her blood. Excess quantities of troponin 1."

"What does that mean?"

"I think someone electrocuted her. Probably after they shot her."

"Jesus. A taser?"

"Well, I doubt she was messing around with a circuit box after the bullet cut her open. She also had severe lacerations and bruising. Looked like she got beaten up badly before she was shot. She must've gotten some treatment because there was a bandage on her left thigh. Some of the other bruises were fresh, though."

They didn't just shoot her, Seamus realized. They tortured her. "Anything else?"

"I'm afraid so." Fender pressed his hand against his forehead. "Paramedics who found her said she was—" He paused. "She was naked, below the waist."

"Was she sexually assaulted?"

"There's no medical evidence of it. But someone sure made her think she was going to be. Why would anyone do that?"

"I don't know. What does she say?"

"Next to nothing. Cops have been here quizzing her, but she's tight-lipped. Says she doesn't remember much. Which could be true. Shock like that could easily erase memories. Took a week before she could communicate clearly." Another pause. "But I suspect she's deliberately keeping quiet."

"Why protect her assailants? That's bizarre."

"You haven't heard the most bizarre part yet." Fender rummaged through the clutter atop the credenza behind his desk. "As soon as she was sufficiently stable, we did an MRI scan to see if she'd suffered any brain impairment."

"Did you find any?"

"No. But we did find...this. Implanted in her head beside the left temple."

Seamus took the plastic bag and scrutinized the contents. The mechanical device was tiny, but he knew what it was. He'd seen them before.

Why would anyone put a subcutaneous tracking and eavesdropping device in Leilani Kahale's skull? Who had the technological capability to do that?

The same people who could employ the Aprilynne decryption algorithm.

Seamus didn't know who was behind this. But they were major players. He didn't know what they wanted, either. But if they were capable of torching a retirement home, torturing this woman, and destroying a military installation to achieve their goals—what couldn't they do?

"JUST A FEW MORE THINGS I want to cover before I go under the knife," Mr. X said. If she was nervous, she wasn't letting it show.

Dylan listened attentively. Even in a hospital gown, she still spoke with authority.

"Those people have already started building your set. It's made of interlocking parts, like a giant jigsaw puzzle. Once you know how to do it—you can put it together quickly."

"I want them to practice every day between now and when we go into action. Once we're done, we want to eliminate all traces we were ever there. Quickly."

"Understood."

"And now—Dr. Giep and Dr. Reacher are waiting for you. Don't be worried."

"I'm not."

"Giep is the most advanced surgeon in his field. His use of bioengineered stem cells to heal surgical scars and accelerate recovery is nothing short of revolutionary."

"You'd bloody well better have done your research right. This is my face he's messing about with."

Yes, Dylan thought, and it's such a treasure. Most people in her situation would give anything for this opportunity.

He heard a knock on the conference room door. The doctors gestured for her.

She gave Dylan a sharp look. "Don't get any ideas. I'll only be unconscious a short while. Xavier and his men will be watching you constantly."

She'd be out something like twelve hours, but there was no point to correcting her. "Fear not. I'll be much too busy to cause any trouble. As soon as—"

He was interrupted by a piercing scream from the main entrance.

He whipped his head around. Through the glass walls of the conference room, he observed a slender blond-haired woman being dragged through the door by Xavier's brutes.

"Get your hands off me, you freaking apes. Let go!"

For a tiny woman, she had considerable strength. Not enough to overpower those two, though.

"I said, let go of me!" She kicked Marco in the shins, and when he tried to slap her, she grabbed his arm and twisted it behind his back.

Mr. X rapped on the glass wall. "Xavier."

The Russian giant appeared out of nowhere. He wrapped his thick arm around the woman's throat, choking the fight out of her. In a few seconds, they had her under control. But even Xavier couldn't prevent her from expressing her opinions.

"I'm going to rip every one of you apart!"

They hauled her down the corridor where Dylan knew she'd be put in a holding cell, at least for a time.

Mr. X cleared her throat. "So that's your encryption expert."

Lovely. Another innocent forced into their insidious web—and it was his fault. "What did you do to get her?"

"Does it matter?"

"I suppose not."

She wrung her hands. "Let's get this damnable operation over with." She stared at Dylan with abruptly narrowed eyes, tiny slits barely large enough to permit the passage of light. Before he knew what had happened, she slapped her hand against his chest, hard. "This had better be absolutely necessary, Dylan."

"It is."

"Had my tonsils removed when I was eight. Didn't care for it."

"Did they give you ice cream?"

"I don't like ice cream."

"Come on. Everyone likes ice cream."

"I don't."

"When you get out of surgery, I'm bringing you a banana split. You'll love it."

"I will not love it, and don't do me any favors, and stop flirting. You're not my type and I'm not that stupid skinny Barbie doll you've been screwing. So leave me alone and do your job!"

Dylan allowed himself a small smile. His plan was working.

CHAPTER
THIRTY

WHEN SEAMUS ENTERED the private hospital room, Leilani Kahale sat upright in bed. She had an IV connected to her wrist. She'd arrived almost dead and had been unable to eat or talk for a week. They were still giving her an intravenous nutrient laced with some pain medication. She wore a hospital gown, but he was impressed by the fact that she was clean and groomed, something he knew was not always easy to accomplish in a hospital--especially when you were tethered to an IV. She had a small computer in her lap.

As soon as she saw him, she closed the lid.

"Pardon me for intruding," he said. "I'm Seamus McKay. NCTC." He flashed his badge.

"The nurse warned me you were coming."

"I'd like to ask a few questions about what happened to you. And your boyfriend."

"I don't know much," she replied, "and I've already told it to the police, several times. Plus some guys who said they were with the FBI. But I guess I can tell you, too."

"I'd appreciate it."

"It's pretty simple. They opened the door and shot me. I don't know why. I thought they planned to rob me. All I know is I fell on the floor, bleeding and unconscious. I don't remember much more. When the ambulance arrived, Dylan was gone."

"You assume he was kidnapped?"

"He wouldn't have left me in that condition if he had any choice."

"I see."

"I'm sorry I can't be of more help."

"I am, too." Seamus turned to leave, then paused. "Oh, I did want to ask you one more question."

"Yes?"

"Why are you lying?"

He watched as Leilani's face traveled from surprise, to concern, to denial. "Why would you think that? I have no reason to lie."

"Apparently you do. Because you are."

"You can't know that."

"I can. Don't make me go into all the boring details. The way your eyes traveled up and to the left when you said you don't know why they shot you. The way you broke eye contact when you said you don't remember anything after you hit the floor. And the obvious indicators in the record."

"The police didn't mention any obvious indicators."

"They may not be as good at reading between the lines. But I've had a lot of experience with liars who are, quite frankly, a lot better at it than you."

She turned away. "I don't have anything more to say."

"All right then. Let me tell you what happened."

He could see he had her attention.

"Your assailants had been watching Dylan's condo for some time. Every room. Even the bedroom. They watched you make love and then, when you were both most vulnerable, they burst in. There was a struggle. Furniture was damaged and you were hurt, though not as badly as you would be later. They could've killed Dylan, but they didn't, so they must want something from him. And it isn't money, because there are much wealthier people in this city who would be easier to intimidate. They want him to do something for them. He refused and tried to escape, even getting himself arrested to get away from them. But it didn't work. Neither of you could escape. They planted a tracking device in your head and probably in Dylan's, too. Finally, to coerce him, they killed his elderly friend, assaulted you, shot you, tasered you, and threatened to rape you."

He paused. "How am I doing so far?"

Leilani did not reply. But her eyes were noticeably wider.

"I understand your reluctance to speak to the police," he continued. "You don't trust them. If I were in your situation, I wouldn't trust them, either. They're too unreliable, too easily bought. Dylan's abductors probably told you they had people on the inside, and the truth is, they may well have."

Her left eye twitched.

"But I have resources the cops don't. I have all the high-tech gizmos and databases. And I have experience dealing with some of the meanest, nastiest bastards on the planet." He paused. "I can help you. If you'll let me."

Her lips parted. She almost said what was on her mind—then retreated at the last moment.

Seamus filled the silence. "You're worried about Dylan. They told you that if you said anything to anyone, they'd hurt him. Or you. And you believe them. I get that. But I also know this, Leilani. When they're done using Dylan, they'll kill him. His only hope is that you help me find him before that happens."

He watched her hands tighten on the handrails of her bed. She wanted to talk. He was sure of it. He just needed something else. Something to convince her she could trust him.

"I know how you feel in a way no one else can. I...loved someone. Once. And she was taken from me by people just like the brutes you're up against now. It destroyed me. I felt helpless, angry—and worst of all, guilty. All the emotions you're experiencing now." He paused, watching her eyes. "I know what you're going through. And I'm determined to help." He drew in his breath, then slowly released it. "Won't you please let me help you?"

Her lips parted so slowly it seemed eons before she spoke. "I know they've been watching me. They said they'd kill Dylan if I talked."

"They'll keep him alive until he's served their purpose. I need to find him before they're done with him."

Her chest rose and fell. Her eyes drew closer together.

"No one else is going to do it," Seamus continued. "We're the only ones who can help him. You and me."

At long last she spoke. "You promise you'll try to find him? No matter what they do?"

"I promise I *will* find him. But you have to help me."

Her eyes welled up. "You were right. About everything. How did you know they attacked us in the bedroom?"

"Found traces of listening and recording equipment. And I saw that someone—you, I'm guessing--scrubbed the floor so hard the woodwork lost some of its varnish. Blood, right?"

"Yes."

"The missing security guard?"

"They killed him." She told him the whole story—from the initial break-in to the final assault in the cabin.

"Is it possible Dylan knew they were coming?"

"Of course not. Why would you ask that?"

"The police suspect that Dylan shot you, then disappeared."

"That's total crap."

"I know. Do you have any idea why these people wanted Dylan?"

"He never told me. I think he thought I would be safer if I didn't know."

He was right. "And you don't know who these people were? Or who they worked for?"

"No." She described Marco, the one she saw the most, in great detail.

"Doesn't sound like anyone I know. What about the leader? The giant."

She shrugged. "I didn't see that much of him. Said his name was Xavier."

"An obvious alias. Can you describe him?"

"Muscular. Abnormally large. Pumped up and then some. Medium height. Buzzcut. Foreign accent. Russian, I think."

Seamus' eyes widened. "Dark hair?"

"No, blond."

"He could've bleached it. Square jaw? Like Dick Tracy square?"

"Yeah."

"Birthmark right here?" Seamus pointed to his neck.

She thought for a moment. "Yeah. Do you know him?"

"I might." He bit down on his lower lip. "I hope to God I'm wrong. For Dylan's sake." He thought another moment. "But it makes sense. Only someone completely vile could do what he did to you. I want to help you, Ms. Kahale. I know after what you've been through, it must seem as if they're unstoppable, invincible—"

"No, you're wrong."

Seamus stopped short.

"They're not invincible," she continued. "They're mean, and resourceful, but they make mistakes like everyone else."

"Why do you say that?"

"At the cabin. While I was bleeding out and Marco was torturing me. I heard Xavier tell Dylan that he'd severed my spine. Crippled me for life."

"Yes?"

Leilani sat up straight and set the laptop on the table beside the bed. "He didn't. He missed. He was only off by an inch, but that inch was enough to save my spinal column. I've been walking for almost a week now. The doctors think I'm pushing too hard. They've insisted that I stay in the hospital under observation. But I'm not going to let those people win. Dylan is too important to me. I never felt close to anyone in my life before him. I'm not going to lose that."

Instinctively, Seamus put his hand on her shoulder. This woman had strength of a caliber he had rarely seen in over twenty years of intelligence work. "Ms. Kahale, I'm going to find this Xavier. Before he can hurt anyone else. I'll start now and I won't quit until the job is done. That's a promise."

He started toward the door. "I'll check in with you whenever I can, and—"

"Like hell."

"Uh—what?"

Seamus pivoted around. To his astonishment, Leilani tore the bandage from her wrist and, with a single stroke, jerked the IV needle out of her arm. "Those sons-of-bitches hurt me. They...played with me. And they took the man I love."

"I know, but—"

"You said you couldn't do it alone."

"But I meant—"

She swung her legs around and pushed onto her feet. "If you're going after those bastards, I'm coming with you."

CHAPTER
THIRTY-ONE

DYLAN CHECKED all around him for scrutinizing eyes. He thought he was alone as he left the barracks where he slept and headed for the conference room in the main building. But it was impossible to be certain. He would simply have to take a risk. And hope for the best. He was no coward.

But he wasn't stupid, either.

Mr. X and Xavier waited for him in the main conference room. She liked the morning briefing to start at nine o'clock sharp. Dylan's personal guards remained at his office. Others would attach themselves when he entered the building. He was still potentially observable, even as he crossed the short space between the two structures, but over the past several weeks he'd located the surveillance cameras and knew how to avoid them. He couldn't escape. But he could gather information.

If he was careful.

A few days ago, he'd spotted a patch of camouflage green peeking out behind a warped sideboard. There was nothing he could do about it then. Too many eyes were on him.

He approached the side of the building.

He bent the plywood siding back so far it snapped. Clumsy. He hadn't intended that. He didn't want to leave any traces of tampering.

But the broken piece revealed another layer beneath the siding. That

wasn't just camouflage green he spotted—it was military green. The
original wall of this building had been stamped with a distinctive logo.
The logo of the US Navy. But not the current one. Dylan knew this
emblem had been phased out shortly after World War Two. He'd seen it
in some of his father's scrapbooks.

Had the terrorists taken over an abandoned military post? If so, that
limited the number of places he could be. If he could figure out where
he was, he'd be one step closer to figuring out how to escape.

He heard a shuffling noise in the main building. Someone was
heading his way.

He pressed the broken piece back against the wall and it held, at least
for now.

He scurried toward the back door just in time to meet Xavier.

"You late."

"Sorry. Wool-gathering. We creative types do that."

Xavier squinted. He peered into Dylan's eyes with more than the
usual degree of suspicion.

"Shouldn't we be getting to the meeting?"

Xavier stared a few more moments, then abruptly turned on his
heel. "Hurry. We have surprise for you."

LEILANI PEERED over Seamus's shoulder at the large plasma screen
computer monitor.

"No, his face was wider. And older."

Seamus punched a few more keys. The computer moved sluggishly,
but that was because he was remote-accessing the facial reconstruction
software in the FBI's database. The NCTC's budget was too puny to
afford their own.

Having spent most of his career in the field, Seamus was better with
guns and fists than high-tech gizmos. But he'd learned that this program
was invaluable. Made the days of sketch artists seem downright
primitive.

Leilani insisted they start by recreating Marco's face, because she had
a much more vivid recollection of his appearance. They spent almost

three hours on that one—and when they submitted it to the law enforcement databases, they got no hits. Apparently Mraco had never been in trouble with the law or tagged as a "person of interest" by anyone in the intelligence community. So they turned their attention to Xavier.

"You've got his hair too long. Shorten it."

Seamus complied by clicking the proper icons.

"He had almost no hair on the sides. And it needs to be lighter. Don't forget the birthmark on his neck."

"Right, right."

"Make his chin squarer."

"I know. Dick Tracy."

"Pump up the muscles. All over his body."

The panel on the right side of the computer screen gave Seamus a choice of facial features in each category. It also provided a template for every imaginable physical trait. He could enhance image accuracy by choosing among different hair tones, facial markings, hats, headwear, and eyeglasses.

"That's it. Except he isn't mean enough. Can you make him meaner?"

Seamus turned the corners of his mouth slightly downward and added a frown line between the eyebrows.

"That's it! That's him!"

Yes, it was him, all right. The man he had known as Dmitri Yevtushenko of the Russian mafia, but that probably wasn't his birth name any more than Xavier was.

"Do you know who he is?"

"I think so. Let's submit this portrait and see what happens."

Seamus saved the file, transmitted it to all available law enforcement databases, and waited for a match. This program did more than create a sketch. It automatically generated a Biometric Alphanumeric Code for every facial characteristic. The 56-digits in the BAC represented specific facial features. He'd sent that digital fingerprint to DHS, Secret Service, FBI, CIA, Interpol, and a host of others. Even though Seamus thought he knew who this Xavier was, he had no photograph in his files.

"It's out in cyberspace," he told Leilani. "We'll give it a few moments and—"

A ping from the CPU's internal speaker told him he had a hit.

"We got mail," Leilani said, leaning forward.

"I'll bet it was Interpol or—"

He stopped short. Long ago he'd learned how to multi-task, an essential field-combat skill.

The match had not come from Interpol, or the CIA, or anywhere else he might've expected. It came from a military database. The US Navy.

"Can you blow it up larger?" Leilani asked.

He double-clicked the photo.

"It's him," Leilani said. "I'd swear to it. How many people could be that large? But—what's he doing with the Navy?"

Seamus shrugged. "Maybe they have him under surveillance."

"I don't think so. Look." She pointed toward his shoulders. Distinctive stripes. A Navy uniform. "How can that be?"

"Says he served as some kind of consultant. No longer active." There was a name attached, another obvious pseudonym.

Seamus fell back into his chair, massaging his neck. "But here's the primary point of interest, Leilani. He's not in their database because they think he's a threat. He's in their database because he used to be one of them. Maybe he still is."

CHAPTER
THIRTY-TWO

"I DON'T UNDERSTAND," Leilani replied. "How can a guy go from the Russian mafia to the US Navy? Why would our government want someone like that?"

"If you have the right skill set, our government will overlook a great deal."

"Is this the guy you thought it would be?"

Seamus pursed his lips. "It's the right guy. Just the wrong name. The guy I knew grew up in an orphanage at the foot of the Ural Mountains. But the orphanage was actually a soldier factory for the Red Army. They experimented with children. Pumped them full of steroids and other chemical enhancements. Tried to create an elite military force of perfect warriors. What they ultimately created were monsters."

"That's a good description of him."

Seamus nodded grimly. "He went to military school, then had a long career in government service doing Soviet dirty work. Started out in the Interior Ministry forces. Participated in the initial invasion of Afghanistan. Then he moved to GRU. Military intelligence. Then to the KGB, the civil police force. Became a commissar. Worked in Nagorno-Karabakh, back when Azerbaijan and Armenia were fighting over it. Taught at the KGB Military Counterintelligence School in

Novosibirsk. After the Wall fell, he was with the Russian mafia. Did a stint in Iraq before and during the war with the US. That's when I bumped heads with him."

"What happened?"

Seamus paused, contemplating just how much he could tell this civilian. He was willing to give her some superficial information because he wanted her help. But she didn't need to know all the details. Especially the ones that pertained to Ingrid.

"It was in the early years of the second Iraq war. Just after Bush declared 'Mission Accomplished' and just before he made the disastrous decision to dismantle the Iraqi army. Chaos reigned supreme in Baghdad and the surrounding areas. Your Xavier was doing a work-for-hire gig for Islamic extremists. I was with the CIA, rooting out threats to the security of our troops."

"Like him."

"Exactly. We had...an encounter. A conflict of interests, you might say."

"Who won?"

"Oh, I defeated him. I had the military might of the US on my side, and he had employers who didn't like to show their faces." Seamus paused. "My superior ordered a military strike. I thought it was overkill, but it wasn't my call. The strike took out this man's home in Sabaa. Blew it to smithereens."

Leilani followed him to the window. She still limped, but given what she'd been through, Seamus was amazed she could walk at all. "Bet that pissed him off."

"Yeah," Seamus said quietly, glancing down at his desk. "Especially since his wife and infant son were still in it."

Leilani's lips parted.

Seamus fingered a few loose papers on the desk. "A very ugly bit of business. Had to be done. But it left him with a serious bad-on for the good ol' U.S. of A. It would be more convenient to hate him. But unfortunately, I know too much about him. Once you know how the monster came to be, it's hard to feel anything but pity."

"I felt much more than that when I saw him. I felt fear."

"Yes. No matter what happened in the past, today he's a ruthless and brutal killer. One of the most dangerous men I've ever known."

"Why would he be consulting with the Navy? And why would he kidnap Dylan?"

"I don't know. But he hates the United States. Hates it with a passion. It wouldn't take much to recruit him into a plot against us. He might even do it for nothing, just for personal satisfaction." Seamus looked up at her, his eyes crinkling. "And with him on the team, there's a damn good chance their plan will be executed. Successfully."

"Wow," Dylan said, gazing down at the conference table. "When you said you had a surprise for me, I never imagined anything this spectacular. Samsonite luggage. Am I getting a lovely parting gift from the *Hollywood Squares*?"

Mr. X smiled. This was the first time Dylan had seen her since the surgery. He was amazed at the transformation. Her face was so changed that, but for the red hair, he would never have recognized her as the woman who once crushed his gonads. Her face was not healed, but the hideous scars were gone. Her face was soft and smooth and feminine, with delicate features and even a pleasing smile.

"Just open it."

Dylan flipped open the latches on each side. "I normally prefer to pack my own—*Gahhh!*"

Dylan leaped backward as something sprung out of the suitcase. Correction: As some*one* sprang out of the suitcase. An impossibly small bundle of flesh unfolded itself midair and turned into a person wearing a tight black unitard. A very small person, but a person, just the same. He did a half-somersault and landed squarely on his feet.

The little man grinned. "What's the matter? Never seen anyone jump out of a suitcase before?"

"Maybe in a circus," Dylan said, recovering his sangfroid. "But I'm pretty sure those clowns were coming through a trap door."

"Amateurs." He was extremely muscular, despite his size, perhaps four foot eleven and, by Dylan's estimation, no more than a hundred pounds. He was brown-haired with strong features—just smaller than everyone else's.

"I'll say this," Dylan said. "You know how to make an entrance."

"Show business is in my blood."

"Dylan," Xavier said, "meet Tolga Sarica. Turkish by birth. Spent past five years performing at Tivoli Gardens."

Dylan cautiously took Tolga's hand.

"Also moonlighted as operative for Copenhagen mafia."

"There's a Copenhagen mafia?"

"Run by an American used-books dealer. Big secret."

Felix jumped in, as always talking while simultaneously clicking his laptop keyboard at the speed of sound. "What Xavier is trying to say, Dylan, is that Tolga is the contortionist you requested...and a professional thief."

"I'm looking forward to working with you," Tolga said. He had an accent, but it was slight. He spoke English well. "Xavier gave me some of your books to read on the plane. Very entertaining."

"I'm glad you—"

"If totally unrealistic. That scene in *The Daedalus Dilemma* where Fargo Cody escapes the fire through a natural gas pipeline? No way. I tried to get through a pipeline in Morocco once. Didn't make it. And if I couldn't do it, your guy wouldn't have a chance."

"Fargo is very resourceful."

"Fargo is six-foot-three and two-hundred-and-twenty pounds. I doubt he could get his head through that pipeline."

"Well, there's a big difference between fiction and real life." A lesson Dylan was learning incrementally every day.

"Could we return our attention to the matter at hand?" Mr. X asked. "I assume you'll be ready to go on PFD, Dylan?"

"I've done everything required. Is the set ready?"

"Completely."

"The doctor? The drugs?"

"Also ready."

"The makeup artist?"

Xavier jumped in. "Will persuade him tonight."

Dylan tried not to contemplate what that meant. "I have concerns about the blonde encryption expert I see your men dragging to breakfast every morning. How can I trust her in the field?"

"She's stubborn," Mr. X explained, "but she'll do as she's told. The consequences of noncompliance would be extreme. And she knows it."

Dylan wondered what they were holding over her. Did they torture her lover? Cripple her grandmother? He knew he would have to make sacrifices if he were to have any hope of stopping these people. But she didn't. He was choosing her sacrifices for her.

"I'd like to talk to her personally."

"I don't think that's wise."

"I'm not taking her into the field until I'm certain I can rely upon her. You know as well as I do how fragile this illusion we're creating will be. There's no margin for error."

Mr. X frowned, spoiling her pretty new face. "Very well. I'll tell her keepers you're allowed to communicate with her." She took a deep breath—and caught her reflection in the glass pane. Dylan could see her studying herself, the new line of her face, the smooth skin.

"What do you see when you look at your reflection now?"

Her reply was surprisingly gentle. "Someone I haven't seen for a long time."

"I'm sorry."

She whipped her head around. "Don't be."

"Did I strike a nerve?"

"You haven't even tickled one."

"You've lost someone."

"Bollocks."

"Or maybe..." He thought another moment, then looked deeply into her eyes. "You're afraid you're going to lose someone."

"I'm not afraid of anything. Except, perhaps, that your infantile efforts at psychoanalysis will derail our plan. So stop it, immediately, or I'll let your girlfriend stop another bullet."

"Is this the part where you indulge your fondness for groping genitalia?'

"No. This is where I remind you that although we could have done so, we have not as yet killed every single person you love. But I can guarantee you this, Dylan. You screw this mission up, and we will." She turned on her heel and stomped out of the conference room.

He'd pushed her to the limit. And there would probably be consequences. But Dylan could accept that. Because, despite her best efforts, he'd obtained his first useful bit of intelligence about her.

CHAPTER
THIRTY-THREE

SEAMUS RETURNED to his office and found Leilani hard at work.

"I brought some more files and photos I'd like you to review." He was still hoping for an ID on Marco or the other man Xavier had working for him. "If you will—"

He paused. Leilani's head was down. She wasn't paying attention.

"Did you hear me?"

She looked up abruptly. "Sorry. I was engrossed in this report."

He glanced at the file open on the table. CARTWRIGHT. "I didn't give you that."

"I found it in your desk."

"You were going through my desk?"

"You told me to be thorough, didn't you?"

"This is a high-security office. We're in the intelligence-gathering—"

"We're looking for Dylan. And I'm not going to overlook anything that might help find him."

"Listen to me, Miss Kahale. You are not an NCTC agent and you do not have clearance for intelligence work. You will look at what I ask you to look at and nothing else."

Leilani hobbled right up in his face. "Now you listen to me. Those bastards tortured me and stole the love of my life. If you want my help, fine, but I'm your partner, not your lackey, and if you can't live with that, I'll leave right now and start my own investigation. And I'll probably find Dylan before you do, because I've already spotted something you and your pals missed!"

They stared each other down for several seconds.

"I don't believe you found something I missed," Seamus said finally. "Prove it."

"Nice try. But I'm either in all the way or I'm out. Which is it?"

They stared each other down for several more seconds.

"You went to the senior prom alone, didn't you?" Seamus finally said.

"Stop trying to distract me." Leilani paused. "I was an awkward-looking teenager."

He shook his head. "The boys were afraid of you."

"You're still not answering my question."

"All right, you're in. But I'm in charge."

"I can live with that. As long as you don't do anything stupid."

"What is it you think you've discovered?"

"You told me the explosion at the Cartwright Institute might be connected to Dylan. You thought maybe the terrorists were after the enriched plutonium stored in the basement."

"That's a possibility."

"Then why did they kill the scientist on the fourth floor?"

Seamus stopped a beat to process. "I believe many scientists were killed."

"In the explosion, yes. But this one was murdered. Before the explosion. And none of the nuclear materials were taken."

"The operation didn't go down as planned. Something went wrong —they probably mishandled the K4—and they ended up blowing the joint sky high while they were still on the premises."

"Or some of them were. I don't think they were after plutonium. I think they were after this scientist."

She showed Seamus a file photo. He remembered glancing at it earlier. Dr. Johann Karelis. Late sixties. Born in Germany. "An expert in theoretical physics? Terrorists don't blow up buildings to get to theoretical physicists."

"About eighty years ago, a theoretical physicist came up with the idea of splitting the atom. He changed the future of the world."

Seamus grudgingly granted her the point. "You can't assume Karelis was murdered. Almost everyone in the building was killed."

"Did you read the ME's reports?"

"I glanced at them. Not much to say. The cause of death was obvious."

"I would agree with you," Leilani said, "in every case but one." She pulled the Karelis report out of a thick stack. "Karelis was found in his bathtub, and to some extent, that porcelain encasement protected his body. Enough was left to conduct a reliable autopsy. Which, being a trained paramedic, I know how to read."

"Let me guess. Traumatic shock due to massive K4 explosion."

"He drowned."

"What?"

"No doubt the body went through massive shocks. His skull was crushed. But his lungs were full of water." Leilani pointed to the key line in the autopsy report. "Guess he stayed in the bath too long, huh?"

Seamus grabbed the report. "You can't drown yourself in the bathtub."

"But someone else could drown you. Or threaten to drown you, to extract information. Just before they blow up the building. To disguise their true objective."

Seamus hated to admit it, but what she said made sense. "Why would anyone go to all this trouble to kill a physicist?"

"That's what we need to learn. I know you're primarily a desk jockey now, Seamus. But like it or not—it's time for you to go back into the field."

LENNY BAKERSFIELD LEFT the location shoot and headed back to his car. It had been an exhausting day. The latest of many. He was used to working long hours. When a movie was in full production mode, eighteen-hour days were not uncommon. Actors were always going on talk shows, complaining about early-morning calls. But the makeup team

had to be there before anyone. And as the head of the makeup department, he had to be there first.

People always assumed makeup men were lightweights, that it was a
sissy-boy job for people without any real talent. Glorified Max Factor
salesmen. As far as Lenny was concerned, it was the toughest job in the
business. It required true artistry, an eye for color, an understanding of
lighting and cinematography, and a talent for detecting and emphasizing
the line of the face. Plus it required the greatest gift of them all—the
ability to deal with actors' egos.

He had an Oscar on his desk for his work on *Nemesis*, but that was
because it was a period picture and they tended to draw awards in
makeup and costuming. His Oscar should've come for dealing with the
lead actress on his current picture. Yes, it was hot here in Hawaii. Yes,
sometimes the sun was in her face. Not to worry. He had her back. She
wasn't going to sweat, she wasn't going to freckle, and she wasn't going
to look bad when fanboys bought her on Blu-Ray and put her up on
their 80-inch 4K screens. So chill, already.

He tossed his makeup kit into the passenger seat and slid into his
car. Location shoots were the worst. Directors rarely anticipated all the
complications of shooting where environmental conditions could not
be controlled. Why do it? These days, they could greenscreen or CGI
any background they wanted after shooting the whole movie in the
comfort of a closed set. And yet, movie directors always wanted location. Said it helped capture the ambience. Now even tv people were
doing it. Ever since *Lost*, everyone wanted to film in Hawaii.

He tried to distract himself as he drove home, but his mind was
stuck in a rut. He had to shift mental gears. He didn't want to inflict
this mood on his family, even if in all likelihood they were already in
bed. He had to switch his brain to the positive.

This industry had given him a fat bank account. And best of all, a
wife, something he was convinced he would never have. Now they had a
little daughter. Whenever he had trouble hauling himself out of bed in
the morning, all he had to do was think of her. The women in his life
made it all worthwhile.

Lenny pulled into his driveway and parked. He walked to the front
door, slid a key into the lock—and froze.

A cold blade pressed against his throat.

Turning his head slightly, he saw a muscular man with the darkest eyes he had ever seen.

"Wh-wha-what's going on?"

The man grinned. "Is showtime."

CHAPTER
THIRTY-FOUR

THE INSTANT LEILANI entered the laboratory, she spotted a familiar figure decked out in a full-length white lab coat, bolo tie, magnifying lenses over his eyeglasses, spinning a Frisbee on one finger.

He hadn't changed a bit.

"Patrick?"

"Leilani!" The Frisbee flew off his finger and crashed into a beaker containing a blue viscous fluid that spilled out onto the countertop. Smoke rose as the fluid burned into the table.

He grabbed a fire extinguisher and squirted the mess. The smoke cleared, revealing a vast array of Bunsen burners, test tubes, petri dishes, and Erlenmeyer flasks.

"Sorry about that. Practicing an experiment for class. It's a demonstration of torque." He dabbed at the mess with a towel. "What brings you on campus?"

She accepted a gentle embrace. "Actually, you."

He beamed. "I'm flattered. Have you been missing those late-night food fests at Sam Choy's?"

"Patrick, I'm here on a...professional matter. I need your help."

"You need the help of a physics teacher? That's not something I hear often."

"It's not something I've ever had occasion to say before. Or expect I ever will again. But you're doing yourself a tremendous disservice." And he was. He held the Harold K. Boyes Chair at Hawaii Pacific University, the largest private school in the islands. No small thing for a man in his early forties. "We both know you're much more than a science teacher."

"I'm guessing you're referring to my kissing technique."

"I'm referring to your extensive knowledge of all things relating to the world of physics. This is actually very important. A dear friend of mine's life may be in danger."

He frowned. "The writer?"

"How did you know?"

"I've seen you with him in the newspaper. Attending gala events, arm-in-arm. You haven't been totally off my radar since you broke it off."

"I need to know about a physicist who died a month ago. A Dr. Johann Karelis. Have you heard of him?"

He shoved his hands into his pockets and fidgeted with his cell phone. "Sorry. I always forget to put this on vibrate before class. Yes, of course I knew Karelis. I'd be a pretty sad excuse for a physicist if I didn't." Deep lines etched their way across his forehead. "What you haven't explained is—why in God's name should I help you?"

CRAZY IDEA, Seamus mused, as he approached U of H Student Union. Let's split up and talk to physicists! How had Leilani talked him into this? He still didn't see how a physicist's murder could be connected to the disappearance of Dylan Taggart. Which explained why he'd had so little success explaining it to Eustace. He suspected his boss would not tolerate this investigation much longer unless he came up with a concrete threat to national security.

Dr. Louis Scheimer worked for the US Navy—another of several arrows pointing the same direction. And he worked with Karelis. Given the multiple levels of approval Seamus needed before he could speak to the scientist, the project must be top secret. Weapons research, most likely. He still wasn't allowed into Scheimer's lab. He had to settle for a half-hour meeting at a nearby coffee shop, where Seamus knew several guards would be watching at all times.

Curiouser and curiouser.

Scheimer was a German immigrant, balding, covered with liver spots, and unless Seamus was mistaken, miserably unhappy. All the smarts in the world couldn't cure depression. In fact, sometimes Seamus suspected smarts were the carrier of the disease. He'd talked to Scheimer for ten minutes without hearing anything useful. Scheimer didn't know Dylan Taggart, didn't know Xavier, and had no idea who these people were. He was simply conducting theoretical research on neutrinos.

He decided to shake up the conversation.

"How was your recent trip?"

"Trip? They never let me go anywhere."

"Yes, they did." He stared at Scheimer. "They let you go somewhere extremely cold."

"How—" Scheimer stopped himself, but it was too late. "Why would you think that?"

"First tell me if I'm right."

"I...can't."

"Okay, let me fill in the blanks. I don't think they'd let you leave the country. And since this is late summer, you must've been to Alaska."

The slight widening of Scheimer's eyes told him he was correct.

"The trip must've been related to your work. I'm guessing an experiment, something that had to be performed outside but couldn't be done where anyone might see."

"And...what would that be?"

"If I wanted to go into full Sherlock Holmes inductive-logic mode, I'd say you conducted a weapons test. Something that didn't involve radioactive fallout, so the Bikini Islands weren't necessary. Only privacy."

"You're a gifted agent, Mr. McKay."

"Nah. You've still got severe tissue damage, broken capillaries, around your ears. Didn't pull your cap down low enough, I guess. Sometimes takes months for that to heal. And when you opened your briefcase, I spotted empirical antibiotics and diuretics." He paused. "You got frostbite."

"And it still hurts."

"So tell me what you were doing in Alaska."

"I can't. I'm not allowed."

"Was Dr. Karelis there?"

"Maybe."

"You've never done government work before."

"And for good reason." He looked down suddenly, as if afraid he'd said too much.

"What changed your mind?"

A tiny smile played on Scheimer's lips. "A call from the master."

"Karelis?"

"No. The dead master."

Seamus thought a moment. "Einstein."

"It doesn't matter. I now believe I made an error in judgment. But I am...unable to leave my work unfinished."

Translation: the military had him where they wanted him and they wouldn't let him go. "We all have regrets. But you can't turn back time. Was this experiment a success?"

Scheimer's eyes darted to one side. Seamus knew he was mentally weighing how much he could say. "More successful than our wildest imaginations."

"Is that why Karelis is dead?"

Several gulps of coffee were swallowed before the scientist answered. "I hope not."

"But you don't know? Or you don't want to know?"

Scheimer pushed away from the table. "Our time is over."

"Our time is not half over." He grabbed Scheimer's wrist. On both sides of the room, he saw guards flinch. He removed his hand. "Tell me what happened in Alaska."

Scheimer's voice dropped to a whisper. "Do you know what Oppenheimer thought at Trinity?"

Seamus did. "He quoted the Bhagavad-Gita. 'Now I am become Death, the destroyer of worlds.'"

"Oppenheimer was an amateur. We have taken his blunderbuss and given it precision tuning. We have made death as easy to implement as to contemplate."

CHAPTER
THIRTY-FIVE

"PATRICK, PLEASE. THIS IS IMPORTANT." Leilani could see this interview was going to be difficult. Asking favors from someone she once dated was probably a bad idea. But he was the only physicist she knew.

"You know what? I'm important, too. And you hurt me. I really thought we had something."

"I wasn't the right one for you."

"You mean because you didn't know the difference between a quark and a quasar? I didn't care about that. I cared about you. And you dumped me. By email, no less. That's about as cold as it gets."

"I was trying to make it as painless as possible."

"You failed. You made it as hard and impersonal and pain*ful* as possible. I thought we had a real connection. And you just walked away."

Leilani reached out and took his hand. "Patrick—I'm sorry. I screwed up. Maybe we could've made it if I hadn't been a coward. I've... had a hard time allowing myself to get close to anyone. And I so clearly wasn't the right match for you. Being with you just made me feel more alone. That was my fault, not yours. But now I have a real chance for happiness. Won't you please help?"

Patrick gave her a long look. He inhaled deeply, then finally spoke. "Karelis is famous in the field of quantum chromodynamics."

"Did you know him personally?"

"I met him once. About a year ago. Here in Hawaii. Puzzling thing. His entire life, he never left his native Germany. Never worked for the government. Never taught. Not once. And then, about three years ago, without any explanation, he moves to Hawaii."

"To do what?"

"None of this is official. But if you get enough people involved, and spend enough money, eventually word is going to leak out. I know he was working for the military—he must've convinced them he could make something they could use. Probably a dodge to get funding for his research. Frankly, Leilani, I think he was crackers. Nut job. Off the deep end."

"Is that your official hypothesis? Speaking as a scientist?"

"It's not an unusual trajectory for a physicist. We start crazy and get crazier. But functionally crazy. Like Nikola Tesla—probably the greatest scientist who ever lived. Obsessed with the number three. Couldn't eat unless he had three napkins. Had to circle a building three times before he could enter. Could only stay in a hotel for a number of nights divisible by three."

"But Patrick—do you have any idea what Karelis might've been working on? Before he died?"

"None." Pause. "Except..."

"Yes?"

"That one time I saw him? He was with Louis Scheimer."

"And that's important because...?"

"Scheimer's specialty is neutrinos."

"And neutrinos are..."

"Fascinating. Did you know that billions of them are passing through your body as we speak?"

She did not. And she didn't much relish the mental image, either. "What can you do with neutrinos? What are the military applications? How can you use them to hurt someone?"

"There's nothing you can do with neutrinos. They're elementary particles. Interesting, but harmless."

"Then what is Scheimer doing? Why would anyone want to kill Karelis?"

"I thought he died when that gas line exploded."

"Yeah. In a watery sort of way. Do you know what these two might have been concocting?"

"I'm sorry. I don't."

"Okay. Thank you for your help, anyway. And Patrick." Her eyes lowered. "I should've treated you better."

"I appreciate you saying that." He picked up his Frisbee. "But it doesn't make it hurt any less."

She nodded. "I know."

LEILANI RETRACED the entire conversation in her head as she crossed the quad to her car. What would she tell Seamus when she reported back? She hadn't learned much. Karelis was working with another mad scientist named Scheimer, who was obsessed with tiny particles that flew through the air and never hurt anyone. Why would the military care? None of it made sense. And none of it brought her closer to Dylan.

She was pleased when she finally found her car, parked in a dubiously legal spot on the north oval. It had been a long hike and her left leg ached. Dr. Fender was calling every day, urging her to return to the hospital.

No chance. She had work to do.

She had almost opened the car door when she felt the barrel of a gun jab into her gut, just below her ribcage. "Don't move."

Leilani winced. The gun poked her where she'd been shot.

She whirled around. The dark-eyed man in the suit jabbed her even harder. "I told you not to move."

Another taller man stood behind him, stoically surveying the situation. Somehow, his lack of expression was more alarming than the gunman's aggressive attitude. "Let's get her someplace private."

"I'm not going anywhere with you," Leilani said. All the memories crashed down on her. The last time someone pointed a pistol at her. And the protracted horror that followed.

The gunman twisted her right arm behind her back, then shoved her forward. It hurt, but she was not going to let that show.

"Move."

They pushed her between two large brick buildings. A minute later, the taller man opened a side door. They shoved her into a dark dusty room. There was only one window, up high, and it was so encrusted with dirt that almost no light crept through. The tall man locked the door behind them.

"What's this about?" Leilani said, holding panic at bay. "What are you going to do?"

The man with the gun shoved her back against the wall. "We're going to finish the job our friends started."

CHAPTER
THIRTY-SIX

XAVIER TOSSED the makeup artist through the door. This shouldn't take long. They only needed him for two days, once for dress rehearsal, once for the op itself. All Xavier had to do was convince the man he had absolutely no choice.

Xavier had intentionally chosen to recruit Bakersfield at home, where his wife and daughter would be sleeping. As with Dylan Taggart, the persuasion process was much simpler when easily threatened loved ones were nearby.

He turned on a lamp and shoved Bakersfield onto the sofa. A photo of his wife rested on the end table. She had jet black hair and full lips. Very attractive. Appeared to be Middle Eastern.

Xavier could see that Bakersfield soon would be asking questions. He wrapped his powerful hands around the man's throat, choking off his words. "Your wife upstairs sleeping. Would be best if she not hear you. If she comes down, she never go up again."

Bakersfield cowered into the cushions, a stricken expression on his face. He pursed his lips as if to form words. Xavier held up a finger. He stopped.

Xavier took a stack of printed digital photos out of his shirt pocket.

"This picture of wife at supermarket," he said, slapping it down onto the coffee table. "Could have killed her there. No one could stop me."

He pulled out another photo. "This picture of wife at gymnasium. Could have killed her then."

Bakersfield's eyes were cold blue sheets. He breathed in short quick bursts, probably on the verge of hyperventilating.

"This picture of wife undressing for shower. This picture of wife leaving shower." He slapped down another. "This picture of wife removing makeup." He tossed down the last photo. "Bitch brushes hair forever."

Xavier leaned into the quaking figure on the sofa, hovering over him. "Wife upstairs now, sleeping. Wearing brown leopard-skin nightie. Needs someone to fulfill needs." He leaned in closer till they were almost nose-to-nose. "Will it be you? Or me?"

Bakersfield spoke in barely a whisper. "What do you want?"

"Need you for job. Two days. Tomorrow we practice. Next day, we do for real."

"They're expecting me on the set tomorrow."

"Tomorrow you will be sick. Doctor will call, say you have contagious flu. They won't want you. Day after that is PFD. No filming. After that, you back, like nothing ever happen. And wife still alive. As long as you keep mouth shut." This was a lie, of course. Xavier knew Mr. X would have Bakersfield killed when she was done using him. That was how it always worked with these recruited specialists. No one could be trusted to remain silent forever.

"I'll do whatever you want," Bakersfield said. "But I don't see what I can—"

"Your job simple. Do what told."

"Do I need...any equipment?"

"Makeup, prosthetics, latex, hairpiece. I have list. We go shopping later."

"I'll need to tell my wife something."

"You leave note. Doctor will call in morning. You are quarantined for forty-eight hours."

"Okay." Bakersfield sweated profusely. Xavier couldn't help but compare him to Dylan Taggart. The writer had tried everything, had been defiant to the last. He was a rod of iron compared to this stick of butter. "I'll do anything you say."

"Good." Xavier grabbed him by the throat and hoisted him off the sofa. "You will need—"

He stopped in mid-sentence.

Someone was coming down the stairs.

Xavier released Bakersfield, giving him a hard look that said in no uncertain terms that he should not speak.

The footsteps were shuffling. Slippers? Someone tiptoeing to avoid being heard?

Xavier reached inside his coat and withdrew his Sig Sauer. He pointed it toward the foot of the stairs and waited to see what emerged.

For once, even he was surprised.

"Daddy?"

The shuffling sound was not the result of houseshoes. It was the padded feet on her pajamas. The tiny blonde girl who stepped into the room could not be more than five years old.

"Daddy? What's hap'ning?"

Xavier readjusted his aim. Directly at her head.

CHAPTER
THIRTY-SEVEN

DYLAN SPOTTED his target as she crossed from the gymnasium to the barracks where her sleeping quarters were located. She'd been swimming. Her hair was wet and dangling around her shoulders. She wore a clinging green cover-up over her suit.

This was his opportunity. Their keepers waited in the main building. Only the perimeter guards could see them, and they weren't close enough to overhear.

He ran forward and touched her on the shoulder. "Excuse me."

Her face was flushed and her eyes were red, not from swimming.

"I'm Dylan Taggart."

She didn't stop walking. "I know who you are."

"And you're Mikala Meilani. I'd like to talk to you."

Her upper lip curled. "Do I have any choice?"

He put out a hand to stop her. "Yes. But I'd appreciate the chance. Five minutes will be enough. Probably the most we'll ever get without interruption or observation."

Mikala inhaled deeply, causing her ample chest to rise and fall. She was tall, appealingly curvy but still muscular, which didn't surprise him. He'd seen how effectively she'd struggled with three security guards twice her size. She was no wimp. She was a beautiful woman, but her face was haggard, worn. She had not enjoyed her first week at the terrorist camp.

"All right," she said. "Talk."

Dylan steered her to the north. "This way, please." He knew where the security cameras were located so well he could position himself outside their ambit without even glancing upward, like an actor who'd learned to hit his mark without thinking consciously about it. "Let's talk here. And please keep your voice down."

A light rain trickled through the palm fronds. She removed her cover-up, then pulled a sweatshirt out of her gym bag and shrugged it over her shoulders. Dylan tried not to stare, but it took some effort.

She reminded him of Leilani.

"Just give me my orders and let's get on with it."

"I don't have any orders."

"Are you going to beat me senseless?"

"Of course not."

"Torture me? Threaten my relatives?"

"Mikala, I'm a prisoner. Just like you."

"Don't try to kid me. You're planning the whole operation."

Is that what she thought? Is that what everyone here thought? That he was one of the terrorists? "That doesn't mean I wanted to do it. I was brought here against my will."

"I thought they never brought anyone here against their will. They just broke your will. They made it so you had no choice."

"Exactly. How did they get you?"

She peered into his eyes. "They went after my father. Killed his dog. Burned his crops. Sent someone out to beat him up and—and they used an—an—electric cattle prod on his—" Her voice choked.

"I'm sorry." Dylan wanted to hold her but knew that would probably be a mistake. "I—" He retreated into passive voice. "There was a need for a decryption expert. An extremely talented one."

"I'm a private-sector security consultant but I've handled many government contracts. I've developed programs that can override the best portal systems in the world."

"You create the gizmos that make it possible to break into buildings with high-tech security systems?"

"I create the gizmos that make it possible to break into NORAD. Our government funds projects at research facilities all across the country. One group of scientists constantly invents new and increasingly impenetrable security systems, while another constantly looks for ways to breach those impenetrable systems. There is no defense that can't be compromised eventually. The government knows this. So they hire me to figure out how to breach their systems before the Russians do. Or the North Koreans."

She turned away. He could see her eyes were watering. "I'd rather be working for the North Koreans than these bastards."

He felt drawn to her. Was it because they both had been turned into puppets by these sick, manipulative monsters? Or was there something more? He had a sense that there were great depths to her, much more than was visible on the surface. The key question was how much he could trust her. "They did something similar to me. Attacked my girl-friend. Shot her. Tortured her. Threatened to—" He stopped short. "You don't need all the details. We're both prisoners."

"Then why are you in charge?"

"Believe me, I am not in charge. They're using me, just as they're using you."

"They seem to trust you."

"They do not trust me. And they shouldn't." His voice dropped a notch. "There's a way out of this. Out of here. And I plan to find it."

"Why are you telling me this?"

"Because I want your help. I *need* your help."

"Why should I help you?"

"I won't lie—what I'm planning is difficult, dangerous, and could well end with both of us dead."

"You're a really poor salesman."

"But I think we might pull it off. We can thwart their plan—and escape in the process."

"How do you know I'm not working with them? A mole."

"You could be. But I don't think so. I've been watching you care-fully and I'm usually pretty good at reading people."

"What is it you want me to do?"

"I need you to...overlook something. And then you're going to drive the getaway vehicle. In a manner of speaking."

"But you've already outlined your plan. I've read it."

"Yes." He glanced over his shoulder. They needed to start walking toward the main complex. If they delayed any longer, it would create suspicion. "But there are going to be a few plot twists they don't anticipate."

"You're going to beat these people? I don't see how that's possible."

He laid his hand firmly on her smooth shoulder. "As it happens, surprise endings are my specialty."

CHAPTER
THIRTY-EIGHT

LEILANI FELT a flash of pain in her still-healing stomach wound, an aching reminder of what happened the last time she was on the dangerous end of a pointed gun. "What are you talking about? What friends? Finishing what?"

"Don't play dumb with me," the man with the gun said. His tall companion stood behind him, watching carefully but remaining silent. "Tell me everything you know. Starting with why you're asking questions about Dr. Karelis."

How did they know about that? The doctor took the listening device out of her head. Was it possible there was another one? Was there no escaping these people?

"I still don't know what you want. Who's Dr. Karelis?"

"Look, lady, we can do this nice, or we can do it the hard way. Your choice. Personally, I don't care. We're going to get what we want, one way or the other."

Because they always got what they wanted, didn't they? Or so they thought.

Her eyes scanned the room, searching for some means of escape, or something she could use as a weapon. This appeared to be some sort of storage area. Lots of packing boxes and crates. No potential weapons. Certainly nothing that moved faster than a bullet.

"Stop the bull and start talking, lady."

"Or what? You'll rough me up? Maybe you'll do that anyway, once we're done talking. Because that's what you do, isn't it?"

She turned her head in disgust—and saw a large chrome box-end wrench resting on a crate about two feet to her left. Was it possible...?

One thing was damn sure. She wasn't going down easy this time. She wasn't letting these bastards rip her clothes off and torture her. Not without a fight.

He pushed the gun forward. "Last chance, lady. Why are you checking up on Karelis?"

Time to put on the frightened kitten look. "Please—Please don't point that gun at me. Guns scare me." A terrified expression on her face, she backed away from him—toward the wrench. "Don't hurt me. I'll tell you anything you want to know."

"Then start talking!"

"Of course I will. I'll start with...this." She grabbed the wrench and flung it toward him. Her aim was good. It hit his hand and knocked the gun away.

While he stumbled, she ran to the door. She knew it was locked so she didn't waste time with the knob. She rammed her fist through the window. Shattered glass flew everywhere. She knocked away the remaining pieces that clung to the frame. Her arm was cut, but she ignored that. Once she'd cleared enough space, she pushed her head and arms through the opening and tried to dive through.

Someone grabbed her feet.

She pressed her hands flat against the outer door, trying to stop the backward movement. She flexed her gym-girl arm muscles to the max. But she knew this was a losing battle. She couldn't hold out forever. There were two of them and they had more leverage. And the gun was still somewhere in that room.

She let go. They pulled her back into the room, her jaw narrowly missing the jagged glass. She fell hands first onto the hard floor.

"That was a mistake," the man said, shoving the gun into her face. "Now you're going to pay for it."

"Go to hell," Leilani snarled. She closed her eyes, bracing herself for the impact of another bullet.

"Daddy? I don't unnerstand."

"Don't hurt her," Bakersfield whispered, his voice pleading. "She's only a child."

Xavier stared down the sight of his gun. He had no choice here. Someone that young could never be trusted to keep quiet, no matter what he did or threatened. "She see too much."

"She won't remember anything."

"Cannot take chance."

"Daddy? Who is this man?" Her eyes were wide as saucers, watery, confused. "Is he a bad man?"

Xavier's finger tightened on the trigger.

"Please," Bakersfield said. "I beg you. She's my only child."

"Wife young," Xavier grunted. "Have more."

"She can't have any more." Bakersfield's voice cracked. He fell to his knees before Xavier, his hands clasped as if he were at an altar begging for absolution. "Let her go back to bed. She'll think it was all a bad dream."

"Daddy?" The girl moved toward her father.

Xavier's arm stiffened. "Stop!" The padded feet ceased shuffling.

But he had spoken too loudly. Now he heard more rustling upstairs. From the wife's bedroom.

This operation was rapidly spiraling out of control. Now he regretted his decision not to bring Marco. He couldn't effectively control three people.

He would have to eliminate the two expendable people in the house.

He retargeted the little girl, squinting his left eye. His hand trembled. He tensed his arm muscles.

"Jesus God, man," Bakersfield whispered. "Don't do it."

"No choice," Xavier grunted. Bakersfield grabbed his targeting arm, but Xavier shoved him away.

"Daddy? Are you okay?"

Xavier's nostrils flared. He breathed in short, quick, bursts. Pull the damn trigger already!

Before he could, Bakersfield stepped into the line of fire. "I can't let you do this."

"Move or I kill both."

"I don't think so. You want me to do something for you. And I don't think you have time to find anyone else. So put the gun down or your mission is a failure."

Xavier whipped the gun against the side of Bakersfield's head. Blood spurted out. But he did not budge.

"Move!" Xavier barked.

"I'm not going anywhere."

"Then I knock you down."

"I know you don't want to do this horrible thing."

"I have no *choice!*"

"Daddy?" Tears seeped from the tiny girl's eyes. "Is that a gun? A real one? Why is that man in our home?"

Home. The word thudded into Xavier's head with a resonance he could not have anticipated. This was their *home.*

He'd had a home, once. Only time in his life, unless you counted that orphanage that was not really an orphanage. He'd had a wife not unlike the woman in the photograph, beautiful Middle Eastern features, high cheekbones, full lips, hair that flowed like an ebony waterfall.

And a daughter. Almost the same age as this one. Until that bastard called in the air strike.

Of course, that man undoubtedly told himself he had no choice, too.

A soft sleepy voice emerged from above. "Is Emily down there?"

"She is," Bakersfield replied. "I think she's been sleepwalking again. I'll bring her up in a minute."

Bakersfield looked at Xavier. "Let me put her to bed. I'll assure my wife everything is okay. Then I'll tell her I have to go out on business. I'll be back in five minutes. I promise."

Xavier still pointed the gun. "She saw me."

"She won't remember. She sleepwalks, but she never remembers it the next day."

Xavier peered at the girl standing before him. Then he glanced at the photo on the end table.

He lowered the gun. "You have one minute to get her back in bed. I go with you to make sure you not try anything. Do not speak to wife. If you do, I kill her and I take girl back to friends in Middle East and sell her."

Bakersfield scooped his daughter into his arms. Her head dangled over his shoulder. "Come on, darling. I'll sing you a lullaby. You go back to sleep." He carried her up the stairs and started singing quietly. "Baby mine, dry your eyes..."

Xavier followed him. When he was done, they returned downstairs together.

"You were really going to kill my daughter," Bakersfield said, as he slid into the Hummer. "A harmless toddler. Weren't you?"

"Still might." Xavier had made a mistake. He knew that. But it might work out. Bakersfield's family wouldn't talk. They had little to say.

Probably. He'd put a tail on the wife, just to make sure. And when he made his report, he'd leave out a few details.

This kind of sentiment made a man weak. Ineffectual.

A man in his position could not afford such feelings. Not now. Never. Never again.

CHAPTER
THIRTY-NINE

"I TRIED TO TALK TO YOU!" the man shouted at Leilani, shoving the gun against the side of her head. "Now we have to do it the hard way!"

Leilani clenched her eyes shut, bracing for the agonizing pain she knew was only moments away. She hoped it would be quick. "Goodbye, Dylan," she murmured under her breath.

The crash was so loud she initially mistook it for the report of a gun. She literally rose off the ground, her heart racing. It took several moments to realize she had not been shot.

Someone knocked the door down.

The gunman whirled around, firing, but the figure in the doorway did a low somersault and rolled into the room under the spray of bullets. He sprang up onto his feet, knocking the gun away.

"Seamus!"

He did not stop to say hello. Seamus gave the gunman a knee strike to his upper thigh. The man screamed and crumpled to the floor. Leilani realized he must've hit the common peroneal nerve, rendering the man incapable of standing.

For a desk jockey, Seamus was pretty good in a scrap.

The tall man raced forward, but Seamus crouched low and rammed his shoulder into the man's stomach. He fell backward, tumbling into his partner.

Before either man could so much as roll over, Seamus had his own gun trained on their collective heads. "I'd suggest not moving," Seamus growled. "I'd love to blow a hole into both of you."

They didn't move.

"You okay, Leilani?"

"I'll be fine." She brushed herself off. "These creeps knew I was asking about Karelis. They wanted to know why."

She saw a brief grimace cross Seamus' otherwise impassive face. "Can you hold the gun on them?"

"With pleasure."

"Don't fire. Unless they blink." He passed the gun to her, then reached inside the gunman's jacket and withdrew his wallet. "Now this is interesting."

"Someone else you know? Another professional terrorist?"

"Not exactly." He turned the ID so she could read it. "They're with the United States Navy."

SEAMUS STEERED his Expedition toward the coast, trying to ignore his passenger's fury. She made that challenging.

"I can't believe you let those thugs go!"

"I had no grounds to hold them."

"They hurt me!"

"Technically, you hurt yourself."

"Trying to escape. Okay, they pulled a gun on me."

"They're military investigators working on a national security matter. Not trained to be sweet-talkers. And authorized to use force. Particularly against 'persons of interest.'"

"They said they were going to finish what their friends started."

"They know you were recently assaulted. They were trying to scare you."

"He put a gun next to my head and threatened to shoot!"

"Still trying to scare you."

"It didn't work."

Seamus glanced at her out the corner of his eye but said nothing.

"How did you find me, anyway?"

"You remember that tracking device Dylan's abductors put in your head?"

"Yeah..."

"I put one in your purse."

"You—!" She stopped short. "I guess I can't complain, given the circumstances." Leilani pounded her hands on the dash of the Expedition. "Couldn't you have...I don't know. Sent those creeps to the brig? Put them on bread-and-water rations? Called their superior officers?"

"You saw what happened when I interrogated them. They weren't talking. I can't torture members of the US Navy. Technically, we're on the same team. And I did call their superior officer. All I got was the runaround. National security. Threat to domestic tranquility. Classified. Yadda, yadda, yadda."

Leilani fidgeted with the car-radio dial, even though it wasn't turned on. "Why did they grab me?"

"I think your ex-boyfriend turned you in."

"My—How did you know—"

"The Navy has Patrick on retainer. Anyone asks him questions about Karelis, or Scheimer, or their work, and he sends a signal."

Leilani turned her memory backward. "He did fidget with his cellphone, come to think of it. Right after I mentioned Karelis."

"That's why they grabbed you."

"But why do they care? Patrick told me these crusty old physicists were obsessed with...neutrinos. Said it was all theoretical. Couldn't harm anyone."

"That's funny. Because Scheimer thinks he's the 'destroyer of worlds,' though he declined to provide any details. I'm seriously confused. Someone drowns Karelis, destroys the building where he worked, then grabs Dylan Taggart, a writer, who probably never took Physics 101. Makes no sense. But there must be a connection. And I intend to find out what it is."

"I thought their superior wouldn't talk to you."

"Their boss in Navy intelligence wouldn't. Hit the same stonewall with Scheimer. So I came at it from a different direction. I found someone in the Navy who would talk. Someone who has a keen interest in this situation. Almost as great as yours."

He pulled over beside the safe house where Leilani had been staying since she left the hospital. Seamus didn't think her house was secure. This location was monitored both physically and electronically twenty-four hours a day. "This is where you get out."

"You're dumping me?"

"I have no choice. You can't go where I'm going."

"And where would that be?"

"The United States Pacific Command Headquarters."

"That's the top naval installation in this half of the world. Who's your contact?"

Seamus unlocked her car door. "Dylan's brother."

CHAPTER
FORTY

SEAMUS DROVE THROUGH CAMP H. M. Smith near suburban Salt Lake and Moanalua till he spotted a metal gate stretching before the long flat pinkish building with a raised tower in the rear. He'd reached his destination. The Nimitz-MacArthur Command Center, headquarters of the Pacific Command—PACOM.

He pulled his Expedition to the guard post and rolled down his window.

"Seamus McKay," he said, flashing his NCTC identification. "I have an appointment."

The puffy-faced lieutenant glanced at his clipboard, then made a checkmark in the appropriate box. "We're expecting you, sir. Please pull up to the next stop, where you and any containers you plan to take inside will be screened by a magnetometer. Park in the spot designated B-4. An escort will be waiting for you."

"Thank you."

Seamus advanced to the next station. First they ran him through the security screen, then they scanned the silver attaché he carried everywhere. They were efficient but thorough. Seamus knew they did this dozens of times every day, but no sloppiness had crept into the routine. After they finished, he threaded his way through the parking lot till he found his spot.

His escort met him at the door. "Good morning, sir. I'll take you inside."

"Thank you."

"Commander Taggart asked me to bring you to the briefing room. If that's convenient." It was not a question. The young man led him to the front door, then down the main corridor.

Security was tight. Took him fifteen minutes to get through the front door, perimeter guards watching him at all times, metal detectors flashing, video cameras blinking, guards doing everything short of a body-cavity search to make sure he wasn't carrying anything dangerous. The hallways were busy, as he would expect. Over three hundred officers and enlisted personnel were stationed here from all branches of the military, not just the Navy but the Army, Air Force, Coast Guard, and Marines. PACOM had jurisdiction over half the world, including Indonesia, North Korea, China, Japan, Russia, and India— most of the world's trouble spots and the area military analysts thought most likely to generate the next major threat to the United States.

They arrived at the primary PACOM briefing room. "He'll be with you shortly," the escort explained. He turned on his heel and departed.

Seamus loved this room. The design was fabulous, so 1960s, so obviously influenced by the movies. It looked like something out of an early James Bond picture, with its illuminated maps and mahogany finish. Seamus had never objected to a touch of the theatrical, even when he was doing some of the dirtiest work imaginable in some of the dirtiest places on earth.

The room was dominated by a huge map of what they once called the Pacific Theatre. It had been digitized and modernized, but there was no denying the dramatic power of seeing half the world presented in dynamic, back-lit colors. Above it, a row of clocks showed the time in various world capitals. Was that really necessary? Could they not deduce one from the other by adding and subtracting? Of course they could, but the clock display conveyed a sense of power and global scope. It said: this room rules the world. Even time itself is not beyond our grasp.

"Makes you wish something big would happen, just so you could see it play out on that wall, doesn't it?"

In the corner, Seamus spotted a sturdy man wearing a khaki-colored uniform and a star and three stripes on his sleeve.

"Commander?"

He was in his early forties, Seamus judged. The black half-moons under his eyes made him appear older than he was.

"Robert Taggart." They shook hands. "Hoping to see some action?"

"Not really. I've got enough to do. Thank you for meeting me."

"Always happy to liaise with you boys at NCTC. That's what you're there for, isn't it?"

Technically, he was correct. President Bush had created the NCTC to collect and coordinate intelligence information. In the wake of 9/11, some criticized the intelligence community for failing to share critical data. The NCTC was supposed to prevent that from recurring. But Seamus knew most military officers considered them desk jockeys and thought the world would be safer if the paper pushers stayed out of their way and let them do their jobs.

"You're investigating the Cartwright incident?" Taggart asked.

"Yes. And a murder at the Mahoe Assisted Living Center. A murdered security guard and lawyer. And an assault on Leilani Kahale."

Taggart tilted his head. "Who's she?"

Seamus hesitated. "She's...your brother's girlfriend."

"I didn't know Dylan was seeing anyone. How long have they been together?"

"Two years."

He nodded. "And you believe these incidents are related?"

"I know they are. Commander—are you aware that your brother disappeared about a month ago? I have reason to believe he was taken by extremely dangerous freelance operatives. Leilani was tortured in an effort to coerce your brother into doing...something."

Taggart's expression remained frighteningly phlegmatic. "What do they want him to do?"

"I don't know. But I know this. If we don't find him soon, they're going to kill him. If they haven't already."

"I don't understand. How does this relate to the explosion at the Cartwright Institute?"

Would he really rather talk about that building than his brother? "I think the Institute was attacked by the same people who went after Dylan. Forgive me for saying so, but—I can't believe you don't know more about this. Are you and your brother close?"

For the first time, Taggart hesitated. "Not as close as I'd like."

"Even though you both live in the same city?"

"We grew up here. Our father was stationed in Honolulu when we were kids."

"Your dad was military?"

"Navy. Some work with coalition special forces. He retired a Rear Admiral."

"Do you know why anyone would want to abduct your brother?"

"I don't. But as I indicated, I don't see him much."

"Who in Navy intelligence is investigating the Cartwright matter?"

"I think it's mostly Homeland Security's baby now."

Seamus let that pass for the moment. "You're aware that the Cartwright Institute for Hawaiian Antiquities was a cover for a high-tech scientific-research laboratory."

"I am. But I don't know much about what went on there."

"And you are also aware that the story about a gas-line explosion was a cover. The installation was attacked by terrorists of unknown affiliation."

"Right."

"There was a scientist working there. Dr. Johann Karelis."

"What was he working on?"

"I haven't found anyone willing to answer that question for me. Including his colleague, Dr. Louis Scheimer. I was hoping you might be able to fill me in. Because your brother's life may depend upon it."

"Even if I had clearance to give you that information—which I don't—I couldn't, because I don't know and I have no way of finding out. Scientific research is totally outside my department."

"Seems to be outside everyone's department. At least everyone who will talk to me. I realize the relationship between military brass and scientists is often guarded. They need scientists, but they don't really trust them."

"Sadly, that is often the case."

"But Leilani Kahale—Dylan's girlfriend—was accosted by two

Navy intelligence agents. Because she was asking questions about Karelis."

"I assume they were making sure she's not an enemy agent. Protecting the viability of the project."

"But you don't know what that project is?"

"No."

"And you have no involvement in the Cartwright investigation?"

"I'm mostly in finance these days. Number crunching. If anyone is investigating, it would be Captain Randolph's people."

Seamus made a mental note. "Do you know this person?" Seamus passed a photo he'd retrieved from the navy database. "Currently using the code name Xavier. He's had others. He's Russian in origin, but he's worked for about every enemy America ever had."

Taggart glanced at the photo. "Doesn't ring any bells. Sorry. I'm sure the Admiral would allow you to review our computerized photo files."

"I did. Found the guy at a Navy function. Bunch of dignitaries about to board the Admiral's barge—and I know you can't sneak onto that yacht."

"The Admiral allows the boat to be used for special occasions. We don't run extensive security scans every time it ships out. It has no national security applications. Strictly for PR."

"Well, this time, the Admiral's PR people entertained one of the most vile terrorists on the face of the earth. And he was wearing a Navy uniform."

"Intriguing."

"This man was involved in your brother's disappearance. And I would think that would interest you, even if you aren't close and never have been."

"That last part isn't true." Taggart chuckled. "There was a time when we did everything together. I could get my little brother to go along with anything. We were a team. We two against the world."

"And your father?" Seamus hazarded.

Taggart rubbed the back of his neck, twisting it from side to side. "Have you talked to my father?"

"No. I haven't been able to reach him."

"He travels a lot. Lost his house and his pension. Gambling, I think. So he stays on the road. Doesn't send postcards."

"Hasn't lost his steam?"

"Oh, no. He keeps his fingers in. Calls the admiral with unwanted advice. He did some hard time in Vietnam, back in his younger days. Behind enemy lines. Went through a bad patch afterward, but he also won many commendations and is now considered one of the top military experts on Indonesia. Dad used to be on the President's staff, you know. So you can imagine how he got along with peace-loving Dylan. Who protested against both wars in Iraq."

"How was he as a father?"

"He was...strict. Controlling. Never hesitant to punish. Believed humiliation could be character-building."

"Are we talking about spankings?"

"We're talking about being forced to strip down to your underwear and stand on a table—he called it the Shame Table—for hours. Holding a heavy rock."

"And this would be a punishment for...?"

"Weakness. Any form of weakness. I can still hear his voice. '*Weakness is cowardice. And the only cure for cowardice is shame.*' So he'd make us stand on the table in our skivvies, even with other people strolling in and out. If we tried to sit, he'd whip the back of our legs with a riding crop. He did a lot of other things, too. Stuff I don't even want to talk about." Taggart's eyes seemed to recede. "But he did it for a reason. He wanted us to be strong. Ready to deal with anything. He approached parenting just as he did foreign policy. Carry the big stick and you get what you want."

"Sounds demanding."

"He did tend to believe the whole world should think and be just like him. And if you didn't—you weren't as good."

"I've known people like that," Seamus said. "Egoists. They justify their constant criticism by saying they're trying to help you. But they're intolerant of anyone who's different from themselves."

"That's about right. Our dad was never satisfied with anything we did. Especially not anything Dylan did. He was too much like his mother. That's what the old man always said. As generous as he could be at work, or with friends, Dad was very...cold with his children."

So you, Seamus thought, being the oldest child, dealt with the icy withholding by following in his footsteps, doing everything imaginable to become the man he wanted you to be. A duplicate of the original. And Dylan, the youngest, dealt by rebelling against everything his father represented. "Thank you for talking with me."

"Not at all. I hope you find Dylan."

Seamus started out of the briefing room. Just before he reached the door, Taggart spoke again. "Mr. McKay—what's going to happen if you don't find Dylan? And don't pull any punches because he's my brother."

Seamus exhaled heavily. "Dylan is mixed up with some seriously nasty characters. I don't know what they want, but if he refuses, or he screws it up—they'll kill him."

"And if he complies?"

"They'll still kill him. After they're done with him."

CHAPTER
FORTY-ONE

DYLAN HELD the photograph beside Mr. X's face. "The resemblance is remarkable," he said. "You look just like her."

"And I suppose that makes you proud."

"It makes my plan feasible. I like that." They sat opposite one another at a small side table in the cafeteria. He knew he was taking major risks just being near her, but he did it anyway.

"No, you're thinking of much more than your plan. This is your Pygmalion moment."

"I never cared for *My Fair Lady*. Too much singing."

Mr. X swatted the photo down. "Don't pretend you don't know what I'm talking about. Every artist wants to create something new, right? Just as Pygmalion created Galatea. In your mind, I'm your Galatea. A woman you created. In your image. Or an image of your choice."

"You're making far too much of this. I'm just trying to bring off the impossible."

"I suspect you could've concocted any one of a hundred schemes to accomplish that. You chose the one that stroked your ego."

"I chose the one I thought had the greatest chance of success."

She pushed her tray away. All she'd eaten was a green salad, and not much of that. "Let me make something plain to you, Dylan. I'm not your creation. Even though you've selected how my new face should look, you have not remade me in your image. I'm my own woman and I always will be."

"As you say."

"So if you possess some deluded notion that you'll win me over by transforming me physically, forget it. You're not that talented an artist. You have severe limitations."

Certainly I've become more aware of my limitations of late, Dylan mused. "Aren't I the one you always accuse of playing amateur psychologist? Sounds like you're doing it now."

"It's an easy game. For the smug egomaniac."

"Tell you what. Now that we're both in the game, why don't we establish some rules?" Dylan had no idea how far he could push this before she lost her temper. "You tell me something about yourself," he ventured, "then I'll tell you something about me."

"I think you should go first."

"Of course you do."

"How do I know you won't feed me a pack of lies?"

"Shouldn't I be asking that question?"

"I'm not the fiction writer. What do you want? The traumatic childhood incident that explains all? Real life doesn't work that way."

"Sometimes it does. Sometimes the incident isn't even all that dramatic. But it still hurts."

"What's your inner pain, Dylan? Your mother died early? Your father was cruel?"

"Both true."

"But which one scarred you for life?"

"I didn't know I was scarred."

"Trust me, you are. Deeply. So what's your secret?"

"My father was more than cruel. He was a complete sadist. Made my brother and me do things...deliberately designed to induce shame."

"That's how he got his jollies?"

"He justified it. Said he was instilling discipline. Making us strong. I think that was rationalization. He had some kind of demon inside him. One he couldn't exorcise. So he took it out on his children."

"You left home as soon as you could and built a life opposing every-thing he represented."

"That sums it up concisely. Okay, your turn. Inner trauma."

Her eyes scanned the cafeteria. It was well past one and no one else sat anywhere near them. She could talk freely. The question was —would she?

When she finally spoke, her voice seemed astonishingly quiet. "I was in love once."

Dylan watched as her eyes darted into the distance. "And since this is your inner trauma, I'm guessing it didn't work out."

"Not at first. And not at the end. But there was some wonderful middle."

Dylan found himself smiling. This was a beautiful thing to say— from the most unlikely source imaginable.

"The embarrassing part," she continued, "is how willing I was to change myself, to change anything, to win his love."

Dylan's lips parted. "You didn't join the IRA out of political zealotry. You were chasing a guy."

She bit down on her lower lip. "Embarrassing. But true. What I discovered to my surprise was—I was good at this. And versatile. When they needed an explosives expert, I filled in."

Dylan wanted to ask a follow-up question, but Xavier entered the room. "I look for you everywhere."

"Sorry," Mr. X said. "Dylan and I were having another of our stimu-lating chats."

"Not you. Writer." Xavier grunted in Dylan's direction. "Need to conduct final inspection. Make sure everything ready."

Mr. X rose. Dylan realized the conversation would not be contin-ued. He would have to wait for another opportunity to delve into her past.

"I did my final check already. But you can't be too careful. Lead on."

This really was going to happen, Dylan thought. His plan would no longer exist only on paper. For the first time, one of his plots was coming to life. His storytelling ability would be put to the ultimate test.

And may God have mercy on their souls.

DR. SCHEIMER APPROACHED the janitor with caution. "Joe?"

The skinny man with bad teeth set down his broom. "Something I can do for you, Doc? Need your lab cleaned again?"

"No. I just wanted to talk." He wondered if Joe could smell the alcohol on his breath. Didn't matter. They all knew he drank. It was none of their business. "I'm concerned about security."

"Want me to get Bukowski? He's in the guardhouse outside."

"No, I'd rather talk to you."

"Sir, I'm just the janitor."

"No, you're not, so don't argue with me. I've been watching you for weeks. The government planted you here. You are much too observant for a mere janitor. Every time there's a noise, or a sudden movement, I see your head jerk around. You're watching out for me."

Joe apparently didn't care to argue. "You're very observant. But I'm not watching you." He paused. "I'm watching your laptop."

Scheimer nodded. "That makes sense."

"They fixed it so no one could get information out of you. But they're concerned about your notes. I monitor that laptop at all times."

"Smart. Very smart."

"So what's bothering you, Doc?"

"I met with a man from the NCTC. A determined man. A smart man."

"Did he pry anything out of you?"

"No. But he did not strike me as the sort to give up easily. I was concerned that amidst the chaos of PFD..."

"Don't worry. You're safe here. Guards outside and inside. Video cameras. And me. You and your work wouldn't be safer in the White House."

"That is good to know." He could see that Joe thought he was worried about intruders. What he didn't realize was that he was actually wondering if, during all the revelry, he might escape. Cease performing this work that had become repugnant to him. But of course it was impossible. He was stuck here. Till the day he died.

"You must be proud of all you've accomplished, Doc."

"Yes. Proud."

"I don't know much about it, but I know the brass hats put a high value on you. Must make your heart swell to see all you've accomplished."

"Something like that."

"Pardon me for saying so, Doc, but—you seem a little down. Is there anything I can do?"

"No, it's nothing. I—I hate PFD. Universities should be places of advanced research and learning. Not...loud drunken celebrations of... nothing much."

Joe chuckled. "I know what you're saying. I think you need to get out more. Got a friend you can call?"

"No time."

"Or better yet, a woman?"

His eyes misted. "I had a woman. Once. But that was long ago. And I'm afraid she cannot be replaced."

"Sorry to hear that."

"And I am sorry to have bothered you. Thank you for your time."

"You betcha."

Scheimer wandered back to the lab. He couldn't pour his next shot fast enough. Why couldn't he shake this sense of foreboding? It wasn't just the interview with the NCTC agent. Ever since Johann's death—his murder, in all likelihood—he had felt with inescapable certainty that he'd erred in coming to the United States, sinned in working with the military, and debased himself for an unworthy cause. But he could do nothing about it now.

Kronos had been unleashed, thanks to him. Now the lightning would strike and the world would never be the same again.

CHAPTER
FORTY-TWO

SEAMUS LOGGED into yet another database and prepared himself for more hours of slow-scan boredom. So this was life at a desk job. Hard to make the adjustment. Even harder to keep himself motivated. To convince himself he was doing this for a noble cause. To help those in need. To defend this great nation.

Not for revenge.

He appreciated the modern miracle that was the computer. And CCTV. He appreciated the fact that he had access to some of the best research materials on earth. This new collaborative integration software was extraordinary. Not only did it allow him to search numerous databases with increasingly targeted parameters, it also provided alerts in real time, an invaluable asset when processing related data fields. Information junkies loved it. They could set it up so they received a constant flurry of data about potential threats.

That would drive Seamus mad. When he was working, he didn't like distractions.

Where are you, Xavier? What rock have you crawled under this time, you son-of-a-bitch?

Americans already had precious little privacy, and the combination of increased tech and increased government paranoia would soon eliminate what remained. That was fine with Seamus. In his experience, when people were excessively concerned about privacy, there was usually a reason.

He set the playback speed faster than normal. He had quick eyes and still felt reasonably alert, even though he'd been doing this for hours. He'd already run scans on Johann Karelis and his buddy Scheimer, but he hadn't found anything he couldn't learn from the newspaper morgue or Wikipedia. He knew more than enough about Xavier's past. What he needed was information about where the man was hiding.

"You're taxing the server, Seamus."

Eustace. As smoothly as possible, Seamus dimmed the computer screen.

"Got a call from the Pentagon. Said someone here made an unauthorized breach of their intelligence interface."

"It wasn't unauthorized. I used a password."

"Yes. But it wasn't yours."

"You mean currently."

"If it isn't current, it isn't yours."

"If the Pentagon isn't smart enough to change their passwords periodically, am I to blame?" In fact, the Pentagon did change their passwords and command codes almost every day, but unbeknownst to most, there were back doors that always remained open. Maybe he was the only one who still remembered they existed.

"How am I going to square this with the military brass?" Eustace asked, reminding Seamus why his colleagues called the man "Eustace the Useless."

"We're supposed to share information, aren't we? What's their problem?"

"They don't like people hacking into their server."

"Maybe now they'll tighten security. I've done them a service. Better I show them the loopholes than the Taliban."

Eustace grimaced but dropped the subject. "What are you working on?"

"That Cartwright/Taggart business."

"You've devoted a great deal of time to that, but you haven't produced much. Maybe you should leave it to Homeland Security."

"I'm pursuing leads they don't have."

Eustace folded his arms across his chest. "I'll give you twenty-four hours to produce something concrete. Failing that, I want you to move on."

Seamus knew there was no point in arguing. "Understood."

"Saw Ingrid at the club the other night. She looked ravishing."

"She always does."

"Who's that man she's running around with?"

Seamus' stomach tightened. "I have no idea."

"Do you care?"

"Not in the slightest."

"I can see how you might be bitter."

"I'm not bitter. I'm indifferent. I've moved on."

"I see. Interesting that she turns up in Hawaii not long after you do."

Interesting was not the word Seamus would've used.

"I suppose she always had to work to get your attention," Eustace continued. "A super-patriot like you can be so focused. Difficult to distract with the more...human emotions."

Seamus understood that Eustace was his supervisor, but he felt certain that didn't mean he had to endure this. "Don't mean to be rude, but if I don't concentrate on these images, I might miss something."

"Right, right." Eustace gave him a patronizing look he would've loved to wipe away with a baseball bat. "I gave Ingrid my card. I don't suppose you would mind if—"

"Of course not," Seamus said, knowing Eustace didn't have the slightest chance.

Eustace edged toward the door, suddenly uncomfortable. "Let me know if you get something."

"Of course."

He waited until Eustace left the office, then resumed his search. Super-patriot? Had the man actually said that? Many moons had passed since Seamus thought of himself in anything resembling those terms. He didn't know what he believed anymore. Except he believed Dylan Taggart was involved with some seriously evil people. And he believed in Leilani Kahale. He'd rarely witnessed such strength. She was fighting to preserve...what Seamus had abandoned.

Ingrid called the first night she was in town. Seamus let it ring.

Forty-five more tedious minutes passed before Seamus saw something that looked like Xavier. A stray CCTV image snapped the day Dylan was taken from his condo. In fact, the time-date stamp suggested this was only a few minutes after the attack occurred. Xavier was speeding, so the camera automatically took a pic of his Hummer as he blasted through the intersection.

Seamus froze the image just before the Hummer left camera range. Placing his finger on the touch screen, he brought the crosshairs down until they focused on the back bumper of the car. He hit the Magnify button. Then he hit it again, then again, until he could make out the license-plate number.

And more. Someone sat in the passenger seat. Someone who wasn't Dylan.

Seamus focused on the blurry face and brought it up to the maximum magnification, which only made the blurring worse.

A woman. He was certain of that. Long blonde hair. No wait. He used the color translation tool to make a best guess at hair color.

Red hair. Bright red hair. Almost orange.

Seamus felt a tingling at the base of his spine. Could this be *her*? And if so, what were those two doing together?

He couldn't get much detail on her facial features. But one fact was clear. This woman was disfigured.

Seamus knew why. And unless she'd gotten over it, which he doubted, she would be just as twisted and bitter as ever.

He would run the image through the FBI's face-match computer, just to be sure.

He rubbed his hand against his forehead. Every time he learned something new about this case, it got worse. From dangerous to deadly.

But knowledge was power. Now that he knew who he was after and had an idea how he might find her. She would lead him to Xavier. And then there would be a final reckoning. Accounts balanced, once and for all.

The door opened. Leilani entered.

"Find anything?" she asked.

"Nothing useful, no." It wasn't a lie. Knowing McKenna was

involved was not immediately useful. Didn't tell him where Dylan was. Just told him Dylan was in even more danger than he'd realized. Leilani didn't need to know that. "I spotted some CCTV images of Xavier in Hawaii. Nothing of interest."

"I've been doing the same thing on the other monitor, looking for Marco. No luck."

"He's an underling," Seamus said. "And given what you've told me, probably a relatively new one, inexperienced. Drunk on the power trip. Riddled with perverse sexual obsessions, indicating that he hasn't come to grips with his own sexual identity. People like that don't last long in terrorist organizations. They're redshirts, basically."

"I hope someone puts him on the front line. When I'm on the other side."

"How's your leg?"

"Fine. No problems at all."

Liar. But he wasn't going to call her on it. "Ready for a new assignment?"

"You know I am."

He handed her a scrap of paper. "Here's the tag on the Hummer Xavier drove the night he invaded Dylan's condo."

"You want me to call DMV?'

"I guarantee it's either unregistered, fake, or stolen. But find out what you can. Use the phone and computer in my office. I've put your name on the NCTC rolls as a consultant."

"I'll get right on it."

"If you get an owner, collect anything you can about him or her from the conventional sources. Legal records, FBI database, Interpol..." He waved his hand in the air. "You'll figure it out. I'm already logged into all the databases." He grabbed his coat.

"What will you be doing?"

He pulled his jacket on and headed toward the door. "I'm going to pay a visit to an old friend."

CHAPTER
FORTY-THREE

DYLAN WATCHED his team assemble in the conference room. They looked ready. Yesterday's dress rehearsal had gone down without a hitch. Which said nothing about what might happen during the actual mission—no simulation could fully reproduce the unpredictability of being out in the field, interacting with human targets. But he was encouraged. When he'd first presented his proposal, some wondered if he was joking. And now they were all lined up, ready to bring this plan to life.

The plan as they understood it, anyway.

As he walked the length of the conference table, he felt like a drill sergeant surveying his platoon. Xavier, Mr. X, Felix, Tolga, Mikala, Dr. Giep, the set design and construction guys, and the new kid, the makeup artist. Bakersfield. They looked slick, professional, fit, and ready. They had all the gear they needed, all the equipment, drugs, everything. Despite the manner in which he and most of the others had been recruited, they seemed of one mind and ready to execute the mission.

Marco entered and stood beside Mikala. Dylan's gorge rose in his throat.

"What's he doing here?" Dylan asked.

"We need backup security," Mr. X explained. "He'll remain in the van and will only emerge if an emergency arises."

"I don't want him involved in this op," Dylan said.

"You'll probably never see him."

Marco grinned. "Whatsa matter, writer-boy? Still holding a grudge?"

If this had come at any other time, Dylan would've put needles through the man's eyeballs. But for now he had to remain calm. He didn't want to blow everything, not when he was this close to setting his plan into motion.

"I want this man gone," Dylan said in a steady voice. "I will not work with him."

Mr. X's lids lowered. "You are the planner, Dylan, but not the leader. You do not have the authority to choose my security personnel."

"I don't see the problem," Marco said. "Your girl ain't here." He glanced at Mikala. "And you might need someone to keep this one in line."

"I'm not undermining your authority, X," Dylan said. "But I will not work with this disgusting excuse for a human being. I will not—"

He felt smooth gun metal pressed against his right temple, stopping him in mid-sentence.

"I think you will," Xavier said, his bad breath wafting into Dylan's personal space. "I think you will shut up and do as told, or will be my pleasure to kill you. We have your plan. Why do we need you?"

SEAMUS KNOCKED TWICE, but no one opened the door. He was not surprised.

"I'm not going to bother shouting," he said to the door, "because I feel confident that you're standing on the other side waiting to see if I'll go away. I did see the fiber-optic camera hidden in the porch light, so you know who's knocking. Let me tell you why I'm here. I want information. That's all. But if you don't open the door, I will obtain a warrant and subpoena. The house is surrounded by six other agents so no one inside will have a chance to leave, not even the ones who are not legally in this country or are in possession of items the law says they should not have." He paused. "Decide, Karen. Do we chat? Or do you want to see what a team of federal investigators armed with search-and-seizure power can turn up?"

Once upon a time, a place like this would've been hidden in the rural parts of Oahu, close to the beach perhaps but not the city. These days, pushers seemed to favor the suburbs. Was it because no one would expect anything naughty in this three-bedroom Beaver Cleaver house? Or was it because no one in the suburbs paid attention to anything outside the perimeter of their own neatly trimmed lawns?

Either way, he was not surprised when he heard the door open, or when he saw an anorexically-thin woman in her mid-twenties emerge sporting a nose piercing, a tongue stud, and a barbed wire tattoo around her biceps.

"What the shite do you want?"

Seamus loved what an Irish brogue did to swear words. Somehow, "shite" didn't seem nearly so harsh. Almost like baby talk. "Karen, is that any way to talk to the man who kept you out of prison?"

Her eyes flared. "You held me prisoner for three days without food or water. Till I gave up my friends."

"But did I let them lock you up afterward? No."

"You're a bastard."

"I'm a federal agent, and we tend to look dimly on foreign nationals with links to Al-Qaeda."

"We weren't hurting anyone. We—"

"You were smuggling supplies to people planning to detonate a fertilizer bomb at an American embassy."

"Screw you, anyway."

"Do I need a subpoena? Or are you going to let me in?"

She glanced over her shoulder. He knew what that meant. Company.

Seamus stepped inside and saw two looming musclebound figures, both with shaved heads and wearing white t-shirts, only a few steps behind her. The immediate image that came to mind was Mr. Clean, but Seamus supposed that was a sad sign of his increasing age.

"Who're Wynken and Blynken?"

"Friends," Karen said, closing the door. "So don't try any rough stuff."

"I wasn't planning to. I just want information."

"I'm out of the game."

"Or have you shifted to another game?"

She peered at him with squinted eyes.

"Switching from terrorist flunky to drug mule isn't exactly an upwardly mobile career move."

"I don't know what you're talking about."

"You seem well protected," Seamus said, glancing at the muscle hovering behind her. "Are you expecting a shipment?"

"I said, I don't know what you're talking about."

And he didn't much care. Chasing drug runners was a losing game that fell well outside his jurisdiction. The bodyguards were getting antsy, bouncing up and down on their toes. Time to move along.

"I hope that's true. I need the skinny on one of your old galpals. Fiona McKenna."

When she stood sideways, she was almost invisible. "Fi? Haven't seen her in years. Not since her accident."

"Heck of a coincidence. Both of you being in Hawaii."

"Is she? I had no idea."

Seamus didn't need years of experience to see that she was lying. She had so many tells she was a poker shark's dream. "You knew. I'll bet you know she's been hanging with Dmitri Yevtushenko, too."

He received a blank response.

"Or do you know him better as Xavier?"

The twitch in her eye told him what he needed to know.

"You probably have some misplaced loyalty, Karen. And that's admirable, in a twisted sort of way. But you need to understand that these are very bad people. Very bad people planning very bad things. To be blunt, they are further out of your league than Reggie Jackson is from T-ball. You don't want to protect them. You don't want anything to do with them."

"I don't have anything to do with them."

"We're not talking about throwing bricks through windows or

helping Saudi Arabians get fake passports. We're talking about real terrorism. Is that something you believe in?"

"And what exactly is it you believe in?"

For that, Seamus had no answer. "Fi plans to strike at the heart of the United States. That's treason. Which in case you didn't know, is punishable by death."

"There's no death penalty in Hawaii."

"Treason is in the US Constitution. Federal law. If you don't start talking, you're gonna fry."

"I'm telling you, I don't know what you're talking about!"

"I know better. It will go much better for you if you tell me what Fi's up to."

"Leave me alone!"

Seamus took a step forward and squared his shoulders. "You're lying."

"I'm not."

"Your spoiled-brat act won't get you anywhere. I want to know the truth. And if I have to get insistent, I will." He grabbed her arms and shook her.

"Don't touch her!" An instant later, the Mr. Clean on the left stepped forward and shoved Seamus away. Before he could respond, the muscle hoisted him up and tossed him backward. He lost his footing and tumbled to the ground.

The man reached inside Seamus's jacket and took his gun. He grabbed Seamus' tie and twisted it sideways, choking him.

"Leave now, you pathetic old man. Or I'm gonna be wearing your face for a Halloween mask."

CHAPTER
FORTY-FOUR

THE GUN BARREL pressed against Dylan's face did not increase his confidence, but he held firm. "I guess this is a decision for you, Mr. X. Do you think you still need me? Or do you think Conan the Barbarian here, who pulls a gun at the slightest provocation and blew up an entire building last time you unleashed him, can get you the files you need?"

Xavier was furious. "I can get intel. Anytime!"

"Yeah, but if he brings down the whole university, I'm pretty sure the military will know something's up."

"I want you to come," Mr. X said. "But I also have to make sure we have sufficient security."

Dylan watched her eyes as she spoke. They both knew perfectly well she had enough backup without Marco. This was about power. Control. She was the boss and she didn't like to be questioned.

"I'm the one ultimately responsible for the success of this mission—"

"I thought that was the Supervisor."

She took a deep breath. "The Supervisor is counting on me to make sure—"

"And you don't want to disappoint the Supervisor. You would do anything to avoid disappointing the Supervisor. Why is that?"

"You have no idea who the Supervisor is."

"Maybe I do."

"That's not possible."

"Because I've never met him?"

"I didn't—" She stopped short, as if horrified by her outburst. She pressed her hand against her forehead, visibly collecting herself.

She chuckled, but it was filled more with bitterness than amusement. "Well played, Dylan. Well played. You're good at this."

"I don't know what you're talking about."

"Have it your way." She gestured to someone outside the door. "Get Kalifa. He can take Marco's place."

Marco sputtered. "But—"

"Oh, shut up. And in the future, keep your revolting tongue in your mouth."

The switch was made. Dylan had won a battle. A tiny thing. But it was a start.

Xavier cleared his throat. "Everyone understand rules governing op?"

"I'm sure we do," Dylan said, "but why don't you review them, just so we're clear?"

"Dylan is in charge. You take directions from him. But I am overseer. I will be watching at all times. If there are problems"—he gave Dylan a stern, lingering look—"there is possibility that I assume command. If I do, you take orders from me and me only. Got it?"

Everyone nodded their heads, except Dylan. "What circumstances would require you to take command?"

"Why discuss? Hope won't happen."

"I'd just like to know."

"Gross incompetence. Unexpected developments." His voice slowed. "Deviation from plan. And of course, any attempt to escape or contact outside world. That would provoke immediate intervention and extreme consequences."

"Got it."

"One last thing." Xavier held what looked like a small asthma inhaler to Mikala's face. "Take deep breath." Before she could respond, he squeezed the inhaler. "Sorry. Supervisor says we keep headquarters location secret. Suggest you sit before fall down."

Mikala complied. Five seconds later, she was unconscious.

"What the hell was that?" Dylan asked.

"Chloroform compound. Induce sweet sleep. But also contains smart dust."

"You're joking."

"You know smart dust?"

"I know it's been hypothesized. But it doesn't actually exist."

"You need to update research," Xavier said. "Dust laced with wireless network of tiny microelectromechanical sensors. Just precaution."

"I'm not going to screw this up, Xavier. This is my story now. I never leave dangling plot threads." He meant it. He'd put hundreds of man-hours into this plan, and even though he knew their ultimate objection was vile, a part of him couldn't help hoping the plan was a success. A part that wanted to know he was just as good as Fargo Cody.

"I hope that true. But know this." Xavier walked around Dylan, circling him, never taking his eyes away. "While you were unconscious, after leaving Oahu, our medic—same one who patched up your bitch—also planted something inside ear. Radio-activated nanites, powered with nanobatteries. Capable of emitting heat. Think of them as tiny lasers implanted in cerebral cortex. Where leetle heat can do big damage."

"Like what?"

Xavier shrugged. "Hard to say. One burst will burn off part of brain. Might disable motor functions. Might lose use of leg or arm. Might lose sight. Or all of above. Hard to predict what you lose." His eyes locked with Dylan's. "But you will lose."

"And who can activate these nanites?"

"I have remote controller. I can hurt you from inside your head, anytime I want." He paused. "Do not make me mad."

"I won't," Dylan lied. "Let's roll."

CHAPTER
FORTY-FIVE

THE MUSCLEBOUND CREEP in the white t-shirt hovered so close Seamus was afraid the man would drool on him.

"You understand what I'm saying, old-timer? If you don't get the hell out of here, I'm gonna pound you like mashed potatoes, pour gravy down your throat, and serve you for dinner." He gave Seamus a shove for good measure.

Seamus drew himself up, brushed himself off, and then, to the man's great consternation, smiled. "That's the one chance you get to touch me. Next time, I take you out."

Both Mr. Cleans smirked. Karen stood to the side, keeping her distance. Seamus noticed she wasn't smiling so much. But she had a lot more experience, and probably a lot more smarts.

The Mr. Clean who'd attacked him grunted. "In about two seconds, I'm gonna rip that smile off your face with my teeth."

Seamus gave Karen a long look. "Really? This is what you travel with now?" He turned back to the man looming three feet away. "All right, Bluto, you want a fight, you've got a fight. Fair and square. No weapons. Just you and me. On the count of three. Got it?"

"Got it," the man snarled, tossing his gun away.

"One," Seamus said.

The man bounced up and down on his toes, flexing his muscles, pounding his fists together.

"Two."

Seamus lunged, clapping his palms over both sides of the man's head, shattering his eardrums. The man cried out, and while he was off-balance, Seamus grabbed him by the ears and jerked his head down till it smashed into the brick mantle of the fireplace. Blood spurted from his forehead. While he was crouched over, Seamus rammed his knee into the man's gut. He stumbled. Seamus grabbed a poker from the fireplace and swung it like a golf pro, right into the man's ribcage. He screamed, teetered, staggered. Seamus brought his foot up between the man's legs. That dropped him to the floor, face first on the carpet, blood streaming from his mouth and the side of his head.

Seamus pressed his shoe against the man's head. "If you move, I kick you in the face. You won't like what that does to your pretty-boy looks."

He saw the man's partner hovering indecisively in the background.

"Are you going for it? Or are you gonna be smart and go make yourself a nice peanut-butter-and-jelly sandwich?"

The man continued dancing. He glanced at Karen.

"Oh, leave already," Karen said. He did.

Karen marched up to Seamus, arms akimbo. "You cheated!"

"Excuse me?"

"You said you were going to count to three. You never said three!"

"I was never good with math."

"You're a goddamn bully."

"I'm a federal agent," Seamus replied. "And I'll do whatever I have to do. Your girlfriend poses a serious threat to the nation. And I think you know it."

"I don't! I know nothing!"

"You're lying through your crooked teeth. She was behind the attack on the Cartwright Institute. She was after Dr. Karelis. I know she has the writer. And I know where she is." He took a breath. "She's going down, Karen. The only question is whether you're going with her."

She turned away, pacing in front of the fireplace. Seamus kept his foot on Mr. Clean's face.

"I want you out of my house," Karen said.

"Fine. But I'll be back. With a subpoena. And this time we'll take you downtown. As a foreign national and a person of interest, there's no telling when you'll get out. If ever."

"I'm calling my lawyer."

"I hope your lawyer is more effective than your thugs."

She opened the door. "Get—out!"

He passed through the door, smiling. "Till we meet again."

She slammed the door behind him.

Seamus strolled down the sidewalk, adjusting his tie. Nothing like a hearty workout to get your blood pumping. He didn't mind a little physical activity now and again. But he would've been pissed if the cretin had ruined his tie.

Especially since the wire was planted inside it, woven into the silk fibers.

He walked to the van parked halfway down the street and knocked. "Open sesame."

Leilani opened the door. Behind her, he saw the sound tech working a keyboard, earphones clamped over his head.

"Did you get it?" Seamus asked.

"Every word," the tech replied.

"Did she pick up her phone?"

"About a second after she slammed the door on your ass."

"And you've got the line tapped?"

"I can hear every beep. Give me two minutes and we'll have the location."

Seamus smiled. Perfect.

The sound tech put the audio on the speakers so Seamus and Leilani could hear it in real-time.

"Hello." The voice was Irish. Seamus winked at Leilani. Bingo.

"This is Karen."

"Why are you calling me on this number? I told you—"

"You're in trouble. I just had a visit from that bastard McKay. From the CIA."

"He's not in the CIA anymore."

"He's sure as hell in something, because he knows all about you."

"Like what?"

"He says you were behind the attack on the Cartwright Institute."

"He's guessing."

"And he says you were after some German guy. Weird name. Started with a 'K.'"

"Krakow?"

"No."

"Karelis."

"That was it."

There was a pause on the other end of the line. "What else?"

"Don't ask me why, but he thinks you're involved with some writer."

When the voice returned, it was urgent and forceful. "Karen, hang up the phone."

"But—"

"Right now. I'm hanging up. Disconnect the line."

Seamus nodded at the tech. Smart lady.

"But he said—"

"Write me a letter. Post an encrypted message on the bulletin board. But for now, hang up!"

The line disconnected on both ends.

"She figured it out," Leilani said, frowning.

"Yes," Seamus answered. "But in time?"

The tech was still punching buttons. "I got her position down to a one-mile radius."

"Better than nothing. Where was she?"

"Triangulating now." Seamus watched as an aerial map appeared on the tech's laptop screen. "It's in Honolulu."

That makes sense. Keep working it...

"I'm bouncing off three wireless towers..." The tech stroked a few more keys. "That's weird. It's coming from somewhere in or near the University of Hawaii campus. What would she be doing there?"

"Not studying Irish literature," Leilani said. "Isn't that where you met Dr. Scheimer?"

"Yes," Seamus replied. "Because that's where he's conducting his research. Under heavy guard."

"Then why is she there?"

"I don't know. But if she's there, Xavier might be, too. And if we can find them, we might find Dylan."

CHAPTER
FORTY-SIX

2:10 p.m.
One hour left

DYLAN SAT in a dull gray minivan parked on the edge of campus just off the south oval. They had sixty minutes to pull this off. If they weren't done by then, they never would be. The diversion would be over and security would realize they had intruders.

It wasn't much time. But it would be enough. If the plan worked. If he'd anticipated every contingency.

"Stupid holiday," Xavier grunted. "Why celebrate holiday no one else does?"

Kalifa, a lifelong Hawaiian resident, replied without looking up from his laptop. "Didn't they have holidays back in Russia?"

"Not like this."

"I don't doubt that. PFD—Personal Freedom Day—is a weird little celebration, if that's the right word. It's never been embraced by any government. Originated on this campus. It started with Kuhio Day, a genuine Hawaiian holiday honoring one of the most beloved figures in Hawaiian history. A man who fought for the rights of the people, the homeless, the indigent. To prevent the Hawaiian race from becoming extinct. But on campus, it was too often treated like St.

Patrick's Day and Mardi Gras and other holidays that turned into drunkfests."

"Well," Xavier said dryly, "that explains parade and beer and giant bobbleheads."

"Many thought this was disrespectful and offensive—because it was —and so over time a new event arose, something that could be celebrated any way people chose, because after all—it's Personal Freedom Day. Like Burning Man, only Hawaiian. Flash mob celebrations. A parade here on the main campus, fueled by alcohol and pakalolo. And this is key—with so many events occurring all over the island, the police are stretched thin."

Xavier sniffed. "Still don't like it."

Tolga pulled clothes—later to be shed—over his nylon body stocking. "I think what bothers you about the big heads is that you have to wear one."

"Big head looks stupid."

"Yes," Dylan said, "but if you don't wear it, the guards will realize you're not a college student. Once you put it on"—he glanced out the van window—"you'll blend in with about six hundred other people out there wearing goofy masks and costumes."

Still frowning, Xavier pulled on the polystyrene head. A grinning face with a big up-curled moustache. "Undignified. Make me long for days in Russian mafia."

The parade headed their way. "All right, team," Dylan said, cracking open the rear doors. "Let's rock and roll."

XAVIER JOINED the parade outside Kuykendal Hall, about a block before it reached the new Harrison Elliot Research Lab beside the Physical Sciences building. No one seemed to notice him amidst the floats and marching bands and cheerleaders. The copious quantities of alcohol floating around probably had something to do with that.

Just as he reached the front of the lab, Xavier swerved out of the parade line. A security guard posted in front of the entrance immediately moved toward him.

Xavier staggered like a pro. Anyone watching Xavier would think he was drunk. At the same time, he was not so over-the-top as to attract suspicion. It was a nuanced performance, not vaudeville.

Though remaining friendly and casual, the guard intercepted Xavier before he reached the front door. He grabbed Xavier by the big cartoon head and brought him to a stop.

"Wait a minute, brah. I think you're lost." He was a tall slender man. Xavier could take him out effortlessly. But that wasn't the plan.

Even though the head was plastic, the way Xavier moved suggested extreme disorientation and imminent illness. "My Lizzie dumped me... dumped me on Personal Freedom Day..."

"Broken heart and heavy drinking. Never a good combination. Where do you live? Athletic dorm?"

A logical guess, given Xavier's size. Xavier mumbled an incoherent response.

"Let me call someone from campus security and they'll—"

Xavier held up his hands, pantomiming panic. "Not the cops! Not the cops!"

"Don't worry, nothing's going to happen to you." The guard—his badge said his name was Detwiler—placed his hands on Xavier's shoulders. "They'll just take you somewhere you can lie down and sleep it—"

"Oh my God!" Xavier doubled over and made a retching sound. "I —think I am going to hurl!" He turned suddenly and wrapped himself around the guard's waist.

"Don't do that." Detwiler tried to pull away, but Xavier held fast. "They don't pay me enough for this. Let go. I—"

The guard tried to extract himself, without success.

"Please do not--*Ohhhhhh*!" Xavier pushed a small needle into the plastic bag concealed within his plastic head. He held onto the guard's waist as the artificial vomit spewed out of the mouth hole all over the man's pants. Fake but highly realistic, including the odor.

"Oh, geez, don't--" The guard turned his head, disgusted, and held up his hands, trying to keep them out of the line of spewage.

And that was their cue. While the guard's head was turned and his attention was diverted, Dylan, Mikala, and Tolga crept out from behind a hedge and moved quietly toward the door. Tolga had the forged access card they'd created based on the card Xavier extracted from the former assistant head of campus security. He jabbed it into an electronic reader and pushed open the door.

"WE'RE INSIDE."

Dylan could hear the clickety-clack of Felix's keypad. "Very good. Were you spotted?"

"I don't think so. Xavier proved a great distraction. And the people watching the parade are in another world."

A few more rapid-fire keystrokes. "I'm getting your GPS signal. Smart dust is operational. Coordinating with the schematics for the building. Tolga?"

"I'm here."

"Your entrance is six feet to the left, then three feet to the north. Then up."

They paced out the instructions, which led to a corner in the front foyer of the building, just outside the sweep of the security cameras.

Dylan spotted a panel in the ceiling held fast by four screws. At first glance, he might've thought it was a ventilation shaft. If he didn't know better.

"How long have I got?"

There was a slight pause before Felix answered. "Xavier is keeping the guard distracted. Eventually the man will call security. But you're good for now. I can see the guard and I can hear anything he says into his radio. Nothing's going to happen fast today."

Dylan crouched down so Tolga could step onto his back.

"You've got about eight-point-two minutes before the security guards arrive to take Xavier away," Felix informed them. "Once he's been relieved, Detwiler will return to his station—and if you folks are still hanging around the lobby, he'll spot you."

"Already moving." Standing on Dylan's back, Tolga rapidly removed the screws using a magnetic induction tool Dylan called a magnasonic screwdriver. It used magnetism and ultrasonic waves to loosen screws and bolts exceptionally fast. In fewer than ten seconds, Tolga had the panel off the ceiling. He shed his outer clothing in five.

Mikala peered up into the dark passage. "No way that was meant for humans to slither through."

"No," Felix said, "it was designed for cables and wires to serve the geeks' needs, before the world went wireless. They use robots on a magnetic track to thread the passage. Not humans."

Tolga pushed off Dylan's back and pulled himself into the tiny opening. Rippling arm muscles were visible through his tight black clothing. He might be small, but he was all sinewy tendons and strength.

"I don't think I could even get my face through that opening," Dylan said.

"Artists do tend to have swelled heads." Tolga's shoulders stopped him. With a movement so small that on someone else it might look like a shrug—Tolga dislocated his right shoulder. Then he dislocated the other one. Dylan remembered his struggle to execute a similar maneuver when Leilani was bleeding on the floor. Tolga made it look easy.

"Eeeeewww," Mikala said, stepping away. "I will never get used to that."

Tolga slithered into the tiny shaft and launched himself horizontally through it. Even with his shoulders lowered and compressed, he still filled the tiny area. And yet he managed to creep forward incrementally. It was like watching Silly Putty that moved.

"Mr. Fantastic's got nothing on you," Dylan commented.

"Well, he's got a beautiful wife. And a kickass car."

"Just take the compliment."

"I don't mean to interrupt the jocularity," Felix said, "but the security guards have reached the corner of Hialea. As soon as they figure out how to cut through the parade, they'll be in front of the building."

"Understood," Tolga replied. His feet disappeared up the shaft.

"Good luck, India Rubber Boy," Mikala whispered.

"Good luck indeed," Dylan muttered. "If he doesn't make it, this plan is shot. And we're finished."

CHAPTER
FORTY-SEVEN

2:17 p.m.
53 minutes left

"TOLGA NEEDS MORE TIME. STALL."

Xavier rolled his eyes. Fortunately, no one could see what his eyes were doing inside this big bobblehead.

"This the guy?"

Through the nylon screen just under the chin of the big head, Xavier saw two men in campus-security uniforms approaching.

Detwiler nodded. "Think he's had a little too much party, if you know what I mean. Mixed with some heartache." He glanced at his stained pants. "And, I think, pepperoni pizza."

One of the security officers clapped Xavier on the shoulder. "I'm Sergeant Singer. Let's go to Health Services so you can sleep this off. Then we'll talk about maybe—"

"Can't...go...anywhere," Xavier said, lurching, trying to look drunk or sick, anything to delay the process. He couldn't stop these men from hauling him off. Well, he could, but not without blowing his cover. "Your badge," Xavier gasped, wheezing. "So shiny...doing something..."

Xavier flipped onto his back and thrashed wildly. "I'm...epileptic..."

"Seizure!" The two security officers went into immediate action.

One knelt beside him. "Can you hear me? Do you have medication on you?"

Xavier kept writhing. "Can't...talk..."

"Better get this head off," the security officer said. Xavier felt hands descend upon his polystyrene cover. No, we can't allow that.

"Oh my God!" Xavier screamed, as he used his teeth to pop open the second bag. "Spitting...blood!"

And then the blood—or corn syrup with food coloring that looked like blood—spewed through the mouth hole toward Sergeant Singer. The security officer let out a yelp and jumped away, looking as if he'd been stung by scorpion venom.

"He bled on me!" Singer said to his partner, desperately trying to rub it off.

"You'll live," his colleague replied.

"How do you know? What if he's HIV positive? What if he's got COVID?"

"Then you're screwed. But that's unlikely. Let's take him to the clinic."

"I'm not touching him!" Singer replied.

The partner sighed. "I'll call for medical backup."

And inside the big head, Xavier smiled, because he knew he'd just bought his teammates another seven point four minutes.

THE PROBLEM, Tolga recalled as he slithered, was that two security cameras patrolled the hallway leading to the scientist's quarters, and a guard in a room in the back watched the monitors. Not all that carefully, given the slow response time last week when Felix experimentally spiked the feedback with controlled electrostatic charges. But still. They couldn't count on him being inattentive forever.

One option would be to take out the guard—but there was no way to do that without tipping the government to the fact that they'd been infiltrated. Turning off the power might work, but that would bring more people running to the building too quickly. Instead, he would reorient one of the cameras to allow Dylan and Mikala to slink down the corridor. He could do it from here. Assuming he could get his arms free. And get the lid off the opening. And turn the camera. And do all that in...

"Four-point-one-five minutes," Felix announced.

"You can round off, Spock," Tolga muttered.

Tolga knew only one possible way to make more room in an area that was already filled. He inhaled. And held his breath.

He managed to snap his right shoulder back into the socket. Hurt like hell. He pulled that working arm forward, an inch at a time, each agonizing. His hand pushed itself along, using the friction of his fingertips to gain purchase. In truth, he wasn't sure how exactly he moved or what muscles he was flexing. He just did it.

The arm clutching the magnasonic screwdriver flopped onto the lid.

"Three minutes," Felix said, as if somehow knowing the time might enable Tolga to work faster.

The miracle of this high-tech screwdriver was that it worked as well from the bolt end as it did from the head. Despite the fact that there was no elbow room and his elbow was in his face, Tolga managed to pop all four screws in under thirty seconds. He used his fingers to hold the lid, then tilted it and brought it through the opening. He laid it gently on the surface of the shaft a few feet ahead of him.

Now where the hell was that camera?

He was stuck too tightly. He had almost no room to maneuver. During the practice sessions, he'd known where the camera was supposed to be. But now he had no means of seeing it, much less reaching it.

He needed his other hand.

"The medical team has arrived," Felix said. "You've got one minute, tops, before Mikala and Dylan are spotted."

Gritting his teeth, Tolga wrenched his left shoulder back into its socket.

His face contorted with pain. *What the hell happened?* He didn't know what it was exactly, but something went wrong. Popped a blood vessel? Pulled a tendon? All he knew for certain was that he had never felt anything like that before, and he was glad, because it hurt so much he could barely think straight.

"Thirty seconds," Felix barked. "Do you need me to round that off for you? The guard is walking up the damn sidewalk!"

Tolga closed his eyes and focused. He used his left hand to push himself toward the gap. His right hand still couldn't reach the camera. He pushed even harder. No luck.

He felt as if his entire body had been stuck in a trash compactor set to maximum crush. He stretched his arm so far he was afraid he might inadvertently pop a bone out of joint.

He still couldn't reach the camera.

"Ten freaking seconds till he arrives and your buddies are toast!" Felix said. "What are you waiting for?"

Tolga didn't push with just his arm. He pushed with every muscle in every part of his body.

"*Do it!*" Felix shouted.

Tolga stretched like he had never stretched before, like a human body was never meant to stretch, not even his.

And then he felt it.

DYLAN SAW the guard making his way to the front door.

"Felix....this would be a good time to tell us to go in..."

"Not yet!"

He did his level best to keep his voice flat. "Felix, if he sees us, it's all over."

"If he sees you, it's more than over. You're caught and arrested."

"But he's almost here..."

The pause was in fact barely more than two seconds, but it seemed an eternity.

"Feliiiiix?"

"The camera's adjusted. *Go!*"

CHAPTER
FORTY-EIGHT

2:22 p.m.

48 minutes left

DYLAN OPENED the door and raced into the main corridor. He crossed the hallway, Mikala close behind him. As planned, the camera pointed at the opposite end of the symmetrical corridor. Unless he detected the movement, the guard wouldn't know that he was now gazing at a different wall and that a foot-and-a-half strip along the north wall was not monitored. A strip currently traversed by two intruders.

The third door on the right was the one they wanted. A security card scanner with a ten-digit keypad was attached to the wall. Mikala opened her shoulder bag and withdrew what looked like a hand-held calculator connected by computer ribbon to a credit card. She slid the card inside the pocket and tapped buttons on the device.

"Here's where we see if my decrypting is as good as the US government's."

"I have complete faith in you."

"That won't get you a—" She was interrupted by a soft pinging sound. The numbers on her calculator flashed red.

She smiled. "Can I cook, or can't I?"

Dr. Louis Scheimer, Ph.D. in Physics, theoretical designer of the first large-scale proton cyclotron and the world's leading expert on neutrino oscillation, hated PFD. He also wasn't keen on homecoming, Mom's Day, or anything else that diverted the university from what it was supposed to be: an institution of higher learning and a locus for research. He'd come to the United States after the fall of the Berlin Wall because he felt constricted in Dresden. He needed better equipment, more support, than he had ever been able to obtain in the Fatherland. And to be sure, the climate was sunnier in Hawaii and he wasn't opposed to the occasional sunset walk by the beach. The price of obtaining this had been relatively small.

All he'd had to do was sell his soul.

All he'd gained was the opportunity to work with a natural phenomenon so extraordinary that even Nikola Tesla was astounded by its possibilities.

Had he made the right choice? Yes, it was a breakthrough that made the theory of relativity and the splitting of the atom seem like baby steps. He could not deny the excitement he felt with each new discovery, each breakthrough. But the military wasn't interested in theory. They wanted a weapon. And when they tested that weapon—it proved more powerful than he'd thought possible.

His dream of using science to free mankind from poverty, energy shortage, environmental catastrophe, and daily drudgery hadn't happened. Unprecedented destructive power is what happened.

He was grateful that, in the aftermath of the test, the military agreed to suspend the project. Even they knew that, much as they longed to reshape the world order, they did not know enough to safely control this weapon. But the apparatus had not been dismantled. And the Kronos Key had not been destroyed.

Under duress, he'd agreed to create the Key, a device that could harness the lightning, in a manner of speaking. He'd been curious to know if it was possible. And if he were totally honest, he wanted to challenge himself, to see if he was up to the task. To do something that had never been done before.

He'd accomplished his goal. And regretted it every day since. He tried to live with what he'd done. But every day he found it more difficult. His work gave him no relief. Alcohol gave him no solace. His friends were gone, Karelis probably murdered. Agents asking questions. How long would it be before the truth was revealed and he was held in the contempt he deserved?

He heard steps in the hallway. He wasn't expecting anyone. Detwiler hadn't said anything about visitors. Neither did Joe. Probably Admiral Stewart, here to make his impotent demands, pretending he still controlled this project. Stewart didn't even understand this project.

He flung open the door and found a man with dark close cut hair, smiling. He held what looked like an asthma inhaler up to Scheimer's face.

"Sweet dreams, Doctor."

DYLAN FLUNG SCHEIMER'S limp body over his shoulder fireman-style. Gravity was a serious issue with this physicist. Because he was seriously heavy.

"Grab the laptop." Mikala was already there, trying to open the target files. Unfortunately, as their intelligence had suggested, the files were encrypted. Mikala couldn't hack into it without the entry password—and even then, reading the files would require considerable decryption.

She closed the laptop, then followed Dylan down the corridor and into the foyer. The parade was still in full force.

"We're here, Felix. Send it. Before someone spots us."

The parade and revelry made it easier to sneak in—but more difficult to get the famed physicist out. The parade wasn't going to part while they pulled up their minivan. Only one vehicle could possibly get through.

The ambulance pulled up to the front doors just as Dylan arrived. The ramp lowered and a gurney slid outward. Dylan gently but expediently lowered the scientist onto the flatbed. He didn't want anyone to see who it was.

Detwiler left his station and approached Kalifa, the driver of the ambulance. "What's going on?"

"Research assistant. Alcohol poisoning. We got a call."

Detwiler nodded. "Not the old man."

"I don't know any old man. This guy's about twenty."

"Post-doc." Detwiler shook his head. "Science nerds. Smart but stupid. Carry on." He returned to his station.

As soon as the rear doors closed, Kalifa put his foot on the accelerator. Dr. Giep took Scheimer's arm and administered the first of the drugs, the sodium-thiopental derivative. Next he would inject the hallucinogen. By the time Scheimer awoke at the redressed warehouse two blocks off campus, he would be confused, disoriented, and extremely susceptible to suggestion. And that was critical. Because to avoid triggering the CIA post-hypnotic suggestion, they had to interrogate this man—without him ever feeling he had been interrogated.

The siren blazed as they sped past Gilbert Hall. He hoped the Hollywood boys were ready. The show was about to begin.

CHAPTER
FORTY-NINE

2:28 p.m.
42 minutes left

THE INSTANT THEY ARRIVED, Dylan and Kalifa wheeled the scientist-laden gurney into the warehouse. They did not want to attract attention or cause anyone to wonder why an ambulance stopped here.

They rode the elevator to the second floor.

Dylan pushed Scheimer into the room where the drama would unfold. Perfect. The Hollywood art- and set-design team had recreated the room in the photographs to the last detail. Most of the photos were black and white, but they'd used computer analysis to determine the original colors. If Dylan hadn't known better, he would've thought he'd stepped back into the 1960s. Behind the Iron Curtain.

Mr. X was by the bed, in costume, attending to a few final details. "Felix has kept me informed. Any problems?"

"None we couldn't handle."

"No one suspects?"

"No."

"What about the physicist?"

"Never knew what hit him."

"Tolga?"

"Safe."

"Good. We should be able to—" She paused, frowning. "What are you staring at?"

Dylan realized why Bakersfield had an Oscar on his mantle. Her surgery had been designed to reproduce the general contours of a particular face. But the makeup had made her the living incarnation of the woman she was about to impersonate. "Never did I imagine I would hear myself saying this but—you're beautiful."

Mr. X tucked her chin in. "Don't let yourself be distracted. We have work to do."

"But it's true. I particularly like what he's done with your hair."

"Don't bother turning your alleged charm on me. You're not my type."

Dylan dropped it. But he also noticed that this time she did not resort to threats of physical harm.

Dylan sat Scheimer upright in a chair beside a large mirror. Giep and Bakersfield went to work, like a top-flight surgical team. Giep injected the scientist's face with hypertox, a fast-acting but short-lived botox variant. The toxin paralyzed the nerves in Scheimer's face, erasing frown lines, eye creases, and brow furrows. Bakersfield used a shampoo dye to color his hair. Then he applied makeup to add color and vitality to the man's face, shading to eliminate liver spots and to reduce the visibility of sagging skin beneath the chin. Giep gave him a testosterone-based vitamin injection. He wouldn't revive until they gave him the stimulant, but when he did, he would feel energized.

Young.

After the redressing was complete, the costumers stripped him and applied the final touches.

Dylan could only watch and marvel. Yes, he'd dreamed up this operation. But seeing it come to life was different. This was like watching one of his books being reenacted before his eyes.

DR. GIEP GAVE Scheimer the stimulant, then ducked out of sight. Once he was gone, nothing remained in the faux-bedroom that had not been there in 1968. Dylan and Mikala watched from an adjoining alcove. The bedroom was wired for sound so they could hear everything and they could watch through a two-way mirror. Mikala hacked away at Scheimer's laptop, but she only became increasingly frustrated.

"I need his password," she muttered, not for the first time. "This computer has been programmed to resist any attempt to input random sequences."

"So we'll get the password."

"You seem very sure your plan will work."

"Classic Skinner behaviorism. Provide the correct environmental stimuli and you obtain predictable behavioral responses. How do you get someone to give you something they don't want to give you? By altering the environment. In this case, we're going to recreate the happiest time in Dr. Scheimer's life. Where he feels free to say anything."

"If he believes it."

"He will believe it. Because he will want to believe it."

Scheimer's eyes opened. He blinked several times. Dylan could hear him whispering "Where am I?" even though his lips were not moving. He slowly rose, propping himself up with one arm.

When he saw the room, his eyes widened. He looked as if he had fallen through the rabbit hole—and in a sense, he had.

"How can this be?"

A soft pad of footsteps turned his head. His entire body stiffened. "No."

Mr. X emerged from the shadows. "Hello, Louie." Her German was perfect.

"Liesel!"

She sat on the edge of his bed. "Of course, darling. Who else would it be? Are you feeling any better?"

"But—it isn't possible. You can't be here."

She smiled slightly. Dylan could hardly believe the cruel woman who had tortured and threatened him could be so convincing in this loving, caregiving role. Her brain had to be a masterwork of compartmentalization. Her mimicry of the voice tapes was too close to be doubted—especially by a man currently under the influence of several mind-altering medications.

"Surely you didn't think I would leave your side?"

"But my Liesel. This must be a dream." He paused, his mind obviously in conflict with itself. "You're dead."

"*I'm* dead? You're the one who's been sick these past weeks. Why would I die?"

"You had a cancer." He tilted his head to the side. Anyone in his situation would be confused, and the drugs magnified the disorientation.

"You've had scarlet fever, darling," Mr. X said. "It almost took you. Last night, we thought...well. The fever broke and here you are."

This story had been carefully scripted. Scheimer had in fact suffered from scarlet fever when he was a young man and it almost killed him. When he was twenty-four. And his wife was still living.

"But that was so long ago."

"No, darling. You're confused. That's understandable. Lie back down."

"But—"

She gently but insistently pushed him back to the bed. "Take a moment to gather your thoughts."

Which would be impossible, with all the chemicals coursing through his head.

"But my Liesel." Despite his difficulties, Dylan noticed Scheimer was squeezing her hand. "That was so long ago. When I was young."

"You're still young."

"I'm not. I'm old. I remember—"

"You remember a dream. A fever dream."

"No. There were years. Decades."

Mr. X laughed a little, a high-pitched trill. "No, my darling. Just a terrible nightmare." She took a hand mirror from the table by the bed. "Look at yourself, Louie. Is this the face of an old man?"

He took the mirror in both hands. And gasped.

"But—this cannot be. I remember aging. I remember--" He looked at her. His eyes watered. "I remember burying you."

"It wasn't real."

"I remember moving to the United States."

"The United States? Louie—look around you. Are we in the United States? Is this not the same flat where we have always lived?"

He looked all ways at once. So far as he could tell, he was a young man again, with his much beloved wife, in his old apartment.

"Liesel...it's like I've been given a second chance. It's a miracle!"

She softly brushed his hair from his forehead. "Louie, with you, every day is a miracle. And this one may be the greatest of all."

CHAPTER
FIFTY

2:37 p.m.
33 minutes left

DYLAN WATCHED through the two-way mirror as Mr. X comforted and calmed the addled and disoriented scientist. She was delivering a magnificent performance. He had chosen her for this role thinking that, if someone had to have surgery to make them resemble Scheimer's deceased wife, it might as well be the woman whose face was marred by extensive scar tissue. He had not counted on how truly impressive her thespian talents turned out to be.

As good as she was, she still hadn't obtained the information they needed, and time was running out. Mikala listened to every word of the conversation, typing every possibility into Scheimer's laptop. But so far —no hits. That worried Dylan. Because learning the password was the primary purpose of this elaborate charade.

Dylan had conducted extensive research on how most people chose their computer passwords. The most sensible approach was to create a password made of gibberish, a random collection of numbers and letters. But most people don't do that because it makes the password too hard to remember. Most people choose a word or phrase that has special meaning to them. A wife's name, a pet's name, their birthday. Something they would always recall, maybe with a number or punctuation mark added.

Felix had uncovered a redacted transcript of a CIA meeting in which Scheimer, in response to a security check, said his password was something "no one else knew—at least no one still alive."

That was the hint Dylan needed. By far, the most significant deceased person in Scheimer's past was his wife. He hoped that recreating the happiest time in the scientist's life would induce him to unwittingly reveal the password.

"I'm so confused," Scheimer said, in a soft, broken tone. "I cannot believe all this is true. I can recall an entire life. Can an entire life be a dream?"

"Apparently so, Louie."

"I remember my travels."

"And I know you have traveled nowhere, because I have been standing watch over your bedside for weeks."

"It seems incredible—but it must be so. This room of ours, you, even me—" He glanced at himself again in the mirror. "Nothing has changed."

"And nothing ever will, my love." She kissed him lightly on the cheek. "Not so long as we are together. Focus on the happy times. That will chase away the nightmares."

Come on, Dylan thought, glancing at his watch. Get him to talk about what matters most to him.

"The happiest day of my life was the day I met you, Liesel."

"Tell me about it."

"But you were there."

"I want to go there again. Tell me the story."

He smiled a little. "I was thinking about a problem posed by the master. His early work in robotics. I was strolling past the Brandenburg Gate and there you were. In the heart of the city, and in my heart as well, from the first moment I laid eyes upon you."

Out the corner of his eye, Dylan saw Mikala typing in every possible word of any significance. Brandenburg Gate. Master. Good thing she understood German—and the laptop didn't penalize for incorrect guesses. She still hadn't found the password.

"Do you remember our first date?" Mr. X asked.

His smile brightened. "Of course. Springtime. Alexanderplatz. Rumors that Americans would bring down the Wall. So much going on in the world. But all I cared about was you."

Mikala kept typing. Without success.

"And of our happy moments together, dear. Which do you cherish most?"

His eyes moistened. "The day you agreed to be my bride. And our wedding day. The French Cathedral at the Gendarmenmarkt. Music streaming from the Concert Hall next door. You in my arms. So much future we had. So many plans. We were going to buy a home. We were going to start—" He stopped short.

The expression on Scheimer's face triggered a thought. Dylan knew what Scheimer was about to say. Because he and Leilani had said it too.

"What were we going to start, dear?"

He placed his hand over hers. "It doesn't matter."

"Did you mean—a family?"

"I would've been a horrible father."

Dylan had done extensive research on this man's life, but there was no record that he ever had children. Not with his deceased wife or anyone else.

"Don't be foolish. You would have been wonderful. If—If—"

He lowered his head. "If she had lived. I am sorry for reminding you. I know how much it hurt you to lose her."

"Get a name," Dylan whispered into the transmitter.

"It did hurt," she said. "But I thought there could always be another."

"The doctors said no. So tragic to lose a child. When there can never be any more. We never spoke of it. Not to others. Not to one another."

"But we never forgot her. Our little..."

"Of course not. How could we?"

"But my baby," Mr. X said, her voice cracking. "My poor sweet little..."

"She had her mother's eyes." Tears flowed.

Dylan looked at the clock. The time allotted for this masquerade had already elapsed. "Get the name!"

"I remember," Mr. X said, "how your voice trembled the first time I heard you say her name out loud."

He nodded, pulling her tightly to him. "When they let me hold her, ever so briefly, ever so still."

"Say it, Louie. Say it again for me."

He held his hands up as if holding an imaginary infant. "My little Elise!"

Dylan's head whipped around. Mikala was already typing. E-L-I-S-E. She hit Enter.

Nothing happened.

She typed it again, then added a "1" and an exclamation point.

The screen turned white, then resolved into a desktop with many file folders.

"I'm inside," Mikala whispered.

"Can you read the files?"

"Not yet. But I can begin encrypting."

"How long will it take?"

"You know I can't predict that. Stop talking to me. I'm working."

"We have what we needed from Scheimer," Dylan said into the transmitter. "End it."

Mr. X put her arms around the scientist, his eyes glazed and wet with confusion and sorrow. "You are a good man, Louie," she said. She removed the inhaler from her pocket and held it to his face. "Go to sleep."

XAVIER WAS in the emergency medical room in Health Sciences. A nurse took his pulse and blood pressure. The two security guards stood nearby, just in case he caused more trouble. He was ready to bolt, but he couldn't do that until he heard...

The voice in his head. "Lani and Dylan are heading back to the university. You can go now."

And not a moment too soon—the nurse was talking about removing his plastic head.

"No," he informed her, "we will not do that."

Xavier removed the blood pressure cuff from his arm.

"Wait a minute," the nurse said. "We're going to need a reading before we put in an IV."

"I am fine."

"Fine? A few minutes ago you were spitting up blood."

One of the security guards stepped forward. "Mister, you need to do what she says. Just lie down and—"

"Do not give me orders," Xavier said directly. He could see they were taken aback by the sudden absence of drunkenness in his voice. "I am your superior."

"My—what—?"

"I am working special university task force," Xavier said matter-of-factly. He pulled out Detwiler's wallet—pickpocketed when he grabbed the man's legs—and flashed the ID. "Boris Pushkin. This has been test."

"A test?"

"And am pleased to say you passed with flying colors."

That slowed him down. "I did?"

"You all did. You are to be congratulated. I will recommend all for promotion. And big hike in pay."

There are few things as sad, Xavier thought, as a man accustomed to being in control who suddenly realizes he has no idea what is going on. "Could you just—explain what you're talking about?"

Xavier did his best to sound serious, despite the fact that he was still wearing a cartoon head he had no intention of removing. "Very simple. University has received large grants from US government to conduct secret intelligence-related research."

The guard nodded. "So?"

"We asked to conduct exercises to test officers. You showed impressive efficiency and great capacity for dealing with unexpected."

The man wasn't arguing, but Xavier could see he was struggling to understand. "We have been through extensive training..."

"It shows. I was instructed to use whatever means available during chaos of parade to distract you from job. But I could not. Brilliant work, men. And you, madam. Brilliant."

"Well....thank you."

"I must be going. I will ask you to keep quiet until exercises completed. Don't give advance warnings to other personnel. You will be contacted when it is all over. And you will find reward is worth wait." That should buy their silence. At least until it didn't matter anymore.

"Sure. I can keep a secret."

"I know you can." Xavier clapped both men on the back. "Now if you will pardon, I must wear this head to nuclear physics lab. Damn thing weighs ton. Carry on with excellent work."

THE POP-UP APPEARED on Joe's computer screen. He set his broom down and slid into the carrel.

Someone was trying to access Scheimer's laptop files. Possibly Scheimer. But then again, possibly not. The good doctor had expressed concern that an enemy agent might pursue this information.

He'd been hired by the Navy to make sure Scheimer's research was protected. His primary function was to check every half hour on the laptop. It didn't word process, it didn't compute, and it certainly never went on the Internet. All it did was make sure Dr. Scheimer's data was safe. The laptop had an internal spider that even Scheimer didn't know about. A cuff fastened around the hard drive equipped with wireless transmission capabilities. When certain activities occurred, Joe got a message.

Joe couldn't read Scheimer's files, but he could tell when they were in use.

Most importantly, he could tell anytime someone tried to copy the files. Or typed in the wrong password.

Which someone had done twenty-seven times in the last half hour.

Not even Scheimer was that bad a typist. At least when he was sober.

Fortunately, Joe could lock the files remotely. Then no one could access restricted files or copy anything.

He sat down at his keyboard. Should only take a few minutes to freeze the files.

Then he would go down to the lab and find out what was going on.

CHAPTER
FIFTY-ONE

2:44 p.m.

26 minutes left

DURING THE DRIVE back to the university, Dylan watched Bakersfield remove the hair dye, the make-up, and change Scheimer's clothes. The hypertox faded on schedule. The wrinkles returned. All traces of the deception disappeared and the GHB Giep administered would have its intended amnesiac effect. When he woke, Scheimer would have a severe headache, but he would remember nothing. Neither he nor the CIA would know he'd been interrogated. In a way.

Kalifa drove the ambulance to the designated point on campus, parked, and switched to another car. Dylan threw Scheimer over his shoulder. Mikala placed a huge serape over Dylan's head.

"Unless someone looks really closely, they can't tell you're carrying a passenger."

"I can," Dylan grunted. "Let's hurry."

They ducked behind a hedge while Kalifa drove his car—technically, his float—toward the parade. A campus security officer held back the spectators. Dylan eavesdropped through the listening device inside Kalifa's mouth.

"What's your story?"

Kalifa had an elaborate tale prepared, but it wasn't necessary. "Sorry I'm late. I made a wrong turn on Pine. This is my first time to drive a volcano."

He was indeed towing a volcano—one made of papier mache and tissues, padded in the center with foam rubber. Glitter lights provided the illusion of lava flowing down the sides.

The officer rolled his eyes. "You'll have to wait for an opening."

"Whatever you say, sir. Appreciate it."

A few moments later, the cop jumped between two floats, held traffic for a few moments, and let the volcano join the line.

"Hurry," Dylan muttered into his mic. "This guy weighs a ton."

"Kalifa's approaching the physics building," Felix answered. "Yes. Here he goes."

From their secluded position, Dylan watched Kalifa weave in his lane—in effect, getting into character. He wondered what the ultimate charge would be. Drunk and in charge of a volcano?

Without warning, Kalifa floored it. The car—with the float still attached—veered to the right, off the road, and straight toward the physics lab.

Detwiler rushed out. The car weaved back and forth in the lawn. Kalifa took a sharp left, forcing Detwiler to leap out of the way of the jackknifing volcano. The car barreled into a tree.

Kalifa feigned a head injury. Detwiler ran to the car.

And while Detwiler and everyone else had their eyes fixed on the idiot who just collided with a tree, Dylan and Mikala sneaked back inside the lab.

———

DYLAN DROPPED Scheimer into the chair by his desk, letting his head fall forward. He would be asleep for at least another ten minutes. When he woke, he'd have no idea that he'd leaked his password.

"How's the encryption working?" Dylan asked.

"Done," Mikala replied. "Downloading. Started with the eighth file first, as you requested. But we have a problem. We've been detected."

Mikala pointed to a tab at the top of the screen. "It popped up as soon as I finished decrypting."

"What does it mean?"

"Someone with a remote connection is trying to shut me down."

"How is that possible?"

"I don't know. But see the parallel lines." Mikala pointed to two horizontal indicators inching across the screen. "The longer one shows the progress of my download. The shorter shows someone else's progress toward shutting me out. I'm ahead. But he's moving faster."

"You'll be locked out in about a minute."

"Right. And I won't be done for at least..."

"A minute and forty-three seconds." Felix's voice crackled in his ear.

"You understand what's happening?" Dylan asked Felix.

"I sure as hell do."

"Is there any way we can stop it?"

"No. Your cyber-supervisor appears to have override capacity."

Dylan and Mikala exchanged a somber look. "Then we're dead."

CHAPTER
FIFTY-TWO

2:51 p.m.
19 minutes left

THIS WAS strange and getting stranger, Joe thought, as he watched the progress of his lockdown order. No one could access Scheimer's files wirelessly or through the Net. No one could get inside this building without clearance. So what was going on? He knew Scheimer was fond of his sour mash, but he usually didn't start this early in the day. Was he doing wild and funky things to his laptop without knowing it?

Didn't matter. His job was to secure those files. Then he'd go to the lab and investigate.

He clicked Return a few times, which of course had the same effect as impatiently punching the Close Doors button inside an elevator. None.

The problem was, there were eight separate files. He could only close them one at a time. And it took a while for the close order to be transmitted via the spider, which was slower than an internet connection would be. The database wouldn't be secure until they were all locked.

Take a deep breath, Joe told himself. Like the students say—chill.

The Navy established a protocol for this scenario and he was following it. The hard drive would shut down soon.

There was no cause to worry. No one could possibly get to those files. And even if they did—they couldn't possibly escape.

Tolga slithered through the open portal head first, grasping the edges with his arms. Both shoulders were now relocated, but the left ached with an intensity that made it difficult to focus on his remaining tasks. Tensing his entire body, he executed a perfect head-tuck somersault and slowly lowered himself to the ground. He released the ceiling ledge and dropped the remaining four feet.

Thank God he was out of that sausage grinder. Felt good to be able to take a deep breath. Being stuck in a passageway built for some pint-size R2D2 was painful. Miracle he could still move, much less breathe. Now all he had to do was stay out of sight until Felix gave him the all-clear.

"Tolga? Are you there?"

Tolga almost jumped. Did the man not know he was speaking from the inside of his mouth? There was no need to raise his voice.

"Tolga? We have a problem. Are you in the electrical room?"

"Isn't that where I'm supposed to be? So I have access to the corridor once Dylan and Mikala are finished?"

"Yes, but that's not the only reason you're there. Dylan planted you as a backup in the event that—"

As if he didn't know. "What happened?"

"Someone is trying to shut Mikala out of Scheimer's laptop before she can download the files. And he's going to be successful in...thirty-nine seconds."

He scrutinized the breaker boxes. "What do I do?"

"I'm sending the schematics to your iPhone."

Tolga retrieved the device from between his butt cheeks. Embarrassing, yes, but the only place it could go without creating an obstruction while he slithered through the passageways. "Got it." He moved to the second box. "Sixth switch from the top?"

"Seventh! For God's sake, be careful!"

"Maybe I should trip them all, just to be safe."

"That wouldn't be safe. That would be stupid. If you shut down all the power, it will attract attention all over campus. Just eliminate the problem."

"Understood." Tolga counted down seven black switches. "Should I do it now?"

"No, take your time. You've got thirteen seconds."

Tolga hated sarcasm. Perhaps because English wasn't his first language. "Throwing the switch...now."

DETWILER WAS SEARCHING for his wallet when the lights in his guardpost went out. *What now?*

This had been a hell of a day. First that drunken lunatic in the bobblehead, then a moron crashes into a tree, now an electrical outage. Actually, come to think of it, the last PFD had been worse. But still. Who needed this?

He checked the building. The interior lights were still on. Maybe they just tripped a breaker. Overloaded a circuit. Those scientists might be geniuses, but they had about as much common sense as his cat.

He'd better check it out. He hated to leave his post, especially with the parade running. But he would be remiss not to investigate. He could be in the electrical room in a couple of minutes. Then he could see for himself what was happening. And take care of the problem. Whatever it might be.

"THAT WASN'T THE RIGHT SWITCH!" Felix screamed into Tolga's ear.

"I did the seventh one! I did what you told me!"

"These schematics must be out of date. Try the eighth one."

"Are we just going by trial and error now?"

"No, I'm consulting a psychic. Have you thrown the switch yet?"

"Should I?"

"Lani will be shut out in five seconds. Do it!"

"You mean it? You're not being sarcastic?"

"Throw the goddamn switch!"

"Throwing the switch..."

DYLAN FOUGHT against the panic rising in his throat. He had not anticipated every contingency. He had not foreseen the possibility of someone shutting down Scheimer's files remotely. And he had no idea how to deal with it.

He finished setting the stage. He ran through the lab smashing quantitative equipment, electroencephalographs, a magneto-optical trap, and something he thought was a femtosecond comb.

"How's the download coming?" he asked, trying to keep the urgency he felt out of his voice.

"Not fast enough," Mikala replied.

"Felix, help us."

"Working on it," he growled back.

Five, four, three...

The top horizontal bar disappeared.

"You did it!" Dylan cried.

"I didn't do anything," Mikala said.

"I did," Felix crowed. "With an assist from Tolga. How much longer till the files are downloaded?"

"About fifty seconds," Dylan replied. "Shouldn't be a problem."

"I beg to differ."

"What do you know that I don't?"

"What would you do if your power went out just after you spotted an unauthorized intrusion into top-secret government files and tried unsuccessfully to shut them down?"

Dylan's heart sank. "I'd check it out."

"I've hacked into the building's CCTV. Someone is headed your way. He'll be there in less than a minute."

"How do I get out without being spotted?"

Felix was so succinct Dylan wanted to slap him. "You don't."

CHAPTER
FIFTY-THREE

3:01 p.m.

9 minutes left

"GET OUT OF HERE," Dylan told Mikala. "Now."

"But—"

"It will be much simpler for one person to escape than two. I'll bring the files when the download is finished."

"We should just take the laptop."

"If we do that, they'll know they've been robbed."

"They'll know they were robbed if they catch the robber!"

"I won't get caught."

"But—our plan--"

"Mikala, it's better this way. Now you won't be responsible for... what I'm about to do."

"Dylan, don't—"

"This is an order. Go."

"But I—"

"Don't argue. Just remember everything I told you before. Go!"

She disappeared. He waited until the last file downloaded. While he waited, he opened the eighth file and absorbed as much as he could.

Fortunately, a lifetime of voracious book consumption had made him a fast reader.

"The computer monitor stopped in the front lobby to talk to the guard," Felix informed him. "You've got maybe another minute."

Good. He kept reading. The fundamentals on how the weapon worked. For anyone who had the Key. And where it was located. Critical equations.

When he'd read as long as he could afford to, he closed the file.

He right-clicked on the eighth file. And chose Delete. Then he emptied the recycle bin and told the computer to reboot. He placed it on Scheimer's desk, just under his head.

When everything was in place, he removed the flash drive and ran.

———

AFTER HE LOST POWER, Joe had been tempted to call his Navy contacts. But they would undoubtedly ask him to stay put till they arrived. He decided to show them how proactive he was by taking the lead.

He'd almost made it to the main corridor when he bumped into the security guard posted outside the front entrance.

"Gerald Detwiler," the guard said, extending his hand.

"Of course." He did not return the handshake. He didn't do handshakes. He saw no reason to share germs in such an unnecessary manner. "What brings you inside?"

"Power went out in the guardpost."

Joe's nose crinkled. "Same thing happened in the library. Which I thought odd. But if it's happening everywhere..."

"Probably some absent-minded Einstein left his Bunsen burner on too long. Scheimer blew the circuits last week with an unauthorized experiment."

"Yeah. Probably something like that."

"Still, thought I should check it out."

"Of course. We must be vigilant."

"Absolutely. Keep the drunken students away from the mad scientists."

Joe laughed. "You check the electrics. I'm going to the lab. That's my protocol in the event of any potential computer interference."

He nodded. "Call me if there's anything wrong."

"Believe me, I will."

***

"Did Mikala get out safely?" Dylan asked.

"She did," Felix replied. "But what about you?"

"I've got the files. I'm halfway down the central corridor."

"You won't make it in time."

"What do you mean?"

"In ten seconds, you're going to have company."

***

Ten minutes ago, Tolga's left arm had ached severely. At present, there really was no arm. Just one big long hurt radiating from the ulna to his fingertips.

"Are you back in the interior passage?" Felix asked.

"Is the sausage back in the grinder?" Tolga replied, swearing under his breath, pulling himself along by inches. "Yes, in fact I am."

"That's good. Because the guard is entering the electrics room."

Tolga swore silently. A few seconds slower and he would've had a difficult situation to explain. Probably the last explaining he would do in his entire life.

"But this leaves you a clear path out front. The guard is not at his post. You can escape."

"Fabulous. I should be there in a couple of minutes."

"Except that you need to pause along the way and readjust the camera. Remember—no traces."

Right. "Will Dylan and Mikala be able to escape?"

"Mikala is already gone. Dylan can't go out the front. Someone's in the corridor."

"Then—"

"Just worry about your part, okay? I can only solve five or six major crises at once. This op is unraveling like virus-infected code."

Tolga continued slithering through the impossibly narrow passage. He reached forward with his all-but-useless left arm—

Too far. His arm wouldn't move. Wouldn't move at all. Something had severed, some nerve ending had short-circuited.

He was sandwiched inside a passage too small for a medium-sized dog, unable to move. He wouldn't get out in time. Which meant he would be captured. Dylan would be captured. The mission would fail.

And he knew all too well what the price of failure would be. Xavier would kill them all.

CHAPTER
FIFTY-FOUR

3:05 p.m.
5 minutes left

JOE DIDN'T KNOW what to expect when he entered the lab, but he thought he was prepared for anything.

He was wrong.

The lab looked as if a tornado had blown through. Breakage everywhere. Test tubes shattered. Papers scattered. Tables upended. A chair atop a worktable. Shards of glass made the floor a chaotic mosaic. He could barely walk.

A telltale bottle of sour-mash whiskey rested on a countertop. And Dr. Scheimer was hunched over his desk.

Joe took a whiff. He could smell the alcohol a foot away.

He knew the doctor liked to end the day with a drink. Or six. As long as he got his work done, no one cared. But this was early in the day for him.

Joe recalled the doctor mentioning how much he hated PFD—the noise, the distracting revelry. Looked like he retreated to his favorite coping mechanism. And went on a rampage. Not the first time that had happened.

Scheimer's head rested on the keyboard. That would explain the false password entries. Hard to type properly with a drunken forehead.

He walked the length of the lab, casting his eyes around. No one else was here. No one in the corridor. No one on the surveillance camera. Just a scientist who decided to celebrate the holiday with a binge.

He supposed he should be relieved, but it was hard not to feel somewhat disappointed. He was hoping to show those Navy boys how alert he was. Might've gotten a promotion out of it.

He decided to wait in the lab till the doctor awoke. Just in case.

He wanted to make sure he hadn't missed anything.

DYLAN HEARD someone stomping around the lab. He lay flat on his stomach, trying not to make any noise. He'd put a chair on a worktable and pushed through the insulated paneling overhead to escape. He hovered in the narrow air passage between ceiling and roof, hoping the man downstairs didn't get suspicious about the chair on the table.

Dylan slithered like a snake till he reached the access panel leading to the roof. He pushed upward and crawled through the opening.

He was out of the building. But hardly free.

"I must hand it to you," Felix said, in a voice that was beginning to irritate the hell out of him. "Good thing you memorized the building schematics."

What Felix and Xavier and everyone else—except Mikala—didn't know was that Dylan had planned to leave this way all along.

Looking down the street, he saw the last of the parade floats streaming by.

"Any idea how you're going to get down?" Felix asked.

"Does it matter? I can wait till nightfall. I can wait till Tuesday if necessary. Just so I'm not seen."

"That could be a problem."

The short hairs rose on the back of his neck. "Why?"

"Something I just picked up on radar and confirmed on television. Channel 7 News is covering the parade. Their copter will be in range in about two minutes. No way they won't see you. And photograph you. Might even land and ask you some questions."

"I won't answer."

"That's correct. Because Xavier will shoot you before you have a chance."

Tolga was drenched in sweat, but that was good, in a perverse way. The increased moisture lubricated his passage through this insanely narrow chute. He was advancing by inches, half-inches even. All he had to do was get out before the guard returned to his post. But Tolga wasn't moving half as fast as he'd planned.

My God, it hurt. His arm ached like nothing else he'd felt in his entire life. When Xavier gave him a chance to improve his financial situation, he thought, why the hell not? Why spend the rest of his days performing for kids who'd rather be at home playing videogames? How much longer could he handle piddling little Copenhagen capers?

Xavier didn't have to tell him what would happen if he were caught. An organization like this one didn't survive by being merciful or by taking unnecessary risks.

He had to make it out.

"The guard has flipped the power back on," Felix announced. "You've got about one minute to depart before he returns to his post."

Tolga tensed every muscle in his body, pushing forward with every ounce of energy left to him. *Come on...*

Just ahead, no more than five or six feet—he saw light.

He was almost there. The same ceiling panel he'd used to enter.

He could do this. He had to do it. Push. *Push!*

Tolga made it in just under a minute. He was getting so good at manipulating the screwdriver with one hand he could do it in his sleep. He popped the bolts, popped the lid, and eased himself out head first.

He tried to grip the ceiling and leverage his way out, but his right hand was too weak and his left wasn't moving at all. He fell hard and clattered to the ground.

He sprang up, poised, ready to fight. He looked left. He looked right.

The guard wasn't there yet. No one had heard.

He didn't wait any longer. He reattached the lid and got the hell out of there.

"I'm free," he whispered. He reversed his black shirt, turning it into a university T. He headed straight for the parade and blended into the crowd. "So where's Dylan?"

There was a pause before Felix answered. "You'll never guess. And don't look when I tell you."

XAVIER OPENED the back doors of the van. "Where the hell is he?"

"Up on the roof," Felix answered.

"How will he get down?"

"That is the question. The one that seemingly has no answer. And he's about to be spotted by a news copter."

"Unacceptable." Xavier knew Dylan had planned for every possible contingency. He must've known about the roof access panel. So he must've known it was a possible escape route.

That was the reason for the foam rubber.

He bolted out of the van. Just as he suspected—Mikala was hustling toward the car. The one Kalifa crashed.

He raced beside her and clamped a thick hand down on her shoulder. "I do not think so."

She was so startled she jumped. "But—Dylan—"

"Yes. He needs rescue. And then the two of you drive away into sunset. No." Before she had a chance to scream or otherwise attract attention, he threw her into the backseat and locked the doors. Then he slid inside and turned the ignition.

The guard, Detwiler, walked toward them. Good thing he'd never seen Xavier without his bobblehead. Smiling, he told Mikala, "If you do not stay quiet, I kill you and Dylan both. Then your father."

She kept her mouth closed.

Xavier rolled the window down. He raised the pitch of his voice and did his best to sound American. "Security. Just cleaning up."

"Good. I was afraid I'd have to figure out what to do with that thing."

"Be gone soon."

And he would. As soon as he circled back in front of the physics lab.

***

"Twenty seconds till the news copter is in range," Felix announced.

Dylan bit down on his lower lip. There was no good solution here. Only one option. He'd seen Xavier start the car. He was now pulling it —and its cargo—into range in front of the lab.

"You sure you can't distract the copter? Make something explode off campus?"

"I'm sure. Ten seconds."

"How much foam rubber did we put in that volcano?"

"Does it matter?"

"I suppose not." He took one more look, closed his eyes, then raced across the rooftop. "Cowabunga!"

***

Seamus McKay stepped out of his car, removed his sunglasses, and focused his binoculars.

Was that who he thought it was? What the hell was he doing up there?

***

Dylan leaped off the edge of the roof, plummeting into the mouth of the faux-volcano. Two seconds before impact, he thought, Shouldn't my life be passing before my eyes? All I can feel is my heart thumping in my chest...

He hit the foam rubber with a thud. His back hurt like hell. But he was alive.

When he crawled out of the volcano, the handful of people who'd noticed his descent applauded. They apparently thought it was planned programming, the big finish.

A ham fist slapped down on his shoulder.

"Nice try, Dylan. But I outsmart you, like always." He held a gun inside his jacket. "Give me files."

Dylan passed him the flash drive.

"Now we return to van." He shoved Dylan forward. "Then headquarters. For review of operation. You used to getting reviews, right?" He pulled Dylan close and whispered into his ear. "This review I think you not like so much. Your story exciting. But climax was big flop."

CHAPTER
FIFTY-FIVE

AFTER THE DEBRIEF, the other members of the team were dismissed. Only Dylan and Mikala remained, flanked on the opposite side of the conference table by Xavier and Mr. X. Marco and Kalifa stood behind Dylan and Mikala, making sure they didn't move.

"It was indeed an impressive operation," Mr. X said. "You got inside the university, you abducted Scheimer, and you persuaded him to provide the information we needed. Without being detected."

"Thanks," Dylan said. "I suppose you'll be giving me some kind of bonus and severance pay."

She ignored him. "Which makes it all the more difficult to do what we now have to do."

Dylan's brows moved closer together. "What are you talking about?" He saw her fingers tense, squeezing air. "I got what you wanted."

"You tried to escape."

"Wouldn't you have done the same thing?" He paused. "Wouldn't your IRA lover have done the same thing?"

"Perhaps. But that's not your only sin, is it?"

"We got the data you wanted."

"Did we?"

"Yes. What's the problem?"

Xavier pressed his thick hands against the table. "Problem is that you not keep agreement."

"I did everything you asked. Everything and then some."

"It is 'then some' that causes problem."

"I don't—"

All at once, Xavier lashed out, barely missing Dylan's face. Mikala instinctively jumped back.

"Did you think us idiots? Imbeciles?"

"I—got—your information." He had to play dumb. "I did —everything—"

"Bullshit." Xavier shoved Dylan backward. He was caught by Kalifa and Marco, who kept a tight grip on him. "Eight files on Scheimer's laptop. You brought home seven."

"You're wrong. There were only seven."

"No. We have all information we need about weapon, how to operate it. But targeting information is in eighth file."

"You're wrong."

Xavier turned to Mikala and put his right hand around her throat. Her face became pale. "You saw computer. How many files?"

"I—don't remember."

He shook her so hard Dylan was afraid he might snap her neck. *"How many files?"*

She looked at Dylan, then back at Xavier.

This was why Dylan had recruited her. This was why he'd asked her to help him. He needed someone to drive the escape vehicle, true. But more importantly, he knew he couldn't delete anything without the encryption expert knowing it.

"Answer!" Xavier barked. "Seven files? Or eight?"

"I—I'm not sure…"

He pulled out a gun and pointed it at her head. "You try to escape. That alone grounds to kill you. Then I kill father. Slowly." He pulled back the hammer. "Last chance to live. Tell me truth!"

"She doesn't know," Dylan said, cutting in. "I sent her away before the encryption was complete. All she ever saw were seven files." He could tell Xavier was not satisfied. If he was going to save Mikala, he would have to give more. "I'm the only one who ever knew there were eight."

"*What—were—you—thinking?*" Xavier shouted. He shoved Mikala aside and came at Dylan, snarling like a wild beast.

"I was thinking I have a moral compass," Dylan said, teeth clenched. "I was thinking I refuse to help you slaughter thousands of innocent people."

Xavier shoved him in the chest with the flat of his hand. "You were thinking like stupid fool!"

Mr. X walked up to Dylan, glared at him a moment, then swiftly brought her leg up between his. The kick landed with a rippling intensity. Dylan clenched his fists, stifling the pain.

"No," she said. "Not like a fool. He was thinking like an insufferable egotist who, despite all evidence to the contrary, still believed he was so much cleverer than everyone else that he could trick his way out. Isn't that right, Dylan?" She leaned into his face. "Do you think you're the only person capable of foreseeing the future? I was making life-and-death plans when you were writing essays on *Finnegan's Wake!*"

"I just want to see Leilani," Dylan whispered. "Don't you remember what that felt like? When you were willing to do anything—lie, cheat, or kill—to be with the person you loved?"

She slapped him. Her nails drew blood. "Did you really think we wouldn't know you deleted a file, Dylan? When you delete anything from a hard drive, it isn't really gone. It's just moved to another location. And it remains there until the data space is overwritten. Do you know how hard it was for Felix to recover what you deleted? It took him about three minutes."

"I—don't know what you're talking about."

"I've played these cat-and-mouse mind games with you long enough to know that you're not stupid. Solipsistic, yes. Mired in fantasy, true. But not stupid." An abrupt smile came to her face. "Of course. You knew we'd discover the deletion. You did it to distract us, to make us think we'd figured out your secret plan. To prevent us from finding something else."

"You're delusional," Dylan said. "I didn't have time to do anything else."

"You did. And this is the last time I will ask. What else did you do? What are you trying to distract us from? What is it you don't want us to see?"

"Nothing, damn you. I didn't have time."

"Apparently," she said, "the maiming and near death of your so-called true love—the one you're supposedly so desperate to see—was not enough to make you understand the situation. Apparently someone has to die."

Xavier jerked his head back. "Do you remember what I said? What medic put in your head?"

Dylan tried to twist away but Marco and Kalifa held him fast.

Xavier reached into his pocket and withdrew what looked like a small detonator. "Burn."

Dylan felt a fire ignite inside his brain. All at once, he lost control of his body. His legs turned to ribbons and he crashed to the ground. He fell forward, thrashing, as if the electrical circuitry in his brain had gone haywire. He tried to right himself, but his body would not respond. He fell sideways, drool spilling from his mouth.

"Nanites are eating your brain," Xavier explained. "Severing connections. Eroding neural network that transmits commands from brain to body. You are having brain damage, Dylan. Because you did not do what you said you would do. Because you could not follow your own plot."

Dylan squirmed helplessly on the floor. His tongue spilled out of his mouth. His arms twisted backward at an unnatural angle. He urinated on himself.

"Stop it," Mikala said. "You've punished him enough."

"I barely begin." Xavier signaled two security guards in the rear. "Bring in prisoner."

"Not my father," Mikala said. "Please, God, don't hurt my father."

Dylan tried to speak, but the effort was impossibly hard. "Don't... punish...her..."

Xavier glared at him. "Would you rather we killed *your* father?"

Dylan could not reply.

The wait was only a few seconds but it seemed like hours. Dylan's heart pounded, threatening to rip through the pericardium and burst through his chest. He tried to twist his head around so he could see who was coming, but he couldn't control his body. He could barely slither on the floor.

The two guards returned.

Dragging Commander Robert Taggart between them.

"Bah-bby," Dylan said, sounding like an infant learning to speak. His brother wore his Navy uniform, but there were blood stains on it. His face was covered with purplish bruises, as if he had been beaten for a long time. His right eye was swollen shut.

"Dylan?" Bobby whispered. His eyes were unfocused. He was only marginally conscious. "What's...happening?"

Fight it! Dylan told himself. But he couldn't move a muscle. Couldn't twitch an eyelid. His body was no longer his to command.

"Dylan...why are they doing this?"

"Try-ing...."

"What?"

Xavier jumped in. "Your brother is explaining that he tried—unsuccessfully—to be hero. And only thing he accomplished was to destroy his brother."

"Couldn't...let you....kill..."

"So brother dies instead. Bitch had to pay for your sins with her body. Brother will pay with his life."

Xavier kicked Robert in the back of his knees. His legs buckled. Xavier shoved him down to a kneeling position. A moment later, he pulled out his gun and pointed it to the back of Bobby's head.

"Don't!" Mikala screamed. "Please don't!"

Dylan writhed on the floor. He wondered if the damage was progressive. Soon he might not be able to talk at all.

Xavier slid back the cartridge on the .45. "I am counting to ten. If you have not told me what else you did by time I reach ten, brother dies." He looked at Dylan levelly. "One."

Dylan scanned the room. "Did...nothing..."

"Two."

"Bah--by," Dylan said, struggling with every syllable. "Didn't mean to...hurt...."

"Three!"

Dylan tried to scoot closer to Xavier, but he couldn't control his muscles.

"Can't you see he's helpless!" Mikala shouted. "He can barely speak."

"He talk good if he want. Tell us what we want to know. Four."

Dylan glared at him but did not reply.

"Five."

"I'm...there's nothing..."

"Six. How much are you willing to lose, Dylan?" He removed the controller from his pocket. "Enjoy this."

Xavier pushed the button and a bomb exploded in Dylan's brain. He flipped backward. His back arched to an impossible degree. His neck muscles were so constricted he could barely breathe.

"Stop it!" Mikala screamed. "You're killing him!"

"Maybe all Taggarts should die," Xavier said. "Seven."

Dylan squirmed sideways. He needed all the concentration he could muster to form a syllable. "Can't...tell...what doesn't exist."

Xavier adjusted his aim slightly and shot Bobby in the leg.

Mikala screamed. "No!"

Bobby fell, bracing himself with one arm. Xavier shoved him onto the floor, a limp sack of flesh, moaning like a wounded dog begging to be put out of its misery.

Dylan and Bobby stared at one another, both heads on the floor.

"Have answer for me, Dylan?"

"Will never help you...if you kill...Bobby."

"Beg me not to hurt him. Beg me."

Dylan did not beg.

"Eight."

Mikala fell to her knees. She wrapped her arms around Xavier. "Please. Don't do this!"

Xavier shoved her away. "Nine." He jerked Dylan's limp body up by the collar. Dylan was unable to resist.

Xavier pressed the gun into Dylan's hand.

"Beg me, Dylan. Beg me to stop this."

Dylan pressed his lips together. "Never."

"Ten."

"*No!*"

Xavier closed his fist over Dylan's hand, forcing him to pull the trigger. The gun fired. Blood splattered everywhere. Dylan shut his eyes. He heard his brother's head smash against the floor, dull and wet.

"You...bastard," Dylan gasped. "You...filthy...bastard."

Xavier released him. He fell to the floor, eyes glazed over.

"You are broken, Dylan. I know that look. It cannot be playacted. You are broken and beaten and you will tell us what we want to know. Before we kill someone else!"

"I—I—"

"Going after your bitch. *Now!*"

Tears sprang to Dylan's eyes. "I changed...the location. The weapon. It's...actually under Kohala." The life drained out of his voice.

Xavier let his head fall to the floor, wiping blood spatters from his face. He motioned to the two security guards who'd brought Bobby in. "Get him out of here. Then clean up mess." He looked down at Dylan. "Pathetic thing is—Felix would have detected change. But this saves us much time."

Mr. X rose. "Tomorrow will be the start of a new phase in our ongoing operation. We'll meet in the conference room at nine to determine how to proceed." She looked down at Dylan, helpless, drooling on the floor. "We'll send a wheelchair for you. I hope you'll have a few ideas to share with us."

She crouched beside him. "You will never leave this organization, Dylan. Not alive. So you can live here happily and be well treated, or die. But you will never leave. Do you understand?"

"I...understand."

"Good." She rose. "See you all tomorrow morning."

Everyone departed, leaving Dylan alone, sprawled on the floor, unable to move.

He felt something wet rush against his face. Was he crying, without even knowing it? Had he wet himself again? It tasted dark and coppery on his tongue, sticky and—

And then he realized.

He was lapping up his brother's blood. It flowed onto his face, into his eyes, into his mouth. All over him.

He had not anticipated every contingency. They had seen his plot twists coming. They were the ones who pulled off a surprise ending. They'd destroyed him, left him nothing but a pathetic puddle on the floor.

They'd beaten him.

Again.

PART THREE
THE CONSUMMATION

"An unhappy childhood is the best early training for every writer."

ERNEST HEMINGWAY

CHAPTER
FIFTY-SIX

Two Weeks Later

"I HAVE ANOTHER IDEA," Dylan said, bracing himself against the conference table.

"'Bout time," Xavier grunted. "G20 conference soon."

"Hush," Mr. X said. "Let's hear what the man has to say."

"The problem confronting us," Dylan continued, "is that we know this weapon exists and what it can do. We know where it is. But we can't aim it. We know how to input coordinates via an external computer, but we don't have the schematics to build a key. A targeting device. Something to convert coordinates into the equations necessary to send the lightning bolt where we want it to go. So we have only one option." He paused. "We steal the Navy's Key."

"I've read the files you stole, several times over," Mr. X said. "The Navy's targeting device—what they so dramatically call the Kronos Key —is kept in a vault at PACOM—the Pacific Command Headquarters. Probably the most tightly guarded facility this side of NORAD."

"I know."

"If you think you can break into PACOM like you did the university, you're delusional. And if you think you can break into their vault, you're flat-out insane."

"I don't think we can break into their vault. But we can get the Key."

"It's impossible."

"I've never let that stop me before. Felix has done an amazing job of obtaining information about this top-secret installation—but most of the news is not encouraging. First, PACOM is swarming with personnel. Over three hundred. Even at night there are more than a hundred people onsite at any given time. We cannot possibly elude detection in a place so heavily populated."

"Exactly," Xavier said. "Impossible."

"Second. PACOM is protected by a high-tech sonar intruder-detection system. And third, the Key is kept in a bank-style walk-in steel vault protected by heat sensors, pressure-sensitive floor tiles, and a magnetic array that can only be deactivated by entering one of over a million possible combinations into a keypad. Any attempt to tamper with it will release a glycol-based opaque fog which will instantly reduce visibility to zero. The vault can withstand over fourteen hours of drilling, even if you could get close to it, which you can't." He paused. "Those are the obstacles we must overcome to achieve our objective."

"And that is impossible," Mr. X said. "You'd need massive weaponry and an army."

"No," Dylan said. "But you'd need an ingenious plotline. Detailed research. And lots of character development. In short—you need a writer."

THE FIRST DAY after Bobby died—the day after he shot Bobby— Dylan couldn't move his body at all. They forced him into a wheelchair, but he couldn't sit upright. He was a jellyfish on wheels, unable to speak clearly or even nod his head. He could barely breathe. The medics debated whether the nanites would eventually disable his autonomic functions. Many predicted he would die in his sleep.

And he hoped they were right. He had failed. Again. He had not anticipated every contingency. He had not escaped. Even as he cursed and despised Mr. X, he knew she was right. He had been an egomaniac.

He had thought he was smarter than everyone else. Yes, his writing skills had proven to have some real-world usefulness. But they hadn't been enough to escape. They hadn't been enough to stop him from pulling a trigger on his own brother.

Dylan lay fitfully in the bed where they placed him, eyes open wide, all through the night. He was certain that if he closed his eyes he would die.

He did not die. But neither could he move. They pushed and carried him through the day. Mr. X forced him to attend all meetings, even though he drooped sideways like a Dali watch. Mikala and the others avoided his gaze.

Kalifa and Marco were his personal detail. They pushed him from one appointment to another. They fed him mashed foods like a baby. They even put him on the toilet and waited until he "finished his business."

But he did not die.

The next night he slept. And when he woke in the morning—he could wiggle his big toes.

It wasn't much, but it was a start. Gradually, one muscle at a time, his brain reasserted itself. The medical staff theorized that other parts of his brain were compensating for the damaged areas, much in the way the brain of a handicapped person will reroute commands to circumvent nonfunctioning cells. At the end of the week, he took his first tentative steps.

Eventually, he regained most of his motor functions, though he still didn't feel right. His body moved awkwardly. He felt at times as if an alien skeleton had invaded, one he could not altogether master. He was not the same as before and he knew he never would be. Body and mind, inside and out, everything had changed. But he could move. And most importantly, he could think.

A new Dylan Taggart entered the conference room this morning. One that even Xavier trusted. Because he had been broken. So utterly destroyed that he could no longer resist. Especially since Xavier still had that detonator in his pocket. No one thought Dylan would survive another nanite blast.

At long last, they had the idea man they wanted.

Or so they believed.

He knew the deletion of the eighth file would be detected. He knew the escape plan would probably not work and he would have to tell them about the true location of the weapon. Those were all diversions. Level-one and level-two bluffs. He knew they would punish him afterward and he had an idea what the punishment would be.

They had no clue what else he planned. And that gave him an edge. That gave him a fighting chance.

Dylan had made mistakes. He saw that now. The only upside of total immobility was that it gave you time to think. A good novel had three critical elements: plot, structure, and character. When he first tried to outwit Mr. X, all he had was plot, a series of Fargo Cody tricks. The second round, he added structure, concocting an elaborate sequence of events that anticipated everything—except character nuance.

The key to any good story was character. If he hoped to devise a winning tale, he would have to understand who he was dealing with and how he could use them. He had to arrange not only events, but people.

Act One and Act Two had gone to Mr. X. But this story was not over yet.

"CHARACTER DEVELOPMENT?" Mr. X narrowed her eyes. "Any characters in particular?"

"Sonics expert," Dylan replied.

"I know one who will do whatever you want for the right price," Mr. X replied. "What other characters would you like to develop?"

"I need a helicopter pilot. And a copter."

"Xavier is an excellent pilot. Anyone else?"

"Yes. One absolutely critical character who requires additional research. A character not even Xavier could recruit, but one we need working for us just the same."

"And who would that be?"

"The head of PACOM. Admiral Charles "Swifty" Stewart." He slid a photo across the table. "Find him. Then watch me do the impossible."

CHAPTER
FIFTY-SEVEN

MR. X JOINED the Supervisor in what she liked to call the Aerie, an attic-like room with an expansive window surrounding the third floor of the complex. The door was locked and guarded at all times and only a few had clearance to enter. A secret side entrance and spiral staircase allowed the Supervisor to visit without being detected.

From here, they could see all the way to the Pacific Ocean, the most gloriously blue water found anywhere, just off the jagged volcanic coast. They'd spent a good deal of money ensuring that this installation, built on the ruins of an abandoned WWII Navy post, was not visible from land or air. It was camouflaged with visual and radar interference signals so it would blend into the surrounding brush. They employed high-tech imaging technology to prevent accidental detection.

Mr. X always met the Supervisor in the Aerie. This allowed the Supervisor to give her instructions in person without risking identification. So far as Mr. X knew, everyone else was asleep, or at least in their personal quarters.

She looked forward to these talks. They helped her keep the operation on track. Xavier might be in charge of field operations—anything that required guilt-free brutality—but she controlled him. And the Supervisor controlled her. The Supervisor supplied money, seemingly infinite amounts of it. The Supervisor recruited Mr. X and Xavier, then gave them instructions on who else to obtain and how to recruit them. As they approached the final stage of the operation, the Supervisor was understandably concerned.

She refilled both their glasses. She didn't know enough about brandy to fully appreciate what they were drinking, but she knew it was good, probably the finest in the world. The Supervisor was not one to settle for second best.

"So," the Supervisor said, "you think Dylan is totally ours now?"

"I do," Mr. X replied. "I've watched him carefully these past two weeks. I think watching his brother die, coupled with the loss of his own body, made a decisive impact."

"That was a nasty business. The execution. Right in front of him. Brutal."

"But effective."

The Supervisor nodded. "You had no choice. We need him planning this finishing stroke. We need him one hundred percent."

"I agree. Unpleasant though it may have been." She gazed at the palm trees swaying in the gentle tropical breeze. Somewhere, she heard a gecko making its distinctive call. She loved life here in paradise. She never missed home. All it held for her were unpleasant memories.

"How are you liking the new face?" the Supervisor asked.

"I preferred the old one."

"Don't be absurd. Dylan did you a great favor."

"He did nothing." She drank in the night air. "My previous face told people who I really am."

"If you say so. Did someone take care of Bakersfield and Giep?"

"Of course. We couldn't allow them to return to their normal lives. Not after all they'd seen."

"Indeed. Despite your confidence that Dylan is ours, I assume you still have all the protocols in place?"

"I do. Every fundamental brainwashing procedure has been systematically implemented."

"His food is treated?"

"Every meal."

"Gas pumped into his cell at night?"

"Synthetic oxytocin. Leads to feelings of bonding."

"Temperature modulation?"

"We induce mood swings and use them to our benefit."

"Hypnotherapy."

"Every night. Sometimes twice a night."

"He has a strong mind, you know. You can't expect these techniques to manipulate him as easily as they might your average street thug."

"I have no reason to believe he's resisting. Honestly, I don't even think it's possible."

"Good." The Supervisor took another sip. "He has a creative mind. And a considerable ego, like all artists. Too big to believe he couldn't trick us, couldn't outsmart us. At first."

"He's lost his cape. He knows he's not invulnerable."

"That's a tough nut for anyone to swallow."

"He's already outlined how we get the Key. He's requisitioning equipment. Has Xavier researching an admiral. I expect him to submit a detailed plan soon."

"I expect him to be carrying a gun and leading the charge. That's what I've wanted all along."

"You won't be disappointed." She paused. "I would do anything for you."

"You would, wouldn't you?" The Supervisor leaned forward and kissed her. She returned the kiss, pressing as hard as she could—but it was never enough.

"I won't let you down," she gasped.

"I know you won't." The Supervisor unsnapped her jeans and yanked them down.

"I will never ever *ever* let you down," she murmured, pulling her blouse over her head.

"You need to let go of the pain of the past." The Supervisor snapped a handcuff around her wrist, then snapped the other end to the arm of her chair.

"What's that for?"

"A new sensation. A pain borne not from guilt and recrimination but from love."

The first blow hit the left side of her face. The next hit her on the right, knocking her head back with such force that it crackled.

"Without pain, the heart becomes hollow. And the flesh becomes weak. But we are not weak, are we? Every revolution requires sacrifice."

"Yes," Mr. X said. Blood trickled from the corner of her mouth.

"We are united in a common purpose. There's no room for slackers. We will make the world a better place together, you and I."

"Yes," she said, her chest heaving. "Yes, we will."

Their bodies pressed together, churning. "I love you," the Supervisor said. "And our love will transform the world."

"Yes!" she replied, hips thrusting. "Oh God, Oh God, yes! I love you! Yessssss!" She cried out, her words echoing through the Aerie, delirious, ecstatic.

That night she slept soundly for the first time in as long as she could remember.

CHAPTER
FIFTY-EIGHT

SEAMUS AND LEILANI hunched over Dr. Kurosagi's shoulders.

"Why is this taking so long?" Leilani asked, tapping her foot impatiently.

The forensic scientist exhaled. "Normally I work without an audience."

"But this is important!"

Seamus laid his hand on her arm and nodded. Give the doctor a moment of peace. We'll both get out of here sooner.

"All he's doing is watching the computer crunch data," she whispered.

"This isn't my field of expertise," Seamus whispered back, "but I believe there's a little more to it." In truth, seeing Leilani tap her toes gave him a good deal of pleasure. She was walking as well as anyone. There was a trace of a limp, if you watched carefully, but she had no trouble moving and had even started going for short runs in the morning. He'd seen other people recover much less successfully from gunshot wounds—including himself. He was impressed.

"Getting some matches," Kurasagi said, gazing intently at his computer monitor. He ran his fingers over the keyboard at breakneck speed. "Things are definitely lining up..."

"Matching?" Leilani said. "What does that mean? Is it him or not?"

"I'm sure he'll tell us as soon as he knows," Seamus replied.

"But I want to know now!"

She was like a kid on Christmas Eve, but she'd earned the right. She'd been waiting for this a long time.

A chiming sound emerged from the computer. The images on the screen flashed red.

"What does it mean?" Leilani asked.

"It means the computer is certain. The DNA in the blood sample from the lab matches the blood sample on the bedsheet you gave me."

"It's Dylan!" Leilani shouted.

Kurasagi nodded. "Indeed."

She grabbed Seamus by both arms. "You were right. He must've cut himself when all the lab equipment was damaged. Which means that was Dylan you saw flying off the roof."

"I thought so. But that leaves two big questions. What was he doing atop the science building on PFD? And where is he now?"

Kurasagi swiveled around. "I may be able to help you with that last one."

Seamus tucked in his chin. "How?"

"This blood sample you brought me has some unique properties."

"Such as?"

His eyebrows danced. "It's alive."

Two weeks before, in the immediate aftermath of the parade, university officials refused to allow Seamus into the highly guarded Harrison Elliot lab. And since Eustace had ordered him to drop the investigation, he couldn't call for help. Fortunately, he still had friends at the CIA who not only owed him a debt but knew how to do things discreetly. They brought him two important bits of information. First, no, they wouldn't let him interrogate the lab scientists, and second, the reason they wouldn't is that the lab was the nerve center of an ongoing clandestine research project being conducted by the US Navy.

The same people who accosted Leilani when she spoke to her old scientist chum. The same people who were conducting research at the Cartwright Institute.

Since the official channels weren't working for him, Seamus resorted to another standby from his intelligence-gathering days: subterfuge. Although going to the top was often more expedient—going to the bottom was often more productive.

Around nightfall on PFD, he found the lab security guard, Detwiler, taking his dinner in the Student Union. Seamus introduced himself, flashed his badge, and launched into a conversation.

"Was anyone in the lab today who shouldn't be?"

"I'm afraid I can't talk about my work." Detwiler took a swig from his coffee and grimaced. "Worst java on the island."

Seamus removed a flask from his coat pocket and poured something into the coffee. "See if this helps any."

Detwiler sniffed it, then took a sip. "Definitely an improvement. But I have to go back on duty in ten minutes."

"I won't tell anyone." And he wouldn't. That would defeat the point of bringing the flask. Which he'd done because he found it more useful than a rubber hose. "So you didn't see anyone inside the lab?"

"Not at all," Detwiler replied. He was eating a pastrami and rye, with salt-and-vinegar chips. Apparently the gift was mellowing him, or he'd decided Seamus was not a threat to his livelihood. "A little activity on the front lawn. Drunks who lost their way. A wayward float. Par for the course on PFD."

"But no intruders?"

"I'm stationed at the only entrance and we have video cameras monitoring the interior corridor at all times. You can't get anywhere without being seen."

Seamus noodled that over for a few moments. "Nothing unusual occurred?"

"We had a power outage, but we corrected it quickly."

"What caused that?"

"Can't say for certain. But our resident scientist was in a bad way, so anything's possible. He's run experiments that shut down half the campus."

"You're talking about Louis Scheimer?"

"The one and only." Detwiler took another bite of his sandwich.

"And when you say he was in a bad way…"

Detwiler made a drinking gesture.

"Started the cocktail hour a little early?"

"Hates the ruckus. Probably told himself a drink would be medicinal. He's fond of the sour mash. Washes down egg-salad sandwiches with it. Disgusting, I know. By mid-afternoon, he'd trashed his lab and passed out."

Seamus's eyes narrowed. "He trashed his own lab?"

"Did a good job, too. Hundreds of dollars in damage. And created cleanup detail for several work-study students."

"Could I see the lab? Before it's cleaned."

"I'm afraid it's off limits to anyone who doesn't have clearance."

"I have clearance. I'm with the NCTC." He poured a little more from flask to mug. "I promise to be fast."

Detwiler picked up the mug and tilted it toward Seamus. "Fifteen minutes."

"Done."

FIFTEEN SECONDS AFTER ENTERING, Seamus knew that the trashing of Scheimer's lab had been staged. The job was probably sufficient to fool the casual observer. It gave no one any reason to look harder. But it was much too deliberate. Even a violent, sloshy, staggering drunk would not do so much damage or rearrange so much furniture.

And then there was the matter of the chair on the lab table. That just made Detwiler roll his eyes. But then, he hadn't seen a man fly off the roof.

Seamus climbed up on the table, then the chair, and pressed the ceiling panels.

As he suspected. Roof access.

Did Dylan plan to leave that way? Or was he improvising?

What was Dylan doing here? According to everyone he'd interviewed, nothing was taken. So what was the point?

He needed to speak to Scheimer, the man around whom so much attention was focused.

Seamus searched the lab as carefully as possible, but he still didn't know why Dylan came here. When he climbed down from the lab table, however, he noticed something he had not spotted before.

Blood. Partly on the table, partly on a shard of broken glass.

And he had a hunch it did not belong to the scientist. It belonged to whoever set the stage.

He scraped a sample into a plastic vial.

On his way out, he noticed something else. A light brown smear, almost invisible, on Scheimer's desk.

He rubbed his finger in it, then held it to his nose. It wasn't chemical. It wasn't poisonous. In fact, it reminded him of Ingrid.

He'd have to run a test to be sure. But he thought it was makeup.

He searched his most reliable database—his brain. A few days before PFD, a film makeup artist named Bakersfield had disappeared, saying he was ill and quarantined. He never returned.

Curiouser and curiouser.

TURNED out the blood was even more helpful than Seamus had imagined. He'd not only confirmed that Dylan Taggart was there—he'd possibly twigged onto a means of locating him.

"There are tiny digital sensors in this blood," Kurasagi explained. "He's been injected with what people in the intelligence community call 'smart dust.'"

"For real?" Seamus had heard talk about smart dust, but he'd seen no evidence that it actually existed. They certainly didn't have any at the NCTC. Unless Eustace was holding out on him. "How does it work?"

"The sensors emit a trackable signal."

"Could we pick it up?"

"If we knew the frequency. Unfortunately, we're not talking radio here. We're talking about a combination of the infrared spectrum, magnetic resonance, and heat signatures. So there are millions of possibilities."

"Can you figure it out?"

"I can try. But the signal fades over time. It's probably already fading. I may only be able to give you a general location. And it may take weeks."

Seamus looked at him directly. "I can give you forty-eight hours."

Kurasagi frowned. "Guess I won't be bowling tonight."

"Thanks." Seamus turned toward Leilani. "Are you following all this?"

"Well enough. But I don't know if I can wait two days to find Dylan."

Seamus led her toward the door. "I have an activity in mind that might help you pass the time. While I make another probably futile attempt to pry information out of the people at PACOM." Seamus had called about two weeks ago to request a repeat interview with Robert Taggart—only to find the officer had disappeared and no one knew where he was.

"What do you want me to do?" Leilani asked.

"Not much. Just set up a chat with the world's most closely guarded military scientist. Louis Scheimer."

CHAPTER
FIFTY-NINE

"PUT YOUR ELBOWS ON THE TABLE," Dylan said into the microphone.

Xavier, listening through the transmitter inside his mouth, murmured a reply. "Bad manners."

Xavier had no problem with abduction, torture, and assassination, but he didn't want to put his elbows on the table? "Is that something your mother taught you?"

"What mother?"

"Okay, your wife."

"Irina was not—"

He didn't finish the sentence.

"She the girl back home?"

"No girl. No home."

"There must've been at one time. What happened?"

Mr. X interceded. "Stop your infantile attempts at psychological profiling and stick with the mission."

Dylan obeyed. "Get your elbows on the table."

Xavier rested his elbows so the outside of his hands faced the man eating across the aisle and one booth down. Admiral Charles "Swifty" Stewart.

"That's it," Dylan said. "I've got him."

He could see the leader of PACOM ordering his burger at this 50's-style diner. Xavier had been following him since he left the base. Dylan could observe as well, because the "gemstone" of the ring on Xavier's left hand concealed a tiny digital camera, an Aviflex 21-X. The transmission streamed to Dylan's laptop. So long as Xavier kept his hands pointed the right direction, Dylan could follow the admiral's every movement.

Dylan suspected the admiral came here often because the waitress knew him. They chatted amiably for several moments. She already knew what he wanted. Cheeseburger and chili cheese fries. Vanilla malt.

Mr. X watched over Dylan's shoulder. "We'd best move quickly."

"Why?"

"The way that man eats, he'll soon be dead of a heart attack."

"He's a widower. Got no one to cook for him. Burgers are comfort food."

"He's going to comfort himself into the grave."

"Shh. What's he reading?"

On the laptop screen, they could see that the admiral had brought a newspaper. "*Honolulu Advertiser.*"

"What section of the paper is he reading?" Dylan asked.

"Sports," Xavier replied. "Football." He appeared to be reading every word with intense interest.

A few minutes later, Stewart set down the paper and picked up a hardcover book.

"What's he reading now?" Mr. X asked.

"Vince Flynn," Dylan replied. "The admiral likes thrillers with a conservative, pro-military slant. That's too bad."

"Because he's not reading one of yours?"

"Because it means I can't steal any ideas from Vince Flynn. Stewart will see them coming."

"I'm sure you'll manage."

The waitress returned with Stewart's food. After a few more pleasantries, he withdrew a small bottle from his pocket.

"Purell hand sanitizer," Dylan noted.

"Admiral worried about germs," Xavier grunted. "Wimp. Maybe I should start conversation."

"Under no circumstances," Dylan said. "You do not need to be on his radar."

"I would get more information. And faster."

"Once he hears your accent, you won't get anything out of this cold warrior. Just sit and watch."

The admiral consumed half the malt before he started on the burger and fries. He used the squirt bottle to get a quantity of mayonnaise almost equal to the quantity of fries.

"Good God," Mr. X said. "My cholesterol is rising just from watching the man eat."

Dylan barely heard her. He was distracted by an entirely different observation. Stewart ran through five napkins in the course of consuming his meal. He rarely took a bite without wiping both hands and mouth.

"How can he lead men to battle?" Xavier asked. "Afraid to get hands dirty."

"Yes," Dylan said quietly. "And the key word there is, 'afraid.'"

When Stewart finished his meal, he again sanitized his hands. Then he read a bit, chatted with the waitress, paid his bill with a credit card, and left.

"Should I follow?" Xavier asked.

"Yes," Dylan said. "Follow him home. You never know what you might learn. But," he added quietly, "I think I have what we need."

Mr. X's eyes narrowed. "What do you mean?"

"Our admiral has mysophobia."

"Talk to me in English, Dylan."

"He's a germophobe. Afraid of dirt, bacteria."

"Maybe he's worried about COVID."

"Nah. That wouldn't explain the way he eats. This is a good thing. This gives us a door."

"I don't see the knob."

"Surely an experienced terrorist like you knows the best way to control someone is through fear."

"True."

"Fear communicates directly to the amygdala. The fear center. Affects neurolinguistic programming. Influences the brain, autonomic responses." He leaned back in his chair. "If you can influence someone's fear reactions, you can persuade them to do anything."

"Why are you smiling?"

"Because I know how we're going to get that Key. I need you to recruit a doctor."

"What kind?"

"A specialist," he said quietly. "A specialist in fear."

CHAPTER
SIXTY

SEAMUS LEANED FORWARD, his fingertips pressed against the admiral's desktop. "There must be something you're not telling me."

"I can assure you there is not." Admiral Stewart was a ruddy, portly man, but still distinguished in his own way. His silver hair was slicked back in a manner that recalled the stereotypical millionaire playboy of another era. He was tan, but not from working outside. This man sat at a desk and he didn't play golf. Judging by the fact that Stewart was not brown under his chin, Seamus inferred that he sunbathed, perhaps on his lunch break, trying to hide the wrinkles and recapture the flush of youth.

"So you're telling me a senior member of your staff disappeared and you're doing nothing about it?"

"That is the exact opposite of what I told you, Mr. McKay, and to be blunt, I'm not going to repeat myself. After three days of not reporting for work and not calling in, we initiated an investigation into Robert Taggart's disappearance. We found no trace of him. We searched his home and office. We communicated with the police. We simply don't know where he is. He seems to have vanished off the face of the earth."

Seamus had heard that before. "You realize he's probably dead."

"I make no assumptions."

"I'm not making assumptions. I'm employing common sense." Seamus scanned the row of diplomas on the wall. Stewart had graduated from Annapolis. Given many years of loyal service. Repeatedly promoted, particularly during the second Bush administration. Nice photo of him shaking hands with Dick Cheney.

"Listen to me, Mr. McKay. I'm a busy man. I'm only talking to you because you're NCTC and I try to honor the requests of other governmental agencies, even when I don't know what they do and suspect they don't, either. I can assure you I can find any number of national crises to occupy my attention to such a degree that my assistant will not be able to fit you into my schedule until next December."

Message received. "I'm sorry, sir. It's a frustrating case."

"Imagine how I feel. One of my top commanders gone. That won't look good on my monthly report."

"No. I suppose it won't." Seamus stepped in a little closer. "Do you think it's possible Commander Taggart has been captured by foreign agents?"

"I have no reason to believe so. He has high-level clearance, but he's not the man I'd go after if I were working for North Korea."

"Maybe the others are too hard to get."

"An operation like that would make ripples. Someone in the intelligence community would've heard something."

Yeah. And the same thing would be true if suspected terrorists started taking flying lessons in Florida, right? "You realize his brother disappeared only a few weeks before."

"Of course I do."

"Have you investigated that?"

"Not as such. But I've talked to the authorities who have. No one seems to know much about it."

"Doesn't that suggest some sort of pattern?"

"Not really."

"Then allow me to be blunt. I know the Navy has some sort of secret project underway. A weapons project. I've spoken to Dr. Scheimer. I won't waste time trying to get you to tell me about it. But if I know, others do, too. My associate asked a physicist friend a few questions about the work of Dr. Karelis, and some of your security people apprehended her."

"And could have held her forever, if I'd wished it. But I didn't."

"I think someone is trying to get your weapon. Maybe you think your security is so tight you don't need to worry about it. But I'm telling you, if you don't do something fast, your weapon may fall into enemy hands. And the next Navy officer to disappear may be you."

"I'll ask you not to resort to melodrama." Stewart leaned forward. "How much do you know about the Taggart clan?"

"Not as much as I'd like."

"I wouldn't want this to get around. A senior naval officer has to protect his own. We hang together or we hang separately."

"I know how to keep a secret."

"The truth is—the Taggarts are a weird bunch. Always have been. I've tried to work with Robert, but it hasn't always been easy. He would've gone a lot further if he hadn't been related to his father."

"You didn't like his father?"

"More to it than that. He's a hard man—and an even harder dad, from what I gather. Never seen a man who could be so stone cold, so strict. 'Course he came by it earnestly. Taggart saw some tough duty. In Vietnam. 1970. He was attached to Charlie Company, 11th Brigade, 24th Infantry Battalion. Military intel believed the Viet Cong were holed up in a hamlet called Son My. They coptered in some troops for an assault. Taggart guarded the only footpath into the hamlet. His orders were to stop or kill anyone who tried to pass through."

"What happened?"

Stewart pursed his lips. "Children. Five or six VC kids, maybe eight years old. This was after My Lai and civilian casualties was a touchy subject. Everyone knew kids could be used by the enemy, but still. Kids. Taggart didn't have the capacity to hold them prisoner. But he couldn't bring himself to kill them. So he let them pass."

"And?"

"The kids were spies. They gave away the battalion location and the enemy called in an air strike that night. Over two hundred casualties, killed in a few minutes, most of them burning to death, screaming in pain. Every single member of the battalion died—except Taggart himself, because he was still out in the field." Stewart's eyes hardened. "One moment of weakness. Of human mercy. And as a result—all those deaths hanging over your head. Haunting you. For the rest of your life."

"So Taggart vowed to never allow himself another instant of what he called weakness. And he taught his boys to be just as strong. Came down hard on any sign of weakness."

Stewart picked up a file on his desk. "Did a little reading on you, Agent McKay. You used to be CIA, right? Worked in Afghanistan, other places. You must know something about the way the world works."

"I like to think so."

"You can rattle on about peace all you want—the only way to get it is by showing the bastards of the world that they can't screw with you. After Vietnam, Taggart got that. He was a solid, no-holds-barred hawk. Ultra-hawk, really. Bit too much for some people. He believed in a strong defense. But his idea of a strong defense was dropping napalm on every target in sight."

"I'm surprised he rose as high as he did in the military."

Stewart waved the comment away. "Oh, hell, that's all about politics, these days. During the Reagan era, he was exactly what they wanted. Clinton administration, not so much. The Bushies could count on him to support invading Iraq or whatever they wanted to do. But you can't make much of a career out of being in favor half the time. You know what I mean?"

Indeed he did. The intelligence community was equally subject to the winds of change, the unpredictable vicissitudes of presidential administrations. Some thought the CIA would not survive the Carter years. Some wondered if there was anything they couldn't do during the Dubya administration. "Are you still in contact with Admiral Taggart?"

"He contacts me occasionally, much to my dismay. From all around the world. Seems to stay well-informed and busy, although with what I have no idea."

"You'd think he would've gotten in touch with you after his son disappeared. The second one, I mean."

"But in that bizarre family, disappearances are not uncommon. The old man used to do it. Disappear for months, no one knows where he is, then he reappears and everything's okay and some high muckety-muck has smoothed it over. I think he had his fingers in the NSA—they were sending him on missions with need-to-know clearance. But that's just my theory. Youngest kid apparently did the same thing. Disappears, then it turns out he was on a research trip and didn't want anyone to know. Didn't want other writers getting the jump on him."

"He is not on a research trip. At least not a voluntary one. And you're not going to find Robert unless you look."

"My resources are stretched to the limit. Do you realize how important PACOM is to the security of this nation? We're the first line of defense against any threat from the Asian/Indonesian region, and just in case you didn't get the memo, that's probably the most dangerous part of the world these days. Some of those maniacs have nuclear capacity. They're barely able to feed their citizens, but they could destroy New York in ten minutes. You think I've got time to run around hunting some AWOL bean-counter from a family of eccentrics? I don't."

CHAPTER
SIXTY-ONE

"BUT WHY INVOLVE ME?" Leilani asked. "You're the superspy."

"Which is exactly why Scheimer will be more comfortable around you," Seamus replied. "You'll have an easier time getting past the guards, too."

"Why?"

"Because you're cute. And you blush readily. And you weigh— what? Ninety pounds, give or take an ounce?"

"Hardly."

"The point is, you look harmless." He winked. "But you're not."

"I still think—"

"He's far more likely to talk to you. Remember, the post-hypnotic suggestion prevents us from using force. He has to want to talk to you."

"Why would he?"

"Leilani, this is the oldest story in the history of mankind. What's the one thing that can make a smart man stupid?" He grinned. "A beautiful woman."

"I thought you were going to say 'ice cream.'"

"No, but that's not a bad idea for a backup plan."

"Fine. I'll do it. I guess." She frowned. "I like you, Seamus, but you can be totally manipulative, you know it?"

Yes, that had been pointed out to him before.

<hr>

WALK WITH AUTHORITY, Seamus told her. And then he made her practice it for half an hour.

If you look the part, he said, if you appear to know what you're doing, there's a good chance someone will let you do it. So she dressed in a two-piece dress suit of the sort that seemed practically a uniform in the halls of the NCTC. She put a stern, no-nonsense expression on her face. And she walked with authority. Even though she was pushing a hotel dining cart.

She approached two plainclothes guards standing at the hotel room door and flashed a fake badge Seamus gave her. "Leilani McKay. NCTC."

The guard on the left scrutinized the badge. "Okay. So?"

"I'm supposed to meet with Dr. Scheimer." She glanced down at the cart. "I'm bringing him a midnight snack."

The guard arched an eyebrow. "I thought he always drank his midnight snack."

"Apparently tonight's fare will be different."

The guard glanced at his clipboard. "We did receive notice that Scheimer would be having a visitor tonight."

"I can assure you I have clearance. Here's my authorization." Leilani passed him a packet of paperwork. Apparently, if you want first-rate forged government documents, the best place to go is another government agency.

"This appears to be in order. I still need verbal confirmation from the admiral, though. Please step away from the door."

"Why?" She grinned. "Are you afraid I'll overpower you and make a run for it?" Seamus said looking helpless was an asset. She decided to combine that with needling the male ego.

"Just need to make a phone call. Might take a while to get through this late at night." He withdrew a cellphone from his pocket. What he didn't know, of course, was that Seamus had already obtained a subpoena so he could search the nearest server for the guard's cell carrier

—and while there, he did more than search. Any call the guard made to the admiral tonight was going straight to Seamus.

"Hello?"

"Sorry to disturb you so late, sir. This is Lieutenant Conrad at the hotel. We have a female Hawaiiian-descent dark hair approximately 110 pounds with ID indicating she's an Agent McKay of the NCTC. She wants to see Scheimer."

"Agent McKay has clearance. Let her in."

The guard looked at his companion and shrugged. "He says she's okay." His friend nodded. "Very well. Good night, admiral. Sorry to trouble you." He ended the call, then redirected his attention to Leilani. "Guess you're good to go."

"Many thanks."

"I still need to search your cart, though. And you."

"No problem." Lieutenant Conrad searched thoroughly. A little more thoroughly than necessary she thought, particularly in her sensitive regions. But when he was done, he opened the door to the hotel room.

She was inside.

SHE FOUND Scheimer sitting at a desk, his head down as if he had fallen asleep while working. She parked the cart in the center of the room.

All at once, he sat up, eyes wide. "Who are you? How did you get in?"

She kept walking. "I have clearance. I'm a friend."

His eyes were red and tired. "I don't have friends anymore."

"You do now."

He replied with a smattering of German she didn't understand.

"I just want to talk."

"Leave me. I'll call security."

"Doc, take a gander. Do I look dangerous?"

"N-No. You look... healthy."

"Thank you. Those hours in the gym paid off."

"*Ja*. Very much so." He rose. "But I must call the guard."

She grabbed his hand. "Please don't. I need information."

"I can't tell you anything. You could be working with foreign powers."

"I'm not. I'm working for myself."

"Then you should find other work. Go home. Talk to your parents. Let them—"

"I don't have any parents," Leilani said, with more intensity than she intended. The words flowed out like an uncapped geyser. "They died in a car accident. We were all three in the car when it careened into a semi. They were critically injured, bleeding to death. I wasn't hurt much, but I was pinned down in the back seat. I couldn't do anything. I watched—" She turned her head away, fighting back her emotions. She had not intended the interview to go this way. "I watched them bleed to death, in great pain, calling out to me. Both my mother's legs were broken. My father was gasping, coughing up blood, spitting his life away. But I couldn't help."

She wiped her eyes and continued. "After that, my life was a mess. Never fit in. I was the orphan kid with serious issues. In school, no one wanted anything to do with me. Eventually I became a paramedic. Trained for EMT service. So next time someone I loved was in danger, I'd be able to do something about it."

Her voice cracked. "But I can't. Even after I moved to Hawaii, I never felt connected to anyplace, anyone. Until I met Dylan. And now the man I love more than anything in the world has been taken, kidnapped, tortured, forced to do things against his will. But this time, I'm not pinned down. I'm going to help him."

Two pairs of sorrowful eyes met. "Dr. Scheimer, if you've ever lost someone you loved with all your heart—please listen to me."

He hesitated.

"You have. I can tell. I can see it etched into every line of your face."

He said nothing.

"My boyfriend has been taken by some cruel, evil people. I know you don't know anything about that. But you're involved, just the same. It has something to do with the project you've been working on. You're my only lead."

Scheimer's face tightened. "You must leave."

"I'm not asking you to reveal state secrets. I'm just looking for information. Anything that might help me find Dylan."

"Why do you think his disappearance relates to my project?"

"The same people who took Dylan also blew up the Cartwright Institute—where your colleague Dr. Karelis worked."

Scheimer said nothing.

"When I started asking about Karelis, I was apprehended by US Navy operatives. Like it or not, doctor, you seem to be in the eye of the hurricane."

Scheimer nodded slowly, a lost expression on his face.

Time to bring in the mood enhancers. "Doctor, you need a pick-me-up."

He glanced at his whiskey bottle.

"No. I have just the stuff. I understand you're a fan of egg-salad sandwiches."

"German egg salad. My mother used to make it."

She lifted the lid off a platter. "*Voila*! Here they are."

He leaned forward, sniffing. "With celery. And bits of bratwurst?"

"Is there another way to make it?"

Scheimer nibbled on one of the wedges. Already he seemed more animated. Perhaps the cliché was true—the way to a man's heart was through his stomach.

Time for the pièce de résistance. "And for dessert"—Leilani removed another lid from a bowl—"ice cream. Vanilla ice cream."

Scheimer's lips parted. He looked like a little boy getting a treat for the first time in ages. "How did you know?"

"A girl's got to have some secrets." Especially when the answer is so simple it would spoil the mystery. When Seamus searched Scheimer's office, he saw what the man had ordered for lunch and from where. He called the deli and asked about Scheimer's favorite sandwiches. And as for liking vanilla ice cream—well, who doesn't? Seamus said its near-universal appeal is because there's vanilla in breast milk. We learn to love it at an early age.

Scheimer finished his meal, eating every bite of the sandwich, then the ice cream, and washing it down with the sour mash. She didn't want

him to become sick or intoxicated. But if the meal loosened his tongue
—so much the better.

He wiped his mouth with a napkin. "Thank you. That was deli-
cious. May I know your name?"

"Leilani. Leilani Kahale."

"Leilani, you have done me a great service. But I still must ask you
to go."

She reached out and clenched his hand. "Doctor, I told you my
name. Now I want you to tell me the name of the woman you once
loved."

He hesitated. "Liesel."

"If you could do anything—anything at all, to bring her back,
would you do it?"

"Of course I would."

She squeezed tighter. "Then you know how I feel. You're the only
person who can help me find my Dylan."

He fell back against the sofa. His eyes seemed to drift to another
place, perhaps another world. "Have you ever heard of Nikola Tesla?"

She scanned her short-term memory. "Didn't he have an obsession
with the number three?"

"Yes. But he was also one of the greatest scientists in the history of
the world. Perhaps the greatest."

"Like Einstein?"

"Far greater. I have always felt Einstein's work is overrated. People
think he invented the atomic bomb. He didn't. Yes, he devised the critical formula, $E = mc^2$, which was invaluable to the nuclear scientists, but
he played no role in the development of the bomb itself. He is best
known for his theory of relativity, which was proposed by Boskovic long
before Einstein. And he is known for the unified field theory, which he
never discovered. Because it probably does not exist."

"Okay. Tell me about Tesla."

"Tesla had the fortitude and intelligence to transform himself from
a poor boy in a large family in a small town in the backwater of the
Austrian Empire into the most famous scientist in the world. He had a
photographic memory, which allowed him to grasp complex physics at
an astonishing rate. He came to America and worked for Edison, but

after his task was completed, Edison refused to pay what he had promised. Tesla went out on his own. Unfortunately, although he was a brilliant scientist, he was no businessman."

"What did Tesla accomplish?"

"Many things. Wondrous things. His work in electromagnetism is why we have electricity in our homes today. He developed the modern standards for AC power, fighting Edison and others who believed DC was the only path. He also performed pioneering work in computer science, radar, x-rays, robotics, ballistics, and nuclear physics. According to your Supreme Court, he's the true inventor of the radio."

"I appreciate the biography, doctor, but what does this have to do with your work?"

He continued as if he had not heard her. "Eventually, Tesla's battles with Edison and others caused him to travel to Colorado. According to official accounts, he was working on the long-range transmission of power. Several years of his work are unaccounted for. Toward the end of his life, he announced that he was working on a weapon. He called it a peace ray, but of course, others called it a death ray. Without providing many details, he said he'd conceived of a 'teleforce' weapon, a directed energy beam of startling precision utilizing charged particle streams. He was unable to get any nation to sponsor his work. By that time, his eccentricities, his obsessive-compulsive disorders, so little understood in that day, caused most people to believe him insane."

Scheimer turned toward Leilani, his face asking if she could be trusted with a secret. "He was not crazy. He was a genius. His recently discovered notes have provided the basis for a weapon of unprecedented power utilizing a fantastic quirk of nature still unknown to the world at large. And the person who controls it, controls the world."

CHAPTER
SIXTY-TWO

DYLAN STARED at the many puzzle pieces arranged on his desktop. He had written each major section of the plan on a piece of a tangram, the Chinese puzzle with seven different components that can be arranged to form many shapes. Visualizing the way they might fit together helped him think through the variables of his plan.

The tangram analogy worked well because, although the pieces would eventually fit together, they would never wholly interlock like a jigsaw puzzle. For a scheme like the one he was concocting, the parts that had to be kept separate were just as important as the parts that had to work together.

One piece represented the front guard station, another the vault, another the perimeter guards, another the sonic alarm system, another the heat sensor, another the motion detectors...

There were about a million-and-five steps between Dylan and the Key. He took his fountain pen out of his pocket—the one Dobie had given him, the only personal belonging he'd been allowed to keep—and made some notes. He told them he couldn't do any creative work without his pen. Told them he'd never had a good idea he didn't write down with that Volta. Mr. X made some remark about "eccentric artists." She'd taken it apart, and when she was satisfied it was just a fountain pen, she let him keep it.

He no longer needed to read Felix's research reports, to view the PACOM schematics, or to consult the personnel files. Dylan knew them all as well as he knew his own name.

The hardest part was preparing for the unknown. This op would be a thousand times more difficult than the university mission. These weren't college geeks and rent-a-cops. They were trained military professionals instructed to accept no deviations from protocol, to be suspicious of strangers, and to contact their superiors at the slightest sign of trouble. Security would probably be tighter than ever in the wake of—

He took a deep breath, then let the air slowly stream between his lips.

In the wake of the recent disappearance of one of their senior officers, Robert Taggart, PACOM would likely implement heightened security measures. He could deal with that. The sonics expert had done his job. All they needed now was the proper frequency. Xavier's observation of the admiral had given him some thoughts on reducing the PACOM night shift.

Pieces were falling into place. They would be ready to proceed on schedule...

Radiation. That was the last tangram piece. They would need something to protect against neutrino radiation...

He stared deeply into a mirror. Yes, it's a good plan. Especially the part he hadn't revealed.

It had to work. It had to. Because there was one thing he knew with absolute certainty.

When they were done with him, they would kill him.

CHAPTER
SIXTY-THREE

"A QUIRK OF NATURE?" Leilani asked Scheimer. "What do you mean? How can you keep a quirk of nature secret?"

"The miracle is that this was ever discovered at all," Scheimer explained. "Because it's deep underground, on the Big Island. In Tesla's day, there was little activity there, mostly agricultural, no science. Grover Cleveland found the islands so unappealing he refused to support bids for annexation. But when his successor, William McKinley, came to office, he had a different attitude. His pro-annexation stance is typically attributed to economic interests who wanted to expand Hawaiian trade opportunities, and the islands' strategic location in the mid-Pacific." Scheimer paused, pursing his lips. "The true story is far more interesting."

Leilani's brow wrinkled. Could this be true? He was a good deal brainier than she. If he believed it, how could she doubt it?

"In the last years of the nineteenth century, a team of surveyors were mapping the islands and, secondarily, determining which volcanoes were still active. While spelunking in the caves at the base of a particular volcano, they discovered something they could not explain."

"The quirk of nature?"

He nodded. "Do you know anything about quantum anomalies?"

"Definitely not."

"Classical theory supposes that the laws of physics will be the same anywhere you go. What we have discovered in the last few decades, however, is that this theory is not always borne out by reality. There are anomalies. Instances in which what we expect to happen does not."

"Like what?"

"The gravitational anomaly, for one. It's a gauge anomaly that invalidates the general covariance of the laws of general relativity."

A deep line furrowed Leilani's forehead. "Any chance you could put that in simpler terms?"

"Gravity goes crazy sometimes."

"That's better."

"Electrical and magnetic anomalies have also been discovered. The surveyors beneath that volcano found that the pull of gravity was greatly reduced. Light objects would float, as if buoyed up by currents of air. Electromagnetism was similarly affected. Compasses spun erratically. Generators pulsed with extraordinary energy, far beyond what would normally be expected."

"What would cause that?"

"They had no way of knowing. Only in recent years have we come to understand that our universe—with its laws of physics—is not the only universe. And our laws of physics are not the only possible laws of physics."

"This sounds like something out of science fiction."

"Now it is science fact. The currently prevailing cosmological theory proposes that our universe was spawned from a microscopic region of a primordial vacuum in a sudden burst of exponential expansion. That same vacuum could continually birth many other universes, and each would have its own unique physics."

"Are you saying that...when those surveyors descended into the cave..."

"They actually passed into a space shared with another universe. We believe that universes can be described as three-dimensional membranes —branes for short. They can touch one another. Or even collide. Overlap."

"Then those surveyors found some sort of...gateway?"

"A rip in the fabric of our spacetime."

"That's bizarre."

"What's bizarre is that at the time this was discovered, no one thought it of any particular value. Some thought it might be a potential tourist attraction, assuming they could persuade people to lower themselves into a cavernous pocket beneath the base of a volcano. The Hawaiian Provisional Government contacted Tesla for advice—and he saw much more than a tourist trap. He saw an opportunity to achieve the impossible. He contacted President McKinley and told him to annex the islands immediately."

"Why?"

"Tesla recognized the possible uses of a place where the laws of physics were different. Many years after annexation, the existence of a new particle, now called the neutrino, was postulated, and Tesla had what he needed to lay the theoretical groundwork for his peace ray. His ultimate weapon."

A shiver ran down her spine. He was scaring her, and she only barely understood what he was saying. "Aren't neutrinos—harmless?"

"Neutrinos are neutral elementary particles produced by radioactive decay and nuclear reactions, such as those that occur constantly in our sun. For example, when a proton decays into a neutron, two extra particles are produced: a neutrino and a positron, the antiparticle of the electron."

"Are you talking about antimatter? I've heard of that."

"Antimatter is involved, but the process is much more complicated than an ordinary nuclear transmutation. The neutrino I described is the electron neutrino, but they come in two other flavors: the muon and the tau. Once an electron neutrino is produced it travels at near the speed of light and continually oscillates from one flavor to another, passing harmlessly through any matter it encounters."

"Doesn't sound like much of a weapon."

"What happens in that underground cave makes it a weapon. Normally, there is no way to control neutrino oscillation. But in that cave it can be done. It *is* done. We know that neutrinos can create wormholes and pass through them. This phenomenon must've opened the gateway to a unique place where normal neutrinos become brane-to-brane-traveling sterile neutrinos. There, we can send a composite neutrino beam out of our brane to reemerge at a chosen target anywhere else in our universe as a stream of antiparticles which destroy all forms of matter on contact. An undetectable, unstoppable weapon."

"How do the antiparticles know where to go?"

"For that, I had to develop what the Navy calls the Kronos Key. The coordinates entered into the Key and the phase of the oscillation uniquely determine where the stream of antiparticles emerges. The set of equations I developed and encrypted into the Key make targeting possible. With pinpoint precision."

"But we have other powerful weapons."

"This one is unique, and not only in its potential destructive force. You don't need enriched uranium or plutonium or any other rare elements. You don't need a ballistic missile to deliver the payload. All you need are some talented engineers and a particle accelerator to create and launch the beam. There is no explosion. Your target simply —disappears."

"That's what you've been working on? You and Karelis?"

"And we have been all too successful. The Key takes the coordinates and, using an orbiting tracking satellite, locates the target, calculates its position, and directs the beam. The first test succeeded beyond our wildest imaginings—or worst fears. This is no blunt instrument, no weapon of mass destruction. This is an untraceable weapon with an unprecedented degree of accuracy. Karelis and I hoped that by tapping the power of the neutrino, we could solve the world's energy problems. What we did instead was create the greatest tool for assassination ever known, one that can pinpoint a group or individual on the other side of the globe and convert their matter into energy. Which destroys them instantly."

Leilani didn't know what to say. No words in her vocabulary came close to encompassing her feelings. Her fear. The people who took Dylan wanted this hideous weapon.

"There's more," Scheimer continued. "We may have called into question the flow of time as we know it."

"*What?*"

"We should have anticipated it. Einstein proved that time was not an immutable constant. During the test, the beam destroyed the target—ten seconds before it was released."

"How is that possible?"

"Because two branes overlapped, each curved and possibly deformed by quantum fluctuations. We can't control when, in our time, the beam emerges because it passes through other dimensions on its way to the target. I would not go so far as to call it time travel. I would simply say the beam takes an extremely unusual shortcut enroute to its destination."

Leilani could hardly believe what she was hearing. "I can see why the Navy shut this project down."

"Pending further investigation. But the apparatus is still in place. The weapon exists, as does the Key. They can be put back into operation at any time. And they will. I know they will."

"Why do they call it the Kronos Key?"

"Kronos was the father of the gods—the father of Zeus, the lightning king. We are tapping into the power of the gods, the very processes that created this universe, and it would seem, many other universes as well."

"It's Tesla's death ray."

Scheimer's eye drifted to the floor. "'Now I am become death, the destroyer of worlds.'"

Leilani felt for him. America turned out not to be what Scheimer expected—the same feeling his hero, Tesla, must have experienced.

Scheimer reached into his pocket and withdrew a flash drive. "I want you to have this, Leilani. Open the ninth file. This is the only copy. It isn't even on my laptop. That file will tell you where to go. Destroy this vile project. Once and for all. Then perhaps your man's abductors will have no reason to hold him."

"I will. I promise."

"I had a dream recently." His eyes remained unfocused, far away. "I remembered a time long ago. When my Liesel was still alive. When my life was filled with love."

"It can be again."

He shook his head. "Now it is filled only with death. Death and failure."

"Doctor, we can fix this problem. Make sure no one uses this weapon again."

"I have sinned." He staggered toward the door. "And now, I will make sure no one ever suffers as you have because of my actions."

Before she understood what was happening, he'd pulled a gun from his jacket.

"Doctor, *don't*."

He ignored her.

"Help!"

She heard an audible commotion outside. Barely a second later, the door burst open and the two guards rushed inside.

Scheimer inserted the gun into his mouth

"Doctor!" Leilani screamed. She rushed toward him. "Please—!"

The report of the gun sent Leilani reeling. Blood and brains splattered her face.

CHAPTER
SIXTY-FOUR

DYLAN KNEW he should be in bed. The planning was over. Tomorrow they would execute the operation. This was his time to rest, perhaps the last chance he would get for some while.

So why wasn't he sleeping?

He sat at his desk, reviewing his notes for the thousandth time. Had he really prepared for everything? Had he anticipated every possible contingency? Did he know his characters inside and out?

He opened his laptop and browsed through the files. He was not going to review his plan. He'd done that more times than he could stand. He could review some of the foundational documents, though. The PACOM schematics...well, truth to tell, he'd memorized those, hadn't he? The various key personnel...yeah, he had them down, too...

He remembered his father discussing the importance of knowing the people you worked with. It wasn't just about making a good impression. It was about being the best at your job you can possibly be. If people liked you, they would give you their best work. He bragged that he knew the names of every man who worked under him all the way down to the lieutenants, and their wives' names, and their children's names, and enough about them to make effective small talk for at least a full minute, should the opportunity arise.

Perhaps Dylan was not the first member of his family to grasp the importance of knowing the characters.

His dad was full of ideas about how to get ahead. Full of ideas about how Dylan could obtain success if he were tougher, like his old man. Full of ideas about how he could make the world safe with bigger and better sticks.

And what was Dylan doing now? He had to admit, there was a certain irony...

He clicked on some of the photos in the file—parties, gala receptions, outings to the admiral's barge. That barge was actually a plush yacht, but apparently that sounded a little too hifalutin' for a military man, so they went with "barge." Its unique black hull had been a familiar sight in Pearl Harbor for more than fifty years. Every president since Eisenhower had ridden on it, as well as many distinguished heads of state. It was a favorite place for formal receptions with noteworthy visitors who wanted to see the USS Arizona Memorial or Battleship Row, particularly spectacular at night.

Dylan wished he'd looked at these earlier, even if they were irrelevant to his mission. Almost made him wish he'd fulfilled Daddy's dream and gone into the Navy. He would've hated the work, but he might've enjoyed the field trips...

Something in a photo grabbed his attention.

Not something—someone.

Someone just barely visible in the background, three rows behind the admiral.

Did this change anything? Or did it explain everything?

SEAMUS HATED interviewing wives whose husbands had gone missing. He'd done it far too many times in his career. It put him in an impossible position. He had to give them hope that their husbands might turn up. At the same time, he knew the chances of finding a husband gone this long were slight. If he was alive, he'd intentionally deserted his family. If he'd been kidnapped, he was almost certainly dead. Which outcome was worse?

Padma Bakersfield was a beautiful woman, which immediately made Seamus wonder what she was doing with that lumpy makeup artist. He must've had a great sense of humor. Or perhaps he just knew how to treat a woman.

Padma's hair was black as night and her eyes were almost as dark. He knew she'd been crying, but it didn't show in her eyes, only in the irritation around them. She had high cheekbones and full lips. He believed she was probably Indian, but he wasn't going to ask.

"You have no idea what happened to your husband?"

"None at all." She was poised, even in her sorrow. "Everyone liked Lenny. I can't imagine anyone wanting to hurt him."

"It's possible he just...left. Thought disappearing would be easier than divorce."

Her chin rose slightly. "Not my Lenny."

"You said the note he left was strange."

"It was an email. Said he was ill. Quarantined. Would be gone for a few days. Would call soon."

"That doesn't sound so strange."

"It does if you know Lenny. He would not have sent a message like that by email. He knows how much I care about him. He would have told me in person, and if that were not possible, he would have called me. Besides—I know he came home. I heard him. He told me not to come downstairs. If he could come home, why could he not talk to me?"

"Did he behave oddly before he disappeared?"

"Not at all."

"Any financial problems? Unpaid debts?"

"Far from it. Lenny's film work is extremely lucrative."

"And when you woke the next morning, he was gone without a trace."

"There were traces. I found blood in the carpet."

Seamus nodded. He'd read that in the police report. "But not much, right? And you have an accident-prone child?"

"True. She sleepwalks. She hurt herself several times before we put a gate at the top of the stairs."

"So she can't come down on her own."

"She can if she opens the gate. Which she could never manage when she's asleep."

"Were you and your husband having any problems?"

"We love each other deeply."

"Yes, but that wasn't the question. Marriage is tough. Sometimes love isn't enough."

"It was for us. We were extremely happy."

"You never fought?"

She tilted her head to one side. "Rarely."

"And when you fought, did he get mad?"

Again the tilt. "Rarely."

"Maybe he was drinking."

"I don't believe that," she replied, and in fact, neither did Seamus. This did not sound like the case of a middle-age man who decided he couldn't stand family life any longer. He did have the sense that Padma was holding something back, though.

"No one wants to believe that their husband is unfaithful."

"My Lenny was never unfaithful."

"Much less that he might get tired of you. Want to move on."

"And do what? Apply makeup under a pseudonym?"

"The facts are tough, but they're all there. He got pissed off about something, decided he'd had enough, and hightailed it. You'll never see him again. Because he doesn't want to see you."

"You don't know what you're talking about!"

"All the evidence indicates—"

"How do you explain the Polaroids!"

"Polaroids?" Seamus settled back into his chair. He hated being a bastard. But sometimes it was the only way to get information.

"I found them on the coffee table, the morning after Lenny disappeared. Five photos of me. I didn't tell the police." She twisted her hands awkwardly in her lap. "I didn't want those men...well. These photos are personal. And I know anything you give the police can end up in the newspapers."

She was right about that. "What was in the photos?"

She reached into the end table beside her sofa, took out a copy of *Leaves of Grass*, and withdrew an envelope. She passed it to him. "Me.

Over and over again. Me shopping for groceries. Me at the gym. Me brushing my hair at night. Even me getting undressed."

Seamus glanced at them. She was almost entirely naked in the last and clearly oblivious that she was being photographed. "Did your husband take these?"

"I assume so. I mean, who else could?"

Seamus, unfortunately, had several possible answers to that question. "Did you ever see Lenny taking these?"

"No," she said, swallowing. "I can't imagine why he would want to take them."

Neither could Seamus, but he could imagine why someone else might. Lenny Bakersfield was being blackmailed, coerced. Just as Dylan Taggart had been. Once again, they were using their target's loved ones to get what they wanted.

These two disappearances were connected. Seamus was certain of it. But what was the point? Why would they need a writer, much less a makeup artist? "Ma'am, is there anything else you can tell me about your husband's disappearance?"

"No, I'm sorry, but—"

A high-pitched voice emerged from upstairs. "Tell him 'bout the big man. The monster." Seamus could see two tiny feet poking out at the top of the stairs.

Padma sighed. "That is our daughter. Emily. She is four and she has a very active imagination."

"Tell him about the monster with the gun, Mommy."

"Emily, please—"

"I'd like to hear about the monster with the gun." Seamus rose to his feet. "Emily, would you tell me about him?"

The tiny girl tiptoed down two steps. Her voice grew even smaller. "He was scary."

Padma stood, trying to intervene. "She's a delicate child. She lives in a fantasy world. I told you she sleepwalks."

"Was she sleepwalking the night before your husband disappeared?"

"I...believe so. I heard her downstairs. That was when Lenny spoke to me. He said he would put her to bed."

"Didn't you tell me that when she sleepwalks, she can't open the gate?"

Padma's lips parted, but she had no answer.

"And she was back in bed the next morning? I'd like to talk to your daughter." Seamus didn't wait for permission. He walked to the foot of the stairs and crouched down to the girl's level. "Emily, why do you call the man a monster?"

"He was big. Bigger than anyone I've ever seen."

"Yellow hair. Cut really short?"

"Yes." Seamus could see she was excited. This was the first time anyone believed what she had to say.

"Thick muscles all over. Mole right here?" He pointed to the side of his neck.

"Yes."

"Did he talk funny? Like he was from another country?"

"Yes!"

Xavier. "Did you say he had a gun?"

"He pointed it at me. But my daddy got in front of the gun. He wouldn't let the bad man hurt me. Not even after he hit Daddy."

Thus producing the blood. Any father would gladly take a bullet to protect his daughter. Seamus talked to the girl for a few more minutes, confirming his conviction that Xavier was involved. But he still couldn't figure out the motive.

And there was an even bigger mystery. If this girl saw Xavier, how could he possibly let her live?

Seamus pivoted, looking even more carefully at Padma. She was Indian, but at first glance, she could pass for Middle Eastern.

She resembled Xavier's wife. The one who was killed in an air strike. The air strike Seamus called in. Xavier's daughter was killed, too.

She was just about Emily's age.

That's why the monster let her live.

"Thank you for your assistance," Seamus said, heading for the door. "I promise I'll let you know if I learn anything about your husband."

He raced out of the house. He'd come here hoping for some clue to Dylan's location or the motive behind the kidnapping. He'd found neither. But he had found something of incalculable value.

He'd discovered his enemy's weakness.

CHAPTER
SIXTY-FIVE

DYLAN FOUND Mr. X in the kitchen making a sandwich. She faced away from the door, gazing out the window. Dylan walked directly behind her. When he was about ten feet away, he heard:

"Hello, Dylan. Shouldn't you be deep in the arms of Morpheus?"

He stopped in his tracks. "You lied to me."

She did not seem particularly perturbed by the accusation. "Can you be more specific? There are so many lies to choose from."

She swiveled around to face him. Her face was bruised. How did that happen? She was using makeup to cover the mark, but he could still see traces. "How did you hurt yourself?"

She shrugged. "It's nothing. Walked into a door."

She was lying, but not because the injury caused her any trauma. Come to think of it, she hadn't minded the scars, either. Did she like being hurt? "You admit you lied?"

"Did you think I was one of those honest terrorists?"

"I'm not sure what you are. I just saw a picture of Xavier. At a reception on the admiral's barge."

"He was doing reconnaissance. Working undercover."

"He was wearing a uniform."

"He was in the Navy."

"But—you told me he was in the Russian mafia. And the KGB."

"And many other places as well. The Navy came after he...retired from those positions. He was recruited."

"I don't believe anyone would recruit Xavier into the US Navy."

"Someone did. A high-ranking official."

"I thought you were terrorists."

"We are. But terrorists who work for the US military."

Dylan stared at her, blank-faced.

"Does that surprise you? Are you stunned? Feel free to sit if your knees are wobbly."

He didn't sit. "Who's in charge?"

"I can't give you names. We work for a relatively small, relatively secret cabal of current and former military officers who are trying to accomplish something they can't get done through official channels. Haven't you ever wondered how we were able to get access to so much government information? Personnel files. Schematics. How we were able to locate ourselves at an abandoned Navy facility. I would have thought it was obvious."

"You're saying this operation was organized by US military personnel?"

"Yes."

"Who want to assassinate world leaders."

She raised a finger. "I may have misled you about our ultimate goal."

"Then what's the big plan?"

She took another swallow of coffee. "Look, just to forestall the usual cat-and-mouse games, let me give you a hint. And this is as much as I'm ever going to tell you. What the people running this operation want is simple. They want the United States to be the strongest nation in the world—at a time when it is dangerously close to losing its global influence forever. They want the US to be strong enough to fight off the barbarians at the gate—meaning, currently, terrorists, insane dictators, Russia, and China. But at present, we are militarily weak, overextended, and financially challenged. So this organization is taking actions to remedy the government's failures."

"What are you babbling about? The US is the strongest nation in the world."

"Was. The US has enemies all around the globe—far too many, with access to major weapons and almost infinite manpower. China's population alone makes it a major threat, not to mention its economy and the fact that it holds the notes on about half our national debt. North Korea is led by a madman who would love to attack the US. Pakistan is run by sociopathic generals. Most of the Middle East cannot be trusted."

"We've been dealing with the Middle East for a long time."

"Ineffectively. They grow stronger while the US grows weaker. Have you studied the Crusades?"

"Not...recently..."

"Read up on the Battle of Neapolis. Fourteenth century. The East crushed the West and brought the long and bloody Crusades to an end. Today, the East is stronger, richer, more extreme, better armed, bent on the destruction of the West and making sharia law a global mandate. Neapolis could happen all over again. We can't sit around and hope everything works out for the best. We have to take aggressive action. We must eliminate these enemies, fast and efficiently. Strike with surgical precision."

"Very patriotic, coming from an Irish girl."

"I've been persuaded that the downfall of the US would not be in the best interests of the world. Much as I might enjoy it."

I would give a great deal, he thought, to know who was doing the persuading. "Shouldn't these alleged employers of yours be lobbying Congress? Writing letters to the president?"

"You're joking, right? Congress? Let's face it—the Afghan and Iraq wars have turned them into pussies. Your government is dangerously cowardly. Look how they helped Ukraine. Gave them everything except what they needed most."

"You told me your target was the G20 summit."

"That was a fairy tale."

"Meaning, a lie?"

"Did you believe it? No, you didn't. You knew there was more and you were right. Our target is indeed on American soil but a place that, although high profile, will not be much missed, and not all that many lives will be lost, relatively speaking. Maybe twice 9/11, tops. Don't you see the beauty of it? If we make a first strike against the United States

with an untraceable weapon, it will spur the world into action. Haven't
you visited Pearl Harbor? Have you forgotten that the US was officially
neutral until the Japanese bombed us? That gave Roosevelt the excuse
he needed to enter the war—and he targeted Hitler first, even though
Hitler had nothing to do with Pearl Harbor. Well, we're going to create
the next Pearl Harbor. To spur the government into doing what it must
to save this nation."

"And you honestly believe this will work?"

"What I want or believe is unimportant. I'm a professional. I do my
job. I leave the big questions to the Supervisor."

"I think there's something you're not telling me."

"You're right. Actually, I made that whole story up."

"Now you're lying again."

"Are you sure?"

Dylan hesitated. "Who's the Supervisor?"

"I can't tell you that."

"Can't, or won't?"

"Both."

"Is it someone I know?"

"You're baiting me. Trying to get me to tell you more than I
should."

"You said you were a freelance terrorist. That you're just in it for the
money. But I think you may have more motivation than you're letting
on."

"How romantic. Am I driven by revenge? Lust? Or am I simply
psychotic?" She laughed. "Why is it so hard for you to believe I'm
working for a living? Everyone else does. In your novels, you may prefer
to have complex, multi-dimensional characters, but in real life, sometimes people are painfully simple."

"If you're only doing it for money, you're not a terrorist. You're a
whore."

Her eyes flared. "I am not—" She bit back the rest of the sentence.
"Oh, well played, Dylan. Well played. It almost worked."

"I don't know what you're talking about."

"I'll tell you this much. I am deeply motivated to see this plan
succeed."

"Because you want to please the Supervisor."

"Don't most people want to please their superior officer?"

"Do you think that will make the scars go away?"

"You already took care of that."

"I'm talking about what turned you into the person you are now. What caused the deep insecurity that lies in the hearts of all bullies. What made you feel unloved. What caused the real scars—the ones plastic surgery can't take away."

"Please spare me your amateur psychoanalysis. I told you about the man. The one I followed into the IRA. The one I instructed in explosives. Was that not good enough for you?"

"It was too good. Too perfect. Like a bit of backstory I might invent for a minor character."

"All right then, Sigmund. What's really driving me?"

His only reply was a thin smile.

"I'm going to miss you, Dylan."

"When you're done with me? After you've gotten everything you want? Because once you have the Key, you're going to kill me."

"That's not for me to decide."

"What happened to Bakersfield, the makeup guy? And the plastic surgeon?"

"They won't cause any trouble. They'll be glad to be rid of us."

"They knew too much. So you killed them. Just as you plan to kill me. Just as you'll kill us all, eventually. Right?"

"The only remaining question is, are you ready and able to go forward with the operation tomorrow?"

"Of course I am. I wouldn't come this far without seeing it through. And I expect everything to go...exactly as planned."

CHAPTER
SIXTY-SIX

SEAMUS STOOD WELL outside the bathroom door, but not so far away that Leilani couldn't hear him. He marveled at how quickly his relationship with his new accidental partner had progressed. When he first approached her at the hospital, she barely trusted him enough to speak. Now she was speaking while she showered.

"I still don't understand why you're showering. Dr. Jerrie is waiting for us."

"If you'd been in military custody for two days, interrogated around the clock, you'd understand."

"I got you out as soon as I could."

He heard the water shut off. "It wasn't soon enough."

"You have to understand their position. This is the second time you've appeared to interfere with a top-secret operation. And this time, their leading scientist is dead. You can see where they might be suspicious."

"I had nothing to do with it. He killed himself before I could stop him."

"I get that. And so do they, now. But they had to be sure you weren't sabotaging their project." He paused. "And they had to be sure he didn't tell you anything important."

She stomped out of the bathroom, steaming in more ways than one, a towel wrapped around her midsection. "I didn't give anything up. Not in two long days. Told them nothing."

That was true. This wasn't the first time Seamus thought she'd make a first-rate intelligence officer. "I convinced them you're my new junior officer working undercover on NCTC business. If I didn't have a high security rating, you'd still be in their interrogation room."

"And they still wouldn't get anything."

"They'd be waterboarding you by now."

She crossed into the bedroom. "Let them. I like water. Have you had a chance to look over those files Scheimer gave me?"

"Yes, and they're fantastic. Complete schematics for the control center. Including a back door entrance that might be useful. Only one problem—nothing in the file tells us exactly where it is."

"But you're going to find it."

"Damn straight. Get dressed. We have an appointment with the doctor."

SEAMUS LISTENED as Leilani spent half an hour detailing everything she learned from Dr. Scheimer before he terminated himself. Dr. Jerrie took copious notes but never said a word. He was a bald man, snowy gray on the sides, with a down-to-earth manner.

Jerrie was not a physicist. The NCTC didn't have enough need to bankroll that degree of specialization. He was a generalist, an all-purpose smart person, which was usually more than enough. Most of the NCTC's science questions related to the construction or dismantling of explosive devices.

"Does any of that make sense to you?" Leilani asked after she finished.

"Sadly, yes." Jerrie batted a pencil against his lips. "Neutrino weapons have been hypothesized for some time. But this underground anomaly has apparently allowed the hypotheses to become realities. Ever heard of a super-collider?"

"Scheimer talked about a particle accelerator."

"That's essentially what a super-collider is, only on a huge scale."

Seamus jumped in. "They were going to build one in Texas, weren't they?"

"Back in the '90s. Someone saw the value in having one in the US, rather than letting Europe have a monopoly. They spent a ton of money on it. But before they could finish, Congress yanked the funds. They were getting flak from the press about the cost, and they couldn't justify it as promoting the national defense, so they killed it. Clinton tried to salvage the program, even though it was a Reagan/Bush initiative. No success. The Congressional tide had turned."

"So it was never completed?"

Jerrie pursed his lips. "Some people high up realized this was too important to be left to the whims of Congress. They initiated a project, quietly funded by the military, to develop a super-collider for military purposes."

"At PACOM?"

He shook his head. "Given what I just heard, I think it must be on the Big Island. Underneath a volcano."

Seamus frowned. "That would cost billions."

"And then some. But theoretically, the super-collider would be big and fast enough to generate a Higgs boson."

"Excuse me?"

"Higgs boson," he repeated, tapping his pencil on his desk. "Elementary particle. Some people call it the 'God Particle.' Supposedly around since the Big Bang. If it's proven to exist, it would solve many of the major mysteries of physics."

"Like what?"

"It explains the difference in mass between the photon, which mediates electromagnetism, and the W and Z bosons, which mediate the weak force. If the Higgs boson exists, it would be pervasive throughout all of matter, throughout the known universe. It sounds as if Scheimer figured out a way to use the collider to generate not only bosons...but neutrino beams."

"Then it's true? You think this monstrosity beneath a volcano generates some kind of death ray?"

"I believe the late Dr. Scheimer was about eighteen times smarter than me, so if he believed it, I believe it. A controlled oscillation neutrino beam, and its potential use as a weapon, is far less theoretical than the Higgs boson. People have known about the neutrino's potential destructive power for a long time. They just weren't able to create an artificial environment conducive to oscillation."

"And now they can."

"Sounds like they don't have to. This naturally occurring anomaly is doing the work for them." He paused. "Seamus, you need to get on this immediately."

"I believe I'm the one who's supposed to be giving Agent McKay his marching orders."

All three whirled around. Eustace stood at the door behind them.

Busted.

"Just for the record, last time I checked, I was still your handler, Seamus, not Bill Nye here. I told you to get off this project weeks ago."

"Eustace—" Dr. Jerrie started.

"Butt out, Jerrie. This isn't about geek science. This is about the chain of command. Seamus has been filing false reports to mask the fact that he's been insubordinate and derelict in his assigned duties."

"And a damn good thing, too," Jerrie replied.

Eustace looked as if he were about to jump out of his skin. "What the hell are you saying?"

Jerrie looked Eustace square in the eye. Seamus was impressed. For a geek, he had some real fiber in him. "I'm saying your agent did the right thing."

"We don't need him chasing after some writer just to please a pretty face."

Seamus was glad Leilani no longer had a cane. If she had, she might have clubbed Eustace with it.

"This is about far more than a missing writer," Jerrie explained. "This is about a terrorist plot to either interfere with or control an experimental weapon that could have power unlike anything this world has seen. The only person who has a clue about it is your agent."

"And me," Leilani said.

"And her," Jerrie added. "So the best thing you can do is get out of their way."

Ever the professional, Eustace suppressed his temper. But Seamus knew it was there, just the same. "When I start taking orders from some pencil-nosed nerd with a pocket protector, they can roll me up and file me under Dead."

"Let's just file you under Impotent. I'm the Senior Officer in my department. Where a state of emergency exists involving a scientific threat, I have seniority. I've declared a state of emergency. That means that, as concerns this matter, I outrank you."

Eustace fell silent. Which Seamus assumed meant what Jerrie had said was true.

When Eustace finally spoke, it was short and succinct. "I took Seamus off this case."

Jerrie looked at Seamus, not Eustace. "I'm putting you back on. And I'll go to Eustace's supervisor, if necessary, to explain why this case is more important than anything else the NCTC is working on. We're not going to dick around with the usual spy games while someone steals a weapon capable of reshaping the geopolitical map."

Seamus' eyebrows rose. Eustace pivoted on his heel and left the room.

"Don't screw this up, Seamus," Jerrie said. "I know Miss Kahale wants to retrieve her boyfriend. But the stakes are much higher."

"We should be able to find the base, given what we now know. How many volcanoes can there be on the Big Island?"

The expressions on the faces of everyone in the room provided his answer.

"Then I'd better get started. Thanks for your help." Seamus' cellphone beeped. He scanned the text.

"Brilliant timing. It's Kurasagi. He's tracked down Dylan's signal."

CHAPTER
SIXTY-SEVEN

MR. X LAID Dylan's outline on the conference table. She was smiling.

"I've got to hand it to you, Dylan. This is brilliant. Absolutely brilliant. Even better than before. The latest refinements are sublime."

Dylan attempted to be modest. "I don't think I'd go that far."

"I would. You've accessed your creative skills and employed them in this new context with amazing adaptive skill. It's genius. Don't you think it's genius, Xavier?"

Xavier shrugged. "Ish."

"Does that mean I get a raise?" Dylan asked.

"Yeah," Xavier said, "we double salary. Double nothing is nothing."

Everyone had thoroughly reviewed his plan and they seemed content. More importantly, they seemed to think it was possible. Not easy, by any stretch of the imagination. But possible.

"May I interrupt this lovefest?" Mikala asked. "I have some serious concerns about my role in this operation."

"Which part?" Dylan asked.

"All of it," she replied. "I don't need to be out in the field again. I can teach you how to do the encryption work."

"Possibly," Dylan responded. "But we have to be prepared for the unexpected. That's why I want you in there."

"As do I," Mr. X echoed.

"I have concerns, too," Tolga said, bouncing on the balls of his feet. "I don't think I can do this. I don't think anyone can do this. You're asking me to achieve the impossible."

"You should take that as a token of my esteem for your abilities," Dylan said.

"I wouldn't mind if you esteemed me a little less. That last mission hurt like hell. This one will be worse."

"You don't have to crawl through narrow spaces."

"I have to dance around thick-necked MPs with big guns."

"You'll be fine," Dylan assured him. "If there are any unanticipated problems, Xavier will be in our ear solving them."

"Which brings us to my objection," Felix said. "I belong inside the van, not outside. This plan requires me to actually remove my fingers from my laptop. I'm not liking that so much."

"No choice," Dylan said. "I need another person on the infiltration team. Xavier isn't an option—he might be recognized. And we may have computer issues. So the logical choice is you. Stop worrying, people. You're pros. We'll waltz through this."

"Why do I not think it will be that simple?" Mikala asked.

Xavier chuckled. "No one think it will be simple."

"Why do you need the GPS chips?" Mr. X asked.

"I'm going to plant one in the admiral's phone. It will help us locate his office later. It will have to be small, and I'll need to know the frequency."

"I don't understand why you need rubber-soled insulated shoes, either. Those are designed for hazardous electrical work."

"I'll be handling the Taser XREP2 pistol." This weapon, as they all knew, could emit a standard electrical charge on contact, or it could fire tiny electrified darts that induced unconsciousness for up to half an hour. "This baby can transmit over 100,000 volts—more than twice the maximum strength of anything you can buy on the legitimate market."

"Which brings us to my suggestion," Xavier said. "I think you should carry gun. Real gun."

"I don't need it."

"I think you do."

"I'll get by with the taser."

"MPs at PACOM will be packing guns."

"And I'm not likely to outshoot any of them." Dylan looked at him levelly. "I'll make this operation a success. But I'm not a murderer. I would never intentionally hurt anyone. And I certainly will not kill. Ever."

Xavier folded his arms and frowned.

"You'll have the tools provided by the medical specialists," Mr. X said. "And then there are other chemicals...?"

"To make a protective spray. We need to be shielded against neutrino radiation. We don't want to risk being contaminated."

"You didn't hear my objection to my role in this operation." This was Marco. Just hearing his voice made Dylan's skin crawl. "My objection is—I don't have a role."

"And you never will," Dylan said firmly. "Not in any operation of mine."

"Don't tell me you still got hard feelings about—"

"I do not have hard feelings," Dylan said, cutting him off. "I simply don't trust you."

"Does not matter, Marco," Xavier said. "You have big role in Phase Two. When I am in command."

"Does that mean I'm in Control of Phase One?" Dylan asked. "*Complete* control? You won't be hovering over my shoulder?"

"Let me explain what will happen if you deviate from plan." Grinning, the blond giant pulled the detonator out of his pocket.

"Don't do it," Dylan said, but he was already too late. Xavier pushed the red button.

Dylan braced himself—

Nothing happened.

"On timer," Xavier explained. "You have twelve hours to complete mission. If you do, good. I shut it off. If you don't—" He shrugged.

"If you don't," Mr. X explained, "the nanites will eat your brain. And this time, it will be a feeding frenzy. They won't stop until there's nothing left." She pulled him close. "We won't have to kill you, Dylan. Because if you haven't succeeded in twelve hours, there will be nothing left of you."

CHAPTER
SIXTY-EIGHT

DR. KURASAGI EXPLAINED his work to Seamus in layman's terms, which was a welcome change. He'd had enough science to make his head hurt for weeks. He didn't need to know the ins and outs of smart dust or how a single frequency can be isolated from tens of thousands of possibilities.

"...so I determined that the frequency was most likely in the high range of the spectrum, indicating—"

Seamus cut him off. "Where is he, Doctor?"

"Well, er, I was explaining—"

"I know, and I'm sure it would be fascinating if I understood it, but I don't. I just need to know where he is."

Kurasagi cleared his throat. "I was getting to that."

"So do it already!" Leilani yelled.

Kurasagi tugged on his lab coat. "As I was saying, I traced the signal from the blood sample you gave me to the Big Island."

"Can you narrow the location a little?"

"Not as much as I'd like. It's been weeks since he got his injection. The signal is growing faint."

"Can you give me anything?"

"Go north."

"How far north?"

"Top third of the island."

Seamus punched that into his iPhone map. "Thanks, Doc, you've been terrific. Come on, Leilani."

She raced out the door with him. "But where are we going? Which volcano?"

He grabbed his coat. "The one with the power to overthrow nations. Before someone does exactly that."

CHAPTER
SIXTY-NINE

4:02 p.m.
11 hours, 15 minutes left

DYLAN CHECKED the rear view mirror in the van. Mikala was behind them in her preposterously big SUV. It made no sense for a tiny person driving alone to have a car like that. But then, that was what he saw every time he went to the supermarket. Maybe people would assume she had children, although if so, she would've had to start when she was twelve. In any case, it would make the helpless-female routine go down easier.

He wasn't worried about it. When those big service-oriented Navy boys got a look at her in that skimpy outfit, they'd be fighting to help. He hoped.

He turned the van left and got in line in front of the PACOM guardpost.

"Ready?" he asked.

Felix sat in the passenger seat in beige coveralls, wringing his hands. He'd removed his facial jewelry and put makeup over his tattoos to give himself a more conservative appearance. Even shaved the soul patch. "Did I mention that I have no field experience whatsoever?"

"About thousand times or so." Xavier sat in another much larger vehicle about five hundred feet away, manning the computers and orchestrating communications.

"You'll do fine," Dylan said. "This should be easy. If we don't run into any trouble."

"That's a pretty damn big 'if.'"

"If it were easy, what fun would it be?" Dylan pulled up to the guardpost, smiling at the Navy MP on duty, and rolled down his window. "Delivery for the admiral. From Los Alamos. I'm Dr. DeWinter."

The guard checked his computer screen. "Yes, you're cleared."

Of course they were cleared. Felix hacked in earlier and added the pseudonym to the log. He couldn't hack into the main PACOM computer network. That was too well protected. But here in the guardpost they used a stand-alone laptop with an internet connection. Child's play.

"You can proceed to Terminal Five, sir. We'll take care of you there."

———

Once it was her turn to pull forward, Mikala reached under the dash and pushed the button that would release the pressure-packed box hidden under the hood. A moment later, white smoke streamed out. She braked several times spasmodically, simulating an engine problem, then slammed her brakes and turned off the SUV.

All right, she told herself, glancing at the mirror. Helpless and sexy, but frustrated. "Frustrated" was the word Dylan had used when he explained her character. "Angry" is off-putting, he warned, but "frustrated" makes guys want to run to the rescue.

She got out of the car and slammed the door behind her. "Not again!"

She popped open the hood, seemingly oblivious to the other cars or the MPs running down from the guardpost. There were two of them, which meant there would be only two left to search Dylan's van.

The driver from the car behind her and the two guards arrived at the same time. All three were Navy officers. She stared into the bowels of the engine, her face the picture of despair.

One of the guards stepped to the forefront. Despite his youth, he had a take-charge attitude that almost immediately made the other two fade to the background. "Yeoman Briggs, ma'am. What seems to be the problem?"

"I wish I knew. This stupid car has been a lemon since the day it rolled off the lot."

"Sorry to hear that, ma'am." The kid couldn't be more than twenty and he was being scrupulously correct, even standing a respectful distance from her, though his eyes were rather less respectful. "You might want to stand back. That white smoke probably means it's hot. When did you last put in oil?"

"Does this car need oil?"

The tiniest trace of a smile crept across Briggs' face. "Looks like you probably take 10W-40. There should be some in the garage. If you'll wait a moment, I'll get it. We'll let the car cool down, then add some oil and water and see if that helps."

"Well...sure. If you think that's the thing to do."

"I do." He turned to his partner. "Marshall, get some water from the kitchen. Then get the oil from Automotive."

"Will do."

Mikala drained a little "frustration" from her face and added some "eternally grateful." "Thank you. I do appreciate this. Perhaps you can let me show my gratitude in some way."

"That's not necessary, ma'am. We'll have to roll your car off to the side, though. Can't let you block traffic."

"Right." Except—that was the whole point. Dylan and Felix could distract two guards at the x-ray scanner. But four might be pushing it. And there was no way they could shield themselves from passing cars.

So she had to make sure there were no passing cars. At least not until Dylan was done.

CHAPTER
SEVENTY

4:12 p.m.
11 hours, 5 minutes left

DYLAN PULLED his van up to the x-ray device. It was, he knew, similar to the scanners at airports, except larger and more powerful, and built to accommodate sizeable objects.

"Sorry for the inconvenience, sir," the guard said. "But we'll have to scan any containers you plan to bring into the facility."

"No problem."

"That includes your…"

He could see the guard was trying to avoid the word "purse." "Messenger bag," Dylan supplied as he handed it over.

The guard scanned it, looked puzzled for a moment, glanced at Dylan, then looked away. No doubt wondering why a man with such short hair carried hair spray. Let him wonder. It didn't violate any security protocols.

"Anything else you're bringing in?"

"Yes. We've packed everything we'll need into this case. Bart, can you help me?"

Felix slid out a silvery steel case, like an attaché except much larger, about three feet long and a foot wide. They each took a handle and made it appear as if it were heavier than a dwarf star. They slowly lowered it onto the scanner.

Dylan and Felix waited patiently while the second MP inspected the insides of the case. "Is that...radioactive?"

"It is," Dylan answered, "and it's decaying." He watched the man's eyebrows rise. "But you won't die just because you drop it."

The guard nodded. He switched off the machine. "You can take your case now."

"Thanks." This time, unlike before, Dylan lifted it by himself. The strain was evident.

"Need some help with that?"

"No, I got it." He swung the case high into the air...almost all the way to the van...then collapsed.

"*Ahhh!*" Dylan dropped the case. It slammed to the pavement with a thud. He rolled forward, clutching his chest.

"Sir!" Both MPs rushed forward, crowding around him. "Is something wrong?"

"It's...my heart." He gasped for air. "Need...pills...bum ticker..." Did he really just say "bum ticker?" Too bad there was no chance to edit.

"Call the EMTs," the first guard said. The second activated the walkie-talkie on his shoulder.

"Feel like...I'm gonna explode..." That was better dialogue. Not much better, but a little.

"Hang on, sir. We've called for help."

"I—I—I—" Dylan grabbed a stiffened left arm. "I—feel faint."

"Sir, please do not attempt to move. Can you breathe? Is your respiration obstructed?"

"I—I—I—"

"Can you speak to me?"

"I...think I'm going to be okay." Dylan began to breathe more normally. "Maybe I should stand—"

"No," the guard said. "Don't exert yourself."

"I don't wanna be any trouble..."

"Please listen," the second guard said. They were both hovering over him, oblivious to anything going on behind them. "My father died of a heart attack. It's nothing to take lightly. Wait for the experts. They'll tell you if you're okay."

"I guess there's no hurry." Dylan closed his eyes and struggled to take another deep breath. "If you're sure. Don't want anyone to think I can't do the job. I need the work..."

"I understand. But let's be sure first."

"All right." He glanced beyond them. "You okay, Bart?"

"Geez, Sam, don't worry about me." In this scenario, Felix's nervousness seemed appropriate. "We're ahead of schedule. Just rest till the docs arrive."

Dylan closed his eyes. He would take it easy until the EMTs descended and declared that there was nothing wrong with him. Because there never had been.

But in the thirty seconds or so that Dylan monopolized the guards' attention, Felix had switched the case with an identical one from the van. One that hadn't been scanned.

YEOMAN BRIGGS TRIED to shift Mikala's car into neutral. "Don't know why I can't shift gears."

She did. Dylan had installed a lock that wouldn't budge until she pushed a button under the driver's seat. "I don't know why I bought this car," Mikala said. "What a lemon."

"Can't roll it away. I'll call for a tow truck." Briggs did. Before the truck arrived, his partner returned with the oil and water. They added both as quickly as possible. Cars piled up behind them. Mikala could see he was anxious.

"Probably ought to take the car back to the dealer, ma'am. If it really is a lemon, they have to give you a replacement. Or a refund."

"That would be good." In the distance, she saw Dylan and Felix move past the inspection area. As soon as she shook this guy, she could leave.

"But for a car to start smoking like this..." Briggs shook his head. "Might be something seriously wrong. Maybe inside the engine."

"Let's see if it will start. I'll take it straight to the dealer."

"I wouldn't. Not safe to drive. And if you can't shift gears—"

"I can't just leave it here. Look how I've tied up traffic already."

"Didn't you have some business inside? I could escort you."

"I couldn't possibly put you out of your way like that. I've already missed my appointment. I texted them and rescheduled. Let's try the car again. It stopped smoking."

"That doesn't mean—"

Mikala slid behind the driver's seat and put the key in the ignition. It started immediately. Of course. She'd surreptitiously pushed the button under the seat and she was able to shift gears. "We're good!" She waved her arms at the cars behind her, motioning for them to back up so she could turn around. "I really am grateful for all you've done."

"But your car—it isn't safe—"

She lurched into Drive. "Seems to be fine. You're a miracle worker." She leaned out the window and waved. "But I'll drive straight to the shop."

"Okay, but—"

Lani drove off, not looking back, feeling more than a little repentant. He was a nice boy and he probably was disappointed he hadn't scored more of a reward for his gallantry. But by tomorrow morning, everyone at PACOM would have something far more important to worry about.

CHAPTER
SEVENTY-ONE

4:31 p.m.
10 hours, 53 minutes left

A YOUNG LIEUTENANT named Collins escorted Dylan and Felix into the main building, then led them to the admiral's office on the second floor. It was an expansive office divided by an acrylic wall with a door in the center. Through the acrylic, Dylan could see the outline of a large vault.

"Right. Here we are." Collins opened the door to the admiral's office. Admiral Charles "Swifty" Stewart sat behind his desk with his feet propped up.

He rose. "Gentlemen. I understand you have something for me."

Dylan extended his hand. "Dr. Jonathan DeWinter, admiral." They shook hands. Afterward, Stewart surreptitiously turned his back, withdrew a moist towelette from his pocket, and wiped off his hand. "Where's Dr. Marple?"

"Out sick. He asked me to fill in, just in case a medical emergency arises. I think the top brass is still afraid your project might present some undetected health risks."

"I prefer Dr. Marple. No offense."

"None taken. I think the world of Richard. He's the one who got me the gig at last year's Army-Navy game."

"You were the team doctor?"

"I had that honor."

"You're the one who got Kosinski back on the field for the fourth quarter?"

"He's a strong boy."

"You won that game for us! Our first win in six years."

"The team had more to do with it than me."

"Still. It's an honor to meet you, doctor. An honor."

"The feeling is mutual, sir. The best part of my job is getting to meet the best people." Which, he thought, is particularly pleasant if you've done the right research.

"What's in the case, doctor?"

"You know the project has been shuttered."

"Of course."

"Now it's being dismantled. And this is the coffin. Special compartments to make sure nothing vital is damaged. I understand they want you to take it to the project site at the end of the week. In the meantime, it should be given maximum security."

"I understand," the admiral said. "The thing is—I already received a container like this from Los Alamos this morning."

Dylan didn't blink. "As I understand it, the powers-that-be felt it would be good if you had a back-up. You know how surprised we were last time."

Stewart nodded. "Prudent. And more helpful than what I normally get. Most of the people I deal with in Los Alamos act like refugees from *Abbott & Costello Meet Frankenstein*." He chuckled. "Great movie. I'll take it from here, Collins."

The lieutenant nodded and excused himself, closing the door behind him.

Dylan took a quick look around the office. Classical music played somewhere—Beethoven's Fifth, if he wasn't mistaken. The dividing door was slightly ajar. Through the door, he could see a portion of the vault.

To his left, a silver panel on the wall flickered. That would be the heat sensor. Not active at present, but after hours, if any warm-blooded body came near, it would trigger an alarm. The tiles beneath his feet were wired to release security fog. When these devices were active, he wouldn't be able to get close to the vault.

"May I have it?" the admiral asked.

"Of course." Dylan held the case toward Stewart. "But I warn you, it's heavy. That's the containment-field generator."

"I'm sure I'll manage." Stewart took the case—and immediately dropped it. "You weren't kidding when you said it was heavy."

Felix cleared his throat. "I don't mind helping."

"Appreciate it, son. But no one can be back there when the vault is open but me. I'll have to manage." He placed both hands on the case and with considerable effort dragged it into the other room. Dylan imagined there would be several wet wipes following. "Don't normally have to do much physical labor once you become an admiral. I have to close the door behind me and lock it. Required protocol, any time the vault is open. No offense."

"None taken," Dylan replied. He was counting on it.

"You wouldn't believe how much certain people would like to get inside this vault."

As soon as Stewart was on the other side and the door was closed, Dylan went into action. Moving as quietly as possible, he removed the hair spray from his bag and sprayed the heat sensor for ten seconds. Then he took what looked like a small contact lens solution bottle from his bag and squirted two drops into the coffee mug on Stewart's desk. A second after that he was behind the desk, removing the top tissue from a small packet of Kleenex. He rubbed down the arms of the admiral's chair.

Stewart had a photo on his desk of a woman who must be his late wife, and several pics of his now-grown daughters. On the credenza behind the desk, Dylan spotted spread fans and a samurai blade that suggested a tour in Okinawa. To the right, he saw the radio—the source of the classical music. It was tuned to FM 88.5.

He was standing by the door waiting when the admiral returned. "All done, gentlemen. Safe and secure in the vault. Appreciate your assist." He massaged his left shoulder. "Hope I don't have to carry that out by myself." He grabbed another towelette and wiped his hands.

"My pleasure, sir," Dylan replied. "If you don't mind, I've got a few forms that must be completed."

"Of course. Where would the military be without paperwork? We could dismiss half our personnel."

"Seems like bureaucrats are taking over sometimes."

"And there's no one on earth I have less respect for than bureaucrats." Stewart sighed. "But despite everything, I still believe there is good in all people."

Dylan arched an eyebrow. "Anne Frank?"

"You've got a good ear. Loved that book when I was a kid. Still can't read it without tearing up." Stewart sat at his desk, resting his hands on his chair. "Where do I put my John Hancock?"

Dylan pointed.

"Of course. Right in front of my face."

"A little sleepy, sir?" Dylan said, planting the suggestion.

"Do I look tired? Didn't sleep well last night. Be glad when this project is dismantled once and for all." He reached for his coffee mug and took a long swallow. He continued signing the forms, but barely ten seconds later, his head began to weave. He slapped a hand down on the desk, trying to steady himself. "Feel...dizzy," he murmured. "But..." And his head fell flat onto the desktop.

"Good drug, that rohypnol," Felix observed. "And not just for dating anymore."

"This was a particularly fast-acting variant our resident pharmacist concocted," Dylan explained.

"How long will he be out?"

"Only a minute or two. But when he wakes up, he'll feel sick."

"Excellent."

Dylan checked Stewart's arms. A rash was forming where he'd touched the tainted chair arms. The epidemiologist had provided a fast-acting skin irritant that looked like the plague but would fade on its own in twenty-four hours.

Dylan had barely lowered the admiral's arms when the man began to squirm. He made a groaning sound, followed by a long yawn.

"I thought you said a minute or two," Felix hissed.

"Stewart's a tough old coot," Dylan answered. "Pretty sturdy for a hypochondriac germ freak. Ready?"

"I'm here, aren't I?"

"Remember. We're selling fear. And the best way to sell fear—"

"Is with a straight face."

Stewart sat up, blinking. "What—What happened?"

"I don't know, sir," Dylan said. "You passed out in mid-sentence. Do you feel well?"

"I feel...nauseous."

Nauseated, Dylan thought, but he decided not to correct. "You don't look well. Your face is pale. And you're sweating." He took Stewart's wrist.

Stewart snapped it away. "What are you doing?"

"I'm a medical doctor, sir. Let me take your pulse." Stewart grudgingly complied. "Your heart is racing."

"It is?"

He placed a hand on Stewart's forehead. "And you have a fever."

He looked terrified. "Probably just a cold."

"Do you normally pass out when you have a cold?"

He didn't have to answer.

"Pardon me for being presumptuous, sir, but the commander of PACOM needs to be in top shape." Dylan had practiced this expression in the mirror. Just enough emotion to convey concern. Without sliding into theatrics. "Sweet Jesus. Let me look at your arms."

Stewart tentatively, guardedly, extended his arms.

Dylan turned them palm-side up. Blue-black blotches covered both hands and arms. "How long have you had this rash?"

"I—I don't know. I never noticed it before."

Dylan glanced at Felix, then back at his patient. "This is bad. Very, very bad." He reached into his bag and pulled out two surgical face masks. He tossed one to Felix, then hastily wrapped the other over his nose and mouth.

"Why are you doing that?" Stewart could not disguise the urgent tone in his voice. Beads of sweat trickled down his face.

"We received a memo this morning telling us to watch out for people exhibiting precisely these symptoms."

"Why? What is it?" Stewart was doing his best to hold it together, but that wasn't going to happen, not if Dylan understood his character.

Felix cleared his throat. "I think we should call this in. Immediately."

Dylan nodded.

"What is it?" Stewart cried.

"I suppose you have a right to know," Dylan replied. "We've been told to watch out for a weaponized strain of the avian flu."

Stewart's lips parted wordlessly.

"Avian flu is deadly enough on its own. But this strain has been mutated for implementation as a biological plague."

"By whom?"

"By the enemies of the United States, of course."

"Why me?"

"Isn't it obvious? If they can take you out—they could potentially take out this entire base."

"PACOM? But—"

"How long have you been here today?"

"Since nine."

"Who have you stood close to?"

"Absolutely no one."

"Good. Then there's a chance it hasn't spread. And one central ventilation system provides air for the entire building?"

"Yes."

"But there's no telling what you might've touched." Dylan drew himself up to his full height. "Everyone must be tested. Anyone who tests positive will be taken to a safe place where they can be monitored. Anyone testing negative will be quarantined to their homes. No one can leave home until given express permission by the Disease Control Center."

"That's impossible. I can't—"

"With respect, sir, do you want to infect the entire island?"

"Of course not. But—"

"How many people work on this base?"

"About three hundred."

"If three hundred infected personnel go out to dinner tonight, tomorrow ten thousand more will be infected. The island will be saturated by the end of the week. And inevitably, some of that will creep onto the mainland. If you don't want to bring down the entire nation, sir, you will go home immediately, order your staff to do the same, and remain there until you receive further instructions."

"I can't leave the base unmanned!"

"Are there any staff members who have not breathed the air in here?"

Stewart considered a moment. "The guards posted outside."

"How many?"

"Thirty or so."

"Fine. Leave them in place. PACOM can survive with a skeleton crew for one night. I want you to go to the lab and give them a blood sample. I'll have it tested. The incubation period is only twenty-four hours. I'll be able to tell you tomorrow whether the test is positive."

Stewart wrung his hands.

Dylan looked at him sternly. "Sir, have you seen anyone die from the avian flu?"

"No."

"I have. It isn't pretty. In fact, it's about the most gruesome, painful death imaginable. And that's the normal non-weaponized strain. This could be a thousand times worse."

Stewart's face seemed to melt. "But—I have a duty—"

"To this country, sir. Which demands that you go home and stay there." Dylan leaned in for the kill. "Do you realize that at this very moment there may be thousands of avian flu viruses coursing through your bloodstream? Germs that do not belong there. Germs that are nibbling at your internal organs, your immune system. Do you want to give them a chance to multiply? Reproduce?"

Stewart was visibly trembling, leaning against his chair to steady himself. "Is—Is there any cure?"

"We're working on a vaccine. But we have to confirm my suspicions. So get to the lab and give blood. Then order your people home. And get home yourself. Before it's too late."

Stewart's hands went to his face. Blood trickled between his lips. He opened his mouth. His gums were bleeding. "Good God!"

"Get to the lab! I'll collect the sample when you're done."

Stewart raced out of his office.

Dylan gestured toward the wall behind the desk. "Cut the alarm cord. Pry that window open." He sat down at the admiral's desk and opened the laptop. "I'm going to do a bit of internet research. Then let's get out of here."

Felix gave Dylan an appreciative smile. "Nicely played. How did you make his gums bleed?"

"I didn't. He did that to himself. Probably grinding his teeth." Dylan tapped the side of his head. "The power of fear."

CHAPTER
SEVENTY-TWO

12:00 a.m.
4 hours left

BY MIDNIGHT, the interior of PACOM was dark. Only a few office lights were on—the central security office, the MP station, and a few others. Everything on the second floor was dark.

The silver case inside the admiral's vault began to shimmy.

Tolga popped the internal switch that opened the case. And sprang out of it.

Every joint in his body ached. He removed the oxygen mask and tank he'd used to breathe. There was enough air in the vault to keep him alive for a while. What he had to do now was find the switch that shut off the security system—specifically the floor tiles and the magnetic sensor array. All vaults of this model had failsafes in case someone inadvertently locked themselves inside. Presumably they didn't anticipate anyone hiding inside a suitcase and getting put there on purpose. He pushed against the walls, searching for the switch.

"How are cramps?" Xavier asked.

"I no longer have any feeling below my neck," Tolga replied.

"That could interfere with love life."

"Right now I just want to make it out of here alive. I can worry about my love life later."

Xavier chuckled. "Dylan's team is on move. Building quiet. Except for skeleton crew left on patrol. Hurry."

"Already searching," Tolga said, grunting. It was pitch black in here. Fortunately, he'd practiced this many times. He could Braille his way through the entire operation. "You know, this is not my idea of a good time."

"Rather be back in circus, doing tricks for snot-nosed kids?"

"Good point." Tolga continued searching.

Dylan had gotten at least one thing right. This vault was impossible to break into. But it was considerably less difficult to break out of.

———

DYLAN WRAPPED his lips around the regulator mouthpiece and dove.

The Pacific Ocean was cold. He wouldn't mind that on a sunny day, but this time of night the chill wind blew in and he wished his wet suit were not so wet. Mikala and Felix would be along later, as soon as he found the entrance and made sure the path was clear. They remained separate to minimize the risk if, God forbid, he should be caught.

He was making decent progress. None of them had received nearly as much scuba instruction as he would've liked. But they didn't have to swim that far, either. All they had to do was get to the PACOM shore, about eight thousand yards down the beach, without being spotted.

He was surprised at how quickly Mikala and Felix had taken to scuba diving. As far as he could tell, Felix rarely exercised anything other than his fingers. Nonetheless, the kid performed well. Perhaps this was the start of a new era for the laptop-bound boy. Next time Dylan devised one of these plans, he'd have to come up with a reason to send Felix bungee jumping.

Except of course, he reminded himself, there would never be another plan. Not after this one.

A few minutes later he reached a point where the land jutted out into the ocean, creating a natural curve. He knew the primary PACOM building was nearby. The blueprints suggested that the entrance he sought was most likely going to be found there.

Dylan flippered in closer. He redirected his head lamp, providing enough illumination to see in considerably greater detail—but not so much that anyone would notice from the land.

Something copper-colored glinted to the left. What was it?

Dylan redirected the beam and swam in closer. Some kind of iron bars...

The sewer grate. It was protected by a grille that allowed water to flow through—but not much else. Didn't want the fishies swimming into the pipes.

Dylan pivoted, paddling against the current. He tugged at the grate. It was cemented to the side of the cliff. He wouldn't be pulling that out with his bare hands.

Fortunately, like any good planner, he'd come prepared.

He opened the flap on his water-resistant bag, reached under his emergency floatation vest, and grabbed the K4.

CHAPTER
SEVENTY-THREE

12:22 a.m.
3 hours, 38 minutes left

DYLAN CLIMBED up an iron-rung ladder through the access shaft, with Mikala and Felix close behind. Once he reached the top, Dylan took out the magnasonic screwdriver. Turned out it worked just as well on manhole bolts as it had on university access hatches. A minute later all three of them climbed onto the surface.

They were on PACOM grounds, at the rear coastal side of the building. And as far as Dylan could tell, no one had seen them. Yet.

Dylan assembled the sonic disruption unit. He shoved it into the soft wet ground and pushed it below the surface so it would not be seen. Mr. X's expert said this would disrupt all sound and motion detectors within a square mile radius, for at least an hour. If you knew what frequency they were using. Which was tricky, because it was reset each day by the admiral. Fortunately, Dylan had figured out where he recorded the daily frequency.

"I tried a radio after we left," Dylan explained earlier. "And 88.5 was not a classical-music station. The dial on Stewart's radio was not connected to the tuner. We were listening to a CD. The dial is the admiral's way of reminding himself what the current frequency is."

"Wouldn't it be safer to hide the number in a desk drawer?" Mikala asked. "Or in the vault?"

"He didn't want to open the vault twice a day. And no, hiding things where enemies expect to find them is not always smarter. The admiral wanted to be clever. It's called steganography. Hiding in plain sight. Like 'The Purloined Letter.'"

Dylan activated a spark-gap transmitter to take out the security radios. It wouldn't prevent the guards inside from talking to one another, but it would make it impossible for them to reach anyone on the outside, should they have occasion to try. If Dylan or his friends were discovered.

He used a grapple gun to shoot a silken cord up to the second floor. Then he reached into his pack, withdrew a mechanical belay lock, and snapped it onto the line.

"Everyone remember how the repelling lessons went?"

"Hope so," Xavier growled. "Because you have two minutes till guards reappear. Then you're blowfish."

CHAPTER
SEVENTY-FOUR

12:39 a.m.

3 hours, 21 minutes left

DYLAN WAS the last to crawl through the window into the admiral's office.

"You're sure the sonics are off?" Mikala asked.

"If they weren't, we'd have been arrested already. Tolga has deactivated the vault's defenses from within. I killed the heat sensor earlier with hair spray. So get to work on the vault."

Mikala inserted her forged key card into the slot behind the vault's keypad. The card was connected by thin computer ribbon to her pocket computer, which was small but more powerful than most of the laptops in the Pentagon. It was capable of generating all the random number and color combinations that could be punched into the keypad at the speed of light. In less than two minutes, it would cover every possible combination.

"Got it," she said. Dylan heard a clicking sound and, a moment later, she was spinning the handle. The huge steel door swung open.

Tolga spilled out, gasping for air. "Thank God. I was suffocating."

"You should complain," Felix said. "Try scuba diving in the dark when—"

"Boys, we don't have time for this now. We'll determine who's suffered the most later." Dylan shone a flashlight into the vault. "The Key should be right—"

Dylan stopped short.

"Yeah," Tolga said. "I was hoping I missed it because of the darkness."

Dylan entered the vault, shining his light every which way, pushing and prodding, scanning for hiding places. "It's not in here."

"What is going on?" Xavier asked.

"We have a problem. The Key isn't in the vault."

"After all this trouble to get inside PACOM and open vault, there is no Key?"

"Like I said. Problem."

"That's not the only one," Mikala said, glancing at the door. "We're about to have company."

She didn't have to explain. Dylan could hear the footsteps approach. He closed the dividing door and motioned the other three into the vault. He pulled the door not quite closed.

The footsteps stopped outside.

The guard wiggled the doorknob.

Don't come in. Don't come in.

The guard opened the door. Light flooded in from the hallway. Through the crack in the vault door, Dylan saw a medium-height, stocky man wearing an MP uniform.

Dylan held his breath and tried to be quieter than he had ever been in his life.

The guard switched on a flashlight and shone it around the room. Then he opened the dividing door and eyed the vault. The flashlight beam passed over the window they'd crawled through—then stopped. Dylan knew why.

There was water on the floor. They tracked it in when they came through.

The guard pulled out his gun. "Is someone in here?"

He swept his flashlight around. "No point trying to hide. I got three buddies in this wing. You're not going anywhere."

He pointed his flashlight on the vault door. "Hands in the air!" The guard reached for the radio on his shoulder.

Dylan knew if he waited one more second, the guard would call his friends and there would be no way out. So he pushed open the vault door and came out swinging. The guard stepped aside just in time to miss the door and Dylan's fist.

The most urgent problem was that gun. He didn't have time to get into his pack—so he slammed it down on the guard's wrist. The gun clattered to the floor.

The guard lurched forward, throwing a punch. Dylan managed to dodge it, but before he could throw one of his own the guard brought his other arm around and drilled it into Dylan's stomach. He fell backward, closing the vault door.

Dylan was on his own.

The guard hit him again. Dylan fell to his knees. He tried to push himself up but before he could, the guard hit him in the chin, sending him tumbling back again.

"Stay down!" the guard bellowed, and Dylan thought that would be good advice under any other circumstances. But here it was a death sentence. He struggled back to his knees. The guard grabbed him by the throat.

Once again, his lungs craved air. He choked, his stomach convulsing. Got to get into that backpack...

Dylan tried to throw a punch, but it didn't have much impact. The guard tossed him back, kicking him in the stomach for good measure.

Through blurry eyes, Dylan saw the MP scrambling for his gun. That could not happen. He grabbed the man's leg and yanked on it, hauling him back.

"Would you give it up already?" The MP kicked backward. Dylan hit the floor hard. The MP, obviously angry, launched another kick into Dylan's groin. Dylan rolled sideways—and used the moment of freedom to get into his pack.

He pulled out the taser and pressed it against the guard's chest.

The MP spasmed uncontrollably as the full brunt of 100,000 volts rippled through his body. He flailed back and forth, unable to control himself. Dylan knew that after about ten seconds of this punishment, he should black out.

It took almost twenty. Tough guard.

When he was sure the MP was unconscious, Dylan opened the vault.

Felix rushed forward. "That sounded intense. Are you okay?"

"Yeah." Dylan pressed his hands against his abdomen. He was in serious pain, but it would pass. He took a step toward the door that turned out to be more of a lurch. He was taking way more punishment than he'd intended. And that was a problem, because he was going to need every ounce of strength for the grand finale.

He locked the outside door. That should prevent anyone else from entering. At least for a few seconds.

"Tolga, tie the guard up and gag him. Felix, start hacking into the secured files on the admiral's desktop computer. Mikala—help me search. Apparently the vault was a red herring, but I'm confident the Key is in this office somewhere. We've got to find it. Before it's too late."

XAVIER LISTENED CAREFULLY to everything that happened on the other end of the audio link. They weren't doing a good job of narrating, but he got the general idea. And he was impressed. Dylan in hand-to-hand combat? When that guard walked in, Xavier was sure this game was over.

Dylan might make it to Phase Two.

Even if Dylan had no idea what it would be. Even if Dylan knew nothing about the most important parts of Xavier's plan.

CHAPTER
SEVENTY-FIVE

1:04 a.m.

2 hours, fifty-six minutes left

"IT ISN'T HERE?" Dylan asked.

"Nowhere," Mikala replied.

"You're sure?"

"Positive. Searched every nook and cranny."

Felix cut in. "I'm not having any luck on this computer, either."

"You're supposed to be an expert hacker."

"My hacking is fine. There's just nothing here that relates to the location of the Key."

Dylan paced around the office. He knew the sonic dampener would not protect them forever. Neither would the spark-gap transmitter.

He saw the admiral's radio, the one that had given him the clue to the frequency. The admiral liked hiding in plain sight. He had this huge vault nearby, but he chose to record the frequency on a radio behind his desk. Because any thief or terrorist would be looking at the vault.

Misdirection.

And he favored hiding in plain sight...

Dylan pulled out the desk drawers but found nothing useful. He removed them from the desk, checking for secret compartments. He found none. He went through the files in the credenza, without success.

"Come on," Tolga said. "We've got to get out of here."

"Not without the Key." Dylan noticed a tall bookcase against the far wall.

He approached slowly, squinting in the darkness to read the spines. Mostly thrillers, Tom Clancy and Clive Cussler and a little Lee Child. Macho stuff. Man's man books.

With one exception.

The Diary of Anne Frank?

What was it the admiral had said? It was his favorite book when he was younger. He still can't read it without tearing up.

Which, Dylan supposed, demonstrated that no character was one-dimensional, no matter how much people tried to squeeze them into cliché compartments.

He tried to remember everything he could about Anne Frank. He'd read the book in high school, not since. Saw Natalie Portman do the part on Broadway. Nazis. Genocide. Persecution. The secret annex.

Something clicked in his memory. The secret annex was hidden by a false bookshelf. One that disguised a door, that made a door look like a wall, so no one would guess there was an attic on the other side.

He tugged at the bookshelf. He felt it give slightly, but it didn't leave the wall. Something held it fast.

He knew he was getting close. What was the solution? *Think*!

The admiral also mentioned his fondness for *Abbott & Costello Meet Frankenstein*. Which Dylan remembered much better than *Anne Frank*.

The main gag in that movie, repeated over and over again, was secret doorways. Hidden passages. Revolving bookshelves.

Dylan tugged at the Anne Frank volume on the top shelf. He felt a spring release.

The bookshelf swung away from the wall.

"You found it!" Mikala cried.

Dylan pulled the bookshelf open.

There was a small safe inside. With an alphanumeric keypad.

"This seems too simple for something so important."

"No, it's brilliant. He created all these obvious safeguards to divert attention, while he hid the Key in the last place most people would think to look. Is there some way to know what the safe's combination is?" he asked.

"Not unless you're the one who programmed it," Mikala replied.

"Some kind of...default setting?"

"No."

"Can you use your computer card?"

"The safe doesn't have a digital reader. Ironically, its simplicity makes it more secure. From us, anyway."

"So it's hopeless?"

"I didn't say that." She scrutinized the safe. "Yes. I thought this was my model. The last iteration. I designed this baby."

"And?"

Her eyebrows danced. "Back door."

"I'm assuming this isn't a sexual proposition."

"The security protocol has a back door. I programmed the device to respond to a secret code that even the buyers wouldn't know about."

"Do you hear those footsteps upstairs?" Tolga stared at his wrist-watch. "The patrol is early."

Mikala stared at the keypad. "I think..."

"Thirty seconds, people! I can hear someone coming down the stairs!"

She began pushing buttons.

"I assume you programmed the back door in case someone forgot their password."

Mikala focused on the keypad. "Mostly so we'd have a way to retaliate if someone didn't pay their bill."

"Ten seconds," Tolga announced.

"You remember the combination?"

"Of course I do. It's my birthday, plus fourteen other digits. You want to enter it?"

"Just do it!"

She did. The green light came on. Dylan opened the safe.

The Key was about a foot long, two inches wide, and cylindrical, like a high-tech rolling pin. The ridged exterior was designed to slide into the targeting computer and feed equations to the mainframe.

Dylan placed the Key tenderly inside his bag. "Let's get out of here." He motioned everyone toward the window.

They'd barely taken a step when he heard pounding on the outer door.

"This is Security. Open up. Now!"

CHAPTER
SEVENTY-SIX

1:15 a.m.

2 hours, 45 minutes left

DYLAN COULD SEE a silhouette on the other side of the door. Another MP. He'd been fortunate once. He couldn't count on overpowering another one. And besides, his companions had fulfilled their roles.

"You three go out the window. Take the cord and disappear beneath the water. I'll distract."

"Dylan," Mikala said, "that doesn't make any sense."

"It does. It's part of the plan, promise. Tolga can use my scuba gear. I'll keep this guy busy until you're clear."

"Then give us the Key."

Dylan shook his head. "That's not how the plan works."

The pounding at the door intensified.

"Go," Dylan commanded.

"How will you get out?"

"I've got my own ride."

"But—"

"I'm in command of this op, remember? Get the hell out of here!"

The three reluctantly complied. Dylan passed through the acrylic divider just in time to see the outer door kicked open.

A burly MP stood on the other side.

He was holding a gun. Pointed at Dylan.

He spoke with an eerie, authoritative quiet. "Hands in the air. If you move, I will be forced to shoot."

Dylan couldn't think of anything useful to say. He knew if he advanced with the taser, the guard would fire. "Look, this isn't what it seems—"

"Quiet."

"Let me explain."

"You'll have your chance. After I've called for reinforcements." He reached for his shoulder walkie-talkie.

If the MP called for help, it was game over for Team Taggart. "Don't do that. You don't need—"

"Stay where you are." He thrust the weapon forward. "I *will* shoot."

Dylan gritted his teeth.

The MP pushed the Talk button. "Command, this is Sergeant Walker. We have an intruder, possibly—"

The instant his eyes diverted to the walkie-talkie, Dylan rushed him. He executed a horizontal flying dive and landed with a somersault. The MP pulled the trigger but Dylan was below the line of fire. He pushed up on his feet and knocked the gun away. The bullet ricocheted off the vault door.

The MP had the advantage of height, but Dylan had leverage. He wrapped himself around the man's knees and knocked him to the ground. Another bullet flew into the ceiling.

The other sentries would have to be deaf not to hear.

The MP rebounded with impressive quickness. He tossed Dylan three feet off the ground. Dylan wasn't surprised. He didn't suppose the Navy chose MPs who couldn't handle themselves.

The MP thrust his fist toward Dylan's chin. Dylan dodged, then threw a punch of his own. The MP caught it with his left hand and twisted his fist almost 180 degrees. It hurt.

Dylan flailed at the guard's ribcage with his free arm. The MP swatted it away.

Dylan had to do something fast. If this turned into an Iron Man competition, he wasn't going to win. He managed to grab the man's neck and squeezed. A little pressure on the carotid artery never did anyone any good.

The MP knocked Dylan's hand away. That hurt too, but it gave Dylan a chance to get the taser and apply it to the back of the guard's neck. He stiffened, then burst into violent spasms. A few seconds later, he was unconscious.

Dylan knew where he had to go. He would probably have the entire skeleton security crew breathing down his neck any moment.

"Xavier, it's time for Plan J."

"Understood."

"I'll be at the rendezvous point in one minute."

"If late, I cannot help you."

"Tell me something I don't know."

Dylan raced down the corridor and started up the stairs.

CHAPTER
SEVENTY-SEVEN

ONCE DYLAN WAS in the uppermost part of the building, he locked the door and sealed it with a coolant spray that froze on contact and made the lock impossible to turn. But he knew that wouldn't keep the MPs out forever.

Dylan ran to the wall-length window, but almost immediately heard heavy footsteps pounding up the stairs.

"Open the door or we will fire!"

Dylan knew they wouldn't, at least not until they had permission from their commanding officer, and that would take...oh, thirty seconds or so. Plenty of time.

He flipped the latch and pushed up on the window. It wasn't hermetically sealed, but it wasn't easy to budge, either.

"We've been authorized to shoot if you don't open the door in ten seconds."

Dylan didn't have time to struggle with the window. He tossed a chair through it. Tiny pebbles of safety glass flew everywhere.

Furious pounding on the door. "You are on military property and we will take immediate action to secure..."

"Where are you, Xavier?" Dylan murmured. He'd lost radio communication, probably because Xavier was aloft.

Overhead he heard the slow approach of helicopter blades.

As soon as the copter entered PACOM airspace, it would be detected by radar. That's why they didn't come in that way. That's also why Xavier couldn't afford to linger. Every second he was a potential target.

"Thank God," Dylan murmured. "I'm ready when you are."

Outside the door, he heard assault rifles being armed. "Gentlemen, fire!"

A barrage of bullets ripped through the door.

"I'm out of here." He walked to the far side of the tiny room, took a deep breath, and ran.

He hit the window and jumped into the cold night air.

A bullet whizzed by his head, so close he could feel the burn.

He was in midair. With nothing to protect him.

He overshot the mark and the rope ladder slapped his face. He grabbed for it, but his arms went around it, not through it. He fell.

He twisted in midair, trying to grab a piece of rope before it was too late. He managed to thrust an arm through one of the last rungs, stopping his descent with a jolt.

He heard a voice shouting from above. "You like being bulls-eye? Climb up!"

Obnoxious as ever, but his point was well taken. He forced his arms, even the aching one, into action. He climbed while bullets flew around him.

He scrambled through the open hatch, pulled the rope after him, and slid the door shut.

He was not alone.

Xavier sat at the front piloting, but the copter held twelve other men, six on each side, most of whom he recognized. They were the toughest men in the organization and armed for combat. Marco and Kalifa were among them. They had enough weapons to arm a battalion. Guns, assault rifles, grenades, even a high-powered bazooka.

Mr. X sat opposite the pilot. Dylan almost felt sorry for Xavier. She had to be the worst backseat driver imaginable.

"Bruise your pretty face, writer-boy?" Marco asked.

"Just doing my job," Dylan replied. He found his seat and strapped himself in.

"You were detected," Xavier shouted. "We lost element of surprise."

But they'd always known that was a possibility. The plan was to get the Key to the particle accelerator before the Navy could reinforce it with more troops. "You have the EMP gun?"

"Mounted on base of copter. Firing...now." Xavier threw a switch and a ten-gigawatt electromagnetic pulse surged downward from the rotors and blanketed the PACOM facility. The UH-60 was a larger, laser-sighted version of a tool commonly used by law enforcement agencies when battling computer crime, or to stop car chases before they became dangerous. The dish mounted to the copter's chassis emitted a highly concentrated EMP that would fry everything electronic below, including phones, hard drives, and land, sea, and air engines—thus complicating the Navy's response.

"They may guess where headed," Xavier said. "They may try to track us, though copter stealth-equipped. But there is little they can do. We be there in twelve minutes. Before they increase security. Weapon will be ours."

Yes, Dylan thought, and there will be no power on earth that can prevent you from bringing your plans into full and final reality.

Except me.

CHAPTER
SEVENTY-EIGHT

SEAMUS STARED at a wide array of computer monitors, hoping to find something of use.

Leilani whispered. "This is making me dizzy."

It was having the same effect on him, but he wasn't going to admit it. "Take some Dramamine."

"I can tough it out. I had a light breakfast."

After Dr. Jerrie's conversation with Eustace, Seamus had been promoted from rogue agent on a wild goose chase to premier savior of the Western world, at least at the NCTC. He didn't miss the irony. After all, this neutrino project had been instigated by the US military. But the Navy brass were stonewalling, stalling, hedging, withholding information. Seamus wasn't sure if that was because they wanted to maintain secrecy or because there was cause for embarrassment, something that needed covering up. He and Leilani travelled to the Big Island to find out.

"The mad scientist told you so much about the accelerator, including all means of entrance and egress. Couldn't you have gotten him to tell where it was before he offed himself?"

"Sorry. I didn't realize that info wasn't in the file."

With his newfound authority, Seamus had managed to find an officer who could patch him into the live satellite feed from the National Reconnaissance Office. They studied aerial views of the Big Island. Slowly and painstakingly, they'd zeroed in on the larger volcanoes on the top third of the island. Even if the accelerator were underground, it would be impossible to hide all traces of something so monumental.

Particle accelerators, Seamus learned, had existed since the early twentieth century. In their simplest form, you could find particle accelerators in any cathode-ray television set. On the opposite end of the size scale, the Large Hadron Collider beneath the Franco-Swiss border was twenty-seven kilometers in circumference and accelerated protons to energies of 1.2 trillion electron volts. Some scientists speculated that the Hadron project may have reached the peak for compensating for synchrotron radiation losses. They suggested that the next generation of accelerators would be liniacs—longer but not curved accelerators, which would be easier to construct.

Seamus longed for simpler days—bribing desert barbarians and smoking megalomaniacs out of caves.

"Zoom in closer," Leilani said.

He squinted, trying to sharpen the fuzzy image. Was she seeing something he didn't?

When the image resolved, he was amazed by the clarity. The technician told him these satellites had the ability to target a particular automobile and read the license plate. That didn't augur well for personal privacy, but it was a big assist for intelligence work.

"Something's going on down there," Leilani said. "Around Kohala."

Seamus saw what attracted her attention, but he couldn't make out exactly what it was. Kohala was in the midst of a large patch of undeveloped territory. There were few access roads. But not everything surrounding the volcano was natural. He could detect a glint of metal. "Can you get in any tighter?"

The satellite technician took a deep breath. "I can try."

His efforts were impressive. It appeared to be a wind farm, energy collectors powered by giant turbines. Seamus knew Hawaii was at the forefront of alternative energy exploration—seawater, biomass, geothermal, solar panels, and tidal power.

Seamus spotted semitrailer trucks. A concrete mixer. And people. He caught a glint off those moving heads, too, which meant either hard-hats or helmets. Either way, it was informative.

"Something's going on at that volcano," Seamus murmured.

"You mean, beneath it." She pointed to a tiny dot on the screen. "That's the center of activity. I'm betting it's an elevator shaft. Going down."

"That must be where they built the collider. That's where the physics anomaly is located." She turned to the technician. "Can you get any closer?"

"Sorry. This is the best I can manage here. I can save this data, though, and process it through a high-res filter. That will get you a better image. But the compilation will take hours."

"Do it," Seamus said.

"Are we really going to wait for that?" Leilani asked. The tone in her voice made it clear she did not want to wait for anything.

"No. But he'll call me when he has something. It still might be useful." Seamus returned his gaze to the screens. Motor vehicles moved toward the volcano. Difficult to be certain, but he thought they were jeeps.

"How much do you know about volcanoes?" the technician asked.

Seamus shrugged. "I'm new to the islands."

"I'm no geologist, but in Hawaii we get Volcano 101 in grade school. Here's one thing I remember. The island volcanoes were created by hotspots—mantle plumes caused by tectonic-plate boundaries converging on one another. But the disruption to the surface is not all above ground. These upheavals typically create huge caverns beneath the surface of the earth."

"Huge enough to house a particle accelerator?"

"Definitely."

"And if the cavern was the source of a unique anomaly, which allowed them to do something they could not do anywhere else on earth, it would be worth the trouble." That settled it. Time to go. "As soon as you have a clearer picture, send the images to my cell."

"Will do."

"Let's get going," Leilani said, urging him toward the door. "We don't have a moment to spare. Not if we want to stop these people." She paused. "Not if we want to save Dylan."

CHAPTER
SEVENTY-NINE

2:01 a.m.
1 hour, fifty-nine minutes left

XAVIER OPENED the door of the helicopter the instant it landed, even before the blades stopped churning. His men poured out behind him, locked and loaded.

"Give me Key. Now."

Dylan complied. "You need to be sprayed. Everyone does."

Xavier grunted.

Dylan retrieved the spray bottle from its compartment on the copter. "Neutrino radiation will give you a suntan that doesn't go away. Until it kills you."

Frowning, Xavier allowed Dylan to spray him and his soldiers.

"Follow me. But remember, Dylan." Xavier glanced at his watch. "Less than two hours before nanites explode in brain. Do not try to escape."

"I won't."

"After we finish mission, I turn nanites off. Not before."

After we finish mission, Dylan thought, you'll kill me. But he'd known that all along.

Dylan followed Xavier down a dirt road toward a square-cut building. It looked like a huge cinder block with a door. Xavier and his men carried AK-47 assault rifles, bayonets attached.

They rounded a corner on the walkway. Dylan could see the front entrance—and what looked like five guards stationed in front. They were watching, armed and ready.

"They heard the copter," Dylan said.

"As we knew they would." Xavier held Dylan back with the palm of his hand. They struggled for a moment—and Dylan quietly slid his hand into Xavier's pocket. "You remain here. Safe. When I give you signal, come." Xavier waved his men forward. "Move out! Fire on sight!"

They raced onward, guns blazing. Dylan knew the Navy sentries would be insufficient to stop this army of bloodthirsty killers. Apparently, the pulse worked. These men had received no warning from PACOM.

Dylan kept his distance from the gunfire. He wished he could prevent the bloodbath that was sure to follow. But that wasn't possible. The best thing he could do was stay clear. So he could implement the next phase of the plan.

Bullets flew on both sides. Even from a distance, Dylan could see blood splattering. He heard the death cries, the lethal impacts, the thunderous sound of gunfire. This was perhaps the most horrific spectacle he'd ever witnessed—but only a shadow of what might occur if Xavier and Mr. X obtained control of the weapon.

AFTER THEY SCALED THE FENCE, Seamus and Leilani observed the sandstone building he guessed was the top level of an elevator descending to a liniac particle accelerator.

How could he get in? There was no one he could call, no one he could beg for a pass. How could he ask for a pass into something he wasn't supposed to know existed?

And while he pondered this imponderable, a large assault copter landed near the front entrance. At least a dozen of what appeared to be paramilitary troops poured out of the copter. Shortly after, guards streamed out of the building to meet them.

Seamus retrieved his binoculars and took a closer look. A major battle was being fought. All hands were firing, but the military guards were outnumbered.

"Leilani, you need to go back."

"Would you stop with that already?"

"I'm serious this time. If I don't make it out, someone has to report back to NCTC. That's gonna be you."

"You may need my help."

"If I do, I'll call. Meanwhile, I want you to get back in that car and drive away. At least ten miles away. Somewhere safe."

"But—"

"Leilani, just this once, listen to me. You're the backup plan. I can't operate effectively unless I know you're safe."

Her eyes narrowed. "I don't like this. At all."

"But you'll do it. Because you know I'm right. And like I said, if I need help, I'll call." But he knew that no circumstance on earth could ever make him call.

He turned her around and gave her a little push toward the fence. She kept walking, with obvious reluctance.

Good. Now he could proceed. Because, thanks to Leilani, he knew how to get inside. Through the back door. The one even Dylan and his handlers couldn't know about. But thanks to Dr. Scheimer, Seamus did.

THE ENTIRE FIREFIGHT took less than a minute. The military guards were well-trained, but they were also outnumbered and outgunned.

As soon as the gunfire faded, Dylan bolted toward the sandstone building. Xavier was helping Marco haul a corpse off the path. As he passed, Dylan yelled, "I'll get the elevator started while you clean up."

Dylan didn't stop running, didn't turn his head. It took perhaps five seconds for Xavier to realize what he was doing. Then Dylan heard the thud. He'd dropped the corpse. He was running after Dylan.

Dylan hoped his daily beach runs would help. This wasn't going to be a long-distance race. He had to get to the elevator before Xavier did. His life depended on it. His life, and the lives of untold others.

He had not been able to train regularly since he joined the terrorists. But he knew how to push himself. He knew weakness was cowardice, and revolution required sacrifice. He knew how to energize every sinew and fiber.

He slammed into the elevator, sweat flying from his brow. He hit the down button. The doors opened. He entered.

Behind him, Xavier, perhaps fifty feet away, ran hard.

The doors began to close. Without stopping, Xavier pulled out his pistol and fired.

Dylan lunged to the side of the elevator. Bullets hit the back wall. But the doors closed and the elevator descended.

As soon as the elevator arrived at the lower level, Dylan would disable it. He didn't kid himself that he could prevent Xavier and his team from following, but he could make it more difficult. He could slow them down.

He hoped that would be enough.

CHAPTER
EIGHTY

SEAMUS SEARCHED for his back door. The entrance was midpoint on the volcano wall. Unfortunately, the Navy removed the ladder when it shut down the project. Fortunately, Seamus was an experienced rock climber, another skill he picked up in Afghanistan. But volcano climbing was different. The primary material was basalt, which breaks easily. He had to be careful.

He ran to the western wall. He knew the primary elements of any sheer ascent were balance and grip. Find a safe place to lodge your fingers and toes and don't let go until you have a suitable replacement. And don't fall backward. Because there's no net.

He hooked his attaché to the back of his belt, hugged the volcano, and climbed.

Below, he heard a commotion. Glancing down, he saw someone racing toward the elevator shaft. He was certain it was Dylan Taggart. Making his move, at long last.

All the more important that Seamus get in there as soon as possible. So he could help Dylan when he needed it.

The wall was warm and slippery. So focus, he told himself, as he reached for higher ground. Climb. Like your life depended upon it.

Sweat dripped down his face, running into his eyes, making it difficult to see. He had to free a hand to wipe them clear, and that was almost as risky as impaired vision. He rated the grade about a 75, meaning the slope of the incline was greater than forty-five degrees, but still not a totally sheer ascent. He flexed his fingers whenever possible. He knew over-gripping could be dangerous. The surface was craggy and rough, but most of the indentations were vertical, not horizontal, which made it challenging to find a safe hold. His legs ached long before his fingers did. But he kept on pushing.

He came to a sheer expanse of volcano, almost ninety degrees, straight up. He could find no place to put his hands. No way to get higher.

Further above, he spotted what looked like a natural rock ledge. That must be the entrance. But he couldn't reach it. He wasn't long or tall enough. The only way to get it would be to pull his feet out of their secure niches. To jump. To violate another tenet of safe rock climbing.

If he made it to the ledge, he might be able to pull himself the rest of the way up.

And if not, he was dead.

He tensed his muscles. He took a deep breath.

He jumped.

Seamus grabbed the ledge, just barely. His left fingers tickled the edge, but his right hand had a more secure grip. Swinging like a pendulum, he managed to get the rest of his body up, feet first.

On the ledge, Seamus found what appeared to be a natural rock formation. He saw several stones lying beneath it. But one of them, he knew, was not natural. One was a trap door, something the designer installed in the event that fire or cave-in made the front door impassible —a reasonable concern when you're playing around with astronomically powerful forces.

He found the portal stone, recognizable due to its distinct oval shape. He stood on it. When he felt the click, he stepped off.

A moment later, a two-by-two foot rock pivoted. It looked as if it were swinging along natural fissure lines, but Seamus knew better. It was a hidden entrance.

Beneath the opening, Seamus spotted a narrow flight of stone steps leading downward. He knew what was on the other end. The control room. Which would normally be guarded. But thanks to the thugs below, not today. All the guards on duty had been slaughtered.

He started down the steps. A stone handrail helped him guide himself. When he moved onto the fifth step, the door closed behind him.

Slick. And scary, if you didn't have a flashlight. But he did.

He knew it was all engineered by an elegant system of weights and counterweights hidden beneath the surface of the rock, controlled by levers and cables and cogwheels. He was glad he didn't have to design it or even understand it. All he had to do was take advantage of it.

Seamus descended into the darkness.

AFTER DISABLING THE ELEVATOR, Dylan entered the control room, which was precisely as it had been described in the eighth file.

He knew the room had a radio frequency distinct from the rest of the facility to prevent outside interference. Its other unique aspect was the small aperture in the ceiling. A passageway for the neutrino beam, when activated, to enter the outside world. The ceiling was sealed with a thick membrane to prevent solar radiation or any other white noise from comingling with the radiation generated within. The walls were coated with a stiff mesh of titanium-enriched lead fiber. Plexiglas transparent dividers separated the various rooms: the lab, the mechanicals, the research area.

In the center he found a large console covered with blinking lights and computerized display panels. Dylan couldn't help but think of the bridge of the starship Enterprise. He'd seen the command room at PACOM and he'd toured NORAD, but this was something else again. The clear Lucite panel sparkled, but Dylan knew this had not been engineered for its beauty. This was the targeting panel, with its own energy source, a hydrogen fuel cell tethered to a detachable housing station. In the upper right corner of the panel, he spotted a two-inch diameter indentation. The activation port for the Kronos Key.

Fortunately, he'd swiped the Key back from Xavier while they tussled.

Directly behind the panel, the floor was shielded by a ten-by-ten-foot square metal plating. Dylan knew that was installed so the operator would be grounded when the weapon was triggered.

Hovering above them, attached to the ceiling and pivoting on a revolving platform, a long mechanical arm with a clear tip pointed upward. The launching device. The barrel of the gun, so to speak. The neutrino beam would come out of that tip and travel wherever the Key told it to go. All he had to do was insert the Key and feed it the coordinates.

He could study this room for hours, but he didn't have time. Xavier would be close behind him. He flipped the starter switch and heard the engine warming up. He inserted the Key into its designated slot. In only a few minutes, it would be ready for targeting. He tapped at the monitor screen—

And heard footsteps.

Damn. He didn't think Xavier and his soldiers would arrive so quickly.

He removed the taser from his satchel.

"Dylan? Dylan Taggart?"

He whirled sideways. The intruder was a large muscular man, mid-forties, holding a silver attaché.

"You work here?" Dylan asked.

"No. The staff was dismissed when the project was shut down. Only a few guards are on duty. They're probably dead now."

"Then who are you?"

"My name is Seamus McKay. I work for the government. NCTC."

Dylan's eyes narrowed. Was it possible? Had he finally found someone who could help him? "What are you doing here?"

"Looking for you. I've been hunting ever since you disappeared."

"You took long enough."

"You're welcome. I know what happened—at least some of it. I know the people who've been holding you. I'm going to help you escape. We're going to shut down their whole plot and make sure they can't hurt you or anyone else again."

Seamus took a step toward him, but Dylan held him back with a wave of the taser. "How do I know I can trust you?"

"Have you got any better offers? I know you're making your move. Let me help."

"Still don't know whether I can trust you."

"I came with Leilani."

Dylan's heart skipped a beat. "Leilani? She's here?"

"She's somewhere safe nearby. She's been searching for you all this time. She told me what happened."

"How is she?"

"Amazing. She bounced back from the attack with astonishing resilience."

His eyes widened. "You mean—she can walk?"

"Like you wouldn't believe."

"They told me—"

"They lied. She barely even limps. You've got a real winner there, Dylan."

"I know." Leilani. Healthy. God, he wanted to see her. But first—

"Leilani was the one who learned about the back door to this facility —the one I used to get in," Seamus continued. "She got the intel from Dr. Scheimer. A secret that wasn't in the files you lifted from his laptop."

Dylan arched an eyebrow. "You know about that?"

Seamus nodded. "How have you stayed alive so long?"

"They need me. And they think I've joined them. Surrendered."

"And have you?"

Dylan paused. If Leilani trusted this man, he decided, that was good enough. "Surrender to the bastards who hurt Leilani? Buried Dobie? Who want to create some insane Pearl Harbor incident?" Dylan's jaw set. "I won't surrender to them until they put me in my grave. Maybe not then."

Dylan heard noises in the elevator shaft. He had to make a decision. Was he going to let this man help him or not?

He had to make a choice.

He pointed to a steel wheel on the north wall. "Help me."

The wheel lowered the titanium-reinforced slab that sealed off the control room. Dylan assumed it wasn't used often because it was stubborn and slow. They both poured their strength into it, but it barely moved.

"Keep trying," Dylan grunted.

Down the corridor, Dylan saw Xavier emerge from the elevator, followed by about a third of his goon squad. He had perhaps twenty seconds before they would be inside.

"*Push!*"

They both leaned in hard. The gate slowly made its way downward.

A bullet ricocheted just above his head. Idiots. No telling what a stray slug might do in this room.

"Harder!" Dylan knew Xavier could see the slab lowering, but he didn't break his stride. By the time he approached, it was almost to the floor. Xavier threw down his assault rifle, then slid like a runner heading for home plate. He managed to glide under the slab just before it thudded to the ground.

Instead of trapping Xavier outside, Dylan had trapped him inside. With them.

CHAPTER
EIGHTY-ONE

2:35 a.m.
1 hour, twenty-five minutes left

DYLAN HEARD a hail of bullets pounding the titanium slab to no effect. The goon squad could fire all night. They wouldn't even dent the lacing. They'd need a ballistic missile to get through that and he was fairly sure they weren't packing one.

Xavier quickly absorbed the situation. "Now this is homecoming, no?"

Dylan motioned Seamus to stay back. "Be careful. This man is—"

"I know who he is." Seamus' eyes narrowed. "I also know he's been chemically enhanced since childhood. We're not going to outmuscle him."

"What is wrong, Dylan?" Xavier said, sneering. "I thought we all one big happy family now."

"Fooled you," Dylan murmured.

"Fooled no one. I knew you would try something." He laughed. "So predictable. From the start."

"If I'm so predictable, why are all your goons trapped outside?"

"We encountered unexpected resistance. No matter. Supervisor will soon be here. He will get others in. He will take care of you. And your new friend." He turned to Seamus. "I will take from you everything you have, Mr. Secret Agent Man. Like always."

Out the corner of his eye, Dylan saw Seamus' fists tighten. The fact that he despised Xavier was more than enough to convince him they should be working together.

"I'll take care of this man," Seamus said.

"No, he's mine," Dylan replied. "This bastard shot Leilani. Had his goons torture her."

"This bastard fucked my wife."

Dylan drew in his breath. He wasn't sure who had the revenge trump card now.

Xavier laughed. "Ingrid wanted it."

"You used her," Seamus said, "to get to me."

"You had nice home," Xavier replied. "You did not appreciate what you had."

"That might be true. But it's no excuse for what you did."

"You called in air strike. Killed my wife and child."

"Not intentionally. They were inside a legitimate military target."

"I could have killed your wife like you did mine. But instead I did worse. I spoiled her. I spoiled your home. I ruined only thing you cared about."

Seamus glanced sideways out the corner of his eyes. "He's mine, Dylan."

"Maybe we should take him together."

"Deal." Dylan whispered something to Seamus under his breath.

They both advanced. Xavier pivoted on one foot, reached down to his boot, and came up with a small pistol.

Seamus ran faster. Xavier adjusted his aim and fired.

Seamus was fast but not quite fast enough. The bullet caught him in his upper chest. He crumpled to the floor. Dylan raced forward while the gun wasn't trained on him. He tackled Xavier around the waist, knocking him over.

For weeks, this man had tormented him, manipulated him. All his pent-up rage, long suppressed, spilled forth. They slid into the back wall. Xavier's pistol skidded across the floor.

He saw Seamus roll onto his side and pull out his pistol. He was trying to get a bead on the two men wrestling on the floor, but he could barely move and the targeting station blocked his line of fire.

Xavier pushed Dylan away. Dylan took a swing at him, but his fist went wide. Xavier got him in the stomach, still sore from his battle with the MP. He dodged Xavier's next blow but teetered sideways.

He remembered what Seamus said. He wasn't going to win a battle of strength. Dylan would have to be smarter. He wrapped himself around Xavier's waist, pushing him back against the wall.

"Pathetic," Xavier said. "You fight like writer."

Dylan grabbed the man by the throat, trying to choke the life out of him. Xavier resisted, but Dylan held fast. He squeezed tightly, wrapping his fingers around Xavier's larynx, fingernails piercing the skin. If he could deprive the man of oxygen, it would deplete his strength.

Trickles of blood broke out. Dylan could see Xavier's face turning pale.

All at once, Xavier brought his other arm around and clubbed Dylan on the inside elbow, breaking his grip. Xavier pushed him onto the floor, then sat on top of him. He grabbed Dylan's ears with both hands and thudded his head onto the floor.

"So smart, yet so stupid." He swung a fist into the side of Dylan's face. Blood oozed into his mouth. "So strong, yet so weak." He hit him again on the other side. Dylan's head swam. He knew he was on the verge of unconsciousness. He wanted to fight back, but he couldn't focus his strength. "I will enjoy killing you."

Xavier grabbed Dylan by the collar and hauled him into the air. Dylan hung suspended like a rag doll. Xavier leered at him, then tossed him away. Dylan skidded across the floor till he collided with the targeting center, his head smashing into hard metal.

His eyelids flickered. He was losing the fight.

Xavier hit him again. Blood spurted out of his mouth.

"We used you." Xavier spat into Dylan's face. "You did what we wanted. You stole the Key. Now we are done with you."

Behind them, Dylan heard a sound. Somehow, Seamus had pushed himself onto all fours. He was crawling forward, trying to get a clear shot.

"Now you die," Xavier said—then something hard smashed into the side of his face.

Dylan pushed himself to his knees, still holding the hydrogen fuel cell in his hands. The control panel could do without energy for a few minutes.

Xavier tumbled backward, stumbling, trying to recover. Dylan hit him again in the face, even harder. His nose broke. Blood sprayed.

Dylan hit Xavier again. He lurched forward. He brought the metal canister down hard on the back of Xavier's head. Xavier looked as if he were about to collapse. Dylan raised the fuel cell again to deliver the final blow.

Xavier's hand suddenly flew upward and blocked it. A second later, Xavier grabbed Dylan by the shoulders and head-butted him so hard Dylan stumbled back against the control panel. The fuel cell fell to the floor with a clatter.

Like cutting the head off a chicken, Dylan thought. This bastard just won't stay down.

"Finished?" Xavier asked, his teeth coated with blood. "That all you got?"

SEAMUS HAD BEEN SHOT BEFORE. More than once. But he was no longer a young field agent. The blow to the shoulder had knocked him to the ground and caused temporary disorientation. Brief unconsciousness. He had to fight his way back.

Dylan needs you, you tired old warhorse. Leilani needs you. You haven't come all this way to fall apart now.

He mustered every ounce of strength left and pulled himself to his feet. He wasn't sure how long it took. A quick scan of the control room revealed Dylan locked in combat with Xavier. And Dylan was losing.

Seamus lurched toward them, toward the targeting panel. With each step, he felt more adrenaline coursing through his veins. He'd always found the muscle when he needed it. This would be no exception.

Xavier hovered over Dylan, about to deliver the death blow. In a split second, Seamus remembered what Dylan had whispered to him.

Get him onto the metal plate. The plate was behind the targeting panel. How could he do it?

Bakersfield's wife. His little girl. Both still unaccountably alive. That was the solution.

"Dmitri!" His voice gurgled a bit, but he kept it steady. "Dmitri!"

Xavier jerked his head around. "That not my name."

"I know. You change names every time you change masters." He paused, just long enough. "Can't keep a wife, though, can you?"

Xavier's head shook. "You killed Evona. You killed my little Karissa."

"They died because they had the misfortune to be with you."

Xavier's head whipped back and forth between Seamus and Dylan.

"Did I tell you I watched them die, through the satellite link?" Seamus continued. "They suffered. They cried out, pleading for you to help them. But you were nowhere near. You let them down when they needed you most." Xavier's shoulders heaved.

"Yeah," Seamus continued. "I killed them. And I enjoyed watching them die."

Xavier bellowed and raced toward Seamus—stepping onto the metal plate. Seamus knew what was coming and knew he couldn't stop it. He braced himself.

Xavier hit him so hard he literally flew into the air. When he thudded back to the floor, he skidded for ten feet. After that, he didn't move at all.

XAVIER WAS CONSUMED WITH RAGE, crying like a wild beast. "I will kill you both!" He whipped his head back toward Dylan. "I will start with you. You are finished."

Dylan's head throbbed. Xavier rushed him, grabbing him by the throat and pinning him down.

"You think you're so smart." Xavier pulled a knife out of his boot and pressed it against Dylan's neck. "Bet you didn't plan on this."

"No. But I've learned how to improvise." Dylan dug into his pocket for the only item that still remained to him. Dobie's fountain pen. He jabbed it nib-first into Xavier's neck. "The pen is mightier than the sword, you bastard."

Xavier screamed. He staggered away, clutching at it. He eventually got it out. Blood spewed.

And yet, he did not go down.

Dylan swore. Damn that steroid-infused homunculus.

Xavier grinned, his face covered with blood. "That all you got? You finished?"

"I am…just getting started," Dylan said, leaning against the targeting panel. He returned the fuel cell to its housing station. "I've been playing with you, you grunting Goliath." He pulled out his taser.

"You do not scare me, Dylan."

"That's been your mistake all along."

"I been tasered before. It will not stop me."

"You might be surprised. Remember my request for rubber-soled shoes?"

"Wimp. Afraid of power surge."

"Didn't you wonder why I needed the highest-powered taser?"

Xavier spat blood onto the floor. "You wanted to stop opposition without killing. Because you are weak."

"That anti-radiation spray?"

"More of same."

"Did you really think there's such a thing as anti-radiation spray? And you called *me* stupid."

"But—"

"What I sprayed you with is methyl isobutyl ketone, easily made from the chemicals Mr. X provided. And easily ignited by a taser."

Xavier's eyes widened. "I—I know all your ideas. I read plan many times."

"A good writer knows how to plant clues so they're in plain sight— but the reader misses their importance. And you're standing on a metal surface, you highly flammable son-of-a-bitch." Dylan touched the taser to the floor and stared into Xavier's eyes. "Burn."

A second later, Xavier burst into flames.

Xavier ran, screaming, his entire body engulfed in fire. The smell of burned clothing and flesh permeated the room. He made it to the wheel but hadn't the strength to open the door. He collapsed on the floor, smoldering, crying out in pain. A few moments later, he stopped twitching.

Dylan made a mental note to recover the detonator in Xavier's pocket as soon as it cooled off. He still had a few minutes left before the nanites consumed his brain.

Seamus hobbled toward him. "Christ, Dylan. I am so glad I'm not your enemy."

"Thanks for luring him onto the plate."

"My pleasure."

"How badly are you hurt?"

"I'll live." He didn't look good. His shirt was covered with blood. "Give me my attaché. I've got a blood clotter. Bandages. And a stim. I'll make it."

Dylan brought the case to him. "I've got to get you out of here."

"No, I've got to buy you time to dismantle this weapon. I can hear Xavier's men outside. They'll break through that slab eventually."

Dylan knew it was true. He'd seen a bazooka on the copter capable of doing the job.

"I'll go back the way I came," Seamus grunted. "Create a diversion. Give you time to shut this down permanently."

"You'll never make it in your condition."

"The hell I won't. I'll be fine." He spent about a minute bandaging and treating himself. "Here, you keep the gun. You might need it."

Dylan took the weapon.

"See you on the other side." Seamus hobbled to the back door and disappeared.

Dylan returned to the control panel. The targeting computer started rebooting when he reinserted the fuel cell. In just a few minutes, it would be ready.

He heard something.

He stopped, then slowly turned.

Mr. X stood directly behind him. With a gun pointed toward his head.

CHAPTER
EIGHTY-TWO

DYLAN WASN'T DISTURBED NEARLY AS MUCH by the gun as he was by the fact that Mr. X was smiling.

"Drop your gun and kick it away," she said. He reluctantly complied. "Don't bother trying to lure me onto that plate. Toss the taser."

Dylan did. "How did you get in?"

"I was here before you. Sneaked past the guards during the shootout."

"Why didn't you stop me from killing Xavier?"

"Because I don't need him. He's been a loose cannon ever since he destroyed the Cartwright Institute. He's questioned my authority twice in front of others. It was time for him to go. Thank you for taking care of that."

Dylan bit down on his lower lip. "Happy to be of service."

"You've given me everything I needed, Dylan. Now I'm going to kill you."

"I know."

"I'm glad this isn't catching you by surprise." She raised her gun.

"You're not going to kill me."

"I'm fairly certain that I am."

"In fact, you're going to help me shut this project down once and for all."

She laughed, a surprisingly shrill, high-pitched twitter. Dylan realized this was the first time he'd heard her laugh.

"For all your foolish mind games, Dylan, you've haven't learned the slightest thing about me."

"I think I have," he said, taking a tentative step forward. "That's what you've never understood. You kidnapped me because you thought I had a gift for ingenious plots. But a novelist has to know more than plot. He has to understand characters." He took another step forward. "And that's what I've been doing all along. Understanding you."

"You know nothing about me."

"I understand why you're doing this. Why you're so devoted to the Supervisor."

"You have no idea who the Supervisor is."

"I do," Dylan said, looking at her levelly. "And I know who you really are, too."

NORMALLY, coming down the mountain would be considerably easier than going up. But less so when a bullet had recently pierced your chest. Didn't matter. Seamus clenched his teeth and got the job done.

The soldiers, the ones who were still alive, hovered around the elevator shaft. Seamus thought they were lowering someone down, maybe more than one. Given enough time, they would all go down, and then they'd blow the door and kill Dylan. He had to prevent that from happening.

Inside the assault copter, he found a treasure trove of weapons. He knew the soldiers were well armed, but they'd left enough behind to arm another platoon. Guess they weren't taking any chances.

Seamus smiled. If there weren't so many lives on the line, this might actually be fun.

"Excuse me, Ms. Kahale."

Leilani whirled around. Her eyes bulged. "You!"

"Yes. Good to finally meet you."

"But—what—what are you doing here?"

"I've asked myself the same question. I don't normally like making personal appearances. But something has gone wrong inside, so it seems I have no choice."

"But—why *you*?"

"Don't you know? I'm the Supervisor."

Leilani didn't even know what that meant. But a chill trickled down her spine, just the same. "Does that mean—you're behind this whole operation?"

"That's what it means." There was a blur of movement, and Leilani saw light glint off the barrel of a pistol. "And you're now critical to my success."

CHAPTER
EIGHTY-THREE

MR. X SHOOK HER HEAD, apparently amused. "I'm sure you could lead me on a merry mental chase, Dylan. But I don't have the time."

"Here's something I learned from my father," he said, ignoring her. "Something he told me after a tough day on the playground. Bullies suffer from low self-esteem. As an adult, I learned that the biggest book snobs are always the least well-read. It's all about insecurity. So I asked myself what caused you to do horrible things to people? Why do you have such a compelling need to dominate? And how could you none-theless give such a convincing performance as Dr. Scheimer's wife?"

Mr. X seemed to ignore him. "The Supervisor will be here soon. And he will expect me to have this weapon fully operational."

"The weapon is operational. All it needs is more warm-up time and the coordinates from your laptop. I assume you brought it with you."

"I did."

"The question, then, is whether you want to complete this plan." He paused. "*Fiona.*"

Her head jerked upward. "Why did you call me that?"

"Because it's your real name. Fiona McKellan. Right?"

She glared at him. "How can you possibly—"

"Did a little Internet research while I was at PACOM. Didn't take long. I knew what I was looking for. I already had most of it figured out. Just needed to fill in some blanks. I didn't believe your story about the boyfriend who blew himself to smithereens. Too pat, too much like something a novelist would invent for a minor character, cheap transformational backstory. That's why you thought I'd buy it. But I didn't. You didn't lose your IRA boyfriend, because you were never in the IRA. In fact, you're not even Irish."

"Have you gone balmy?"

"You do a decent brogue, but there were many times you used American terms when an Irish citizen would've said something different. You didn't grow up in Dublin. You tried to invent a glamorous background far different from your prosaic past. You were raised in Dubuque, Iowa."

She looked at him coldly.

"You traveled to Ireland after your undistinguished college career as a finance major. You tried to get into the IRA, but they wouldn't have you. And you weren't motivated by politics. You were in love with an Irish IRA lad. Kenneth Burke. But he wasn't interested in you, no matter what you did, no matter what you offered. Probably slept with you a few times, but not many, because he just didn't care enough. Why would he? He was a terrorist trying to bring justice to his people. You were a bean counter with a plain face and a hick accent."

"Lies. All lies."

"You were never a terrorist. More like a wannabe. A stalker."

Her gun arm trembled. "Liar."

"When you pretended to be Scheimer's wife, you were playing the role you'd imagined so many times. A woman who was loved just as much as she loved."

"You don't know what you're talking about."

"After the IRA plan flopped, you decided to reinvent yourself. Create a new persona. You came to Hawaii, far from anyone who could expose your lies. You learned the brogue. You learned the terrorist trade. You looked for work, not because you wanted money, but because at some base pathetic level, you thought if you could make yourself look like a terrorist, Kenneth would love you. Or be sorry he hadn't."

"I will shoot you where you stand," she said through clenched teeth. But she didn't fire.

"You got into the drug trade. Not exactly terrorism, but at least it was criminal. Had a few arrests, then tragedy struck. You were caught in a fire when a weed farm ignited, horribly scarring your face. You didn't care. That just made you look the part you'd imagined for yourself. All this drew you to the attention of the Supervisor. A real terrorist, or at least someone with terrorist plans. As soon as you met him, you transferred your unrequited love for Kenneth to him. You would do anything for him. And you did."

Mr. X thrust the gun forward. "I'm sick of your games."

"I'm not finished, Fiona."

"My name is Kayleigh. Kayleigh McKenna!"

"I can see why you were attracted to the Supervisor. He's just like your Irish lost love. They're both visionaries. Want to make the world a better place. Unfortunately, they both believe violence is an acceptable means to accomplish their goals. With the Supervisor, for the first time ever, you felt that someone cared about you. That you were loved. Even better—that someone thought you were important. You would follow him anywhere. You would do anything he asked."

Her gun arm sagged.

"I don't blame you," Dylan added. "But there's a problem, Fiona. Love is dangerous. It makes you vulnerable. And the fact is—the Supervisor doesn't love you. He's using you. Just like you've used me. And when he's done with you, he's going to kill you. Just as you plan to kill me. Just as he's killed everyone who's played a role in his schemes when he was done with them."

"You're wrong," she said. The brogue was gone. "You don't know anything about him."

"Did he tell you weakness is cowardice?"

Her neck stiffened. She didn't have to answer.

"Did he tell you there's no room for slackers in the battle for world peace?"

Still no response.

"Did he tell you every revolution requires sacrifice?"

Her voice was barely more than a whisper. "Yes."

"That means he's going to kill you."

Without warning, a voice crackled over the intercom, so loud it startled them both.

"Talk to me, Dylan."

The new voice was static-ridden and faint, but still familiar.

"It's the Supervisor, Dylan. I want to talk to you."

CHAPTER
EIGHTY-FOUR

3:01 a.m.

59 minutes left

ONCE HE HAD EVERYTHING READY, Seamus started the copter. That would get their attention.

In his current condition, he couldn't possibly outrun all those soldiers. But the whirring of the copter blades, and the possible loss of their ride home, might catch their attention.

He glanced out the side window.

It worked. Eight armed men, all the soldiers currently visible, were scrambling in his direction.

Leaving the copter running, he crawled out the door on the opposite side and ran for cover.

A few moments later, the men reached the copter. He pushed the detonator.

The copter exploded in a titanic cloud of smoke. Metal and glass flew through the air, sizzling hot. Even from this distance, he could smell blood.

When he finally took a look, there was no movement amidst the destruction.

That should buy Dylan some time. He hoped it was enough.

DYLAN HEARD A TREMENDOUS EXPLOSION OUTSIDE, but he had to focus on the intercom voice. "How did you get here?"

"I repaired the elevator," the voice replied. "Did you not notice? Perhaps you were busy with other matters. I'm standing just outside the titanium-slab door."

"I'm not going to let you in."

"I'll get in soon enough."

"I'll destroy the weapon long before that."

"Could I possibly persuade you to reconsider?"

"No."

"There's no harm in talking."

"No."

"Even if you destroy the weapon, you must realize that as soon as we get in we're going to kill you."

"And you must realize that the Navy has already sent troops, so your time is limited. If you were sure you'd have the slab up before they arrive, you wouldn't be talking to me."

"I'm not alone, Dylan."

"I imagine you travel with your own goon squad."

"I have Leilani."

Dylan's heart raced. "Prove it."

He heard a rustling on the intercom, then a new voice. "Don't give in to them, Dylan."

He'd know her voice anywhere.

The Supervisor returned. "You have thirty seconds."

Dylan didn't reply.

"Hasn't she suffered enough, Dylan? Does she have to face this final indignity? Used by my men, one after another, like a cheap piece of meat, then sliced up like a beef cow? Do you want to add her to the list of people who've suffered because of you?"

A million thoughts raced through Dylan's head.

"Twenty seconds."

"If I let you in, how do I know you won't kill me?"

"You don't."

"How do I know you won't come in armed?"

"I will. Fifteen seconds."

"I'd have to be a fool to raise the slab."

"My hand is around her throat." Dylan heard a hideous gurgling sound. "My, but her neck is soft. Such a shame she dies so young, so cruelly. A waste."

"You're sick. Insane."

"Ten seconds. Her face is turning white. She'll be gone soon."

"Stop it already, you son-of-a-bitch. I'm raising the slab."

Dylan tugged on the wheel. It moved more easily this time.

As soon as the first figure appeared, he reversed the wheel, but four people made it through before he could lower the slab.

Marco had Leilani by the throat. Kalifa stood beside him.

And standing in front was the Supervisor. Dylan's one and only brother. Commander Robert Taggart.

Alive and well.

CHAPTER
EIGHTY-FIVE

3:21 a.m.
39 minutes left

BOBBY SMILED. "Good to see you again, bro."

"Leilani, are you okay?"

Marco jerked her head back. She could not respond.

"I hope to God you haven't hurt her. For your sake."

Marco laughed in his face. "Ooh. Mr. Scary Writer-boy. I'm tremblin'."

"He hasn't harmed her," Bobby said. "Yet. But he will, the instant you try anything."

"Aren't you supposed to be dead?"

His brother spread his hands wide. "Surprise! What you saw was a well-staged bit of theatre. The blood was fake—squibs hidden in my hair and clothes. The gun just made noise. When it went off, you blinked, right? Turned away? And when you looked back again, I was crumpled on the floor with what you thought was blood and brains everywhere. Just pretend. Remember when I played *Man of La Mancha* in college and had that great death scene?" He grinned. "I still got it!"

"Why fake your death?"

"Because maiming your girlfriend hadn't been enough. You obviously had to experience an even greater loss before you would pour your whole heart into this enterprise. You had to lose the only other person we had any reason to believe you cared about. Me. I let them execute me right before your eyes, then I stayed away from my apartment and PACOM, just in case you checked up on me. Of course, I could always reappear after you were out of the way. The Taggarts have a history of vanishing mysteriously for unexplained reasons, right?"

"That's...sadistic."

Bobby shrugged. "'There's no room for slackers in the battle for world peace.' That's what Daddy always told us, right? Surely you realized it had to be someone on the inside. Who else would know about the Kronos Key? Who else could infiltrate Navy operations, provide you with intel and schematics and everything else you needed?" He laughed. "Who else could fund it? My job put me in the perfect position to embezzle from the biggest bankroller on Planet Earth—the US government."

"If you had everything you needed, why did you drag me into your scheme? Surely you could've found the Key on your own."

"Perhaps. But I didn't know where the Key was till you liberated Scheimer's files. And you saw how tightly Stewart controls access. I needed someone with imagination."

"Why me?"

"Why not you? Haven't we always been a terrific team? Don't you remember how it was when we were growing up? No matter what, you and me, we were always solid. We worked together. Who figured out how to ditch school without getting caught when I wanted to run off with Wanda Sue Herman? Who figured out how to erase my grades when Old Man Ludwig was trying to deep-six me? I set the goals and you figured out how to achieve them. It's the same now."

"There's more to it than that. A lot more. To put me through what I've endured these past weeks? You must resent me bitterly." Dylan paused. "Have you involved Dad in this?"

"No. But I like to think he'd approve."

"Because it involves killing a lot of people?"

Bobby sighed wearily. "You never did get Dad, you know that?"

"I got that he thought torture was an acceptable means of child-rearing."

"You didn't understand him at all."

Dylan's lips tightened. "He tormented me. And you. He's a mean, disapproving bastard. His idea of discipline was cruel. It damaged me." He paused. "And I think it damaged you even more."

"You were always his favorite. And you are so undeserving. I had to work twice as hard to get half as much from him."

"Oh, spare me the Daddy-loved-you-best crap. That isn't what this is about. I never did anything that pleased him, and so far as I know, neither did you. He always had some critical remark, some fault to find. Some reason why no one else was ever good enough. Because we weren't just like him."

"But it hasn't stopped us from trying, has it?"

"I didn't go into the Navy. And no one forced—" Dylan stopped short. "Oh my God. That's what this is really about, isn't it? That's the real cause of your insane bitterness. Because I escaped. And you didn't."

"You always got off. Always!" Bobby's voice soared. "Even when we were kids. Even when that man kept us on the Shame Table for hours. You could escape into your own mind."

"I—don't know what you mean."

"I used to watch you on the table. You weren't really there. And then, when Dad released you, you'd go write another story at lightning speed. Because you'd been plotting it the whole time you were on the Table." He was shouting. "Dad destroyed me. But he *made* you! He made you what you are!"

Dylan stared at the tragic, insane man before him—who for once was speaking the absolute truth.

Bobby approached the control panel. "I see you've already armed it. Good. Fiona?"

Mr. X nodded. "Yes?" The brogue was back.

He passed her a scrap of paper. "Here's a list of the five targets and their current coordinates according to our tracking satellites."

"Five?" Dylan snatched the paper away before she could get it. He scanned it quickly. "The President of North Korea. Predictable. President of Russia. Sure. The Saudi Arabian who's been bankrolling most of the world's terrorism. Understandable."

"See, Dylan? We're going to make the world a better place."

Dylan kept reading. "The Chinese banker who controls half of Congress." He paused. "*And the President of the United States?*"

"You got it."

"I thought you were trying to help this country."

"I am. He's a weak-kneed loser and he has to go."

Dylan gave Mr. X an icy glare. "I thought you were creating a new Pearl Harbor."

"That's exactly what this will be," Bobby replied. "We'll take out all of America's greatest enemies at once. And since the President will be one of the victims, no one will suspect the US is behind this. No one will know what happened. It'll be over before it's begun. Literally, given the time anomaly. We'll be on top again. The world's greatest super-power, now and always."

"Are you working with some secret cabal within the military?"

"Indeed. A small but committed group of true believers."

"But they don't know you're planning to take out the president."

"No. That's my own brilliant idea."

Dylan gave Mr. X another fierce look. "Do you hear what he's saying?"

"She's heard it all before." Bobby wrapped his arm around her waist. "We're kinda close. Look, Dylan—did you vote for this president?"

"No."

"Do you approve of his foreign policy? His domestic agenda. His lies? His bizarre conspiracy theories?"

"No."

"And you know those other guys on the list are trouble. Let's you and me make the world a safer place. Just five targets. Then I'll stop. Then you can take the weapon apart and bury it."

Dylan shook his head. "You don't have the right. And even if you did, even if I thought this might lead to peace—I know you won't stop at five targets. Not once you've gotten a taste of that kind of power. You'll never quit."

"I will."

"You won't. And how could the Navy—or anyone—stop you once you're in control of this weapon? You'll go on picking people off, thinking this will be the one that finally makes Daddy appreciate you. Which will never happen. You'll go on killing until there's no one left to kill."

"All I want is peace. That's what I said, just before my feigned death, remember? 'I just want peace.'"

"You'll never find peace, Bobby. You're too messed up. It may be Dad's fault. But it's my problem now."

"World peace, Dylan. Imagine. We can make it happen. We have an obligation to make it happen."

Dylan glanced at the control panel. Barely two minutes till the Key would be ready for coordinates and the beam could be unleashed.

"This is going to happen. This is going to be the end of the world as we know it. All made possible—by Dylan Taggart."

CHAPTER
EIGHTY-SIX

3:46 a.m.
14 minutes left

DYLAN STARED AT HIS BROTHER. "You know you're insane, right?"

"All great men are accused of insanity. All visionaries are ridiculed. Until the world can appreciate the wonders they've wrought."

Bobby kept his gun trained on Dylan. "I have to say, little brother, I'm disappointed. You've always been difficult. Stubborn. But I wanted you to be a part of this. I wanted the two of us working together once again. Even if I had to force you to participate in a plan you never understood."

"But that's where you're wrong."

"What do you mean?"

"You're not as clever as you think."

"Because Dad always said you were the smart one? So you can't allow me one moment of triumph. Give it up. I beat you, Dylan. I brought you into this and you had no idea I was involved. You thought I was dead."

"No, I didn't."

"Bullshit."

"I knew your death was theater. Because I knew that you were the Supervisor. Yes, I pretended I'd been cowed. That was part of *my* plan. But I was always one step ahead."

"That—That isn't true." Bobby's fists clenched. "You just can't stand to admit that I won. That I tricked you into helping me take out America's enemies. Hell, when you were a kid, you wouldn't even kill spiders. Dad put you on the Shame Table because you wouldn't hold a gun. You can dress it up by saying you're a pacifist, but I know the truth. You're weak! And weakness is cowardice." He turned. "Fiona!"

"Yes?"

"Start with the president. He's giving a speech in Honolulu. He should be easy pickings."

"Got it." She handed Bobby her gun, then connected her laptop to the control panel and typed in a set of coordinates. "That should do it."

"Those are the wrong coordinates," Dylan said. He pulled a folded piece of paper out of his pocket and handed it to her. "You're going to kill us all when you're done here, aren't you, Bobby?"

His brother frowned. "Certainly not everyone. But every revolution requires sacrifice."

Dylan gave Mr. X another long look. "Then at least let me say goodbye to my friends." He pulled a cellphone out of his pocket.

Bobby snatched it away. "I don't think so."

"It's not going to happen, Bobby."

"Can you stop me?"

"No. But this mad scheme won't—"

"What are you going to do about it?" Bobby laughed. "You couldn't hurt a fly."

Dylan watched the control panel tick down the seconds. Ten, nine, eight...

"This is your last chance to give up this insane plot, Bobby. You don't have to do this."

"I do. For the good of humankind. And you can't stop me. You said so yourself."

"Why would you believe anything a fiction writer says? Fiona, feed in the new coordinates."

"What?" Bobby said. "*What?*"

Fiona's fingers hit the keyboard. The tip of the firing mechanism turned bright red.

"I chose these coordinates, Bobby. And the target isn't the President of the United States."

Bobby's face blanched. "What's the target?"

"A GPS chip. Which I hid in that phone you just took from me."

Bobby's lips parted. "You would never kill me."

"You're already dead, Bobby."

"Do you think I'm an idiot? You haven't pressed the Launch button."

"Funny things happen when neutrinos pass through another dimension."

The beam was invisible, but Dylan believed he could feel heat generated by the conversion process burn a path from the tip of the firing mechanism across the room to his brother. Bobby started to run, but he was much too late.

A nanosecond later, Bobby disappeared. As if he had never been.

A few seconds later, Dylan pressed the button.

CHAPTER
EIGHTY-SEVEN

DYLAN COULDN'T SPEND a second grieving for his brother. "Leilani—are you all right?"

"I'm okay." She whirled around. "But I've had enough of Marco to fill a lifetime." She brought her leg up and kicked him in the crotch. He doubled over, gasping. She knocked his gun out of his hand, then brought her knee into his stomach. He fell to the floor. She kicked him in the face.

"I've been waiting a long time to do that," she said, wiping her mouth. "Now stay down, asshole." She kicked him in the ribs for emphasis. "Stay down or I'll use you for a piñata." She kicked him again, even harder than before. He did not move.

"Leilani," Dylan said. "I think you've changed."

"Have I?"

"Yes. You're scary now."

They both grinned. She raced into his arms. He picked her up and swung her around.

"My God, I've missed you," he whispered.

"I missed you, too, Dylan. Can we leave now?"

"Second that motion," Seamus said, hobbling toward them.

Dylan's eyes widened. "Where did you come from?"

"Back door. Looks like I missed all the fun. But I took out most of the troops." Seamus glanced uneasily at Mr. X. "Should I be worried?"

Dylan exchanged a glance with her. "I don't think that's necessary."

"Good. Probably still a few of Xavier's men out there. Be careful about raising the slab."

"One thing first." Dylan returned to the control panel.

While Dylan worked, Leilani did a full circle. "Something's happening outside. I—"

The explosion was thunderous. It deafened them and sent them tumbling to the floor.

The titanium-slab door opened. And a few moments later, when his hearing returned, Dylan detected movement.

Three of Xavier's men raced through the entrance, rifles aimed and ready.

"Think a minute before you fire," Dylan said. The men formed a semi-circle around him. "I don't know why you're involved in this operation, but I can tell you this. There will be no payroll at the end of the month."

They stopped, looked at one another, eyes questioning.

"The Supervisor is dead. Xavier is dead. The operation is over."

Mr. X stepped forward. "He's telling the truth."

Kalifa sharpened his aim. "We can still kill you, Taggart. And your woman."

"That's true," Dylan replied. "You can. But there's something else you need to know." He gestured toward the control panel. "I'm determined to make sure this weapon is never used again. By anyone. We're not ready to have this kind of power, and we probably never will be. That means I have to not only take out the super-collider—I have to take out the whole cavern. The geophysical anomaly. So I've restarted the weapon, and this time, the target is itself. I've triggered a timed-release so I don't actually have to be here pushing a button. I'm going to make this weapon disappear. But that will eliminate a lot of structural supports, which will probably trigger a massive collapse. This whole place is going down in..." He glanced at the panel. "Four minutes, I think. But given the time reversal effect, I can't be entirely sure. So do you want to stay here and die? Kill me to accomplish nothing for masters who are dead? Or do you want to run and have a slight chance of seeing tomorrow?"

They only considered a moment. "It's over," Kalifa said, throwing his rifle down. The others followed him out, including Marco.

"Come on." Dylan looked at Seamus.

"Don't worry about me. I've been in worse shape. Let's go!"

He was grateful Bobby fixed the elevator. They returned to the surface and ran for cover. They were barely out of the complex when he heard the sizzling sound that told him the weapon was firing, this time with far more power and intensity than before.

The sky exploded with a brilliant burst of light. "Close your eyes!" He clenched his eyes shut to protect them from the intense glare. He could still tell the light was shifting, first to gold, then to a bright purple. A thunderous sonic boom shook the ground, followed by a fiery roar. A moment later, a tornado-like burst of wind knocked him to his feet. He fell forward, cradling Leilani.

He slowly opened his eyes and glanced behind him.

The base was gone. Totally gone, as if it had never been. And a huge chunk of the surrounding volcano was missing as well.

The ground rumbled beneath his feet. This was going to be bad. The sudden destabilization affected the entire area.

Seamus leaned out from behind a semi-trailer truck. "Get back here!"

Dylan carried Leilani behind the semi before the next explosion erupted. The boom seemed loud enough to shatter their eardrums. Half the volcano appeared to implode. Magma flew up. Debris thudded against the opposite side of the truck. The ground felt as if it might crumble beneath their feet at any moment. Another explosion followed, then another. The explosions were like popcorn kernels in a hot pan. Once one burst, it triggered another, then another, each bigger than the one before.

They clung to the side of the semi, hoping it wouldn't fall on them. Leilani wrapped herself tightly around Dylan.

"This is going to get worse before it gets better," he said. "We need to move farther away."

He grabbed Leilani's hand and ran, Seamus close behind. Barely seconds later, they heard the semi slide backward into a newborn chasm. The sky was filled with a pyrotechnic display. Magma-based fireballs crashed around them like meteorites.

"Keep running!" Dylan shouted. "Don't stop!"

They reached the crest of a rocky promontory and dove. Behind them, the entire area disintegrated. Smoke and dust rose in huge clouds, making it hard to see and harder to breathe. Dylan and Leilani clung to the ground, hoping Mother Nature's revenge was over.

He heard screaming. Someone was trapped in that unfolding disaster—but still alive.

"You stay here," he told Leilani.

"Dylan, no! It isn't safe."

He was already gone, sprinting back the way he came, toward the nearest crater. It was a long shot, but there'd been so much death, so much carnage. If he could save one life, it was worth the risk. He pushed his legs to the maximum, using all his remaining strength to get there as quickly as possible.

He slowed as he reached the crater. Someone clung desperately with both hands on the rim.

Dylan reached down. "Grab my—"

He stopped.

It was Marco.

"Help me!" he screamed.

Dylan's hand wavered. "Give me one good reason why I should."

"It's—It's what Fargo Cody would do!" Marco stared upward, eyes wide. His hands were slipping. He was barely hanging on by his fingertips.

"Do you remember what I said, when you hurt Leilani? Do you remember what I promised?"

"Help me. *Please!*"

Dylan kicked Marco in the head. Marco lost his grip and tumbled into the abyss, screaming as he plummeted out of sight.

I'm not Fargo Cody, Dylan thought as he watched the man fall. I'm stronger than Fargo Cody.

Dylan raced back to safety. The crater was spreading, widening.

There was no way of knowing how far it would go, how long he would have to run before it stopped.

Together, they ran until at last the explosions stopped. There was a moment of eerie silence, followed by an ominous rumbling.

"It's over," Dylan said. "I think. The weapon and the cavern are gone. Destroyed. Forever."

"Good," Seamus replied. "I don't think the world needs any gateways to alternate universes."

Leilani laid a hand on Dylan's shoulder. "Were you able to save...?"

"No," he replied, without explanation.

Dylan peered into the distance. A gigantic sinkhole had formed, as if some subterranean vacuum had sucked the earth away, leaving an enormous canyon in its wake.

"Everyone okay?"

Seamus was lying down, still clutching his attaché. "Depends on how you define 'okay.' I made it out alive."

"What the hell is in that damned case that's so important, anyway?" Leilani asked. "You carry it with you everywhere."

"I've been wondering that myself," Dylan said.

"Funny you should ask," Seamus said, sitting up. "Because I've been waiting a long time to tell you..."

PART FOUR
THE AFTERGLOW

"No matter how much we try to convince ourselves differently, no book is ever truly finished."

ERNEST HEMINGWAY

CHAPTER
EIGHTY-EIGHT

One Week Later

DYLAN TRIED to get comfortable in the chair opposite Seamus's desk at the NCTC, but it was a challenge. His body had taken too much damage. His ribs were wrapped but he was still broken and bruised and aching in places he never knew had muscles. It would be a long time before he fully recovered.

And he didn't care. He was glad to be free, in any condition. After they left Kohala, the NCTC, the Navy, and various other agencies had put him through an endless series of debriefings and rebriefings. Over the course of the week, as additional evidence was gathered, he'd had the pleasure of watching their initial disbelief turn into stunned acceptance.

And now it was over. Seamus was cutting him loose. To reclaim his life. To go home, see friends.

And to visit Dobie's grave.

He didn't write a word. Fargo Cody was over. He wanted to reclaim Dylan Taggart, the human being.

"We found their headquarters. Base. Hideout. Whatever you call it," Seamus explained. "Once you told us it had been constructed from an abandoned Navy post, the possibilities became much more manageable.

Turns out, you hadn't gone far. Unfortunately, by the time we arrived, there was not much left."

"Felix? Tolga?"

"Probably not their real names. Gone."

Dylan found himself feeling almost nostalgic about them. Criminals, yes. But they'd worked together as a team. And they'd worked well.

"We did snag Mikala, though. Thanks to you vouching for her, there will be no charges. She's been returned to her home. Her father is safe. I asked if she wanted to speak to you, but...she passed."

"I understand."

"I don't. She owes you a great deal. You saved her life."

"After I endangered her." He lowered his eyes. "After I used her as a pawn in my chess game."

"The important thing is," Seamus said, coughing into his hand, "the secret cabal has been exposed. We've traced the funds that were embezzled from the military to finance the operation." Dylan noticed the charitable shift to passive voice. "There won't be any more insider plots to steal super-weapons. At least not from that source."

"No trace of Mr. X?"

"No. She disappeared during the explosion. Probably killed."

"I doubt it. She's too smart to die so stupidly." He thought a moment. "I hope she's happier in...whatever life she constructs for herself next. And I hope that with Karelis and Scheimer dead and the geophysical anomaly destroyed, this will be the end of the superweapon."

"I hope so, too." Seamus didn't have to add the rest. History told them that if enough minds worked hard enough on any scientific problem—eventually they would solve it. If people wanted this weapon badly enough, they'd find a way to recreate it. Even without the Kohala anomaly.

Seamus changed the subject. "You know they were drugging you."

"They were trying. I didn't eat any more than necessary. I didn't sleep in my bed, so I didn't inhale the gas or hear the subliminal messages. I only drank from a bottle. They were trying to induce the Stockholm Syndrome. Make me feel I was one of them. After they staged Bobby's death, I let them think they'd won. Most of them bought it." He stopped. "And then I really did kill Bobby."

"You acted in self-defense. And don't lose any sleep over Xavier, either. He was first-class scum."

"You and he have history."

"Yes." Seamus's eyes seemed to lose focus for a moment. "He held me responsible for the death of his family. So he took his revenge. He tracked down my home, my family. My wife. She wasn't happy. She was an easy target. Started an affair that got more crude, more violent as it progressed. Eventually became so degrading it robbed Ingrid of every ounce of self-esteem. She left me, then embarked on a long string of cheap, meaningless affairs. Every time I move, she follows. Like she wants me to see, wants me to be reminded of what she's become."

"Love makes you vulnerable."

"Yes," Seamus said quietly. "Every damn one of us." He smiled abruptly. "You should be proud of yourself, Dylan. You did an incredible thing here, against insurmountable odds. You brought down a major terrorist organization, one that was totally off the intelligence radar. You outsmarted them."

Dylan shook his head. "I didn't, really. I just..." He paused. "I wrote a better story. I want to thank you, Seamus. I wouldn't be alive now if not for you."

"Your tax dollars at work."

"A bit more than that, I think."

"I couldn't let one of Hawaii's greatest cultural treasures be co-opted by a bunch of wannabe revolutionaries, could I?"

"You could. But I'm glad you didn't." Dylan reached for his messenger bag. "I have a little something for you. To show my appreciation."

Seamus waved his hands in the air. "That's not necessary. I was just—"

He stared at the tall stack of paper now resting on the edge of his desk. "You read my manuscript!"

"I had a strong suspicion I would find paper in that attaché of yours. I've seen the hungry look of the aspiring writer many times before."

"You seriously read my manuscript?"

"Better than that. I line-edited it."

Seamus gasped.

"From start to finish. And let me tell you something. It's good."

"You're just saying that because I saved your life."

"No, I just edited it because you saved my life. The book is solid."

Seamus picked up the manuscript and hugged it to his chest. "I can't tell you how much this means to me."

"Least I could do."

"No," Seamus replied. "The most."

CHAPTER
EIGHTY-NINE

DYLAN ROLLED over on his side, wrapping his arms around Leilani, squeezing her tightly.

"I've been waiting a long time for that," he said.

"*You* have." Leilani's lips turned up at the edges. "Think about me."

So much time had passed since he'd seen her, much less in bed, unclothed, with that radiant expression on her face. He'd almost forgotten how good his life was—when he didn't have terrorists and psychopaths trying to control him. She was a gloriously beautiful woman. Especially now, wearing nothing but the splint around her twisted ankle.

"Leilani—I'm sorry. For what happened."

"You didn't do it."

"I couldn't stop it."

"No, you couldn't. And just for the record, I don't think anyone could have. Not you. Not Seamus. Not Fargo Cody. No one."

"You're kind. But the fact is—I failed you."

She sat up and took his head in her hands. "If you'd given up, that would've been failure. But you never did. No matter what they did to you. That's why you're a hero. My hero."

Dylan pressed a hand against hers but said nothing.

"I know what's bothering you. It's your father. That bitter old hardass has plagued you your entire life, and now he's got a new way of getting to you when you're most vulnerable. You're worried that he'll say you failed, that you were weak. That he'll be hateful when he finds out—what you did to Bobby." She inhaled deeply. "When are you going to understand this, Dylan? He doesn't know who you are. He never did. And that's not because you're so unfathomable, either. It's because he doesn't want to. You don't fit into his tidy, tiny little world view. That's his problem, not yours."

She pressed his hand to her breast. "But I get you. And I love you. That's why I tracked you down. Because love like ours is a gift. And when God gives you a gift, you don't let it slip through your fingers. You fight for it."

"You are definitely a fighter."

"Damn straight. I'll always be in your corner. Come what may."

"And I'll be in yours."

They held each other for a long moment.

"Good," she said, rolling over. "Now that we've got that settled, show me some more of your genius. Read me like a book. Send me into orbit."

"But we just—"

"We're making up for lost time, lover boy. And we're starting a family, remember?" She pulled him close and kissed him for a very long time.

DYLAN HAD BEEN STARING out the window since he awoke, not sure what to do with himself. Leilani was deep asleep. When he first returned home, he felt as if he had the world at his fingertips. And ever since then, he'd watched his options become either non-existent or overwhelming. Trying to put a life back together after all he'd been through.

Something was missing. He'd tried writing, but didn't know what to say. Fargo Cody had been a joke, a cheat. Just as his own life had been. Maybe God was a novelist, and he was just an underdeveloped character who only thought he was real.

He sat down in front of his computer and wrote: *The bitter subzero wind chilled Dr. Scheimer—but not nearly so much as the thought of what they were about to do....*

No. Maybe later. Not now. Dylan stared out the window, watching the tide roll in, weighted down with inertia, utterly unsure what to do next.

Until his cellphone buzzed.

"Seamus?"

"Hope you don't mind my calling so early. What are you doing?"

"Staying busy. You know how it is. Tons to do."

"I can imagine. Writing anything?"

"No, not...I don't know...I just...no."

"Look, I don't want to take up your time, but I had this thought. Crazy notion. But I couldn't stop thinking about it. I've been reviewing the NCTC ops reports for the past month and—how can I say this? They're pathetic."

"What do you mean?"

"I'm convinced that if most of our nation's enemies weren't so poorly organized and underfinanced, we wouldn't stand a chance. There's something going on in Pakistan right now and no one knows a damn thing about it. We need to infiltrate their military, but no one can figure out how to do it."

"Sorry to hear that."

"In this day and age, it's not enough to react. Or even to try to stop enemy plans. We need to anticipate them."

"Seamus—why are you telling me this?"

"Call me nuts, Dylan, but—we need an idea man."

Dylan felt a stirring in the pit of his stomach. "You must be joking."

"Look, I know you're not doing anything. Come work for us."

"Seamus—"

"Why not? You've proven you have an aptitude for this line of work. You were just on the wrong side."

"I'm a writer!"

"That's exactly what we need."

"No."

"We can pay you—well, the pay is crap, but you don't need money, and you'd still have time to write—"

"No."

Seamus sighed. "Will you at least think about it? Call me if you change your mind."

"I won't be calling you." He ended the call.

He stared at the ocean for another hour, his mind wandering, but not in a positive, creative way. In a haunted, obsessive way. Every time the waves crashed, he saw Leilani thrown into the air. Every time he saw a family stroll by, he thought of his father.

And every time he heard a loud noise, he thought of Bobby. Disappearing.

He flipped on the television. Unfortunately, the news was on.

"...and the president expressed concerns about the growing number of military hotspots. In addition to the ongoing fighting in the Middle East, there have been outbreaks on the India-Pakistan border and in parts of China, both near known nuclear-weapons facilities. The President of North Korea has said he will restart his nuclear tests despite..."

As Dylan stared at the screen, he couldn't prevent his brother's words from returning to him. *World peace, Dylan. Imagine it. We can make it happen. We have an obligation to make it happen.*

Was Bobby right? Had he cheated the world out of its only opportunity to know a true and lasting peace?

And more importantly—had his father anticipated this possibility, months ago, when he sent the letter?

Dylan pulled it out of the pages of *Treasure Island*, where he'd hidden it, though by this time he could almost recite it from memory:

Dear Dylan:

I'm sure this letter comes as a surprise, since we haven't talked in years. But I had to warn you. I think you know that, even while traveling, I've kept my hand in Navy affairs. My contacts tell me they've developed a weapon that makes the atomic bomb look like a slingshot. After the first test, they discovered it was more dangerous than they realized, so they retired the project. Unfortunately, a secret group within the Navy is not content with that decision. These people are dangerous and must be stopped.

You're probably wondering why I'm telling you this. I believe Bobby is involved in this shadowy confederacy. In fact, I think he's running it. He's a smart man, as you know, and he's in a position to divert huge quantities of government money. That gives me two worries. First, that he might actually use this weapon. And second, that he might try to involve you. Because that's how it's always been, hasn't it? The big brother cooks up the schemes, and the little brother figures out how to make them work.

Don't do it, Dylan. No matter what he says or does. He's going to end up dead, and I don't want you to go down with him.

Dad

P.S. Did you ever wonder why your second book hit it big? I didn't want you to have another bomb. So I bribed someone for a list of bookstores that report sales to The New York Times, *then placed orders for over thirty thousand copies. That's what happened to my pension fund. I bought you onto the list.*

So stop telling people your mean old dad never did anything for you.

FROM THE INSTANT he was taken, although he played dumb, Dylan suspected the operation related to this super-weapon—and that his brother was behind it. His father had given him a vital heads-up. His father also gave him the strength he needed to survive the ordeal. That first night, when Xavier strung him up by the neck, what was that but the Shame Table all over again? His father had instilled an innate aversion to weakness that made it impossible for Dylan to give in, no matter how horrible the circumstances.

He'd spent most of his life hating his father. But his father was the only reason he was still alive.

LEILANI WAS ASTONISHED to see the time. Ten in the morning? She knew she'd been tired, but how could she possibly have slept so late?

She rolled over. Dylan was not in bed. He'd probably arisen hours ago, had breakfast and run five miles on the beach.

She stopped in the bathroom, got a bathrobe, then wandered into the living room to find her lover.

The search did not take long. He was standing on the dining room table, wearing nothing but his boxers, holding a rock over his head, legs stiff, staring toward the sea. He did not move, even when she drew close.

"Dylan?" she said tentatively. "What are you doing?"

His voice had a steely tone. "Thanking my father."

ACKNOWLEDGMENTS

I want to thank the people at PACOM, starting with Jeff Breslau, who guided me on a tour of the facility, including the briefing room, and Admiral Robert F. Willard, who allowed me onto the Admiral's barge for a breathtaking view of the islands at sunset. By the way, if you think I've accurately described the security protocols at PACOM, or that anyone might have the slightest chance of breaking in, you're wrong.

I also want to thank Jerry McCoy and Dale Teeters at the University of Tulsa. Professor McCoy served as my initial guide through the physics in this book and was invaluable in suggesting the use of neutrino oscillation for a plausible super-weapon. Dr. Teeters, the inventor of the nanobattery, was especially helpful on nanotechnology. A special thanks to Scott Holmstrom who read the manuscript and gave me learned scientific advice. He gave the magnasonic screwdriver its name. Don't you wish you had one?

Nikola Tesla is believed by many to be the smartest man who ever lived. His wide range of scientific achievements is unparalleled. He's the primary figure responsible for modern commercial electricity. He invented radio. He made major contributions to electromagnetic studies, computer science, robotics, ballistics, radar, and nuclear physics. He differed with Einstein on the subject of curved space, and that may be the one instance in which even this great genius was wrong. As his life progressed, he became increasingly dominated by obsessive-compulsive disorders, so little understood then that they led to his reputation as a "mad scientist." He also claimed toward the end of his life to have an idea for a so-called peace ray, but could not get funding to develop it.

Physics anomalies, including gravitational anomalies, are a reality. Quantum physics has given us ways to describe them, though not to explain why they occur. Parallel universes, with different laws of physics than the Newtonian or Einsteinian laws we know, have passed from hypothetical to generally accepted in the world of physics. The idea of Tesla discovering such an anomaly in Hawaii is my own invention, but geological pockets or caverns are often found at the base of volcanoes. Historians have long debated the reasons why President McKinley, unlike his predecessor, Grover Cleveland, decided to annex Hawaii. The influence of sugar-plantation economics and the strategic location of Pearl Harbor are usually cited, but I'm not the first to suggest that there must have been more involved to explain the abrupt turnabout.

I'm afraid I completely invented Personal Freedom Day, to avoid incurring the wrath of readers by treating any genuine holiday in such a disrespectful manner. But why not? I think it's more worthy of commemoration than the events that lie behind many modern holidays.

I also want to thank my Hawaiian technical advisors, Judge Bill Fernandez, his son, Don Fernandez, Patricia Wood, and my early readers: James Vance, John Wooley, Barry Friedman, Rick Ludwig, Kim Peterson, Timothy Hoover, and Robin Ware.

Most importantly, I want to thank my children and my cat, who tolerate hours of Dad clicking away at a keyboard because they, like Leilani, know that tenacity is the secret to life, the secret to creating a life worth living.

William Bernhardt

ABOUT THE AUTHOR

William Bernhardt is the author of over fifty books, including *The Last Chance Lawyer (#1 National Bestseller)*, the historical novels *Challengers of the Dust* and *Nemesis*, two books of poetry, and the Red Sneaker books on writing. In addition, Bernhardt founded the Red Sneaker Writers Center to mentor aspiring authors. The Center hosts an annual conference (WriterCon), small-group seminars, a newsletter, and a bi-weekly podcast.

Bernhardt has received the Southern Writers Guild's Gold Medal Award, the Royden B. Davis Distinguished Author Award (University of Pennsylvania) and the H. Louise Cobb Distinguished Author Award (Oklahoma State), which is given "in recognition of an outstanding body of work that has profoundly influenced the way in which we understand ourselves and American society at large." In 2019, he received the Arrell Gibson Lifetime Achievement Award from the Oklahoma Center for the Book.

In addition Bernhardt has written plays, a musical (book and score), humor, children stories, biography, and puzzles. He has edited two anthologies (*Legal Briefs* and *Natural Suspect*) as fundraisers for The Nature Conservancy and the Children's Legal Defense Fund. In his spare time, he has enjoyed surfing, digging for dinosaurs, trekking through the Himalayas, paragliding, scuba diving, caving, zip-lining over the canopy of the Costa Rican rain forest, and jumping out of an airplane at 10,000 feet.

In 2017, when Bernhardt delivered the keynote address at the San Francisco Writers Conference, chairman Michael Larsen noted that in addition to penning novels, Bernhardt can "write a sonnet, play a sonata, plant a garden, try a lawsuit, teach a class, cook a gourmet meal, beat you at Scrabble, and work the *New York Times* crossword in under five minutes."

ALSO BY WILLIAM BERNHARDT

The Splitsville Legal Thrillers

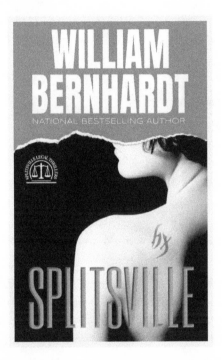

A struggling lawyer. A bitter custody battle. A deadly fire. This case could cost Kenzi her career—and her life.

When a desperate scientist begs for help getting her daughter back, Kenzi can't resist...even though this client is involved in Hexitel, a group she calls her religion but others call a cult. After her client is charged with murder, the ambitious attorney knows there is more at stake than a simple custody dispute.

Exposed (Book 2)

Shameless (Book 3)

The Daniel Pike Novels

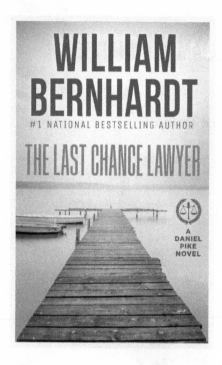

WILLIAM BERNHARDT

#1 NATIONAL BESTSELLING AUTHOR

THE LAST CHANCE LAWYER

A DANIEL PIKE NOVEL

Getting his client off death row could save his career... or make him the next victim.

Daniel Pike would rather fight for justice than follow the rules. But when his courtroom career goes up in smoke, he fears his lifelong purpose is a lost cause. A mysterious job offer from a secretive boss gives him a second chance but lands him an impossible case with multiple lives at stake...

Dan uses every trick he knows in a high-stakes trial filled with unexpected revelations and breathtaking surprises.

Court of Killers (Book 2)

Trial by Blood (Book 3)

Twisted Justice (Book 4)

Judge and Jury (Book 5)

Final Verdict (Book 6)

The Ben Kincaid Novels

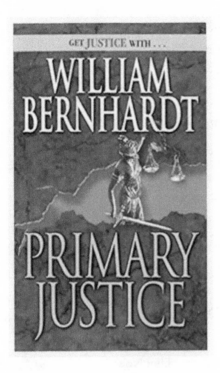

GET JUSTICE WITH …

WILLIAM BERNHARDT

PRIMARY JUSTICE

"[William] Bernhardt skillfully combines a cast of richly drawn characters, multiple plots, a damning portrait of a big law firm, and a climax that will take most readers by surprise."—*Chicago Tribune*

Ben Kincaid wants to be a lawyer because he wants to do the right thing. But once he leaves the D.A.'s office for a hotshot spot in Tulsa's most prestigious law firm, Ben discovers that doing the right thing and representing his clients' interests can be mutually exclusive.

Blind Justice (Book 2)

Deadly Justice (Book 3)

Perfect Justice (Book 4)

Cruel Justice (Book 5)

Naked Justice (Book 6)

Extreme Justice (Book 7)

Dark Justice (Book 8)

Silent Justice (Book 9)

Murder One (Book 10)

Criminal Intent (Book 11)

Death Row (Book 12)

Hate Crime (Book 13)

Capitol Murder (Book 14)

Capitol Threat (Book 15)

Capitol Conspiracy (Book 16)

Capitol Offense (Book 17)

Capitol Betrayal (Book 18)

Justice Returns (Book 19)

Other Novels

Challengers of the Dust

The Game Master

Nemesis: The Final Case of Eliot Ness

Dark Eye

Strip Search

Double Jeopardy

The Midnight Before Christmas

Final Round

The Code of Buddyhood

The Red Sneaker Series on Writing

Story Structure: The Key to Successful Fiction

Creating Character: Bringing Your Story to Life

Perfecting Plot: Charting the Hero's Journey

Dynamic Dialogue: Letting Your Story Speak

Sizzling Style: Every Word Matters

Powerful Premise: Writing the Irresistible

Excellent Editing: The Writing Process

Thinking Theme: The Heart of the Matter

What Writers Need to Know: Essential Topics

Dazzling Description: Painting the Perfect Picture

The Fundamentals of Fiction (video series)

Poetry

The White Bird

The Ocean's Edge

For Young Readers

Shine

Princess Alice and the Dreadful Dragon

Equal Justice: The Courage of Ada Sipuel

The Black Sentry

Edited by William Bernhardt

Legal Briefs: Short Stories by Today's Best Thriller Writers

Natural Suspect: A Collaborative Novel of Suspense